CHARMING
LIKE US

BOOK 7 IN THE **LIKE US SERIES**

KRISTA & BECCA
RITCHIE

CHARACTER LIST

Not all characters in this list will make an appearance in the book, but most will be mentioned. Ages represent the age of the character at the beginning of the book. Some characters will be older when they're introduced, depending on their birthday.

The Oliveiras

Rodrigo & Sônia Oliveira

Oscar – 32

Quinn – 22

Joana – 19

The Highlands

Jack Sr. & Eleonor Highland

Jack – 27

Jesse – 17

The Cobalts

Richard Connor Cobalt & Rose Calloway

Jane – 24

Charlie – 21

Beckett – 21

Eliot – 20

Tom – 19

Ben – 17

Audrey – 14

The Meadows

Ryke Meadows & Daisy Calloway

Sullivan – 21
Winona – 15

The Hales

Loren Hale & Lily Calloway

Maximoff – 24
Luna – 19
Xander – 16
Kinney – 14

The Security Team

These are the bodyguards that protect the Hales, Cobalts, and Meadows.

KITSUWON SECURITIES INC.
SECURITY FORCE OMEGA

Akara Kitsuwon (boss) – 27
Thatcher Moretti (lead) – 29
Banks Moretti – 29
Farrow Keene – 29
Quinn Oliveira – 22
Oscar Oliveira – 32
Paul Donnelly – 27

PRICE KEPLER'S TRIPLE SHIELD SERVICES
SECURITY FORCE EPSILON

Jon Sinclair (lead) – 40s
Ian Wreath – 30s
Vance Wreath – 20s
O'Malley – 27
…and more

SECURITY FORCE ALPHA

Price Kepler (lead) – 40s
…and more

A NOTE FROM THE AUTHORS

Charming Like Us is the seventh book in the Like Us Series. Even though the series changes POVs throughout, to understand events that took place in the previous novels, the series should be read in its order of publication.

Charming Like Us should be read after *Headstrong Like Us*.

LIKE US SERIES READING ORDER

1. Damaged Like Us
2. Lovers Like Us
3. Alphas Like Us
4. Tangled Like Us
5. Sinful Like Us
6. Headstrong Like Us
7. Charming Like Us
8. Wild Like Us
9. Fearless Like Us
10. Infamous Like Us
11. Misfits Like Us
12. Unlucky Like Us

1

Oscar Oliveira

TEN TIMES A DAY, I question why I'm the bodyguard to Charlie Keating Cobalt. The sun just set, and I'm already at number eleven. *Why me?*

Because I can keep up.

Because despite the fact that he's actively trying to lose me in a crowd that's fifty people deep, I'm still six feet behind him. I could lunge and grab his thin, billowing white button-down, untucked from his black jeans.

No one has noticed the famous twenty-one-year-old yet.

Thanks to the fact that Charlie is moving through a crowd of tourists who are all too enamored with the glittering Manhattan skyscrapers. They're too unaware that a celebrity just passed them by, with his unkempt, sandy-brown hair that takes flight with the summer wind.

Charlie veers to the left, suddenly, and his head disappears behind a group of taller men. If it were my first day on the job, I'd think he was trying to lose me in the crowd. But it's not my first day. Not even my second.

I've been Charlie's bodyguard for over five years.

So I don't think it.

I *know* he's trying to lose me.

Here's an annoying fact: His success rate is about 50%.

Here's a less annoying fact: Before me, his success rate was 100%.

Charlie's previous bodyguards were making him look like a gold-star Houdini. They had zero shot to catch up to him. If Charlie wanted to disappear, he'd vanish into thin air.

With me, he has to try a little fucking harder, and that's why I'm still on his detail after all these years. Can't lie, it's not rose petals and holy water over here. It's never stopping. Not for a second. It's stress on stress on stress, and I'm terrified of the day I lose this.

Being his bodyguard.

Because it'll be like going from a hundred million miles an hour to being glued to the ground. I've been at Charlie's speed for so long, I don't know how to stop anymore.

I watch him near a department store, and instead of following his footsteps, I keep walking ahead with the throngs. Officially, I lose sight of him. It's a calculated risk, one with opportunity cost.

And as I make the decision, I know exactly what it's going to cost me…and my client.

I hear overwhelmed, elated, *shrill* screams of a young girl.

"Ohmygod Charlie COBALT!"

Her high-pitched "oh my gods" are probably echoing down the New Jersey Turnpike. Can I blame her? I grew up thinking the Cobalts walked on water. All three famous families are considered American royalty, but the Cobalts are the *gods* among the princes, and now that I protect them, I still think it.

The difference is, I'm not a teenager envious of their flawless intellect and their arm-in-arm impenetrable bonds…their closeness that made my family life seem unspooled and *messy*.

Because I'm older now, and I'm an incredibly *intelligent* motherfucker. And I've come face-to-face with the Cobalts, who are just as messy, just as dysfunctional, just as chaotic as my family still is.

And it made me love the Cobalt Empire even more.

So they still walk on water, but I'm one of several men who picks their asses out of a Great Lake when they slip and begin to drown.

Call me *The Pro*.

The media already does.

More screaming blisters the New York City air, and with a swift turn, I round the corner into an empty alleyway.

I keep a relaxed pace, comms earpiece situated in my ear. The July heat tries to suction my navy-blue button-down to my chest. Curly pieces of my hair brush my forehead, and I push them back and walk. Normally bodyguards alert their lead if they lost sight of their client. Yet, it's pointless, if I radio in.

Fuck, I remember Charlie's past bodyguards and their hysteria over comms.

I lost him. I lost him! Fucking shit, I lost the kid!

He's just gone. I swear I had eyes on him.

I can't…I can't find him anywhere.

Fuck this, I quit.

Having to deploy a search and rescue mission for your client is embarrassing. Epsilon is still licking their wounds after losing the girl squad in Anacapri, which was about a week ago. The youngest girls in the famous families are fledgling teenagers, and they might as well be the *babies*, the treasured irreplaceable diamonds.

You don't lose them.

Charlie is different. For one, he's an adult. For another, he does this all the fucking time. If I asked for a "search and rescue," I know Akara and Thatcher would help me track him, but there's not much they can actually do. They don't have more or better intel than me.

Anyway, I've got it covered.

Halfway down the alleyway, I reach the back door of the department store. I check my watch and then lean a hip against the brick. Waiting. After a second, I pull out my cell to call an Uber Black.

Being the 24/7 bodyguard to a Cobalt, to anyone really, was never my plan, but it also wasn't a far leap from professional boxing.

I love my job.

There's really nothing like it in the world. The fact that every day is different, that it's like being on a drug, adrenaline coursing through my veins, well…the only time I felt like this was in the ring. But it's different here.

Better.

The backdoor swings open. My client's normally messy hair looks even more wind-blown. How many strangers' hands just ran through his hair?

I don't know.

The sleeve of his white button-down hangs limply off his shoulder, ripped and dangling by a literal thread. Popped buttons expose his bare, lean chest, and fresh pink marks mar his fair, white skin like fingernails raked his body.

His neck is rubbed raw and red. I bet someone grabbed him around the throat. Tugging him closer, maybe. *This* was the cost. I knew he'd be bombarded and touched.

Guilt doesn't assault me. I'm not weighed down seeing him hurt. I'm just relieved that I predicted right and he exited *this* backdoor.

When I first started out on his detail, I got sucker-punched with regret. Thinking I could've done a better job. Thinking I should've thwarted this and that touch. But this is the best job *anyone* has ever done for him.

Five years later, I understand there's a bigger picture here.

I have to choose my battles with Charlie.

He meets my gaze, unsurprised by my presence, and casually steps into the alleyway, kicking the door shut behind him.

Charlie lights a cigarette. "I thought maybe you'd take the hint this time," he says and blows smoke into the warm night air.

"You don't want me on your detail anymore, then ask for a transfer." It's the same reminder I give him daily.

We go round and round on this carousel and it never really ends.

"It's not just you." His yellow-green eyes flit to me. "Anyone. I don't need a constant shadow parading behind me."

"Bring that up with your parents then."

He may be twenty-one, but his mom and dad are overprotective, and they're not going to let any of their children—let alone Charlie, the eldest son of the Cobalt Empire—prance around the city without literal protection.

It'll just never happen.

It's a battle he'll lose every time.

It's why he scuffs his shoe against the asphalt and drops the subject. I scan his skin again, noticing blood seeping through his wrinkled button-down. Someone must have scratched him deeper by his ribs.

"You're bleeding," I tell him. "You want me to call Farrow?" He's on the med team.

But mention of my best friend causes Charlie to roll his eyes. Farrow isn't Charlie's cup of tea, mostly for the fact that he's attached to Charlie's *least favorite* cousin, Maximoff Hale. But more recently, Maximoff and Charlie have put their feud to bed.

Charlie will often say things to me like, "You have a strange choice in friends." "You sure you don't want to reevaluate your friendship with *him?*" "Why are you friends with a self-righteous, arrogant asshole?"

Farrow and I go way back.

But I don't shoot the shit with Charlie like *that*.

I'd give him a half-second look and say, "Worry about your own friendships, or lack thereof." He'd take the diss with an impressed smile.

Charlie and I aren't friends.

Let me make this clear.

We.

Are.

Not.

Friends.

I am not a buddy-guard. So when Charlie makes small remarks that edge on lethal injections, I don't play into his hand. He can do that with his actual friends.

In the alleyway, Charlie barely glances at the bloody spot and says, "It hardly even stings." He flicks his cigarette to the side, and I catch a faint note of disappointment in his voice.

I tense. "You at least want a Band-Aid? You're ruining your shirt." My phone vibrates against my ass, but I don't retrieve my cell. It's more likely it's a *personal* text. I swivel the volume of my radio and listen. Seeing if I missed anything over comms.

The line is close to dead.

Comms have been quiet tonight. Not surprising. We all just got back from Italy yesterday, where Farrow and Maximoff had their wedding in Anacapri. Not much is going on now.

Most of the families are resting in Philly. And the ones in New York—mainly three of Charlie's brothers—are safe and sound in their Hell's Kitchen apartment at the moment. Charlie is the only one gallivanting across the city in the middle of the fucking night like a blood-thirsty vampire.

Hey, he is legitimately as popular as Edward Cullen could ever be.

Charlie finally glances at the red stain on his white, shredded button-down. "No Band-Aid. It'll sell more if it has my blood on it." He says it so casually, like that's the most normal reaction in the world.

"CHARLIE!!"

Our heads swerve at the same time. Charlie's adorers have found him, and they're running toward him like he can conjure water in a drought.

I don't ask him where he wants to go or what he wants to do. I grab his wrist and tug him towards the other end of the alleyway.

"Ohmygod OSLIE IS REAL!"

Fuck.

Every tendon in my body tightens, but I don't drop Charlie's wrist. Mainly because there's a 50% chance the guy will let the stampeding pack of fans plow him down if I do. And I've taken his wrist before. I've had to physically *pull* him in my direction plenty of times.

Never did it elicit this reaction.

Never did it hinder my job.

Until those fucking rumors.

Charlie Cobalt and Oscar Oliveira are a couple!

Farrow and Thatcher, two Omega bodyguards, decided to not only date their clients but put a ring on them. And it's fucked me to hell. Because *now* fans think SFO is some pretend security firm as a front to hide relationships with clients. So they think Charlie and I are an item, and it's so far from the truth.

Adrenaline and annoyance make a home in my body. Charlie seems unperturbed but he keeps glancing at me and then back at the girls. We reach the curb just as the Uber Black skids to a halt in front of us. Timing isn't always my friend, but I'm thankful it's in my corner tonight.

Charlie doesn't argue with me as I open the door and guide him inside.

"Where'd you set the address?" Charlie asks me as I shut the door.

"Your apartment."

"Can I have your phone?"

I know the drill. As I pass it to Charlie, I tell the driver. "Frank, we're about to change our destination. Is that a problem?"

The heavy-set man shakes his head. "Not at all. Just give me a second to let the GPS recalculate."

"Done," Charlie whispers to me and hands the phone back. "Your sister texted you."

I can't tell if he's trying to distract me by bringing up my baby sister. Or if he's pointing out that he saw her message to annoy me.

Whatever the case, I take a quick glance at the message while the Uber pulls onto the street.

I found an apartment & roommate on Craigslist. Meeting them tomorrow. Rent is affordable. Im not living at home anymore. I cant do it — **Baby Sis**

Fuck, Joana.
I text fast and feel Charlie's eyes on my fingers.
Just live with me. There's room. I hit send.
She's quick to reply.

I like the Craigslist place — **Baby Sis**

My nineteen-year-old rebellious sister loves to stick it to our dad whenever she can, and I'd say eight times out of ten, he probably deserves the hard time. She's stubbornly set on Craigslist, maybe to cause waves. Because Joana rooming with me will *please* our parents.

I'm the oldest by a longshot. I celebrated my thirty-second birthday a couple months ago, and my sister and brother are a whole *decade* younger than me.

This is a bad time to have a text war with my sister. I'm on-duty. So after I send a brief message saying, I'll call later, I shut out the text thread.

Juggling family life among a never-sleeping job is *hard*. Anyone who says differently hasn't met the Oliveira clan.

My eyes flit to the car windows. Yeah, I have no clue where we're going, but at least we're not being trailed or flanked by paparazzi vans.

I open up the Uber app and glance at the new address Charlie plugged in. My brows furrow.

My veins pump harder.

What the actual fuck?

I figured he'd take us to the airport.

But I'm staring at an address to The Walnut, an apartment building in Philadelphia. It can't be a coincidence that Jack Highland lives there. I rub a hand through the thick curly strands of my hair.

"Why are we going to The Walnut?" I question outright.

Charlie leans back against the black leather seat. "I have an appointment with Jack Highland."

I wait for him to explain further.

He doesn't.

"In the middle of the night?" I ask.

"Yes."

"You didn't think to tell me?"

"I just did."

I'm on a *need to know* basis with my client. And in his world, no one needs to know shit about his life. I get it. He doesn't really want a bodyguard. I'm just the thorn perpetually in his side. But he's got me, and right now I'm on high-fucking-alert.

Highland and I have history.

Okay, that's a lie.

We have zero history.

Because the guy rejected my kiss.

Rejected *me*.

But hey, he still has my fucking bandana, my belt, *and* my sweatshirt that I lent him. So I'm taking this with stride. I'm killing two birds with one stone tonight and coming to collect.

Those clothes are mine.

I want them back.

I may have fallen for a straight guy, but my heart is bricked back up. Duct-taped shut. Jack's not getting anywhere near it, and once I have my clothes it'll cement that shit.

Charlie closes his eyes like he's going to take a nap on the ride to Philly. I should do the same—sleep when I can—which is practically never. But my mind is on high-speed.

I'm about to see Jack.

Again.

I clasp a hand over my mouth, my face hot from what happened between us.

And what's worse—I have no earthly clue why Charlie wants to meet with him. It's like walking into the world's darkest tunnel without a flashlight.

God help me.

2

Oscar Oliveira

THE MOST EMBARRASSING MOMENT OF OSCAR OLIVEIRA'S LIFE

TWO DAYS AGO

THE SKIES SPLIT, rain poured, lightning cracked, and even as the storm subsided, everything felt exactly how it was supposed to feel. Happy, *joyous*. I just officiated my best friend's wedding. I just watched him walk down the aisle in Anacapri and marry the love of his life.

And now…now my urge to be in a relationship has *ballooned* to the umpteenth degree.

Sign me up for sunsets, romantic strolls in the park, sweaty never-ending nights on a dance floor, and mind-blowing sex. Fuck, I'd take average sex at this point if it meant being in a steady love-affirming relationship. I just want the good stable pieces. The thing that seems to slip through my fingertips ever since I joined security.

I haven't been in a real long-term relationship since college and it's starting to grind on me.

But who in the fuck would want to date someone who can't be around longer than five seconds?

Sometimes I wonder if all I'll ever get is the sex. The quick fucks. Easy to come by, but damn the novelty wears off fast.

With the wedding reception in full swing, guests dressed in white are milling about a breathtaking cliffside restaurant. Stuff made for celebrities and for travel writers penning *Top 10 Most Romantic Getaways*. Waves splash against the rocks, oranges and yellows bathing the sparkling sea as the sun begins to set.

Italy can't be more beautiful tonight.

I wander around, doing two things.

1. Trying to avoid my parents and avós. Love them and their gossip, but they'll trap me in their chatty web for too long. I already spent half an hour talking to my mom.

She's been snapping a thousand photos, and she thanked me again for paying for the family's flights to Italy and making this possible. She always expected Farrow to invite her to his eventual wedding, but I doubt she thought it'd be an international destination.

I grew up in a typical middleclass family, and money for travel always went towards flights to Brazil to see our avós.

Farrow said he'd pay for the plane tickets, but I manage my finances well, actually better than he does. His prideful ass will just never admit it.

I set aside a lot in savings before we all got a pay-cut from hell (downside to joining Kitsuwon Securities—a brand new firm).

Another thing I'm doing right now:

2. Trying not to follow Charlie. It's a habit at this point. I'm off-duty, but I trust the temp guards on his detail about as much as I trust a gnat not to zap itself in a fly trap.

Sipping on champagne, I unconsciously spot my client—yeah, we're saying it's *unconscious*. Charlie is kicked back and balancing on two legs of a patio chair, all while Audrey Cobalt talks his ear off. He rolls his eyes at whatever his carrot-orange-haired little sister says.

The one good thing about Charlie being around family—they always try to drag him into their orbit. When he's tethered to the rest of the Cobalts, it's easier to keep track of him.

Really, it makes it easier to relax. To stop leaning on the arches of my feet like I'm two-seconds away from an Olympic sprint after him.

Passing rows of breakfast platters and seafood, I grab a couple shrimp off a tower, gather some crackers in a napkin, and leave the restaurant area.

The wind is warm and the air smells like salt. I'm about to step down the stone steps toward the lounge chairs on the sundeck. The cliffside restaurant straddles a sunbathing area where people can swim in the coves.

Just as I take that step, movement catches my eye in the parking lot to my right. All I can see is the back of a tall guy, sleeves rolled up his arms to reveal sculpted, muscular biceps, and his dark hair blows with a seaside gust.

Like every guest, he's in all-white. The dress code.

That belt is mine.

Lent him that for the ceremony.

I waver for a second.

Fuck it.

I tip the flute back to my lips, and cold champagne slides down my throat, emptying the glass. Slowly, I close the distance between me and the most gorgeous guy at this reception.

Jack Highland is often behind a camera; yet, he looks like he could model for a cologne ad.

It doesn't help that he's bent over the back of a hatchback. Car trunk lifted up while he fiddles with his camera. Ass in perfect view. His athletic build screams *jock bro*. But I wish I knew him better to discern what kind he actually is.

I tend to steer clear of chest-thumping frat bros. But I like a good sports-loving jock. Let's go to a Phillies game. Share a pack of peanuts and complain about the Mets.

My shoes pad along the parking lot as I approach him. His skin is a mixture of light brown and red-gold hues and looks more sun-kissed in the setting light. He's Filipino-American and biracial: Dad is white, Mom is Filipina.

As I near, he turns his head, and his long lashes lift.

"Hey," he says with a smile and a genial nod of his chin. His eyes hold mine for a beat longer. A beat that makes me question every fucking thing. It doesn't help that he does that *thing* that most people do when they're checking me out.

The up-down, imperceptible motion. A one-two movement with his eyes. Up-down. Two seconds flat. Barely noticeable.

Maybe he doesn't even realize he's doing it.

But those two seconds tangle the axons in my brain. Twisting. Pulling. Tying them into a confused knot. So far as I know, he's straight, but sexuality is a fluid thing. He could be questioning, right?

I just don't know for sure.

The parking lot is quiet. No one else here.

I return the nod. "You hiding out, Highland?" I ask him casually, despite the fact that nerves ratchet up. I don't need my Yale degree in Kinesiology to tell me why my heart starts racing or my palms get clammy.

I have a crush on him.

A stupid. Silly. Dumbass crush.

I'm the one who nearly choked on my food when Maximoff used that word. Back at his sister's first Rainbow Brigade outing, he asked me about Jack, *"You have a crush on him?"*

I laughed.

Crush.

I thought crushes were for twelve-year-olds. But I've never been this nervous around someone I like. Is there something different about Jack from all the other women and men I've dated? Or is it just because I know this could be unrequited?

He's probably not even attracted to men.

But the way he's looking at me...

I toss a cracker in my mouth and stand my ground. Not running away from a crush, that's for sure.

Jack twists off a lens to the Canon camera. "Just need to switch these out," he says and then a smile inches across his lips. "Why would you think I'm hiding out?"

"It's a wedding," I say into a shrug. "Sometimes being single at these events royally sucks. I wouldn't blame you, if you needed a minute or two alone."

His eyes hold mine again. He's got this way of staring at you like he *knows* you. Understands you. And I'm not a fucking idiot. A part of that is just his charm, embedded into his DNA. It's what makes him so good at his job. As an executive producer of *We Are Calloway*, he's able to pull out real emotion from the famous ones.

Still looking at me, he wraps the strap of his Canon around his neck and shuts the trunk with a hand. "It's not so bad," he tells me. His smile grows. "You're keeping me company, right?"

He's flirting.

He's definitely flirting.

Someone should just pop out behind the bushes with a huge ass sign that says *yes.*

"Is that what I'm doing?" I say, playing this cool. I pop another cracker in my mouth.

He leans a hip against the hatchback. "You're single, too, right?"

The food goes down rough. "Yeah...single." I glance down at the belt on his waist. *My* belt. When I raise my gaze to his, his eyes flit to the belt he's wearing, and then back to me, down my toned build.

The air feels warmer.

Skin hotter.

He has a couple inches on my six-two height, but as he leans on the hatchback, we're about eye-level. Jack nods slowly to me, and our gazes catch again.

I think he's going to mention the belt.

"It must be hard to date and be a bodyguard," Jack says, treading a flirty line and surprising me a little. It's not often that happens. I always feel ten steps ahead of most people.

I nod just as slowly. "Impossible is more like it."

"What is it all of you guys say...*bodyguards are like spouses to their clients.*"

You guys.

It dawns on me that he's talking about all the bodyguards. I'm lumped in with the lot, even if my style of guarding doesn't match most. I don't really love that phrase. I'm around Charlie more than a spouse would be. I'm not just his husband. I'm his brother. I'm his father. I'm his cousin. I'm every relationship he has all rolled into one.

But I don't tell that to Jack. The easiest way to send someone running would be to announce that I have someone else attached to me 24/7. I mean, technically he knows, but I don't need to spell it out like that.

"Yeah, it's not easy, but I don't want to be single forever," I tell him. "Even if Charlie is my job, and my job is all-consuming."

He lets out a short laugh. "I know the feeling."

Production and security are fire and water. Bodyguards want to extinguish one-half of every smoldering ember the docuseries stokes among the public. We have polarizing goals, but we have to coexist.

As hot as Jack is, I know that crossing any line with him is like stepping into a rigged heavyweight match. But it's nice to hear that he at least relates on this level.

My eyes flit to the camera around his neck. "You have to get back?"

He's here to work. Unlike me. He filmed the wedding and is supposed to be taking more videos of this reception.

I'm distracting him.

"Not yet." He leans his ass more against the closed trunk. "I have a couple more minutes to kill." His eyes flit up and down me again, and he tinkers with his camera as he says, "You know being single at weddings has its benefits."

"Yeah?"

"All the single people start wishing they were in a relationship—or at the very least in someone else's bed."

Can relate.

But I don't get the words out before he says, "Some of my best lays have been at weddings."

"*At* weddings." I grin. "You hooking up in the broom closet, Long Beach?"

He matches my grin. "What are you, a stickler for specifics?"

"Maybe." I toss the last of my food in my mouth.

His smile hits his eyes. "Not *at* the wedding. *After* the ceremony," he clarifies. "One time I didn't make it that far."

Fuck. I'm intrigued. Full-blown, I want to dive into this conversation and never leave. But my muscles have also tensed considerably. Talking about sex and work and weddings without anyone else around feels like stepping out onto a tightrope. One false move and I'm plunging fifty-feet.

"Now you have to tell me," I say.

He shrugs with just one shoulder. "I've *probably* already carved out a spot in hell."

I put two-and-two together, and my grin overtakes my face. "Did you…" I laugh. "Did you fuck in a church?"

"Catholic church. Back pew. The bride was a family friend from California."

I cock my head. "You fucked the bride?"

He laughs. "No. Definitely did not do that, Oscar."

We share a softer smile.

He lets go of his camera, letting it hang. "I'm confirmed Catholic, but I don't go to church as often as I did as a kid." He pauses like he's gauging my reaction. Maybe he cares what I think.

"Same here," I tell him.

We both nod, recognizing in a quiet moment that we have shit in common. More than I think we've both ever even explored or given breath to.

Jack runs his fingers across his strong jaw, slight stubble coming in. Making him look a little older than twenty-seven.

I usually go for people my age or older. I also would usually never even draw *towards* a straight guy like I am him. Look at me, making exceptions left and right for Jack Highland.

"It fit well," I tell him, motioning to the belt threaded through his white slacks. "What would you have done if our measurements were off? Belt was too big for your scrawny waist?"

He smiles. "First off, I'd never be scrawny. Have you seen me swim?"

"I'm suddenly having a hard time remembering. You'll have to show me again."

"Make the date, I'll be there."

Date.

Jack doesn't give the offer time to breathe. "And I knew your belt would fit me. Your other clothes have." He means my bandana and sweatshirt.

I could joke about how the bandana would fit anyone, but he's not Donnelly or Farrow. I don't want to rib him like I would a friend. "If you ever need or want more, I have a whole closet full of pants and tees."

"Just pants and tees?" he jokes with a smile that captivates, that could make the saddest motherfucker on this planet feel some kind of happiness.

"I've already given you more than that, Highland. You think I'd stop there?"

He laughs into a bigger smile. "Maybe I'll just quit packing for these trips. Your clothes always smell good, and you probably have better underwear than me, anyway."

My blood pumps. "Always trying to pad egos," I grin.

He looks me up and down, the suggestion clear to me. "Is it working?"

Yeah. My defenses fluctuate between high and low. "You're doing your LA networking best, bro, but I'm not someone who has anything to offer you professionally."

He opens his mouth. Closes it. He's rethinking something. And Jack isn't a guy that overthinks what he's about to say. He has the charisma of the fucking *sun.* That big blazing ball that is hoisted in the sky and everyone leaves their house to bask in its rays.

It's magnetic energy.

But something traps his words, stumbles him up.

After a second, Jack says, "It's not that...I'm not trying to schmooze you for work or to join the docuseries—though, you'd be *great* in it." He smiles.

I shake my head with a matching grin. "Still never happening." I like maintaining *some* anonymity in the public, and that's already hard these days.

"Really, I just enjoy this," Jack says more quietly, our gazes latched with seriousness. "You and me and..." He breathes in but doesn't breathe out. Our eyes dance along each other, and I find myself stepping closer.

His chest rises in a headier inhale.

My lungs inflate, and I want to take my hand and clutch the back of his neck. To let my fingers thread through his dark hair and up the back of his skull.

For our lips to find each other in a slow, scalding *ache* of a kiss. *I want that.* Warm summer wind whips around us, and tension mounts while we linger, an inch away.

I glance at his mouth. My voice husky as I ask, "Can I kiss you?"

Jack stiffens.

And not like a dick-stiffening kind of way. He morphs into a stone statue, which rocks me back.

Fuck.

Should I be checking myself to make sure I didn't turn into Medusa and cast a spell on the guy?

He blinks.

So at least he's alive.

I actually take two steps away from him. Putting space between us.

"Jack," I say, his name sounding weird on my tongue. I usually call him Highland...or Long Beach. I'm concerned about him, but I'm afraid crowding him will make it worse somehow.

"Uh..." he breathes out. "Thanks, but I'm straight."

I go rigid.

Thanks, but I'm straight.

Thanks, but I'm straight.

Thanks, but I'm straight! It blares in my head.

Concern is gone. I'm just...*fuck.*

My skin scorches from head to toe in deep embarrassment.

He's quiet again, apologies in his eyes.

I want to disintegrate right now. I've *never* been this fucking mortified. I feel like an idiot, and I know I'm not one. An awkward stretch of silence bends around us.

Jack often throws out platitudes to make sure no one in the room is uncomfortable. Well, that's not happening here. He's not saying a fucking thing.

We're both wading in intense, unbearable discomfort.

What was I thinking?

I break the quiet. "Yeah, fuck, sorry," I mumble. "I just...I didn't mean..."

He offers a weak smile. "Yeah."

That one word literally sets my pulse into a panicked race.

Good God I want to run and hide. "Um...cake...has name." I turn around, avoiding his eyes. And I leave with a hot, lengthy stride.

I've never run away from a situation so fast.

Shit, what did I even say? *Cake...has name?* That's not a complete motherfucking sentence! I was trying to tell him there's a piece of cake that has my name on it.

Fumbled the exit.

Fumbled everything.

I'm just mortified I asked him if I could kiss him. It would have been better if I didn't feel like a twelve-year-old. I'm thirty-two, and the way I feel around that guy puts me back to preteen eras. I hate it. I hate what I just did. Most importantly, I'd like nothing more than to never see Jack Highland.

I don't know how I'm going to be able to look him in the eyes ever again.

3

Oscar Oliveira

THE TWO-HOUR CAR RIDE to The Walnut screws me over. It's too much down time to Philly, and I end up replaying the awkward moment in Anacapri over and over in my head. I can't tell if it was actually as bad as I'm remembering or if I'm imagining the interaction worse on each replay.

In any case, I was rejected for a kiss.

I've never been rejected before. Not like that.

Charlie and I are buzzed into the building, and while we ride the elevator to the third floor, I glance at the time on my watch.

1 a.m.

Who has an appointment at 1 a.m. that's not a booty call or something that could put you in jail?

Charlie. That's who.

My ear picks up sudden comms sound.

"Farrow to Omega, I've already left for the lake house. We're trying to make it there before sunrise. Unless some bad shit happens, you probably won't be able to reach me on comms for a while."

I feel my mouth curve. His maverick ass is actually informing our lead about *where* he is. Albeit, after he's already started driving to the Smoky Mountains.

I click my mic and speak quietly on comms. "Have fun on your honeymoon, Redford. Don't be too sad I'm not there to make a good time better."

"I think you mean *messier*, Oliveira."

I stifle a laugh since Charlie is literally beside me and can't hear the radio. I have enough time to say back, "A hundred-and-one tabloids with your face front-and-center would disagree."

"You mean the ones that say I've had the wedding of the century?" I can practically see his smug cheek-to-cheek smile with that ace thrown.

He got me.

Farrow and Maximoff's wedding made every headline, every entertainment site, late-night show, and Instagram feed. I love them, but my friend getting hitched recently, especially to a *Hale*, has been a painful reminder that I'm…alone.

And I'm about to face my crush that last ended like a pie in the face.

I'd joke to Farrow about letting me tag along on his honeymoon if there were time. But the elevator doors slide open, and my *good time* on comms comes to an abrupt halt.

Officially, I've lost the nerve to actually see Jack. Avoidance isn't an option. I'm here for work, not a social outing. The only way to minimize embarrassment is to ignore Jack. Maybe I won't even ask for the clothes he borrowed anymore.

I waffle between the options before I land on one:

Professional.

Keep it professional.

I settle with this plan as we reach Jack's apartment.

Protocol: I answer Charlie's doors and knock on the ones he visits. But before I put my fist to the wood, I look to Charlie.

My client leans a shoulder next to the doorframe, his brows rising like he knows what I'm about to ask. "You'll find out why we're here in five seconds," he says. "I'm not about to ruin the surprise."

"Who said I was going to be surprised?" I knock on the door. I always plan for the unpredictable with Charlie.

The door swings open.

Jack Highland stands on the other side.

I cage my breath.

A yellow sweat-stained Under Armour shirt suctions to his muscular chest like he just returned from the gym. Smart watch on his wrist, one wireless earbud in his left ear, and running shorts all add up.

"We interrupt something?" I ask, worried Charlie didn't have a meeting with Jack at all. It wouldn't be the first time he's showed up somewhere unannounced.

Jack shakes his head. "Not at all. I've been waiting for you guys." He pushes the door open wider, and I slip past him, avoiding his eyes.

He clears his throat. "Sorry I didn't have time to take a shower."

I bite back a comment about how he still smells good. My pulse thumps loudly in my ears. *Professional.* It's usually not hard for me to dip into work-mode. I take my job seriously.

Quickly, I assess Jack's apartment. It's the first time I've ever been here.

My first thought: how does a six-foot-four guy live in something so...*small?*

The space is tinier than even my studio, and I live in Hell's Kitchen. A gray sofa rests against the same wall as a murphy bed (currently drawn up and hidden), and I'm guessing the metal bins in an open-faced cabinet are his dresser, all of which resides under the only window. A surfboard is propped in the corner. One that looks old and used.

Jack surfs.

Didn't know that.

Even if he's born and bred in Southern California, I'm not going to *assume* every Cali stereotype applies, even if they do.

We're all a lot of where we come from, just as much as we are the people who raised us and who we've met along the way.

His place doesn't even have a full kitchen. Just a mini-fridge and microwave. I look around for the TV, thinking he has to have one. He's an exec producer. That's his job. But I can't find it.

I have so many fucking questions.

But that would involve actually staring him directly in the eyes. Not about to do that. My gaze plants on the only window. Just one. Well, that makes my job easier.

Charlie steps into the apartment behind me, and I give him a look. "Stay here."

He nods.

For as much of a pain as Charlie can be, he does listen to me sometimes. I glance to Jack, who's busy locking the door. "Can I sweep your place real quick?"

He doesn't turn around as he says, "There's not much here but go for it."

I slip into the bathroom first, and it's bigger than I expected. I pull back the plain shower curtain. Empty.

A cardboard box is tucked under a rack of towels. Flaps open, I can see some suits and expensive loafers inside. Not sure why he's packing his suits in a box. But I don't stare long or dig through it. I try not to let my eyes roam to Jack's personal belongings. Like his brand of shampoo or the magazines in the wicker basket by the door.

I don't need to know more about him than I already do.

It'll be like rubbing salt into an opened wound, and I just need that shit to heal as quickly as it can.

I check all the usual spots for any mics or electronics that could be recording. Satisfied, I return to the living area. Charlie is already on the couch, and Jack sits across from him on a plastic fold-out chair.

"Do you want it for personal or commercial use?" Jack asks my client.

My muscles tense.

What the fuck are you up to, Charlie?

Floorboards squeak as I walk further in the room. Jack and Charlie glance over at me.

"Everything good?" Jack asks.

"So far," I say. "I just need to check that window."

Jack is currently occupying the middle of the entire room. He stands quickly as I step closer. "You really think I would bug my apartment?" He sounds more curious than dispirited.

"Doesn't matter what I think," I tell him. "It's protocol." Jack might be trusted in the inner-circle, but his place hasn't been cleared today. I slide past his chest, an inch of air between us. I don't know if it was my words or our past that puts an invisible strain between us. But I can tell we're both holding our breaths.

I barely exhale when I make it to the window.

"Personal would be preferred," Charlie tells Jack, replying to his question.

Window cleared and blinds snapped shut, I face them again.

Jack hasn't sat back down, thankfully, because I have to return to the front door. "You could use a bigger apartment, Highland," I whisper to him as I pass again. "You don't fit in this one."

The top of his head is barely an inch from the ceiling fan.

He lets out a short laugh. "I'll take that under consideration. Any other critiques?" His tone is friendly but eager.

Our eyes latch for what feels like the first time tonight. I should ask for my clothes back. But it's not the time or place and the longer he's staring at me, the more my stomach knots. I can't read him. Before, I found it intriguing, now it's almost agonizing. Unnerving.

"Nope," I say and break our gaze to head to the door.

I lean beside the doorframe, giving both of them space, but I'm in earshot. Charlie rubs his fingers over his lips in thought.

Jack refocuses on my client. "I'd love to work with you on it, Charlie, but I can't take on any personal projects right now."

"I can pay whatever you want," Charlie says casually like his checkbook is open on the table. Now I'm a little concerned. *Again, what in the fuck is he doing?* I wish I could ask, but I usually don't get involved unless his safety is on the line.

Jack smiles. "I appreciate that. But it's not about the money. I'm busy these days, so I'm only taking on projects that will land me network and cable contracts."

"So let's say I want you to shop it to a network. You'd take it on then?" Charlie asks.

Pieces are suddenly colliding at a sharp rate, and I have to cut in this time. Not moving from beside the door, I speak up. "You want Highland to film you?" It's an educated guess.

Jack's brows shoot up and he swings his head to me. "He didn't tell you?"

I go rigid. God, I wish I were wrong.

Charlie twists the gold ring on his finger. A Faust Academy crest of a falcon and crown rest in the center. He never had to tell me, but I know that's his father's high school ring.

Charlie's yellow-greens flit to me. "You know now."

"You're already on *We Are Calloway*," I remind him. He also barely shows up to gigs. He'll comply for his segments, but they last maybe two minutes tops. I can't see him staying in Jack's orbit long enough to fill up a whole episode.

He shrugs and tilts his head. "Maybe I want to be the star."

I don't believe him.

Most of the world truly thinks Charlie Cobalt is as narcissistic and self-serving as his father, but I've been around him long enough to know that he has motives. And they're not always egocentric. But does he have the ability to go there? Yeah. It's in him, sure.

He's only twenty-one. He's so young still. I just don't know where he'll really land.

I think on the facts that I do have. "If that were true, Charlie, you would have been the one to bring up the network deal." He wasn't. He wanted this project to be personal. *Private*.

Jack's brows cinch in worry and he raises a hand to my client. "And I don't want to pressure you into doing anything for network TV. I have reliable contacts that would be more than happy to take on a personal videography project for you."

"If you were pressuring me, I'd already be walking out the door," Charlie says, still rolling his ring absentmindedly. "Let's do it. Once you have the footage for a pilot, you can shop it to whatever networks you want."

I grind on my teeth, sawing my opinion down. I have to let him live his life. Make his own decisions without my input. But damn, it's hard sometimes.

Jack hesitates. "This can't be like *We Are Calloway*. If you want to do a show that centers on *your* life, you're going to have to stick around for every scheduled filming. I can't move equipment as fast as you change your mind and run off to Prague."

Charlie snorts. "You mean we're not filming a nature documentary? An up close and personal look at the mysterious beast in his natural habitat."

Jack's face contorts for a second, empathy leaking out. "I didn't want to ask, but I feel like I have to…is there a reason you want to do this?" I'm a little relieved Jack is pressing him on this. I know I won't.

Charlie rolls his eyes. "Do I have to have one?"

"For my moral conscience, yeah," Jack nods. "I need you to give me one. Because I can't film you, if deep down, you don't really want to do this."

Charlie scoots to the edge of the couch. Elbows to his knees. "Deep down," he says. "I don't give a shit if people love me. Or hate me. Or think I'm an entitled, spoiled brat. I'd have to care enough about them to care about their opinions—and I don't give a shit. You want honesty, I have reasons I want my life filmed, but I'm not going to tell them to you. And if you think I'm going to care about exposing myself to the world—I won't. I don't."

I believe that.

Jack looks him up and down, still gauging. "I won't air anything you don't want aired. You can trust me on that, but you're going to get more shit than you've ever received from the public. You'll be the first of the famous kids to step out with their own show. It's like announcing to the world you're going solo."

Charlie lets out a genuine, heartfelt laugh. "Better, even." He rises to his feet.

Jack follows him to a stance. "Everyone knows Cobalts run on loyalty," he reminds him. "To a lot of people, they're going to think this move is a betrayal to your family. I just want you to be prepared for that kind of heat."

"If people think that I'm betraying my family, they're dumber than I thought," he says. "Which is saying something because I think the human race has a chronic case of idiocy."

Jack takes a breath. "We're doing this then?"

"How fast can you get the contract to me?" Charlie asks. "I'd like to start as soon as possible."

Jack nods. "I can have it for you to sign in about five hours."

It's in this moment that it hits me...

I'm about to be around Jack Highland a hell of a lot more. There's no avoiding him. No ignoring him. In fact, I have to schedule a meeting with him. A one-on-one.

I cross my arms over my chest, tensed beyond belief. "Highland," I say. "Whatever time you're thinking of stopping by. Arrive an hour early."

"Sounds like a plan," he says, but his voice is suddenly stilted and lacks the natural warmth it usually carries.

Awkward.

This whole fucking thing.

Charlie's phone rings. A quick glance at the screen elicits an eye roll. Has to be one of his brothers. He silences the call and slides his cell in his back pocket. "See you tomorrow," he tells Jack.

And just like that, we're out of Jack's apartment.

"Where to?" I ask my client as we take the stairs.

There's a long moment of silence before he sighs heavily, almost in defeat. "Home."

4

Jack Highland

HERE'S ONE THING I can always count on: *structure*. Every great film, every cinematic plot has *structure*. Even with the docuseries that I work on—which isn't scripted—there is a story structure. We take our footage and make sure the narrative is in order.

A beginning, middle, and an end.

My life has *always* had structure. I've known how it'd start, where I'd go, and where I'd end up. That is, until Oscar…

My life has never been more jumbled. Confusing. *Messy.*

God, I spent *three* hours in the shower after Oscar and Charlie left my apartment. I just stood there! The hot water ran cold, and I stared at the tile walls in a daze. And I confess, I was thinking about Oscar Oliveira.

I kept replaying how he came into my apartment like a frozen wind. He basically coldshouldered me. Treated me like a co-worker and not a friend.

Were we friends?

I thought we were *friendly*…maybe too friendly. I don't know. But usually when I fuck-up a conversation, I can work my magic and rewind the reel, like nothing ever happened.

Oscar is different. No amount of charm is getting me out of what happened at the wedding reception. I can't flash a smile and expect him to go back to how we were.

I'm terrified of our dynamic changing into something uncomfortable, or worse—something cold and empty. Especially *now*. When it's looking like we're about to be around each other a hundred times more.

I try to take a breath.

Relax, dude.

I'd say I'm rarely uptight. I grew up surfing. Patiently waiting for that perfect wave. Breathing in and out, but fuck if I know *anything* right now about oxygen and patience—because I've never felt more asphyxiated and unbalanced.

I'm in my Mazda. By the time I got out of the shower, I threw on dark jeans, a white crew-neck, and left my apartment, then jumped in my car. No sleep tonight, I'm driving to New York for the early-morning meeting with Oscar.

My cell is docked on the dashboard, traffic a nightmare and the sun isn't even out yet. So I'm even more caught off-guard when my phone rings for FaceTime and the caller is from California.

Long Beach is three hours behind East Coast time. It's basically the middle of the night there.

I answer fast.

Not able to look at the screen while I change lanes.

"Kuya," my mom calls out to me, using a Filipino term that means *big brother.*

I rotate my wheel and check over my shoulder. "Po." I usually say *po* instead of *yeah* to my mom, out of respect.

"Have you heard from Jesse? I can't get ahold of him. He's not in his bed."

Jesse. My seventeen-year-old brother.

I frown, more at the street as a car tries to cut me off. "No, but he's probably just at the beach." *And giving our mom a heart attack.* "I'll call him, Mama."

"He shouldn't be at the beach. He's already been grounded. No surfing for two weeks. And it's too dark outside. It's *late.*"

I glance down at the cellphone. My protective, sweet-natured, generous mom fills the screen on FaceTime. Short black hair molds her heart-shaped face, glasses perched on her nose, and she's in a robe like she hurriedly woke up out of bed.

I smile at the sight of her features. I like talking with my family, but nothing beats seeing their faces. It makes it feel like we aren't split apart on either coast. We try to FaceTime as much as possible. Even when we *all* should be asleep.

She sees my smile. "This isn't funny, Kuya. He could be in trouble or hurt." Worry is etched in her voice. "What if he's not at the beach? What if it's drugs?"

"It's not drugs. I'll find him, rest assured." I'm more confident than concerned.

My brother spills his whole life story to me when we talk on the phone. I literally know when he took a shit yesterday, and not because he called me while he was on the toilet, which he's also done before.

So I'd know if he were snorting coke or shooting up heroine because he can't keep his mouth shut, and he'd tell me in a bout of word vomit.

"You never broke curfew. You told us where you'd be," she says, "and you always came home on time—are you sleeping? Why are there bags under your eyes?"

I glance from the phone to the road. She tries to inspect *my* face through the screen, but I'm further away from my cell's camera.

"It's dark in the car right now, Mama. The sun hasn't risen yet."

"You're working too much?"

I want to say *no*, but again, my life has an outline. I want to work towards something *big*. I always have. And she understands hard work and working hard. I'm just glad she's not asking me about dating.

Or marriage.

Or kids.

That part of my life is starting to be an astronomical who-the-fuck-knows. I blink and picture Oscar, and my heart rate jackhammers.

I inhale and try to stay calm. "My job always has weird hours," I remind her. "I'm gonna call Jes—"

Another voice is muffled in the background. I switch lanes again while my mom turns her head to look over her shoulder.

"Ano ho?" My mom says *what* in Tagalog to the other person in her house. She speaks more in the language.

I figure my Lola—my mom's mom—must've woken up. She's lived with my parents ever since I was a kid. I hear her ask what's going on.

"Utoy?" my Lola questions, using a Filipino term for Jesse which means *little boy.*

I can't hear their exchange until my mom moves closer to her phone and tells me, "Call me back if he doesn't answer you. Ten more minutes and I'm waking up your dad. We'll drive past every beach until we find him."

Jesse has broken curfew before, but that was when he had a girlfriend and snuck into her house. My mom knocked on the door demanding for his return, like the girl's family was holding him captive. Our mom is on our side, always, but she's not afraid to tell us we're doing something wrong. She grounded Jesse on the car ride home.

Our dad slams down the gavel just as strongly, but I'd say that my mom does everything better. My dad would be the first to agree. She's the heart of the Highland family.

"I love you, Ma," I say goodbye to my mom. "Ingat po." *Take care.*

"I love you more, 'nak." 'Nak is a shortened term for *anak*, which means *child.*

We hang up, and I give my cellphone a voice command. "Call Utoy."

You better answer, Jesse.

The phone rings.

And rings.

And I wonder if he's actually at a girl's house. Not the same girl. That one broke up with him two summers ago.

It rings.

He would've definitely told me if he had a crush on another girl… or guy. *He's straight.* He said he's straight before. I said I'm straight.

Because I am straight. I can appreciate good-looking guys, and yeah, Oscar is one of the best-looking bodyguards. If not *the* best.

And I've only had sex with women. All of my celebrity crushes have been women. Whenever I've envisioned my future, there's always been a wife at the end.

But at night, my mind wanders to him. I wake up with a massive hard-on that only goes away when I stroke myself thinking about him.

Doesn't mean I'm gay or bi or anything other than *straight.*

Am I convincing myself or am I really fucking straight? I need a road map to navigate this uncharted place, and I don't have it. I don't know anyone who does.

Oscar.

Yeah right, like he'll help me. Like he'd even want to after I rejected him.

Anyway—I'm straight. There's nothing to ask.

I'm not into Oscar like that.

My nose flares as I bite down on my teeth, and I realize the phone has already rung out with no answer.

Fuck.

I redial for FaceTime.

And he answers on the second ring. "Long time no chat"—we talked yesterday—"listen to this…" He rolls down the window to his Land Cruiser, and I hear the splash of the ocean.

I smile. "Sounds like you being grounded. *Again.*"

"The volume must be broken on this thing. Because that's clearly the sound of the sickest swells."

"Jesse."

"I want to be the first out there when the sun comes up."

My eyes flit from my brother to the road, back to him.

His shaggy hair sticks out in a million different places and he yawns into his arm like he woke up from sleeping in his car. I notice the wetsuit splayed over his headrest and the surfboard in the back. "So you'll tell the parents I'm safe and that I'll see them for breakfast—?"

"Fat chance, wild child, it's a school day." It may be summer, but he has to repeat British Lit for plagiarizing a paper last year.

He has a warm smile while he slouches on the passenger's seat of his SUV. "You look at the calendar this morning, Kuya? I'm impressed." He runs a hand through his dark hair that's long enough to reach the back of his neck. "It's almost like you're a fully functioning adult or something."

I skip over his sarcasm. "Aren't you actually grounded?"

"Like in this moment?"

I laugh. "Yeah. What other moment would there be, Jess?"

He shrugs with a bright smile that could rival mine. "You tell me, *Jack*." He puts extra emphasis on my name like I'm a pirate from the Disney franchise.

Jesse is exactly ten years younger than me, and I love him more than life itself. He's my only sibling, and while my family is still in SoCal, I end up seeing Jesse in person more than my parents. He'll fly out to Philly and stay with me for the weekend at least once a month. My mom and dad would make the trek more often, if their jobs didn't usurp their time.

"You have withstanding groundings," I tell him more plainly.

"Groundings?" Jesse leaves the camera frame for a second. "I mean, I feel like those might have been suggestions." He returns with a banana and slowly unpeels it.

My stomach groans at the food. *Fuck*. After my three-hour dazed and confused shower, I hightailed it to my car without grabbing breakfast. Hunger pains vs. being late. I'll choose the hunger pains every time. Showing up late feels worse somehow. Like knives plunging into my gut.

"You broke curfew three days in a row," I remind Jesse. "I don't think being grounded is a suggestion."

"KuyaI'mseventeen." He mumbles the sentence through his banana-filled mouth.

I laugh. He's an idiot.

He swallows and smiles. "I'm an adult."

"Pretty sure you're one year behind that, dude." I give him a look. "More if we're talking about maturity levels."

He smiles more. "I'm mature. Mama and Dad just miss you, since you're all the way out there and they're keeping their claws in me tight. They were never like this with you."

"Because I didn't break curfew."

"Did you even have curfew?"

"Yeah," I nod strongly. "You were just too little to remember." I switch lanes to take the next exit. "Text Mama right now and tell her you're driving home."

He lets out a huff and peels back more of his banana. "Did you already talk to her?" He sounds more remorseful. "Is she awake?"

"Yeah, and she's worried you're doing *drugs*."

He groans. "Fuck, okay." He sits up straighter and turns on the ignition. Biting a chunk of banana, he tosses the rest over his shoulder in the backseat. "I thought they wouldn't notice if I left—they've been buried in some new development going up in Malibu."

Real estate. It wasn't their first careers, but it's what they've poured everything into for as long as I can remember.

I've inherited their work ethic, the kind that drives me every day to reach higher. Do more. Be more. But it has consequences.

I'd think Jesse breaks the rules just to get their attention, but he probably wishes they forgot about him right now. He's just a free spirit that doesn't like anything tying him down.

But when our parents are working and he thinks he can pull shit over them, I'm usually the one enforcing his punishments from across the country.

"They noticed, and you're still grounded from last time," I say. "That means no surfing. Not even before school. Definitely not during school."

Jesse considers this for a second before setting his phone in a car holder. "You'd think differently if you were here, Kuya. The swells are—"

"Sick," I smile. "You already told me."

His eyes soften, almost sadly. I know he misses me.

I miss him every day.

I sigh heavily. "I have a new project—"

He perks up. "Can I help? Please. I beg of you, Jesus Christ on a cracker, Kuya, I'd do anything." He makes a praying motion with his hands.

My brother wants to attend college for photography. To the University of Pennsylvania. My alma mater. But he doesn't have the grades for Penn, so he's been trying to build his resume. I've let him help me here and there on smaller projects I was hired to produce. Like music videos and commercials.

Never have I let him twenty feet near a *We Are Calloway* production. I trust him, but maybe not with that much responsibility. He's still just seventeen.

"I'm going to have to think about it," I tell him. "It involves a Cobalt." I don't give him more information than that.

"I won't make a peep. I'll just do grip work. *Please*. It's the summer before my senior year. I might not get this chance again."

I haven't filled the grip position yet. Fuck, I haven't picked out any of my crew for the pilot, which is the test episode and will usually become the first episode of a series if it goes to network. It's still so early.

It feels like two seconds ago I was just in my apartment with Charlie having the first meeting. I haven't even slept since then, and he still needs to sign the contract.

And I still need to talk to security about the show. His bodyguard. *Oscar.*

Strange heat blankets my skin. Nerves? Anticipation? I hate not knowing the name to this feeling.

I push it away and concentrate on the details. How I have an experienced, trustworthy group of people that work with me on my production team for *We Are Calloway*. How the plan was to grab some of them to work on this pilot.

"You have summer school," I remind Jesse.

"I can do the class remotely…probably."

"Let me think about it," I say again. "It's a big deal. It's not a small project."

He nods and pulls his SUV out of the parking lot, heading home. "How mad are they?"

"You're definitely gonna get *the look*."

"The one that's followed with, *halika nga rito*." He says *come here* in Tagalog, his voice light-hearted.

"That's the one."

I feel his smile. "I know that look well."

While we're both driving, we stare at the phone screen less, and it's not long before we say our goodbyes.

Jesse always ends the call with, "Talk later, Kuya."

I hit green light after green light, and it feels like I'm flying towards Hell's Kitchen, towards Oscar. I shift in my seat, glance out my rearview mirror. Tendons pull taut in my shoulders, making me sit more tensely than normal.

I feel most comfortable being approachable, being a positive energy when the world clouds and darkens. But for the first time, I'm…

I'm confused.

So confused that *positivity* feels like a fucking farce, and my mind can't stop spinning between my personal feelings and my professional life.

And I knew this project with Charlie would be chaotic on multiple fronts. But adding Jesse to the mix brings it to a new level.

Chaos Factor #1: Filming Charlie Cobalt. It's like trying to catch a firefly on a normal production day, and this show will be anything but routine.

Chaos Factor #2: Being around Oscar Oliveira. At all. For any period of time.

My pulse pounds hard in my neck.

I don't have time to sort out my feelings.

I'm here.

5

Jack Highland

NEW YORK.

Residence to 4 of 5 Cobalt brothers, and in effect, their personal bodyguards. I practically know *everything* about the Hales, Meadows, and Cobalts. Comes with my job title. I'm a treasure trove of their secrets that I'll always keep locked away, and yet, I can't name a single secret of Oscar's that I have.

Nothing man-to-man, person-to-person he's told me that he's never told anyone else. Human connections are usually so easy for me, but after our awkward fallout in Anacapri, I wonder if that's even true.

21st floor of a luxury apartment complex, the deep walls are painted red, and industrial lights hang along the wide hallway.

I pass the gold number: *2166*.

Cobalt brothers live there, and I used to take meetings in the Triple Shield's security apartment right across from *2166*. But ever since Akara created Kitsuwon Securities, Omega has different housing from Alpha and Epsilon.

Oscar is the only SFO bodyguard with a client living in New York, so he's moved to a studio apartment and lives alone.

I've been dealing with the dynamics of security and the families long enough to know how it runs. And if I don't know something, I ask.

But I've never been inside this studio apartment. Something solely belonging to Oscar. The strap of my messenger bag is across my chest, and I glance at the spiral notebook in my hand before slipping a pen behind my ear. Trying to ignore the knot in my chest.

His studio is at the end of the hall. Right next to a stairwell. And he's already texted me about the door being unlocked. To *come on in*.

Still, I knock, and I take off my shoes before entering and set them next to a fake fern inside. "I've arrived," I say lightly, wanting to smile but my rattled confidence flatlines my lips.

"One second," he calls out.

He's in the sleek kitchen, digging in a pantry. I gaze around his place. White marble counters, gray tile backsplash, and dark wood floors—I look up at industrial lights and the loft where a king-sized bed is in view of a living area (leather couch, bookcase, and TV). Yeah, this is *nice*.

Like a five-star bachelor pad. Updated, trendy. Double the size of my shoebox Philly apartment.

I remember Akara telling me security housing in New York costs the most. Weird to think that I'm more friends with Akara than with Oscar. There was a time where I thought Akara and I would butt heads forever, but I fixed that fast.

I don't like having enemies.

While I wait for Oscar, I wander around and pause near the bookcase. A family photo rests in a pewter frame.

Must've been taken years ago. Oscar's little sister Joana looks no older than ten, smiling a wide crooked-toothed smile. Her hands are up in fists while she's perched on the shoulders of a twenty-something Oscar.

His fists are playfully up too, but he's facing his younger brother Quinn, who pretends to box his big brother.

A boxing family.

I know that much. I wonder if he's as close to his siblings as I am to Jesse. I've been around all three of the Oliveiras before. Like at Scotland last Christmas where Oscar, Quinn, and Joana were snowed-in with me and a lot of others.

I frown, remembering an argument between Quinn and Oscar outside a Scottish pub. *Quinn punched Oscar.* I don't know why.

It'd crush my soul if Jesse even tried to swing at me.

Deep down, I wish this show were about Oscar. I have so many things I want to ask him. I have since the first time he called me *Long Beach*.

"Alright, Highland, let's get this over with." Oscar walks closer, a bag of mini powdered donuts in his hands.

I do a literal double-take. His gray gym pants hang low on his chiseled waist. He's shirtless, and my eyes drift along the Latin script inked on his golden-brown skin, placed across his collarbone. He's Brazilian-American, born and raised in Philly, but I know the Latin phrase has something to do with Brazil.

Oscar has the body of an athlete, like me. I've met *many* guys who are just as cut, just as toned, and I never really gave it a second thought. But I'm standing here with a notebook clenched in my hand and surveying his beauty and washboard abs like he's the Mona Lisa.

I wonder what it'd be like to run my hand across his body, his chest, his unshaven jaw. To hold his face and kiss him. He's masculine. Hard. Muscled.

What am I doing?

Get your head in the game, dude.

I lift my gaze back to Oscar's.

He rips open the donut bag, the noise sounding too loud in the apartment. "You know, I'd ask you if you find something you like," Oscar says, trying to be casual but I hear the strained endnote. "But we've already covered that. You're straight, right?"

My throat swells, tongue weighed down. I hate myself for uttering those words in Italy. But I've *never* questioned myself about my sexuality. Not at ten-years-old, not as a teenager, not in college.

I'm twenty-seven. I should have this shit figured out. I should *know* who I am. I thought I did. *I'm straight.* I've only dated women. Only been sexual with women. Only really thought about being with a woman.

But then Oscar entered the picture, and my flirty jokes and banter that I have with just about everyone felt different with him.

I would anticipate it happening again and again. My heart would float like I was breathing in helium. I felt...

I feel...

I swallow hard. He's staring at me. Waiting for me to speak, and I bide time by pulling the pen out from behind my ear and twirling it between my fingers.

You're straight, right? he asked.

I nod slowly.

FYI: I feel chicken-shit scared in this moment. To believe one thing for so long about myself and then have to reassess is not even close to easy.

Uncomfortable silence still hangs, so I try to play it off like nothing's changed between us. "Well, if you did ask me if I found something I liked, I would've told you that I like your look." I motion to the rolled blue bandana tied around his forehead, pieces of his curly hair falling over, and my blood heats. No, actually, my dick *pulses*. "You're an attractive guy, and you'd be good on TV." Do I sound choked?

Oscar pinches a powdered donut between three fingers. "You've told me that before. And the answer still hasn't changed."

Selfishly, I just want to grill the fuck out of him.

He pops the donut in his mouth, and my stomach lets out a loud groan. I'm about to laugh the noise off when Oscar frowns deeply. He rubs powdered dust off his lips with the back of his hand. "You hungry?"

"I had to run out the door this morning, so I missed bre—" I don't even finish my sentence before Oscar is moving back to the kitchen.

"It's fine," I tell him. *Dude, shut up.* Something inside me is utterly enamored with how easily and quickly he just moved into action for me.

"Bro, your stomach is *screaming* at me," Oscar says. "It'd be a crime not to feed you." He bends down to his bottom cabinet. Back turned to me, his drawstring pants pull tight around his ass.

Jesus fuck. My stomach squeezes. And my dick almost rouses. *Stay down.*

I cage a breath. *Don't breathe. Don't speak.* My composure is teetering on the edge of a diving board, and at this point, I'm questioning if I even know how to swim.

Me, Jack Highland, a collegiate swimmer at Penn.

I manage to sit on a wooden barstool across from Oscar without completely losing it. My body acts like he's the hottest thing to ever step foot on this Earth, and my brain has trouble catching up to these feelings.

I'm laps behind.

Tensely, I take off my messenger bag and pull out a contract. I set the paper beside my spiral notebook and abandoned donuts on the marble bar counter.

"I can just have a donut," I end up saying. "You don't need to get me anything."

Oscar stands up with two boxes of cereal. "Baby donuts will hold you over for five seconds."

Baby donuts. I smile.

He shakes the boxes. "Pick your poison, Long Beach."

Organic granola cereal or Lucky Charms.

I hesitate, my smile faltering.

Something intangible stretches the air. I hate that uncertain, uncomfortable feeling because it means other people feel uncomfortable and uncertain. I pride myself on erasing doubts and fears and tension in *any* room.

But lately, I realize, if it's just me and Oscar sharing space, I can't seem to let out the words to ease this *thing* between us. I let it fester for a second too long.

Oscar frowns. "You don't seem like the kind of guy that overthinks things. And not for nothing, Long Beach, but it's just cereal."

"Yeah," I nod. "I just don't know what I feel like."

"So have both." He opens the flap to the Lucky Charms.

My head spins. "You're right, you know. I don't overthink things."

More tendrils of his hair fall over his rolled bandana as he shakes cereal into a bowl. "Look, I didn't want to bring it up and make it more awkward, but I'm not a twelve-year-old, and I won't avoid it." He closes the Lucky Charms box and opens the granola cereal. "I think you're hot, but I think a lot of people are hot. Me asking you for a kiss isn't a big deal. We don't need to make it a big deal."

My stomach overturns.

Disappointment. Devastation. Wrapped up nicely in a little ball.

"It's not a big deal," I say, appeasing him, and then I quickly add, "You're not the first person who's asked to kiss me."

His brows knot as he slowly spins the cap off a milk carton. "But I'm the first *guy* that's asked to kiss you."

My pulse pumps harder. "Well…yeah."

"Good to know," he says in a gruff way that sounds like he actually would have preferred to go to his grave without that knowledge.

Make this better. Jesus fuck.

"It's alright," I tell him.

"Don't do that," he says quickly as he adds milk to the bowl.

"Do what?" I reply, but I know what he's referring to.

He rummages in a drawer for a spoon. His brown eyes keep flitting to me, strands of his hair hitting his lashes. My muscles tense. Why is that so fucking hot?

"You do this thing, Jack, where you try to make everyone feel good. I don't need that kind of emotional baby blanket." His eyes touch mine. A beat passing between us. His brows rise. "I'm good."

"Good," I say, my chest tightening.

He nods. "Good."

The air deadens.

I can't take it. "Oscar, I'm just trying to make this less awkward."

"That's not going to be possible." He pushes the bowl forward, both cereals mixed together. His eyes latch on the contract near the donuts. "Is that one mine?"

"Yeah," I breathe. "I dropped Charlie's contract off to his lawyer on the drive here, and I have a copy for him to sign." It would've been easier to send electronic contracts, but Charlie specified paper instead of digital.

In case of leaks.

While Oscar's eyes journey over the paper, the sun finally starts to rise. Oranges bleed through the window 21-floors high. Bathing the kitchen, him and me, in rays of light.

It brings me back to the wedding reception. When I was bent over the hatchback as the sun set along the coast, and I turned around. The glow of the waning sun illuminated Oscar Oliveira, and he was gorgeous.

I almost told him.

I've told plenty of guys they're beautiful.

But I stopped myself because that moment felt different than those other times. Maybe I just wanted it to be different.

I clutch my spoon, another knot in my chest. Giving him time to read the fine print, I shovel spoonfuls of cereal in my mouth.

After a minute, he starts shaking his head aggressively.

"What?" I question. "It's all standard."

"This says he has to have *at minimum* ten interview sessions. Charlie can barely sit down for one."

This is what I was worried about. "If he wants to do this, he has to put in the time. Either he signs it, or he doesn't. It's no sweat to me."

Oscar doesn't say anything.

I study him, up and down. "Do you want him to do the show?"

"Answering that would require me to know *why* he's doing it. Which I don't. He rarely tells me shit."

"Why is that?"

Oscar gives me a pointed look. "I'm not your subject, Highland."

"I can just ask Charlie."

"Go for it," Oscar says. "I'd love to hear his answer." He stares down at the contract and flips through the last couple of pages. "You have in here that there'll be an additional three people involved in crew. From a security standpoint, I'm a little concerned about all of you getting in my way. *We Are Calloway* filming lasts ten minutes around him. I can't have that all day every day. It's going to be a problem."

"I need a crew—"

"I need to do my job," Oscar cuts me off.

I let out a frustrated noise. "And I don't need to do mine?"

"How hard is yours?" he wonders. "Because mine is fucking difficult every way you come at it. I can't add something else to it. Narrow down your crew or it's a no-go. I'll cut the cord before Charlie even gets the contract."

Confidence radiates from every pore, and his threat is palpable in the room. I've been head-to-head with enough guys on security to not cower. But something about Oscar slowly simmers my blood.

"For the pilot, I can agree to that," I tell him. "But if it gets picked up for network, I can't have a reduced crew."

"I'm not budging from this."

I shake my head. "Out of all the things to push back on…"

"You'll understand when you start filming him," Oscar says. "I'm not being an asshole just for shits and giggles. Just trust me on this."

Getting a series order will happen down the line, and maybe I can renegotiate a bigger crew then. Right now, I just have to get off the block.

"I can agree to—" Static crackles, and I cut myself off, realizing the black radio pack beside the sink, earpiece cord wrapped around the small device, is turned *on*. Volume is so loud that I hear security clearly.

"Farrow to Thatcher, is anyone making a pit stop at the lake house?"

Oscar's hand jolts fast towards the radio. Seizing it. Maybe to power it off or lower the volume so I can't hear.

I'm production.

I'm not a bodyguard.

But as our eyes meet, something stops him. He cradles the radio in his palm.

I dunk my spoon into the milk and ask lightly, "Are Farrow and Maximoff already at the family's lake house?" I heard they were spending their honeymoon there, but I didn't know when they were leaving.

Oscar glances at the rising sun. "Yeah, they should've arrived this morning." His muscles are still flexed. Still rigidly clutching the radio.

I may have gone to an Ivy League, but it doesn't take a genius to know whatever Oscar is thinking, it's not good. But more than anything, I can't get over how he's not shutting me out of comms.

I can't name a single bodyguard who wouldn't pull the plug and turn the volume to negative 100 on me, on *anyone* in production.

6

Oscar Oliveira

WHAT IN THE ever-loving hell am I doing?

Turn the volume down on the damn radio, Oscar.

Put your earpiece in.

Don't let Jack Highland listen to comms chatter.

I've never wavered about this. One girl I slept with was two seconds from hearing a bodyguard talk about Luna Hale. How she was close to flunking high school. I snatched the radio off my end table like it was the last Snickers on Earth, and I shut the girl out of my work.

In this jack-knifing second, my common sense is thrown in the gutter, making way for…what? Idiocy. *No.* No, I'm too intelligent to be that dumb.

Some part of me is instinctively saying, *keep this guy in the loop.* Keep him with you. Keep him close. And he might be production, but he understands sheltering secrets about the famous ones. He's never betrayed them, and I have no reason to believe he'd betray me.

Don't let me down, Highland.

I let him overhear comms.

Thatcher responds quickly to Farrow with a simple curt, "Negative."

I must wear my confusion because Jack asks, "Is that a bad thing?" He swirls around his cereal but looks at me.

"Thatcher is the SFO lead," I remind him as I reach in the pockets of my sweatpants for my cell. *Not there.* I scan the kitchen. "So he should know where every bodyguard is at. We're supposed to report if we make any location changes, and he's saying no one is at the lake house."

"But Farrow thinks someone's there?" Jack asks after another spoonful of cereal.

"Bingo." I'm still searching for my phone.

"By the toaster," Jack points out with the tilt of his chin.

I eye him and his easy-going smile that makes this situation seem less caustic. A grin edges across my mouth in return, but I remind myself not to play the part of *fool* and fall into his allure.

"Is Ripley with them?" Jack wonders.

I grab my phone. "Yeah, they brought the baby." I approach the bar counter that separates his body from mine. Being close causes my gaze to travel along his features: squared jawline, dark thick brows and glittering eyes—and that smile, fuck that captivating, dazzling smile. And I swear he's doing the same to me.

He does this to everyone.

Does he check out everyone?

It's the only thing that makes sense.

Jack asks, "What do you think about Farrow being Ripley's guardian? The baby is six-months-old now, right?" He eats more cereal.

"Look at you, going all 'producer' on me and asking me life questions." I mockingly hunt for his video camera, opening and shutting drawers. Glancing over my shoulder, up at the ceiling.

His eyes are glued to me, lips rising.

"*Your* baby has to be somewhere." I lean over the counter and peer around Jack's body. My biceps flex, and I see his honey-brown eyes trace the carve of muscle. Blood pumps in my veins, especially as our gazes crash together, and he intakes a more confident breath.

If only he wasn't straight.

I'd already be clutching his jaw and kissing the hell out of him. I've thought about pulling his crew-neck tee off and skating my large palm down his chest a painful number of times this morning. Once I started imagining his hand around my cock, I hit *defense mode* on my internal alarm system.

Lock it up.

Slowly, I careen back. Giving us some space.

He runs his fingers through his hair. "My camera is in my car." His voice is just as light as before, and he motions between us. "This is off-the-record."

I touch my chest. "I'm flattered you'd do that for me."

He smiles. "Well, I love to flatter you."

"Oh I know," I say, trying not to sound sexually or *romantically* frustrated.

He keeps dunking his spoon in milk, silence extending before he tells me, "I'm just trying to get to know you better."

Is that a good idea? Against better judgment, my defenses drop. Maybe because I want to get to know him better too. "Ripley is, in fact, sixth-months-old," I answer his questions. "It's still unbelievable to me what happened. You know, Donnelly was supposed to become the guardian, but he couldn't do it. I've known him for over a decade, and the guy is responsible but he's not ready to be a father." *It would've destroyed him.*

"So Farrow stepped in," Jack nods, knowing the history.

Of course he does. I don't know why I forgot that he hears and sees a lot. Plus, the famous ones talk to him.

"Yeah, that's how Farrow is. Everyone wants to be his friend because he looks like a cool motherfucker. He'd do anything for his friends, even if you haven't talked to him in years. If you need him, he'd drop everything and help." I shrug. "Donnelly and I are similar, but we're easier to befriend. And I'm happy Farrow was there to take the baby. He has Maximoff to lean on."

Unlike me.

I don't have anyone else.

I can tell Jack sees the unspoken words in my face. So I drop my gaze and busy myself with wiping down the kitchen counter.

"I'd be a single father," I continue on, "and I wouldn't want that. Farrow *genuinely* wants Ripley in his life. He loves that kid." I begin to grin. "I asked to babysit a few times, but Farrow and Maximoff are fucking attached. It takes a jack-hammer to pull them apart from him."

It's what that kid deserves. Unconditional, never-going-to-leave-you love. But my best friend is unfortunately staring at a legal battle in his future. Ripley is the biological son of Paul Donnelly's thirty-year-old uncle. Who's in prison. And this motherfucker won't sign his parental rights away, probably hoping to extort Maximoff Hale.

It's a fucked-up situation, and I hate that Farrow has to deal with it and that a child is going to be in a very *public* custody battle. Maximoff is famous. Farrow is now famous.

There's no way this won't be all over the news.

"I gather you like kids," Jack says easily.

I nod. "I helped raise my baby sister and brother. I'm used to changing dirty diapers and being spit up on."

"Me too." He explains further, "My parents worked long hours, so I looked after my brother a lot before I left for college."

I want to know more. Like what his parents do for a living. How did his brother take it when Jack left? But my phone buzzes.

Has your location changed? — Thatcher

Before I can answer, another text pings.

I don't want to ask over comms and worry Farrow and Maximoff on their honeymoon. — Thatcher

"Everything okay?" Jack eyes me as I read the messages.

"I can't tell," I say honestly. "I know Farrow better than I even know my own brother." It just came out, and fuck, I can't believe I'm admitting that to anyone, let alone Jack. I swear the guy is made of truth serum. But I just keep talking. "It'd have to take a crater-sized issue for Farrow to interrupt his honeymoon with Maximoff, and if something is going down at the lake house…I wish I were there."

Everyone in SFO is too far away to protect them.

I text Thatcher back: Still in New York

Copy that — Thatcher

My radio crackles in my fist. "Farrow to Thatcher, are you sure security isn't coming here?"

I make an educated guess out loud. "He must see a security vehicle pulling into the lake house." *Why else would he single out security?*

Thatcher replies on comms, "Unless someone is lying, no one should be at the lake house but your family."

Jack stands off the barstool. "Who do you think it is?"

I watch him approach the sink near me. "Maybe Quinn."

Jack frowns, and he's about to wash out the cereal bowl, but I reach for it.

"You're my guest—"

"You already fed me," Jack interjects. "Really, I should've brought over breakfast for the meeting." He runs the water. "I wasn't thinking."

Mention of why he's here—for the show about my client—puts everything in *tense* perspective. The air strains. I scratch the back of my head, feeling the knot to my bandana.

"You think your brother would lie about his location?" Jack asks me.

I lean my waist against the counter. "Probably. He's been imitating Farrow's rebel ass way too much."

At first, I thought it was funny that my brother looked up to Farrow. Mostly because I knew Farrow wanted to be *no one's* mentor. But here he was, stuck mentoring my baby brother.

Now I'm concerned Quinn is taking it too far, but I don't tell Jack that. My brother issues are thick roots that I can't see as they've grown under an old oak tree.

I feel like I have to chop the thing down and dig to understand what's there. And I haven't tried because even trying elicits rage from Quinn.

And I hate meeting his anger.

I shake my head, thinking out loud. "But Quinn has no reason to be at the lake house." I take the clean bowl from Jack and dry it with a dish towel. Ignoring how my hand just brushed against his fingers. "It could be anyone on Epsilon or Alpha…" I trail off because one name latches in my head.

Jack is two seconds from asking.

So I just tell him, "Donnelly." I explain how he'd often crash with Farrow at Yale. He'd even tag along dates. Why not join his honeymoon? Farrow won't care.

I continue with a laugh, "The guy attaches himself to Farrow like he's another appendage. He's practically Redford's sixth toe at this point."

Without a doubt, I love Donnelly as much as I love Farrow.

Jack smiles, but while he leans against the sink, I see his eyes drag across the ground.

Why?

I don't understand that. Facing him, I say casually, "You ever have that *one* friend that's just such a pain in the ass but you love them for it? They could take a shit on your front lawn and you'd laugh about it and tell the story decades later?"

His broad shoulders contract and almost bow forward as he shrugs.

"Come on, Mr. Popular," I say with an edging grin that falters. "Your phone is probably bloated with numbers."

His lips lift. "I'm definitely not starved for those, dude." He takes a step from the sink, closer to me. And like he's polishing a trophy, he adds, "I was Prom King in high school."

Don't give him a once-over.

I nod a few times. "Checks out." My voice is more stilted. I grab my water bottle. "I was Mr. December in a fan's Hot Bodyguard Calendar." I swig my water.

Jack eyes me, the two-second up-down. "That's well-deserved."

The kitchen is fifty-degrees hotter. "I'd say so," I tell him.

Look at me, willingly floating towards the sun like Icarus. If I get too close, *I* deserve melted-wings and a hundred-foot plummet.

I take another hearty swig, then grab my phone.

Mentally, I go back to security, and something isn't adding up. Donnelly has a client in Philly, and I doubt he'd ditch his duty to Xander Hale just to hang with Farrow.

Donnelly is a lot of things, but he cares about the families like we all do.

So I shoot a text to my other best friend: You lying to Thatcher?

His response is almost instant.

Call you later. — Donnelly

That's a yes.

I let out a breath of relief. "Looks like no one is impersonating security. It's just Donnelly."

No idea why he's there, but he'll tell me when he can. More so, I'm stunned at how easily I just informed Jack of security's business.

Again, what in the ever-loving hell.

"What's wrong?" Jack asks.

"Nothing," I say rigidly and return to the contract, pretending to read the thing. I feel his confused eyes on my back.

I just hate how comfortable I am with this guy. I'm already so fucking attracted to Jack, and I don't want to like him even more.

But I'm so used to dating people and meeting solid roadblocks, and I'm starting to realize those don't exist with him.

No guy or woman I take out to a simple dinner can have the details of my job or know what I know about the Hales, Meadows, and Cobalts. It goes against the word *security*.

I've been yelled at for not "opening up" and "sharing" enough with short-term relationships that I thought would last longer.

Can I blame them? *"I can't talk about it"* gets stale fast, and last thing I want is to be stale bread to the person I'm dating.

Not when I'm a motherfucking feast.

In my peripheral, I see Jack move around to his messenger bag on the floor. My phone buzzes again, and I tear my gaze off the exec-producer.

Charlie is texting. Letting me know he'll be leaving in five minutes. It's rare for a heads up or an ETA, which means Charlie must want this show to work.

"You sure you want to do this?" I ask Jack. "Last chance to back out."

He stands fully, and his bottomless honey-brown eyes sink into me. "Do you want me to?" *Christ.* Everything out of his mouth sounds like a come-on.

"Do you always answer a question with a question, Highland?"

His lip quirks into a smile. "You just did the same thing."

"Imagine that," I say casually.

"You don't want me to do the show." It's no longer a question.

"I never said that," I reply. "It's just that I don't think you know what you're getting yourself into."

He can't know. Security history runs too deep.

I've been working in the field since I was twenty-four. First on Ben Cobalt's detail, and I proved myself enough in just a year to land the coveted position as Winona Meadows' bodyguard. Honestly, that caused me more problems than it should've. Jon Sinclair, the current Epsilon lead, was pissed that I was so new and landed with the Meadows family. The asshole still resents me to this day because of it. Then at twenty-six, I was transferred back to the Cobalt Empire to be Eliot's bodyguard. After a successful year with that troublemaker, they decided to toss me into the lion's den with Charlie.

Security literally threw me a funeral.

I'm not Charlie's first bodyguard.

Not even his second or third.

He's left behind a graveyard of qualified men. Some didn't even last a single day on his detail.

Jack may not be filling my role, but he's going to be beside me, and he's in an even worse position. I don't need to get anything from Charlie. I'm protecting him. That's it. Jack has to actively pull out information, interviews, quotes. It's going to be like trying to break into a steel-fortified castle.

Good fucking luck.

7

Jack Highland

MY FIRST FORAY INTO following Charlie Cobalt is taking place in The Vaulted Vestibule, a dimly lit NYC concert venue. I'm holding my Canon, the strap around my neck, but I've expressed to Oscar more than once that I'm not filming.

It's the truth.

His warnings about Charlie have seeped in, and I figure I need to pack on prep work.

Week 1 & 2: test shots and assessing the…situation. That way I can determine logistics without having a crew (okay, a *reduced* crew) around.

Mid-afternoon, the venue only houses stage crew, musicians, and their friends or family. While Charlie stands on stage next to Tom Cobalt, his nineteen-year-old brother, I snap a couple photos.

Their discussion is heated. Tom is the lead singer of an emo-punk band called The Carraways, and he looks the part with ripped jeans, skull-and-crossbones black shirt, and a 90s haircut. And right now, he gesticulates with fervor at his brother, his brows cinched in anger.

While Charlie looks…well, Charlie looks bored.

I try not to judge what I don't know. But his apathy is only pissing Tom off more.

Oscar leans back comfortably in a theatre chair. First row. Right next to me.

We both have front row seats to a Cobalt family blow-up. Even if we're too far away to hear what's said on-stage.

I should be stoked to even have this opportunity, but it's hard to pay attention to Charlie when Oscar is right here.

We haven't spoken.

Not since we arrived at The Vaulted Vestibule. I think we're both giving each other space to do our jobs, but now it feels different.

Like we're consciously deciding *not* to talk.

I'm neck-deep in awkward silence. And I can't take it anymore.

I shift my shoulders a little and pretend to change the settings on my camera. "Does being a bodyguard mean you have to be silent all the time. Or is that just a choice?"

I glance at him from the corner of my eye, and he's looking over. Heat ascends my neck. *Fuck, dude, you should've shut up.* It's easier than treading over my feelings for him…

Whatever those are, I'm not even sure.

"Again, Highland, I'm not your subject," Oscar says casually.

Got it.

Ouch.

My face drops a fraction. He's been forthcoming with me and then sometimes, not at all. Like he's raising and lowering his guards, and every time they raise, I feel like a fresh pile of cow shit.

Like I'm not worthy inside his head. Like I'm not giving enough of *me* to earn him, and then I just want to talk more.

To do *something* to earn Oscar Oliveira. Because I'm an overachiever? Because I like him? Because being on the outs with him fucking sucks, and even though I'm afraid of what I feel, I can't bail. I have to ride the terrifying swell to shore and hope I don't drown.

I pat my camera. "Like I said, I just want to get to know you better. We have to spend more time around each other, so it makes sense. Right?"

Oscar makes a gruff noise that sounds like it died in the middle of his throat.

My dick twitches against my jeans. *Fuck,* fuck. I heat up, and my Adam's apple bobs as I swallow hard. If he were a woman, I'd understand the hard-on.

I'd ramp-up my flirting, and I'd have her number in a second flat. But I'm sitting here just fucking confused why my cock responded to him.

Did I find that noise attractive because I know it's sexy by definition or because I'm attracted to the sound or to Oscar?

That mish-mashed thought has my brain bending like a fifteen-year-old gymnast.

Ride the swell.

I'm about to speak again, but Oscar actually entertains my earlier question. "I'm choosing to be quiet, so I can hear that argument." He nods his chin in the direction of the stage.

Sure enough, Charlie and Tom's conversation has ratcheted up in intensity. Tom places his hands on his head in exasperation.

My brows knit together. "You can hear them?"

"I can read lips…" Oscar pauses and then adds, "If I'm not distracted."

Okay, point taken.

I lean back.

Oscar glances to me. "That wasn't meant for you to shut up. I was just stating a fact."

My lips quirk. "So you do like my questions?"

He shakes his head slowly, and a smile creeps over his mouth. "I didn't say that, Long Beach." *Long Beach.* His tone is sweeter with me when he uses that nickname.

It does something to my heartbeat.

"What's going on with them then?" I wonder.

"Tom's new drummer apparently ditched at the last minute. He's fighting with Charlie over how to replace him before tonight's gig." Oscar looks me up and down. "So this is your friendly warning not to trash talk me across the room."

"I did schedule a trash-talking for later this evening," I say lightly. "I'll let you know what time *not* to be there."

"Oh I'll be there," he says into a grin. "I don't think I've heard you say a mean thing about one person. Ever. I'm not missing the moment a sunshine turns into a raincloud, even at my expense."

My cheeks hurt from grinning like him. "Did you just call me a *sunshine*?"

"Fuck you, dude!" Tom screams, cutting into our banter. Our heads whip towards the Cobalt brothers. "You're supposed to be here supporting me!"

"I am here to support you," Charlie says, voice leveled but irritation sticks to each syllable. Oscar rises to his feet and approaches now, a hand flying to his earpiece.

I follow beside him.

"But if that means biting my tongue when your ideas are bullshit," Charlie adds exhaustedly, "then that's where my support ends."

When Tom sees us approaching, his eyes latch to mine. "Thank you. Jack, can you please tell my brother it's fine if I get someone from Craigslist to fill the drums for *one* night."

"Don't answer that," Oscar tells me under his breath.

I wasn't going to. "What are the other alternatives?" I ask.

Charlie sighs heavily. "Yes, let's hear the other fantastic ideas, you've come up with."

Tom holds up his hands like he's ready to throw in the towel. "With that level of sarcasm, you don't deserve to hear a single one of my *fantastic* ideas. Plug your ears, brother."

Charlie doesn't make a move.

Tom glares.

Charlie's brows rise. "Oh, you're being serious? You do know I'm not a toddler."

Tom lets out a frustrated noise before looking to me. "Option 2 is Eliot's idea."

Eliot Cobalt is Tom's older brother by only eleven months, and they're as thick as thieves.

My team on the docuseries is mostly in charge of filming the older kids of the families, which includes Jane, Maximoff, Charlie, and most recently Sullivan. We'd film Beckett too, but he's private and always declines to be on the show.

So my experience with Tom and Eliot is more limited, but it doesn't mean I haven't filmed them or been around for rifts and family gatherings. Anytime they're together, it's a recipe for drama.

Charlie doesn't stifle his laugh at Eliot's name. "Your option will be better than his."

Tom narrows his eyes. "I take offense to that on his behalf."

"Let's hear the idea," I mediate.

"Instagram," Tom says. "I tell everyone I need a drummer for the night. Give them my location. First guy who shows up and is decent enough, gets the gig. Send the rest home."

"No," Oscar rejects, along with Tom's bodyguard Ian Wreath, who hovers close by.

Tom makes a noise. "It was just an *idea*."

"A stupid one," Charlie adds. "Unless you want to get your show cancelled tonight because you fucked up crowd control outside."

"I'm calling Moffy," Tom refutes. "He'll actually listen."

"Go ahead, call him," Charlie says dryly. "Better yet, call our sister. I'm sure Jane would love to hear your *ideas*."

Tom groans and pinches the bridge of his nose.

"Why don't you play a track?" I chime back in. Akara can also play the drums, but I don't offer him as a suggestion because I know he's way too busy to fill in for The Carraways.

Oscar nods. "Someone can pretend to bang on the drums. No one will know the difference."

"I already suggested that," Charlie says.

"Ethically, I can't play a drums track," Tom tells us. "I'd rather cancel the show."

Charlie smiles, "And that's the other *good* option."

Tom scoffs. "It's also failure."

Charlie rolls his eyes, and then we all turn as a white guy with dyed jet-black hair, styled into spikes, strolls in from backstage, a bass strapped across his chest. Warner, the other member of his band.

"Tom, you figure this shit out yet?" Irritation layers his green eyes. "Cuz this is your fault, you know. Daniel was doing fine on the drums, and I don't blame him for quitting after what you put him through."

"He never practiced," Tom refutes.

"To *your* standards," Warner argues. "Dude, no one can meet them. We're going to go through drummers like fucking M&M's at this point."

"I'm not apologizing for wanting the members of the band to care as much as I do," Tom replies. "*You* live up to my standards."

"Barely."

Cobalts place the bar so high for themselves, they can't see the ground anymore.

Spending so much time with these famous families, I've seen them beyond their fame and money, and I've found pieces of each of them that I relate to.

My job has always been to showcase the human sides of them, and I only hope that when viewers watch *We Are Calloway* they find relatable pieces, too.

So hearing Tom, my heart clenches a little. I was twelve-years-old when I made a binder full of Ivy League colleges that I wanted to apply to. Didn't matter that I still had middle school and high school left to go.

I mapped out my future. Placed the bar for myself in the sky. It's how I've always operated.

Plan and achieve.

Rinse and repeat.

Charlie steps in, his gaze softening a fraction on Tom. "I'm going to take care of it," he tells Tom. "Give me ten minutes."

"How?" Tom asks.

"Eliot's idea but modified." He jumps off the stage and saunters to the abandoned bar in the back of the venue. Oscar and I follow him silently, but I count each heavy step that Oscar takes. Like his presence alone fills up the vacant sound.

Charlie hops up on the counter, his ass right next to a green bottle of absinthe, and he pulls out his phone.

I go for a question I'd ask if we were filming. "What made you change your mind and help Tom?"

Charlie doesn't look up from his cell as he replies, "I was always going to help him."

"You gave him a hard time," I say, urging harder. It's what I do. Push a little. And a little more. I know when to pull back and when to go deeper.

Charlie's eyes flit to me. "You're not filming. So why the questions?"

I wave my camera. "Testing out how this is going to go."

Charlie smiles, but it's a bitter one. "I'm an open book."

"Then tell me something honest about you and your brothers. Something you wouldn't care if the world knew."

Charlie looks from me to Oscar and then back to me. "Ever since Eliot and Tom moved in with me and Beckett, I've been cleaning up their messes. If I'm going to be their janitor, they better know how dumb I think the shit they get themselves into is." He pulls out a cigarette and types on his phone. "So fuck no, I'm not helping them without giving them a hard time."

Oscar cuts in, focus drilled to Charlie's cell. "What's the plan?"

Charlie clicks his phone and jumps off the bar. "It's the best plan I have, but also my last option." He lets out an annoyed breath. "I know this girl who's a big fan of The Carraways. She's also a drummer. She'll fill in for the night, no problem." He turns to Oscar. "Just sent you her info. You've already done a background check on her, but you'll need to do it again. I haven't spoken to her in like three years."

I'm confused, so I prod. "If you knew someone who could fill in so easily, why is she your last choice?"

"Because I don't like calling in favors with girls I've fucked." He sticks the cigarette between his lips and mumbles out. "It's uncouth." He lights the cigarette and walks towards the stage, probably to let his brother know the crisis has been averted.

Oscar hangs back, simultaneously texting and whispering into his mic. Can't believe he named The Carraways. Bodyguards threw out suggestions for Tom's band, and Tom ended up picking Oscar's. It's obvious that the bodyguards care about the famous families, but it's just as clear to me that the families care and appreciate them too.

I stay behind with Oscar and take a few more long shots of Charlie near the stage. Doing my best to resist turning the camera on Oscar and snapping a couple photos of him.

He's been in background shots before, but I'd love to see how he'd look filling the frame right now.

Gorgeous, I'm sure.

Because of course he's gorgeous. Magazines have packed their columns with pics of the now infamous Security Force Omega bodyguards, and those spreads detail how Oscar Oliveira is genetically blessed. They also say that about Quinn, his brother—but I'm not interested in Quinn like that.

Like what, dude?

I fiddle with my camera's aperture, and I look up and zone in on Oscar's nose ring, just a silver hoop. It's hot.

Because of course, nose rings are hot. On anyone. Girls. Guys. People. It doesn't mean I'm not straight. Right?

Like he can feel the heat of my stare, Oscar glances up at me.

I don't look away. "The nose ring was a dare?"

He cocks his head with a look. "You were there for the dare."

I was. Shit.

I was literally at the bachelor party where Oscar was dared. Though, I was invited to go back to the house in Key West, I didn't take the offer and see him get pierced. I had an early call time for work, but the whole night in bed I wished I was there.

I'm usually better with facts, and I can't help but laugh at myself, my smile widening. "I'm an idiot, sorry."

"You're not an idiot," Oscar says in a way that warms my entire body. "But you do ask too many questions."

I smile more. "You want me to stop?" I sound like I'm flirting. *Because I'm flirty by nature.* Fuck, I just want to flirt with this guy. The one with an unshaven jaw, eyes that grin as much as his lips, and curly brown hair that's perfectly messy—the guy that keeps pushing me away.

For good reasons.

He exhales and mutters something like, "Don't ask me that." He scratches the back of his head, then tells me, "You can shoot your shot, Highland. Dunk your questions."

"What if I air-ball?" I quip.

"*Dunk*," he emphasizes.

I like how Oscar always brings me up, even when we're joking around. "Okay, here it is. Why are you still wearing the nose piercing if it was just a dare?"

He could've taken it out.

"Because I look hot," he grins.

My neck heats. It was like Oscar took a personal trip inside my head and captured that answer.

He slides the phone in his pocket. "You have anything pierced?"

"No, but I've always wanted a dydoe piercing."

Oscar's eyes go wide.

I laugh. "That was a joke, dude."

"Let me resuscitate myself for a second." He has a hand on his chest, the other is digging in his pocket. "I had no clue you're an expert on penis piercings." He pulls out a granola bar and rips the wrapper.

My smile hurts. "Not an expert, but I watched a shit ton of porn when I was sixteen—"

"Finally, something in common," Oscar banters. "I was getting a little worried there."

My cheeks flame. We have a lot more in common. Like how our brothers are both exactly ten-years younger than us. But I don't voice this because I'm positive Oscar is just playing around.

"Anyway," I say. "My favorite porn star, Benji Strong, had one." I regret the words as soon as they escape. "So yeah…" I clear my throat. "That's how I know about dydoe piercings. I'm not an expert." My endnote clearly relays a closing of this conversation.

I examine my camera.

But I feel Oscar frowning. Confused at my change in tone.

That's a good thing. It means he's not aware that Benji Strong has mostly been in gay porn.

During my cool-vibes teenage years in sunny SoCal, I used to watch gay porn all the time. Never once did I question my sexuality.

Maybe it was because two of my guy friends told me they also watch gay porn and they were straight, too. Maybe it was because my parents have always been so inclusive and open, and there wasn't a moment in my life that I thought I could be gay just because I liked gay porn.

It just wasn't a big deal, and I hate that I'm making it a big deal in my head now. Because it shouldn't be. I'm just confused about everything.

Am I straight?

Being honest with myself, I don't even know anymore.

I want someone to just appear out of thin air and tell me what I am. Gay. Straight. Bi. Pan. Somewhere in between. I'd be happy with any of them.

But no, I have to figure this answer out on my own, and it sucks knowing that even when I come to a decision, I still may not be a hundred percent certain.

For fuck's sake, I planned out my whole life when I was *twelve*.

I want my binder back. I want to be twelve again and look into the future and rewrite this part of my life out, so I wouldn't have to face these questions. I'd already know the answers.

Smoothly, I excuse myself from Oscar and go grab a water from the bar's mini-fridge. His eyes are on me, then on the double-doors that swing open.

"Fuck," Oscar curses, charging for the door but he slows as he recognizes the nineteen-year-old girl in a Thrashers sweatshirt.

Luna Hale.

I smile in greeting. "Hey, Luna." She must be here for Tom, her best friend. I've filmed segments with Luna and her brother Maximoff before, and I know things about Luna that she's wanted to keep off air.

A Secret about Luna Hale: at 13, a boy left a note in her locker that said, *close your legs, slut.*

Sometimes I feel like I'm their therapist listening to their darkest days and thoughts, but I'm not even close to being a licensed professional. It'd be a lie to say that it's not hard on me. I'm a filmmaker, a producer, a guy with a dream, but I don't want to profit off their pain.

What makes it okay for me is knowing I can be a friendly, familiar safe place when they need one.

Luna waves at me. "Hey. Hi. Heidi. Ho. Howdy." Purple feathers poke from her light-brown hair. And glitter is painted on her arms like a kindergarten class played arts and crafts on her body.

"Like the hair. Looking cool as ever."

She smiles, about to reply.

"Luna from Planet Thebula," Tom calls, using the microphone on stage. "Get up here. Gotta fill you in."

She waves a second time. "Nice to make contact again." And then she slinks to the stage.

I conclude fast that Luna Hale's entrance wasn't on Oscar's radar. He stares down her 24/7 bodyguard, who happens to be *his* twenty-two-year-old brother Quinn.

Quinn is busy shutting the double-doors. Tall and muscled, his floral shirt is tucked in olive-green pants, making him look like he stepped out of a PacSun catalogue. It's a stark difference from the casual east coast look of his older brother.

But they both have tiny scars on their faces from boxing blows.

"What?" Quinn asks him.

"A heads up would've been nice, little bro," Oscar says lightly. He mimes picking up a phone. "Hey, big bro, I'm on my way with Luna to the same venue you're at. Thanks, Oscar, bye. *Click.*" He hangs up the imaginary phone.

I smile and immediately want to film Oscar—for no one but me. Quinn isn't as amused by him.

He fixes his earpiece. "Bro, you're not the lead. I don't need to inform you where I'm going."

"So you told Thatcher you'd be here?" Oscar wonders.

"God, stop nagging me." He watches Luna while he speaks. "That's all you do lately."

Oscar holds up his hands. "I'm legitimately just trying to talk to you."

Quinn scratches his jaw. "It doesn't feel like you are."

"I'm telling you I am."

Quinn shakes his head, his eyes downcast. "I'm on-duty, so..." He mutters something in Portuguese and then walks away. Leaving a motionless Oscar in his wake.

I come closer. "You okay?"

He nods, and then a second later shakes his head. "I swear he's the nicest person to everyone but me. He plays with kittens and puppies like he's a gold-hearted boy next door, won't utter a curse word in front of a child, and paradoxically, he can punch a motherfucker in a ring like no one I've ever seen." He shakes his head again in thought. "But somehow, I'm the *only* gum on his shoe he's trying to scrape off. For...I don't know how long. I thought we were fine when he first joined security." He glances at me. "You know we requested to be separated to avoid in-fighting, and he was put on Jane's detail in Philly while I was in New York. It was going fine too. We put the past to bed."

The past? "Did you two duke it out over a girl or something?" I don't know why that knots my chest.

His shoulders rise. "If we did, he can have the girl. I'd rather just have my brother." He laughs at something.

"What?"

His eyes hit mine. "I just remembered, he slept with the girl I was sleeping with during the FanCon tour. I think it was a shot at me."

"But that's not the past beef?"

"I don't know what is."

I frown more. "So you have no idea what the core of the problem is between you two? Like, what you're actually arguing about?"

"No idea," he admits like he knows it's insane. "Your guess is as good as mine, Highland. So when you figure it out, come talk to me."

Damn, I want to make him feel better, but I don't want to pump him up with niceties just to bolster his spirit. I do that all the time to people, and he's one of the rare ones to call me out on it.

Hard truths, I go with it. "It might be the ten-year age gap between you two. It complicates sibling relationships. Makes it harder. We're big brothers but also mentors and sometimes even father figures."

Oscar lets out a soft laugh. "I don't think Quinn has ever seen me as a father figure. Joana, maybe. Not Quinn." He looks me over. "You good with your brother? He's ten years younger, right?"

"Jesse," I say into a nod. "And yeah, we're good."

"That's good," Oscar says, watching Charlie. "Don't lose that. It hurts when it's gone." He sucks in a heavy breath and almost rolls his eyes. "You're *scarily* easy to talk to, you know that?"

"Yeah, it's a gift and a curse. Getting stuck talking to old ladies on Passyunk while I wait for a cheesesteak is my typical Saturday."

He laughs. "And then I suddenly remember you're from Long Beach, *Long Beach*."

I smile back. "What gave me away?"

"For one, it's pronounced *pash-yunk* not *pass-ee-unk*. And South Philly guys might yell at me for this one, but cheesesteaks on Passyunk are garbage."

I face him more. "I've lived in Philly for years, and they're good there."

He shakes his head vigorously. "No*ooo*."

"Come on." Smiling, I smack his chest with the back of my hand, and the collision of my hand to his body causes both of us to tense like I shot magma in our veins. I don't move though. "You'll have to show me sometime."

"Show you...what?" Oscar asks.

I run a hand through my hair. *Do you still want to kiss me?* "The best place to—" I cut myself off as Charlie bounds over.

We pull apart and return to a professional stasis. Working, both of us.

"I just called an Uber," Charlie tells Oscar, but I zero in on the thick bound manuscript in his hand.

"What's that?" I ask him and follow his footsteps as he pushes into the concert venue's lobby, ticket windows and food concessions in view.

His pace is quick like he wants to GTFO *now*. But the energy that he emits feels more like he's running *from* something rather than towards something.

Oscar is quick to bypass Charlie so he can lead.

"Luna's fanfic," Charlie answers me. "She says people online are giving her shit for some minor grammar mistakes, and she needs someone to edit it."

"You agreed?"

"You ask a lot of questions, Jack," Charlie says. His heeled boots clap against the hallway floor.

Oscar looks back with a smile. "That's what I said."

I'm more amused than offended. "It's literally my job to ask questions."

"Touché," Charlie breathes. "She asked. I said yes. And it'd be easier to edit it on my phone, but we live in a world where little shitheads would love to hack my computer." Luna's fanfic username is only known to her family and security.

I actually don't have access to it.

The world would tear her apart for what she writes. Criticize every microscopic word. Everyone knows it, and I bet that's a reason why security is so highly protective of Luna.

"Why do you think she asked you to edit it?" I wonder.

Charlie laughs and blows out smoke. "Because I'm me." We reach the front doors that lead out into the bustling city. New York is always moving, but he stops a foot short and glances at his phone.

"What does 'because I'm me' mean?" I ask further.

He shrugs with one shoulder. "I'm a genius who doesn't give a shit." His yellow-green eyes flash to me. "I'll edit her tentacle smut without batting an eye, and I don't think the same thing can be said for her older brother."

I've been filming Maximoff Hale long enough on *We Are Calloway* to know he isn't judgmental. He's empathetic to a fault. But he does get in his head a lot. So if Charlie is saying his cousin would over-analyze everything his sister writes, then he's probably right.

But I don't know if that's what Charlie is saying.

And I don't know how to ask him to clarify without a leading question. So I stop asking. We're not shooting right now, anyway.

Charlie sticks his cigarette between his lips. "Car's here."

"Where are we going?" I ask.

"You'll see."

"It'd be better if I knew the location," I say, hoping to have *some* idea. I can hear my crew complaining and griping already.

"I never said I'd be easy to work with."

"But *me* filming you is also helping *you* somehow, right?" I say lightly, trying to be friendly about this. "So let's help each other, Charlie."

He relents. Partially. And just tells me, "We're going out of the country."

Shit.

Fuck, I didn't even pack a bag.

"Bye, Jack!" Luna calls from the stage. She waves with Tom, who yells goodbye to Oscar.

I make the shaka brah hand gesture, and then Oscar and I turn to each other.

Oscar adjusts his earpiece. "Told you to grab a toothbrush before we left, Long Beach."

"I thought you were joking."

"Some days, I wish I were."

It's beginning to be clear that diving into Charlie's life means I've just put myself in the passenger seat to Oscar Oliveira's.

8

Oscar Oliveira

AFTER TALKING WITH THE flight crew, I gather enough information about the spontaneous trip.

Destination: Paris.

Me: Unshocked.

The small private jet hums, and I pass Jack a Gatorade from the cooler on the wall. We sit across from each other at one of the tables. I glimpse over my shoulder to check on my client. Charlie sleeps three rows back, a Cobalt Diamonds-branded mask covers his eyes and bright pink earplugs cancel out all noise.

Jack follows my gaze, and I meet his eyes when I turn back to him. "He's got the right idea," I say. "You should get some sleep now, if you can." He couldn't have slept that much after Charlie and I left his apartment. He had to meet me at my studio in New York like two seconds later this morning. And since then, we've been on-the-go chasing Charlie's shadow.

He uncaps the Gatorade and takes a swig. "It doesn't annoy you that he keeps you in the dark?"

I rarely talk about Charlie. With anyone. It feels too personal.

My reservations must be written all over my face because Jack winces. "I'm not asking as a producer of a show," he clarifies. "I'm just…asking as a friend."

I laugh a little. "Is that what we're calling this?" I dig in my backpack and pull out a bag of Doritos. Snacks are a bodyguard's best friend. Charlie and I keep overnight bags on the plane for his impulsive trips, and I almost wish I knew Jack would be joining. I would've packed more clothes for him.

Then again, Highland *loves* to wear my clothes. And I'd be a Liar with a capital L if I said I didn't like him in them.

Jack frowns. "What would you call us?"

Us.

That word spasms my muscles like I just got zapped in an electric fence.

"Co-workers," I answer. "Production. Security. We're not employed by the same company, but we deal with the same rich, white east coast families, blue-check-marked and verified WASPs."

"Co-workers," he repeats like it's settling in.

"Yeah," I nod.

"Do you ask all your co-workers for a kiss?" he shoots back.

I smile, trying not to disintegrate in my seat from this conversation. "Only the cute ones," I say, popping a chip in my mouth. As smooth as that was, I regret it. *Oliveira, stop flirting with the straight boy.* Holy fucking shit, I'm hopeless.

My phone rings, a saving grace really. Thank the Lord for in-air Wi-Fi.

Caller ID: *Donnelly*

I nod up to Jack. "Sorry, I've got to answer this."

"Yeah, no problem, dude. I'm just going to take your advice." He gives me a smile, and it takes me a second to realize what Jack means. And then I see him pop in a couple earbuds and close his eyes.

I retreat to the jet's bathroom, which resembles a fancy powder bathroom with a rose gold faucet and a shiny rose gold toilet. As a kid, I was just happy to be on a commercial plane flying international to Brazil. That was and still is a luxury for a lot of people.

But this, *this* is like a fantasy made for royalty, and I know for me and a lot of security, it's cool to be a part of it all. Especially guarding the Cobalt Empire, the epitome of lavish extravagance. But we're here first and last because we care about the lives of the families.

I take a seat on the shut toilet lid, a comfortable amount of room here. "Hey." I press the phone to my ear. "What's going on? You alright?" We haven't spoken since his vague text this morning. Sun has set, and we're scheduled to land in Paris tomorrow.

I'm more on edge knowing I left the country before getting answers from Donnelly. But I trust if something is really wrong and time sensitive, Farrow would've checked in with me.

For a lot of reasons, I have a love-hate feeling towards Donnelly not being Beckett's bodyguard anymore. I wish he still were, but I'm also glad he's not for his sake.

Blast to the past, Donnelly used to live with me in New York, while on Beckett's detail, and if anyone asked, I'd probably say he's the worst roommate and to give me someone else—just to fuck with him. But he's not that bad. We saw each other every week. Almost every day.

I miss that.

It's lonely being the only Omega bodyguard in Hell's Kitchen.

"Yeah, yeah," Donnelly replies. "I'm almost back in PA." His South Philly lilt comes out strong. "Just made a mandatory pitstop at Wawa. Where you at?"

"Plane bathroom. Sitting on the rose gold shitter."

He laughs lowly. "Charlie whisk you off to Neverland again?"

"Second star to the right."

"Let me guess, let me guess. *Dubai.*"

"Way off, bro," I say. "Paris." We can play off each other to annoyance, just ask Farrow, and before we get carried away, I add, "I'm serious though. Why were you at the lake house this morning?"

"Yeah, about that…" Donnelly's tone sobers. "I need to tell you before everyone else hears."

My body goes cold. "Tell me what?"

"You know my Uncle Scottie?"

"Yeah…" I'm caging breath.

"I've been visiting him in prison, and I finally got him to let Farrow and Maximoff adopt Ripley. So I brought the papers to the lake house."

"What?" I'm choked.

Emotion tunnels through me. Warring together. I clasp a hand over my eyes that well. Happiness for my best friend. *Farrow and Maximoff are adopting their son.* Deep weighted concern for my other best friend. *What the hell did Donnelly do?*

"Paul…" I scrape my hand from my eyes to my mouth, and my chest collapses. I don't want to diminish the magnitude of what he did for Farrow, who's practically the reason Donnelly is living and breathing—though Farrow will *never* say this to anyone.

I hear him sniff, choked too. "Don't call me that, man. The name's *Donnelly.*" His voice is trying to lighten.

"It's amazing…what you gave him." *Motherfuck,* I'm crying. I wipe my face. "But, bro, what'd you do?" My chin nearly shakes.

He comes from a meth-addicted family. All of them are in prison, except for his father who was recently released.

All I can think is that he convinced Scottie to terminate his parental rights by agreeing to something. So what exactly did Donnelly agree to?

"It's alright," he says. "Like I told Farrow, I'm good. You don't need to worry about me."

"Now I'm worried," I tell him. "He didn't ask you to push drugs?"

"It's not anything with drugs. I'm good. It's all good. Nuthin' I can't handle."

I rub my wet eyes and swallow the rock in my throat. "Can we do anything to help you? I get you keeping shit from Redford while he's on his honeymoon, but I'm on a motherfucking plane. I can't kick your ass if I'm in a different country. Bro, this is the perfect time to come clean."

He laughs softly, but the noise fades.

Leaving heavy silence.

I close my eyes slowly, my grip on the cell intensifying. He's not going to say anything. "Donnelly—"

"It was worth it."

Is that the measure of our actions? Whether they're *worth* something for the people we care about?

A text pings my phone the same time he says, "I've gotta go, Oscar. I'm on-duty soon, and I need to check in with Thatcher."

"Call me tomorrow?"

"Sure thing. Hey, have a crepe for me. Miss those fuckers." Only Donnelly would call a crepe a *fucker*.

We say our short goodbyes, and I check my text messages.

Cancelled the Craigslist meet-up. Still looking around for places. Know anyone in NYC? — Baby Sis

I mutter to myself, "What is it with these teenagers and Craigslist." Between her and Tom, *Christ*. I formulate a text. I already called my sister and talked her out of the Craigslist roommate.

And I learned she doesn't want to live at home anymore because she's A.) nineteen, and B.) employed as a pro-boxer, and C.) sick of our strict dad who pushes her too much as her trainer and father.

Mostly, it's C.

Her going head-to-head with our dad concerns me, so I want her out of there too. It'd be healthier for both of them.

Which is why I said, *come live with me*, again.

She said, *you live down the hall from the most obnoxious Cobalt boy. I'll pass.* I thought she meant Charlie, but then she told me, *Beckett*.

I love that she hates him because he's been trying to hit on my sister since Scotland. And I know what kinds of clubs Beckett goes to, and I don't want my baby sis anywhere *near* that.

Right now, I send her a new text: I know one person in NYC who has a place. Me. Offer is still open. And the apartment is all paid for. You can take the bed. I'll take the pull-out.

Will it be inconvenient? Yeah.

But there are some inconveniences that don't matter in the grand scheme of things. It's a bed, not a college diploma I'm forsaking.

I'm about to put my phone away, but I rub the wet streaks off my face with my shirt and decide to take my mind off everything for a few minutes.

Popping open Instagram, I scroll through Faith's profile. I've been seeing her off and on for the past couple months. Nothing serious. Her hair is dyed a pale purple, and she blows kisses with her hand in most of the pics. No captions, just a couple heart emojis.

Sleeping with her has been fun, but that's all it really is. Nothing there beyond the surface. Against my sanity, I click out of her profile and type in Jack's username.

I may have dug around for that info.

JackStuckOnThe405 pops up. His profile is curated with beautiful landscape shots of Philly and LA, but it's his selfies that get me. His bone structure is can't-tear-your-eyes-away stunning, and I'm almost shocked he's never been an actual model considering all the time he's been in the industry in California.

I skim his bright hundred-watt smile.

I grin back, then cringe.

Holy shit, I'm torturing myself.

I log out of Instagram.

Fuck this.

I delete the app.

I'm about to vacate the bathroom when I remember something. *Benji Strong.*

Jack keeps surprising me. His confession about his porn star crush as a teenager almost annihilated me. Never heard of the guy though.

I could...do some research...

Alright, this is the last time I check up on anything Jack-related. After this, he's not allowed to take up space in my brain.

Quickly, I type in Benji Strong's name in a popular porn site.

Gay.

Gay porn.

XXX GAY PORN.

Tags to the videos.

The actual video titles are more graphic: *Big Cock Bangs Twink.* Benji is definitely the big cock.

I grin into a laugh.

His build is…hmm, we're similar. Not vein-popping bodybuilders, but toned and cut. And the entertainment of this new information slowly fades as *reality* sinks in.

Benji is a gay porn star. Jack watched gay porn as a teenager.

Blood rushes down south, my body ready to jump his bones. Ready to explore Jack and see what's hidden under his clothes, and deeper. To feel his leg slide against mine while I pin him to the bed and fuck him good—yeah, I'm ready.

But really, this doesn't change anything but my attraction to him. Ramping up to the hundredth degree.

He's still straight.

A straight boy that watches gay porn. Or used to watch it. I wonder if he still does.

Wow, I sure know how to fall for them.

9

Jack Highland

STEAM FOGS UP THE SHOWER, water slowly gliding down my temples. Dazed, head light and heady, heat cocoons my limbs. Shutting off the faucet, I grab a towel draped over the glass shower and tie the fabric around my waist. Still drifting, floating, a swelter pricking my nerves.

I shift...a little conscious that...I'm...this is a dream, but I relax and sink back into the thick, steaming warmth.

Quietly, I step onto the cold bathroom tiles, and I look up.

Oscar perches against the sink, coolly. Towel slung over his shoulder. Drawstring pants low on his waist, abs glistening...he's wet from the shower.

His curly hair is damp, the strands brushing his forehead. Already showered, he's in the bathroom with me. My dick rouses, pulsing for a *need*. A hunger for him, and I stroke his body with my eyes. He undresses me with his gaze, even though I'm already buck-naked.

I can barely move, blood pumping in my erection. Like he's already fisting my length. But fog and space separate us, and so I walk over to him in that heady daze.

Dreaming.

Shut that out, dude. I want to see what happens. I want to feel it.

My eyes trace his unshaven jaw, heartrate skipping, and I whisper, "How does this work?"

Oscar grips my hardness with the assuredness I need, and breath hitches in my throat. I clutch his waist, firm muscles beneath my palm.

Our mouths edge nearer, nearer. *Ask me again, Oscar.* I choke out, "Ask me."

He pumps me in a pace that swells arousal, vapor and a tormenting desire wrapping around me. With my other hand, I clasp his hard jaw, but I can barely feel him in my clutch. Dreaming...*just a dream.*

"Ask me," I choke out again, our mouths grazing but not touching. *Ask me if I want to be kissed.*

His hoarse, deep voice says something against my lips. I can't hear him, and I'm dying under the almost-there, the so-close, the one-breath-away of this moment. This second.

"Long Beach..." My nickname is faint.

I glance down at my cock and watch his large hand tug me. Shockwaves ripple through my muscles, my veins, my head—I'm spinning and a groan erupts from my throat.

"Long Beach."

I jolt awake.

Oscar shakes my shoulder, standing in the aisle of the private jet. Our eyes meet, and a new type of heat bathes me. *Mortified.*

I'm on the plane. I fell asleep on the *plane* and had a fucking sex dream! *Dude,* dude, dude, *Jack.* I'm a smooth operator. I flirt, date, and sleep with women without tripping, but around him lately, I want to go for a dive and end up belly-flopping.

Again, *mortified.*

"We're about to land," Oscar says, his hand still on my shoulder and we both suddenly zone in on that fact, his breath and my breath stilted. He pulls back, but no lie, I wish he wouldn't.

Did he hear me groan?

Oscar has a black bandana, already rolled, and begins to tie it around his forehead. "If you need to use the bathroom, now's your chance." His eyes dip for half a second. To my crotch.

I glance down. Oh, fuck, Jesus, I have a *boner.* I'm rock-hard, the outline of my cock pressing against my dark jeans.

And I was worried that he heard me groan. Shit. I shoot to my feet. Embarrassment deflating me more. "Yeah, thanks for the heads up."

He grins, hopefully just at my choice of words. "Hey, it happens to the best of us." He pats my shoulder, and again, the placement of his hand on me catches our breath.

I stare at his hand for a second too long. That hand was just wrapped around my shaft, and it's not just an act I want to stay in my head.

I'm not straight.

I can't be straight with how drawn to him I've been. With how aroused I become, and the attraction is too clear to deny or question. Those clouds are gone.

But the endgame of my future is nothing but a fog. My life's plan— what does that even look like now? I'm used to having the big picture mapped out. High school. Prom King. College. Swim Team. Producer. Wife. Children. Awards. Happiness. Retirement. More happiness.

I've erased essential parts of my map! But the fuck if I even know what a map is anymore. Or maybe, I've added question marks to it. Husband? Or wife? Or spouse? Children???

What even is my sexuality if I'm not straight…I don't know.

Oscar drops his hand.

I slide out into the aisle, catching his eyes. I think about *work*. I'm here to film Charlie, and I can't open the floodgates to me and Oscar in this moment—that's if he'd even want me.

I need to play off what just happened. So I say, "What is that you told me? *I don't need an emotional baby blanket.* Same goes for me, Oscar. Treat me how you'd treat any of your other co-worker non-friends."

He nods slowly. "Nice woodie," he says casually.

"It's even bigger without the pants," I say, just as casually, and then I turn around, hoping he's burning up just as much as I am. Every step to the bathroom feels like crossing molten lava. I can't tell if it's because I'm still mortified or if it's just jacked-up levels of attraction. Probably both.

Definitely both.

10

Oscar Oliveira

NO EARPIECE. NO RADIO. I don't need them. I'm in Paris without anyone from SFO. Officially on my own, and it's just another day at work.

My current office is The Louvre. I've lost count the number of times I've been here, but I try my best not to take these things for granted.

No matter how many times Charlie comes back to see the Winged Victory of Samothrace, a gorgeous eight-foot marble sculpture of a winged goddess, he still has that same awed reverence in his eyes as the first time I saw him here. It's a gift not to become jaded by beauty.

My gaze drifts to Jack.

With a Canon in hand, he's busy talking to Charlie, and I hang back out of earshot, only because it's a busy day at the museum. I had hoped we'd be going to the Musée d'Orsay. It's less crowded. Smaller. Easier to coordinate with the museum's security, and one of Charlie's favorite places in the city.

Landing here, and being on the same floor as the Mona Lisa, isn't ideal.

But ideal went out the window the moment I became Charlie's bodyguard. So here I am, quietly telling a girl in French that she can't get an autograph from him.

She already has a marker in hand, one she dug from her purse. Her crestfallen expression is one I've seen a thousand times. "Cela ne prendra qu'une minute. S'il vous plaît." *It will only be a minute. Please.*

I reply in fluent French, "Pas aujourd'hui." *Not today.*

She can't be older than twenty. Sighing heavily, she stuffs the marker in her purse. I watch as she uses her phone to snap photos of the back of Charlie's head, then shuffles away. Rinse and repeat thirty more times. The only upside I have is that Charlie's less recognized overseas. If this were Philly, he'd have a swarm of crowds already.

It makes it easier to politely bar access to him.

Truth be told, every day is different with my client. Sometimes he won't care if they want autographs. Other times, like today, he asks me to keep everyone away from him. As if he, himself, is radioactive.

Jack leaves Charlie's side, and I watch him disappear down a different hall. It takes all my effort to keep my feet planted and not follow him. *He's not your client, Oliveira.*

He's also *not* famous. Doesn't need a bodyguard. Straight.

Doesn't need me.

Look at me, with this sound logic. I should just duct-tape that mantra to my brain. Then maybe my dumbass can stop thinking he's more mesmerizing than the breathtaking art in this building.

"Hi umm…" Someone taps my shoulder. I rotate to see a twenty-something woman. Hair the color of burnt leaves, American accent, a fashion fanny pack on her hourglass waist—total Instagram Influencer Realness.

She's hot.

Am I interested…? My eyes almost dart to where Jack left.

"Aren't you Oscar Oliveira?" She bites her bottom lip.

On one side of all this SFO fame, I don't need to bat a single eyelash to pick up women or men.

The public knows I'm bi after catching me lip-locked with a man. I was outside a gay bar on my night off, and security isn't supposed to give interviews to press—but the thought of the media theorizing my sexuality didn't sit right with me. So I told the paparazzi, "I'm bisexual" and went home with my arm around a hot one-night *lay*.

Not that picking up people was hard pre-fame. But the new distraction on-duty just makes a complicated job more complicated. And I'm the only one from Kitsuwon Securities in Paris right now. No extra set of eyes when mine wander.

Plus, there's a restriction about fucking the fans of SFO, written clearly in Kitsuwon's 400-page rulebook.

The rule: *do not*.

I think my brother is the only one who consciously breaks it all the time. I prefer not to fuck fans. It ruins some of the chase and foreplay when it's just...so *easy* to get them in bed. A waste of my best pick-up lines.

Have I done it though? Yeah.

I'm not fucking perfect. Far from it.

So I'm staring at the Influencer-styled chick, and she's asking me if I'm Oscar. And I go for the typical response.

"I am," I say. "But I'm busy."

"Can I just have a quick selfie?" She smiles and wags her cellphone seductively.

I shake my head, gaze planted on Charlie, but from the corner of my eye, I notice Jack returning, his confident stride and welcoming aura like a radiant beam of light. Even when I saw his morning wood on the plane and then his embarrassment, he managed to smile and keep cool.

The guy is unreal. Who wouldn't want that kind of luminous joy in their life? *He can't be a part of yours, Oliveira.*

My stomach twists.

Maybe I need to be more proactive in building barriers around my heart. And I can't think of a better way to get over him than to give in to her.

"You know what," I say. "Sure."

Her face lights up, and she lifts her phone. Her hair smells like candy apples, but it's not my favorite scent. She snaps the pic and examines the photo. "We look hot together." Her grin expands. "Could I have your number? Maybe we could take more hot selfies sometime?"

She's bold.

I like bold.

"Hey." Jack steps close, two water bottles in hand. So that's where he went. He casts me a quick glance, then one to the girl. Back and forth.

Her brows draw together. "Who are you?"

"My name's Jack," he says into a short nod, his smile gone. "Who are you?" That was cold for welcome-mat, red-carpet-entrance Jack Highland.

I'm staring more at him than her. He sounds jealous. I'd bet…five bucks on it.

"Everly Adams. I'm here for study abroad and ran into this handsome guy." She winks up at me. "You know he's Charlie Cobalt's bodyguard?"

I look Jack over as he shifts his stance, more closed off to her. He tucks a water bottle under his armpit and uncaps the other. "I know him. Oscar is one of the best bodyguards in the entire fleet, but he's on-duty—"

"Oh, I'll be out of his hair in, like, a couple of seconds tops." To me, she asks, "Think we could meet up later tonight?"

Jack chokes down water.

Now I'd bet a hundred bucks on it.

Before I can answer, Jack smoothly interjects, "We're busy, actually. We have a shoot tonight." He gestures to his camera and tries to fake a smile. My attraction hikes up when his fake smile comes out as a heated glare.

Christ, Highland.

She bristles and turns her back on him.

Even if I bet a grand on his jealousy, it doesn't matter. I have a job to do, and it's not thinking about fucking Jack.

I keep focus on Charlie. He's still staring up at the sculpture.

"So…" Everly surveys my six-foot-two build. "About your number…?

"Yeah, sure." I spout off my number but change the last digit. It's a dick move, but I'm not in the mood to reject her in front of Jack.

I've felt what it's like to be rejected, and I would've died if I had an audience when it happened.

After saving my number in her phone, she politely says, "It was nice to meet you." Ignoring Jack, she skirts off.

Leaving me and him closer together. "A shoot tonight?" I question. "I didn't think you were filming, Highland. It's just prep."

"It is," he says more coolly. "I just thought you needed a wingman." He hands me a water, the tension clear in his flexed biceps. "It's not a big deal."

Then why do you look so nervous?

I almost say that back, but instead, I go with, "I don't know what your friends taught you in California, bro, but wingmen don't run off potential hookups." I touch my ear, but I remember I have no radio in Paris.

"She didn't look like your type," Jack says with the rake of his hand through his dark hair. His eyes sink into me, and my defenses rocket through the stratosphere.

"No offense, Long Beach, but I don't think you know what my type is."

His lips rise in a smile synonymous with a slow stroke of a cock. "Are you sure it's not me?" He's searching my gaze.

I think of all the ways I could shut him down:

It's never been you.

My type is the opposite of you, Jack.

I wouldn't fuck you if you were my last option.

Those ideas pulverize my insides. Hurting him isn't on my agenda. Nowhere near, and so I tip my head back to him and say, "Are you sure I'm not *your* type?"

Mic drop.

Too much passes through his face, and I can't stare. My eyes snap towards a tour group. *Shit.*

The noisy students head towards the Winged Victory of Samothrace sculpture. I've memorized the entire tour schedules, and I know they're early. The moment I step towards my client, he ducks behind a burly man wearing a University of Alabama sweatshirt.

Jack follows close behind as I weave between bodies.

"Excusez-moi," I say, pushing past someone with a sopping wet raincoat. "Excusez-moi." A little girl, no older than five, runs out right in front of me. Elbowing my shins. Jack grabs my arm before I trip over her like she's a lawn gnome.

"Colette!" her mother whisper-shouts. "Viens ici maintenant!" *Come here now!*

Jack's hand falls to my hip, leading me out of their way, while I root a hand between his shoulder blades—guiding him in my direction, further through the maze of the museum.

We breach the packed confines of the crowd, coming into a clear area. Both in lock-step together, we hustle down the hallway without full on sprinting.

When I reach the end, the hall splits towards Greek ceramics and a temporary exhibit hall.

I don't see Charlie.

My pulse stays even, but I'm on high alert. Barely blinking. "We have to split up," I tell Jack. "You take the cerami—"

"I have it, Oscar." He understands, already exiting in that direction.

I shouldn't...but I watch him go. Really, I'm craving to jog after him, but this isn't the time to chase after a crush.

A crush.

That word again, and I almost career my head back in frustration. In reality, I'm more poised for a serious hide & seek game with Charlie. *Where the fuck did you go?*

Carefully and urgently, I sweep the area, talk to the security guards at the exits, and then text Jack a meeting spot when I reach the ground floor beside the information desk.

I don't know whether to be furious or concerned, so by the time I come face-to-face with Jack again, I'm full of pent-up emotion. Charlie ditching me. Fine. Charlie ditching me in the motherfucking *Louvre*. Not fine. Not fine at all.

Jack shakes his head, face fallen in guilt. "I couldn't find him."

"It's not your fault." I pull out my cell.

"It kind of is," Jack tells me while his fingers glide through his hair. "Before all of this, you said not to distract you."

I did give him that threat. Only because I like doing my job well, and that means having clear focus on my client. But I fucked that one up myself.

"You didn't distract me, Highland. I did that to myself when I agreed to take a selfie with a random woman." Shouldn't have done that. Technically, I did do it *because* of Jack. I was trying to get over him. But that's still not his fault.

I dial a number and press my cell to my ear.

"Oscar?" The older man's French accent is thick. "Haven't heard from you in months. I thought maybe Charlie fell out of love with the Louvre."

"Hardly," I say. "And you know I can speak French, Florent."

"I know," Florent replies in English still. "What do you need?"

"Charlie's MIA. Can you see if he left the museum? Last known location was room 703, the Denon Wing."

"It'll take me a couple minutes. Can I call you back?"

"Yeah. Thanks, Florent." I hang up and meet Jack's confused gaze.

"That was the head of the museum's security," I explain. "He's going to check the tapes. It'll save us time from running around the place, if Charlie's already hightailed it out of here."

Jack looks impressed. "And you just had his number on speed dial?"

"If it's a place Charlie frequents, yeah, I've got connections." I check the time on my watch. "It's the only way I can do my job well. Work smarter, not harder, Long Beach. Remember that." I pat his chest, and we both tense.

We keep doing that.

I drop my hand, tension erecting. Thankfully other things aren't *erecting* right now.

Jack smiles a little. "I'll keep it in mind. Tucked right next to *distractions become extractions.*"

I did say that. Right before I told him that I'd extract his ass from a room if his production crew interfered with my job of keeping Charlie safe. But that comment was during a filming segment of *We Are Calloway.* Had to be at least a couple years back, and I'm honestly kind of surprised he remembered it.

I'm about to reply when my phone buzzes in my palm.

I answer on the first ring. "Florent."

"He left the Louvre around five minutes ago," Florent tells me. "Out the Carrousel du Louvre entrance."

Of course he exited to the mall.

Of course.

I grip my phone tighter. "Thanks, Florent. I owe you one."

He says a quick goodbye in French and I hang up. "We have to make up some time," I tell Jack. "How fast can you walk?"

He smiles. "I'm an athlete."

"You're a swimmer," I remind him. "But how are you on land, Long Beach?"

"You just set the pace," Jack says. "I'll follow."

WE SCOUR THE MALL AND ALL OF CHARLIE'S favorite cafés and spots to no avail. Now back at Charlie's two-bedroom apartment in the Saint-Germain-des-Prés neighborhood, I pace the marbled floors and make as many calls as I possibly can.

None of my contacts have seen my client, but they'll call me if he shows up. More likely, a random stranger will spot Charlie and post a pic of him on social media.

But I've got that covered too.

Jack is seated on the black leather couch, gold metal trim running down the side, and with his elbows on his knees, he scrolls through Instagram and Twitter.

He said he'd scour social media before I even asked if he could.

Production. He knows better than most people how the public would fawn over Charlie and post videos to the internet.

It hits me that this is the longest span of time I've ever been with Jack, just one-on-one. I've learned small things about him. Like how he can sprint.

Fast.

Like how he'll hold open doors for every person, and the bright smile he'll give them is never filled with fake kindness.

Like how he didn't prepare for a spontaneous trip to Paris, but before boarding, he grabbed a blue bomber jacket and candy from his car.

He stuffed lollipops in his jean's pocket.

If he were a friend, I'd give him shit for it—out of every piece of candy, a *sucker*—but I still don't want him to be my friend.

Right now, the stick pokes out of his mouth while he scrolls on his phone. He shrugged on the blue bomber jacket, patches sewn in the fabric that say *good vibes* and *totally rad.* Along with a VW van and palm tree patch—he stands out.

To me.

He stands out to me, and I need to focus. "Anything?" I ask him as I slip my phone in my pocket.

"No. Charlie might as well have evaporated." He speaks with the sucker against the inside of his mouth.

My dick between his lips. The image springs up instantly, and heat cascades down my body. It actually helps temper the boiling frustration I have towards my client.

Nope, that comes back.

I cage in an angry breath and stride to the bar. "Well, he's got evaporation down to a science," I say and bend down to a bottom drawer. "But unlucky for Charlie, I know how to find him."

Jack looks up. "So you're not worried?"

"I'm at about a ten percent." I dig through the drawer, full of bottle openers, cork stoppers, and stirrers. *It's somewhere in the back...*

I explain further, "He's good about calling me if something's going down. One time in Holland, he ditched me for about five hours." I pull out a small box. Rising to my feet, I finish the story. "It was during the tulip festival, so more people were around than usual. A few drunk fucks decided to heckle him at a bar, and things turned physical. He called me from the bathroom where he barricaded himself." I leave out the part where Charlie could have called me before they threw a punch. Could have texted before his ribs cracked.

He chose to wait until after.

That story never made the press because I showed up and started confiscating phones and getting NDAs signed. Besides the lead in security at the time, I only told Donnelly and Farrow what happened.

They both asked why my knuckles looked fucked up, and I didn't want to lie.

Jack watches me cross the room to the front door. "How worried were you then?"

I laugh. "Close to a hundred." I look back to Jack. "The whole drive to him, I kept thinking that if my little brother were in his position, I wouldn't have to worry. Quinn's the best fighter I've ever known. Charlie...he weighs—what, a hundred-fifty? Guy's got some lean muscle on him but he's still skinny for my standards."

"Yeah, he's about the same size as my little brother," Jack nods. "Dude, if Jesse called me from a bathroom after a fight..." He takes the sucker out of his mouth and expels an anxious breath. "I don't know what I'd do. Jump a guy...bulldoze everyone, probably."

I don't tell him how I flattened most of the guys on the ground that night.

Instead, I'm grinning. "Long Beach, *you'd* bulldoze everyone?"

He shares my smile. "You think I'm all sunshines and buttercups, but I've got a mean side."

I think about how he made an enemy out of the girl who hit on me, but I don't bring it up. "You're sucking on a lollipop, legitimately."

He smiles more, putting the sucker back in his mouth. "Who doesn't like suckers, *Oliveira*? And you know, you say 'legitimately' a lot."

Guess I'm not the only one noticing habits. "I do," I agree. And while I untie my bandana, I tell Jack, "I'd definitely like to see this *mean side* phenomenon." Flirting again. Twenty points deducted from Slytherin.

The Hale family would be so proud of my geeky ass thoughts.

"What's with the bandanas?" Jack wonders. "You always roll them so they don't even keep the hair out of your face."

"Yeah, but it wicks away sweat."

He nods, thinking that's my full answer.

"I like how I look with them. And I look fucking hot. That's my real answer, Highland." Returning to the small box, I take out a handheld device and attach it to the doorframe.

"What's that?" Jack asks, shifting his sucker from the left to right side of his mouth with his tongue. *Fuck,* I wish he wouldn't do that.

I wet my lips and glance at the wall. "An alarm. It'll alert me if the front door opens, and luckily, this is the only way in and out of the apartment. So while we're out searching for Charlie, I'll know if he comes back home." Installing cameras here would be easier, but it's too invasive. He deserves whatever privacy he has left as an American god.

Jack studies me for a long beat. "You love the challenge of it all?"

I'm a tactical badass, and Charlie is the one person who awakens a specific part of my brain. "I'd say it's more the strategy of it all, and I'd love it more if I knew Charlie was safe." I sweep him up and down. "You're not breaking a sweat yourself."

He smiles brighter. "Sometimes I film Ryke Meadows free-solo. I'm not climbing beside him. Usually I'll be at the top or on the ground doing drone shots, but watching that guy climb his full route with no rope, no harness...man, *that's* stressful. This is a lower tier. Probably because you're with me and you've gone through it all before."

Yeah, but not many guys on SFO would be okay with this situation. Lost a client. He's out in the wilderness of a bustling city. No one to radio for backup. Knowing Jack and I *have* to find him. There is no alternative. No *what if* or *maybe tomorrow.*

It's a lot of fucking responsibility, and not everyone has the confidence to hack it.

I glance at my watch. "Ten more minutes here, then we're going to head to Le Chat Rouge. The show starts at nine."

There's a good chance Charlie will be there. I've never known him to come to Paris and miss some type of performance, whether it's theatre, the opera, or anything in between. Doing the numbers in my head, I realized the longest time has passed since he's been to Le Chat Rouge, one of his favorite cabarets in the city.

"And we can't go in tees and jeans." I open a baroque armoire.

"You keep clothes here?" Jack stands up.

"No, but I'm using his steamer." One that Charlie *never* uses. Guy puts on wrinkled shirt after wrinkled shirt with zero care.

I squat down and rifle through a shoebox where he keeps it. "Pro tip: don't wear tees if you forget a bag."

Jack watches me. "Why is that?"

I grab the steamer and go to my backpack on a Queen Anne chair, digging for clothes. "Let's put it this way, I'd much rather be wearing workout clothes to chase down Charlie, but when I first got on his detail, I had to chase him into a three-star Michelin restaurant." I unzip my backpack. "I didn't pass dress code, and I had to find the nearest department store and buy a suit. By the time I did, he was gone. Went to the airport and flew to Anchorage. I was a real cranky ass over comms that night." I pull out my suit.

Turning around, I face Jack, and I meet his edging smile and honey-brown eyes that dip into me. Like I'm an ocean he's swimming in. "Next time, call me," he says coolly. "I'll drive over with a suit."

"Yeah?" I lick my lips slowly, recalling his apartment. "Aren't all your suits in a cardboard box in your bathroom?" I begin steaming the white button-down, black slacks and suit jacket, catching sight of Jack's widening smile and laugh. "Where's the joke?" I ask.

He shakes his head and pops the sucker out of his mouth. "There's no joke. You saw my Balikbayan box."

My brows furrow. "Your what?"

"My mom's side of the family is from the Philippines. We use a Balikbayan box to send household goods and clothes back to relatives.

I had a couple old suits so I threw them in there. Once the box is full, I'll sea freight it to my uncle's house. He lives in a province in the Philippines called Batangas, where my mom grew up. *Balikbayan* is really a term used for a Filipino who's gone abroad. *Balik* means *came back*. And *bayan* means *country, land, a people, town*." He pauses to add with a smile, "What can I say, I'm a proud Filipino."

I grin more, loving getting to know about Jack and his family, his culture. The biggest worry: the more I know, the deeper I'll fall and I'm already flying too mother-effing close to the sun.

While I finish steaming out wrinkles, I tell him, "From one proud Latino to a proud Filipino, I gotta say I'm most interested in your snacks."

"Filipino snacks?"

"Oh yeah, Long Beach. I need to try them. For research." I check the time on my watch. "And we need to move faster." I throw him the black slacks and white button-down. "Put these on."

He frowns, but pulls his crew-neck over his head, not wasting time. "What are you wearing?"

"The suit jacket over my T-shirt, and the slacks I have on. You're the one wearing blue jeans." I thread my arms through the suit jacket. "Luckily, my pants *might* just fit your thin frame."

Jack chokes on a laugh and extends his arms. "Is this thin, dude?" Bare-chested, his six-four height and sculpted abs tell the story of a letterman jacket jock.

I shake my head with a short motion. My muscles contract in desire that I try to *thwart*. Letting him change in front of me—not healthy. My cock hates me. My emotions are all over the fucking continent. Make that *two* continents, the one we left and the one we're standing in.

"You're hot, Long Beach," I tell him bluntly, mentally checking off everything we have and need. I glance at a missed text from a contact. *No Charlie spotting.* "A classic athletic pretty boy."

He steps quickly out of his jeans, tugging the fabric off his ankles. His eyes keep rising to mine. "I always thought you were the pretty boy between the two of us."

Don't check him out. He stands in tight blue boxer-briefs, and I run a hand across the back of my neck. "I have scars all over my face and body; I'm not a pretty boy."

"From boxing, right?"

"Yeah, hard blows." I request an Uber while he finishes changing.

Jack steps into the slacks, and in my peripheral, I notice how he studies Charlie's apartment. His curiosity grazes the pale-yellow walls and the ornate crown molding.

Most people ask who bought it: Charlie or his parents. Every time Charlie brings someone here, it's their first question.

His reply never changes. He smiles bitterly as he says, "My money is inherited. It doesn't matter. It's all the fucking same."

But I was here the day Charlie walked into this place and signed the contract. His parents weren't around. He was eighteen, and this apartment was his first big purchase as an adult. The price tag is a hundred times higher than what I spent on my first apartment after college.

But his reaction was the same as mine. Like he knew this was a monumental stepping-stone in his life.

I love this apartment for that reason alone. I know what it means to Charlie, and I'm probably the only person outside his family that he's let use it. He's told me multiple times, *Anytime you want to stay here, Oscar, it's yours.* We don't have a buddy-guard relationship, but there is a level of respect and kindness that exists between us.

Despite this current Houdini situation.

"You regretting this show?" I ask Jack as he finishes buttoning his slacks. "Now's the time to back out."

Jack smiles, but it's a weaker one. "I've considered it."

Rare surprise hits me. "Really?"

He slips his arms in the button-down. "Probably not why you think."

"I'm thinking it's because Charlie can be a pain in the ass."

Jack laughs. "I'm fine with that, really. I just don't know if I can put a crew through this. Fuck, I don't know if a crew would *want* to do this."

"Why do you?" I wonder.

He fishes buttons through his shirt. His mouth opens, then closes, then opens again. "Honestly…being a creator of a show has been a lifelong goal. I'm stoked to be where I am on the docuseries, but I'm also just one of many execs on *We Are Calloway*. But *this*…this would be mine." He tucks the button-down in his slacks. "And like, sure, don't attach your dreams to a sinking ship, but I've also never closed a door to an opportunity this big."

I didn't realize how much this means to him. "You were the extra-credit, straight-A high school student, weren't you?" I sweep his frame. "And the category is, *overachiever*."

He looks me up and down. "Didn't you get straight-As? Yale, right?"

I nod heartily.

But the room deadens until I vocally answer, "But I wouldn't call myself an overachiever." Jack and I—we have a lot we can relate to.

Ivy League grads.

Little brothers ten-years younger.

This, though, this is where we diverge. "I don't have lifelong goals that kick my ass up the rungs of a career ladder," I say, our eyes locked. "There is no yearning for more when I have exactly what I want right *here*. I had the whole *fight harder, achieve greater* when I was a pro-boxer, and I landed flat on my face."

I've failed too many times in my life to think sticking any type of dreams on any ship will sail me to shore.

Jack slips on his shoes and tells me, "I can't imagine a life where I don't pursue what I want…" His voice drifts off with his eyes.

Is it selfish to wish he was thinking about me?

I push some curls off my forehead. Jack is so driven, so optimistic, so *hopeful* that he can achieve the pinnacle of success—whatever that is to him, and now I know it's *this* show.

I've felt failure, and it's a shitty fucking thing.

Maybe I can try to make this shit show about Charlie Cobalt actually work—for him and his dreams at least. It's a scary prospect, because for my job, burying this show into the ground would be easiest.

A notification pings my phone. "Our ride is here."

Jack spreads out his arms, my slacks molding his ass and my button-down a little tight on his chest and biceps, accentuating his muscles. "Perfect fit?" His flirty smile causes my mouth to curve up in a grin.

If you were my boyfriend, I'd fuck you.

I nod a few times. "Yeah." My grin fades knowing he's nothing to me, just a guy I'm working with. "Perfect fit."

11

Oscar Oliveira

"MAISON BONDÉE," GASPARD tells me outside the cabaret. "Je ne sais pas s'il est à l'intérieur, mais vous êtes invités à regarder." *Packed house. I don't know if he's inside, but you're welcome to look.*

"Merci," I say as Gaspard lets me and Jack into the side entrance of Le Chat Rouge.

Jack slips me a quick glance, not the first one I've noticed when I've spoken French.

As we move further into the playhouse, I tip my head back and whisper, "Holding in a question, are you coming down with a fever?" I rest the back of my hand to his forehead. Just in a flash of a second.

His smile grows, bending closer to me. "You have a lot of friends in Paris?" That's not the question I expected.

We pass dressing room doors. "They're acquaintances, not friends." I only talk to these people if I need something. Same goes for them. And if they're in New York or Philly, I'm only a phone call away to help them out.

His voice is hushed as he says, "Looks like your phone is bloated too."

I told Jack his phone must be bloated with the numbers of *friends*. It feels like he's telling me his catalogue of friends aren't as close to him as I thought. Can't read his features well in the dark, and we don't have time for a longer conversation.

We follow Gaspard quietly, and Jack leans closer to me, whispering against my ear, "You're fluent in French?" *There's the question.*

His warm breath tingles my skin.

"Yeah," I whisper, "and it's not the only language I'm fluent in. Maybe I'll tell you sometime, Long Beach." I have to face forward more as we roll to a stop. Gaspard led us to a heavy black curtain, which merges to a side aisle in the audience.

Before he leaves, Gaspard tells me that if we find Charlie, we can't stay. Packed house, after all.

This is a mess.

I don't even know if I want to find him. I can't yell at him in public, and I'm going to. Client or not. He's going to hear it from me.

I push aside the heavy curtain to a wonderland of velvet, lace, and 19th century glamour. Champagne soaks in ice buckets on candle-lit tables, chandeliers glinting overhead. Patrons puff on cigars and cigarettes, and under red-tinted lights, they watch artists dance with belle-epoque style feather headdresses that are taller than the women who wear them.

Jewels dangle from costumes and ears. Music thumps the floor as they twirl, melodic voices billowing around the playhouse.

No matter how many times I've been here, it's easy to be swept inside the magic. But I disentangle from the glitz and drama. Le Chat Rouge is a small playhouse, and despite the darkness, I have a good vantage.

My eyes flit from the dancers to the back of the room.

Sitting at his usual table, with a cigarette between two fingers, is Charlie Keating Cobalt. "There he is," I say hushed to Jack.

He follows my gaze. "Should we wait. That way we don't cause a scene." He's thinking from a producer vantage. How would this look to the public?

But I'm not about to wait for the show to end and have a massive group of people in my way *again*. From security's standpoint, I need to be closer, and he needs to know I'm here.

"No," I say. "We're doing this now."

Letting the curtain fall behind us, we make our way to the back of the room. Waiters stroll around the tables, refilling champagne flutes, the atmosphere casual. So I don't feel conspicuous walking to Charlie.

When I'm inches from his table, he leans forward and smashes a cigarette in the ashtray. He stands without hesitation. "I'm ready."

I almost expel a breath of relief. Quickly, I skim his body. *No signs of injury.* I nod once. "You can go ahead." I don't trust him to follow me tonight.

The three of us exit the cabaret. Stars blanket the night sky, a crescent moon and old streetlamps adding light. With Jack walking beside me, I'd call the setting *romantic.*

But the walk home is strained. Quiet.

Silent.

Leftover frustration and ire is bubbling up inside me.

No one says a damn thing, and Charlie casts glances back at me every two minutes like he's worried *I'm* not following him. So by the time we reach the middle of a bridge, I'm not shocked when he stops dead in his tracks and spins to me.

His golden, sandy-brown hair whips around with the warm July wind, a striped button-down half untucked from his pants.

Confusion laces his yellow-green eyes. "I'm fine," he says through his teeth. "Nothing happened. You don't need to give me the silent treatment like I'm five-years-old."

"If I were giving you the silent treatment, I would be the five-year-old," I refute. "I was waiting to talk to you in private."

He lets out a brittle sound. "No one has been on this fucking road for five blocks."

Sure enough, the bridge is asleep. I only hear the sound of a violin off in the distance. Maybe on the other side of the river.

I give Charlie a look and then nod to Jack.

Jack raises his hands. "And I'm fine with staying out of this. I can go on ahead and leave you here to talk—"

"No," Charlie snaps. "You're filming my life; who the fuck cares if you're here or not? I don't." His eyes bore into me. "Vrai?" *True?*

"Fine." My voice grows coarser. "You haven't disappeared on me like that in *months*. And all day, I've been going over it and over it in my head, and I need you to tell me the truth. Tell me if this whole fucking 'show'"—I use finger quotes—"'isn't some elaborate plan to distract me and make it easier for you to go motherfuck-knows-where. Get yourself in troub—"

"Did it look like I was in trouble?" His eyes flame, and he points towards where we left with the cigarette still pinched between his fingers.

"That was one minute out of three-hundred," I tell him coldly. "I don't know what happened..." My voice trails off when he starts unbuttoning his shirt.

"Charlie, stop," I say, my tone tempered. Hand outstretched.

"You want to know what happened in those two-hundred-fifty-nine minutes. I'm going to show you." He tosses his shirt off to the side, pale chest in view. His fingers nimbly unbutton his pants.

"Charlie, what the hell," Jack curses and swings his head around the bridge. No one is here to look or take photos.

"Oscar's worried I let someone lay a hand on me," he explains.

I intake a tight breath through my nose.

The air stills.

Deadens again.

Jack looks to me for answers that I can't give him. All I know is that Charlie could have phrased that a million different ways, but he went with the truth.

No one really *knows* Charlie but Charlie, and probably his twin brother and father. But I have one of the best windows into his life. He's enigmatic and alluring to the world, but what they don't realize is that he's just as destructive as his brothers.

He's simply better at fooling people.

Charlie drops his pants, only in a pair of black boxer-briefs. He extends his arms like he's about to be measured for a suit.

I scan his body out of habit. Not a bruise. Not a scratch. He turns around. His back and legs are just as blemish free.

When he rotates to me, he says, "Satisfied?" He's not mad or angry or anything at all.

"No because I didn't ask you to do that."

"You didn't have to ask," Charlie replies casually and then steps back into his pants. "And you're wrong, Oscar." He fishes the button through and his eyes meet mine. "I'm not doing this show to ditch you. If I wanted to, I could find a better way to do that."

Round of applause goes to this little Houdini.

I let out an unamused laugh. I'm grimacing and I wash away a scowl with the roll of my eyes.

Off my anger, Charlie says, "I'm doing it for you, you know. The show, the one about my life."

Jack shifts his weight, lips parted in confusion.

My brows knot, head cocked. "You did the show for me?" I sound skeptical because I fucking am.

He looks heavenward. "Well...one of the reasons I did it was for you. The more selfless reason, you could say." He picks his shirt up from the bridge.

I shake my head slowly, my whole world on a tilt-a-whirl. "What are you talking about?"

"I know you hate the Oslie rumors as much as me," Charlie says. "I know you barely have time to date because you're following me around the world—"

"It's my job, Charlie. I made that choice."

He glares up at the stars. "No one deserves to have their life attached to mine."

"Charlie—"

"Come back later. When I'm older," he says, his voice cracking. "It'll be easier on my detail then." I know where he'll be when he's older. We both do. He's made a few comments through the years about taking over Cobalt Inc., his father's billion-dollar company.

"I like it now," I retort. "I'm not *coming back*. I'm staying."

He inhales a giant breath like he's trying to suffocate on oxygen before his head dips back down to me. "Then I made the right decision with this show. Aunt Lily always says she can predict love, but she has nothing on me." With another drag of his cigarette, his eyes ping between Jack and me.

I go rigid.

Jack and me.

Pieces try to connect in my head.

Love.

This show?

Me and Jack.

Love.

No.

No.

No damn way.

"You're trying to fucking set me up?" I ask angrily, and I refrain from adding *with a straight guy.*

Charlie shrugs. "Whatever happens, happens. Maybe you two could just be friends. All I know is you're lonely, and Jack looks lonely."

Jack laughs, a bright smile cresting his features.

He's smiling?

I do a double-take, surprised by Highland again, that he's taking this in good humor.

"I take offense to that," Jack says lightly.

Charlie frowns and waves a hand. "Really because your smile is telling a different story."

"I'm just taking this all in…" he explains. "So this show isn't a real thing?" The light diminishes in his smile, reminding me how important being the creator of a show is to Jack.

"It's very real," Charlie says, buttoning his shirt. "I need you to record me. Like I said, I have two reasons for doing this. Ending the Oslie rumors and starting a new one between you two is just an added benefit."

An added benefit. So playing matchmaker and trying to hook me up with Jack Highland isn't the most important reason. That should ease my nerves, but with Charlie, it's just better to be on edge and ready to move.

"You can subtract that added benefit," I say strongly. "There won't be a *single* rumor about me and Jack." *Because we're nothing.*

Uninteresting.

Uncompelling.

Not together.

No kissing.

No fucking.

No holding hands or making love or waking up tangled in bed and smiling about who's cooking breakfast.

I wait for Jack to add in, *I'm straight, Charlie*, with one of his bright, genuine smiles. But when he stays quiet, shock slowly ices my veins.

I'm frozen.

Wondering why Jack isn't piling onto my declaration.

He hangs his head slightly, and as he begins to look at me, my anticipation catapults. His eyes are almost on mine.

Almost.

And then a duck splashes in the river, diverting our attention behind our shoulders. As our eyes are about to come back to each other, Charlie begins speaking.

Guess what? I suddenly hate ducks.

"Still, I need this show to happen," Charlie says, not telling us the main reason why, the one that has nothing to do with me. "We're still set with filming then?"

"I'm fine with it, if Oscar is," Jack says, glancing to me.

Now I have to be around Jack knowing Charlie is trying to set me up with him. As if this couldn't get any messier.

But I think about what this show means to Highland again. What it could do for his aspirations, his career, his life.

I'm not that big of an asshole.

"I'm alright with it," I say.

Charlie exhales a short breath, then tilts his head to me. "If I crossed a line today…"

"You cross them every day, Charlie," I say with no anger. What I've learned in my thirty-two years, there are some fights not worth stewing over. Tomorrow is another day.

His lip rises with a nod of agreement, and he sticks his cigarette in his mouth. "L'enfer est vide et tous les diables sont ici." *Hell is empty and all the devils are here.* I recognize the Shakespeare quote. *The Tempest.*

His gaze does soften. "I am fine, Oscar."

"Yeah, I know."

I've heard it a million-and-one times. But nothing really changes. As long as I'm protecting Charlie, there's going to be a large part of me that has to protect him from himself. He's not the only self-destructive client, but he's the one who runs the most laps around the world.

12

Jack Highland

TWO WEEKS HAVE PASSED since Paris, and I'm still reeling from the whirlwind of events that happened over the course of two days. From the meeting in my Philly apartment to the New York concert venue to racing around Paris. It should be a blur by now, but it's too vivid.

Every frame, every shot that I took with my eyes of Oscar Oliveira, I remember. Like that experience alongside him will be a gold standard for all the others in my life. And I'm not even sure it's *what* I did but just the company I held.

After we got back to Charlie's apartment from Le Chat Rouge, we grabbed our things and left for the airport. We clocked in less than 24-hours in France—and that's normal for Charlie…and Oscar.

How in the fuck is this TV show going to work, dude? I've been asking myself that for two weeks and tossing and turning every night trying to figure out logistics.

And other things…

Let's face it, this pilot has confused my confusion. I now know *one* reason Charlie wants to film a docuseries about his life. He's trying to matchmake me and Oscar together. As friends. As something more? I missed the chance to really *talk* to Oscar in Paris. We fell asleep on the plane. But I woke up early.

Could've woken him up too.

These missed opportunities are so foreign to me. I don't *miss* an opportunity. I've never been scared of walking through an open door.

I mean, fuck, I've rarely been afraid to *talk* to anyone about anything. Not even when I was a nineteen-year-old production assistant, facing a prick of a director who kept spit-screaming at me and the other PAs about moving apple boxes.

And Oscar is lonely? I never saw him as a lonely guy. He has the kind of die-hard, life-long friendships I thought only existed in cult, coming-of-age movies. And he's constantly hit on, and *in* my presence too.

Irrational anger begins to simmer again, just revisiting the memory of Everly coming on hard to Oscar in the Louvre. I've gone on double-dates with Akara; I introduced him to some girls I knew from college. Did I care when Akara and Amber kissed at the end of the night?

No.

No question.

So why did Everly make me want to uppercut a punching bag? And I don't even fucking *box*.

I was so quick to make an enemy out of her, and if presented with the same situation three-hundred times, I know I'd have three-hundred more.

Me, Jack Highland, the guy with *no* enemies.

I guess now I have at least one.

She has his number. Maybe they'll meet up if she finds herself in Philly or New York. Maybe they've already met up. It's not like I've seen Oscar in a while.

Two weeks.

Two weeks of no contact, and what's wrong with me? I've never been so bent-out-of-shape over a short stint of no communication before now.

At least Oscar spent the last week in the Smoky Mountains. He was on-duty with security while the Hales, Meadows, and Cobalts retreated to the lake house. They usually go there on-and-off during the summer, and I heard they were linking up with Farrow & Maximoff at the end of their honeymoon.

The lake house's location is strictly secret from the public. So Everly couldn't have been there.

That should make me feel good enough to coast through the rest of the day, but I just keep picturing this girl at Oscar's studio apartment. Getting down on her knees. Giving him head.

My stomach twists in a pretzel.

I don't know why the image of some chick deepthroating Oscar makes me want to hurl, but I'm at that stage, I guess. The stage where I don't want to imagine my friend—or co-worker—getting off from someone…else.

But me.

I trip over a crack in the Philly sidewalk, and my tray of coffees spills onto the cement and warm liquid soaks my white T-shirt.

"Fuck." I bend down and scoop up the paper cups and plastic lids. Some passersby grimace, their faces saying, *ah, dude, that fucking sucks* and *glad that's not me.*

Spilt coffee isn't a big deal.

Don't sweat the small stuff has been my motto since forever. I've got bigger shit going on.

After tossing the cups and coffee tray in a nearby trashcan, I push into a mid-rise office building. Third-floor is home to the *We Are Calloway* productions.

I come into a small meeting room with a stained shirt and frazzled head. "Sorry, I'm late," I apologize to Ali and Ambrose Miller, both behind laptops and waiting for me at the boardroom-style table, set with leather chairs. I offer a smile, taking off my messenger bag. "I did have coffee for you two, but here we are."

Ali eyes the stain and snorts. "Did you trip? Tell me you caught it on film."

Ambrose laughs while typing. "Now that'd be some camera gymnastics, sis." He's speaking to me, but Ali is also his sister. In their mid-thirties, only a year apart, the Miller siblings are almost inseparable, and they look like Hollywood starlets compared to me right now.

Ambrose has a faux-hawk with a side fade, and I'm jealous of his *clean* yellow button-down. Gold Tiffany bracelets complement his dark-brown skin, and his sister is equally put-together. Black hair gelled back in a curly pony, her trendy jumpsuit is spotless and ready for a red-carpet event.

She's a kickass filmmaker. He's an ace sound mixer. Singularly, they're vets in the industry. Together, they're the best power duo I know, and I'm the lucky producer who landed them on my team for *We Are Calloway.*

"Thank God I didn't have my camera out," I say with a hiking smile, and I walk to the small closet at the end of the boardroom. I keep clothes here when I pull 18-hour workdays. "Broken equipment isn't on the budget."

"Neither is a round of extra coffees," Ali teases.

"Who said *you're* getting an extra latte?" Ambrose banters with his sister. "You're over there scrolling through Pinterest for a honeymoon you've rescheduled *ten* times. At this point, you should wait for tickets to pop up to fly to the moon."

Ali and I laugh.

"Shut it down, I'm so close to scheduling this trip to Barbados," she tells him.

I take a charcoal-gray button-down shirt off a hanger and smile back at Ali. "What happened to Maui?"

"Troy changed his mind."

"And by *Troy*, she means *Ali* changed her mind," Ambrose cuts in. "You should've done what I did and went right after the reception. Flight to Malta. No one but me and Cody and paradise."

Talk about honeymoons is a reminder that I'm very single and surrounded by newlyweds. I attended Ali's wedding, Ambrose's wedding, Maximoff Hale's wedding all within the same year, and it's only July.

It didn't bother me before. *I'll date when I can*, I'd usually say, but now, a hot feeling flares up…a feeling like the one I felt with Everly in the Louvre.

I try to take a breath.

My personal life shouldn't be affecting my work. So I tell Ambrose, "I'd drink to that declaration. But my drink is currently soaked in my shirt." I shrug on the fresh button-down and return to the table, buttoning it closed quickly.

They stare at me a little more keenly.

I take a seat, about to start the pitch but they share a furtive look.

"What's wrong?"

"Your fly is down, sis," Ambrose tells me.

Fuck.

I zip up my pants. Heat swathing my neck. I let out a weak laugh, not even able to recover as smoothly as I know I can.

"You alright, Jack?" Ali asks.

"Yeah." I run a hand through my hair. "Just lack of sleep." *Oscar.*

Really, it's Oscar.

For the briefest second, I almost consider telling them. Asking for advice. Ambrose is a gay man and in a great relationship with his husband. Maybe he'd understand. But it feels pretty unprofessional. We typically talk about our families and weekend plans. Office small talk. No one in production is spilling heartaches and lamenting their struggles to me, and I hesitate to be the first.

Really, at the end of it all, I think I don't mention questioning my sexuality because there's only one person I really want to talk to about it.

And he's not here.

"What's the pitch?" Ali asks, back to business.

"A spin-off of *We Are Calloway*, starring Charlie."

Ambrose's eyes widen. "You're serious?"

"We are talking about Charlie Cobalt?" Ali questions, just as skeptical as her brother.

"Yeah," I smile, actually proud that this project is so close to happening. "It was his idea." I explain the concept and before they ask, I add, "I already went to the network and pitched the spin-off." I'm referring to the premium network that's home to the docuseries.

Ali shuts her laptop, engaged. "And?"

"And they were very interested and want first look. But they requested a pilot before picking up a series order."

Can't fault their reasoning. Charlie is a giant question mark. Ordering this spin-off without footage could be like calling Domino's expecting a pizza, only to be served a cactus. No network wants egg on their face or to waste money.

But there is no crystal ball predicting a hit from a flop. We all have to take chances, and I've never struck out before.

"What about a backdoor pilot?" Ali asks.

I shake my head. "They said *no*. The network doesn't want to mess with the integrity of *We Are Calloway* by hyper-focusing just on Charlie." With a backdoor pilot, essentially one of the episodes of *We Are Calloway* becomes Charlie's pilot, and the network can see how the audience reacts and whether they want to move forward.

I leave out how the network asked, *"What about Maximoff and Farrow?"* They were willing to commit to a series order of a "Marrow" spin-off without any content filmed or even a backdoor pilot.

A straight shot to TV.

I was selfishly happy I could tell the network that Maximoff and Farrow weren't interested in a spin-off, because if they had been...I don't know what I would've done.

Ditching Charlie (who came to me first) just to favor Maximoff for my own gain—that's not the kind of *person* I ever set out to be. But the industry is cutthroat and ruthless, and to most people, that deal would be a no-brainer.

"So no backdoor pilot," Ali considers, "which means whoever works on the spin-off has to work on their own time with no guarantee of pick-up."

I nod. "It's essentially a side project." I go into crew details. "Now, we could film the pilot with two people, but if Charlie's docuseries is picked up for a series order, I'll need a team. Naturally, you're the top two on my list."

Ali rolls forward in her chair. "How big of a team are you thinking?"

We Are Calloway is split into 3 production units. Each one follows a set of famous ones, categorized by age. Which is why I'm attached to the "older kids" who are actually all in their early twenties now.

Each team has 6 people: Producer. Camera Operator. Production Manager. Sound Mixer. Gaffer. Writer/Story Supervisor.

And even then, depending on the shoot, we'll add in more camera operators, grips, and boom operators.

But on filming days, each team tries to keep the number of crew to a minimum. The style of documentary filmmaking we do is cinéma verité. Meaning we're a part of the footage, the narrative. The viewer understands that the famous ones are being filmed in their everyday lives by filmmakers, and the viewer hears our voices but doesn't see our faces.

I prefer operating the camera, if I can.

So how big of a team?

"As small as possible," I answer Ali. "Charlie's bodyguard doesn't want a big crew, and I think we can strike gold with just the three of us, but—"

"I knew there was a *but*," Ambrose says.

"I can't sugarcoat it," I admit. "I shadowed Charlie so I could get a sense of how difficult it'd be filming him longer than five-minutes, and I lost Charlie for hours."

I don't mention how he ditched his bodyguard to give us some quality "alone" time together.

"You lost the kid?" Ali's brows spring up. "During filming?"

"I wasn't filming yet."

"But you would've been," she notes. "And that's *hours* of lost footage and wasted time."

"On the flip-side, I was able to ask him thought-provoking questions, and he answered honestly." I want to explain what he said at the New York concert venue, but it involves Luna's fanfic, which Luna told me in confidence.

So I mention Charlie's apartment in Paris, which no one has ever seen before.

"Was he there when you were shadowing him?" Ali wonders since I did lose sight of him for a while.

"Not at first," I admit.

Ambrose cocks a brow. "This is your pitch?"

"It went better in my head." I smile but it fades, and I tap my pen to the table. "I'm not trying to pull one over on you two. It's going to be a tough shoot. But I need you both on this. You're the best."

Ali contemplates fast. "Have you asked anyone else?"

I shake my head.

"I take it you're settled with just a production manager and a sound mixer? So no gaffer or writer?"

She's a PM (a production manager) on *We Are Calloway* and takes care of logistics like location, budget, and scheduling, but whenever we need an extra camera operator, she takes over with ease.

And I need Ambrose. A whole show can make or break on sound.

My leg jostles underneath the table a little bit. "I figure I can handle the lighting and story myself."

Ali takes a long breath, and her tone changes considerably. "Jack, you know how much Ambrose and I love you."

Fuck.

Ambrose nods. "You're one of the best producers we've ever worked with, especially considering how young you started."

"But," Ali says, "we're already booked solid with side projects. We have two music videos we're doing just this weekend, and Charlie is a risky bet."

"I'm not putting all my chips on him this year," Ambrose agrees. "You know how much a week in Malta costs?"

Ali gives me an encouraging look. "I'm not even sure you need a PM, Jack. It's just a pilot."

"You do need a sound mixer," Ambrose says, and adds to his sister, "Looks like I'm the important one."

She gives him a pointed look. "You wish."

Ambrose reaches for his iced water. "And I thought you were going to date more this year." I did tell him that at his wedding reception, but only after he asked about my lack of a plus-one.

"I'm fine being single," I say, but that hot feeling returns. The only thing that cools it is this project. This goal. *I want it.* So badly.

"You could be playing the field, instead of ignoring the field," Ali notes, and Ambrose nods vigorously.

"This could be *the* one though. The white whale."

We all talk about the white whale. That one project that puts you over the edge. That has your name on it and catapults your career. Being the exec producer of *We Are Calloway* has its merits and accolades, but it's not the one.

Ali shakes her head. "You do know how *Moby-Dick* ends, right?"

Sure. The white whale ends up killing the guy obsessing over it, but I'm not obsessing. I just don't want the whale to swim away before I even have a chance to see if it's the one.

"Hey, maybe I won't die if I have you two on my team?" I flash a smile. One that's opened some doors and driven me further in life.

Ali laughs. "Nice try. I can put you in contact with another sound mixer."

"But he won't be as good as me," Ambrose chimes in.

"No one is," I say with a brighter smile. "But can I trust him?"

Ali hesitates. "It won't be the level of trust like on a WAC production. I'd…make him sign an NDA. And maybe also talk to a lawyer. We're talking about filming Charlie. You can't be too careful."

"Speaking of WAC," Ambrose says, "filming starts for the next season in August, and Google calendar keeps incessantly reminding me that August 1st is in *five* days."

Five days left of pre-production is nothing at all, and with that blanket of urgency, we spend the rest of the time in the weeds of budget and schedule.

No matter the side projects, *We Are Calloway* is the number one job. The production and crew have dedicated years and heart and sweat into this docuseries. And we have the awards to show for it.

If I prioritized a Charlie Cobalt spin-off over *We Are Calloway*, the other exec producers—who are decades older and more seasoned than me—would be irate.

Ali, Ambrose, and I finishing discussing next season and the famous ones before saying our goodbyes. On the table, I bury my head in my arms. I've got to figure this out.

My phone vibrates next to me. Lighting up. I click into the text.

We should talk. Can you meet me at the penthouse tomorrow morning? — Oscar

Blood drains from my body, and my hand falls slowly down the side of my face.

We should talk.

Three notorious words that no one likes hearing or reading. My high school girlfriend said that before saying, "We're going to different colleges, Jack. Let's just do our own thing. We should see what else is out there."

I agreed. Time to move on. Find the college sweetheart. Settle down after the career is built.

But I never found anyone I loved more than my ambition.

But Oscar and I aren't a thing, so he can't break-up with me.

He can bail on the show.

Lump lodged in my throat, I scrape a hand across the back of my neck. But what if he does want to bring up him and me? Our flirting?

I drop my hand and focus on the meeting spot.

The penthouse.

About a month ago, Maximoff, Farrow, Jane, Thatcher, Sullivan, and Luna all moved in together in a glittering Philadelphia high-rise. I've been to their penthouse a handful of times.

Over the years, after filming them for so long, I consider myself friends with Maximoff and Jane, and more recently Sulli. It's not a typical friendship, but they're American royalty. Not much about them is typical.

I stop just staring at the text and my fingers fly over the keypad. I message back: Yeah, no problem. What are we talking about?

Seconds later, like Oscar is poaching my confidence, he replies.

The show. — Oscar

My stomach flops, almost in disappointment. I realize I kinda wish he replied with *us*. My phone pings with another text.

And Jack. Bring my sweatshirt, bandana, belt, button-down, and slacks with you. Thanks. — Oscar

Shit.

I rub my lips. I didn't forget that I had his sweatshirt—something he lent me in Scotland when we were snowed-in. I didn't forget about his bandana that I took when the wind picked up in the Scottish Highlands. I *definitely* haven't forgotten about the belt he let me borrow in Anacapri before Maximoff and Farrow walked down the aisle.

Or more recently, the button-down and slacks from Paris.

I never picked a date to return them. It kind of feels like once those items are gone, Oscar will be gone from my life too. I realize with Charlie's show, we do have more than a few articles of clothing keeping our worlds tethered together, but it's different. The show is professional. Work.

The clothes were personal. Friendship. I almost laugh. Yeah, my daydreams definitely don't put Oscar Oliveira in *friendship* territory.

I'm not straight.

I've known that for the past two weeks. Since the flight to Paris.

And I'm starting to realize my future map can have multiple destinations that I can drive down. Husband. Wife. Spouse. It feels better to take the question marks off those possible futures. Less like staring down the street into dense fog. More like staring at forks in a path. But fuck does it make me nervous.

My stomach cramps the longer I read the text. Every second I wait to reply feels like a depletion of my confidence. I fight that feeling by typing quickly. Yeah, okay. I'll bring them tomorrow. Let me know a time.

I hit send.

13

Oscar Oliveira

I BLOCK OUT LAUGHTER, splashing, and loud chatter on the rooftop terrace of the Philly penthouse. Like the adult that I am, I just went ahead and texted Jack. Told him to meet me tomorrow. My legs are submerged in the private pool, and with my phone cupped in my hand, I stare and stare and stare at his reply.

Yeah, okay. I'll bring them tomorrow. Let me know a time.
– Highland

This is it then. *The end.* I'm still waiting for that weight to lift off my chest. For the big ah-ha moment where I flex my biceps and realize I'm strong. Look at me, setting *boundaries.* Healthy ones. I should be motherfucking happy that I'm a day away from not being jerked around anymore.

But I feel a longing to see Jack again and sadness that it won't be the same after tomorrow.

I let out a long, cantankerous groan, "Estou morrendo de saudade." *I'm dying of saudade.*

Alright, I know I'm being dramatic.

A beer bottle taps my shoulder.

I look up and meet a pair of pierced brows that rise in asshole-ish fashion at me. Wouldn't want it any other way, especially as Farrow tells me, "You didn't just say what I heard you say." Handing me the beer, he takes a seat beside me on the edge and dips his inked legs in the pool where mine have been.

Like me, he's bare-chested and just in swim trunks. Unlike me, his body is covered in pirate and skull tattoos. I've known Farrow since before the neck tats.

"I said it," I say into a hearty swig, and more clearly, I repeat in Portuguese, "Estou morrendo de saudade."

Farrow rolls his eyes halfway around Center City.

"I think your eye-roll passed Fishtown." I push my curls back, feeling my rolled bandana around my forehead. "Better be careful, Redford, the hipsters there are gonna think you're too cool for them."

He cracks a smile that levels-out in concern. After a swig of his own beer, he tells me, "I haven't heard you say that since Darrien."

My college boyfriend. By far the Mount Vesuvius of break-ups that I've ever experienced. I thought he was *the one* at first, but it erupted after an argument over microwavable pizza bites.

I haven't eaten a pizza bite since.

Deep down, it wasn't about the food. After our fight, he dumped me in the fucking Yale library while I was cramming for mid-terms. I failed three of my exams that semester, and I didn't consider the dumping a rejection because I thought about dumping him too.

But the more alone I was afterward, the more I missed him. The more Farrow would take me to bars so I'd stop embarrassing my ass by texting him.

And I'd groan out, *Estou morrendo de saudade.*

There is no direct translation of "saudade" into English. To me, it's always been a nostalgic longing for a love that's missed and gone. When I left for college and missed my brother and sister, sometimes I'd call them and groan out, *Quero que você mate minha saudade.*

I want you to kill my saudade.

I want you to kill this longing feeling inside of me.

"I feel like I'm breaking up with the guy," I admit to Farrow, tipping the beer to my lips. "And all we've done is flirt like kindergarteners."

"Man, what kindergarteners do you know that understand blow-job euphemisms?" he asks in a rising wiseass smile. "You're more like middle schoolers."

I grin. "Yeah, you're right. Your husband is more like the kinder-gartener."

He goes to shove me in the pool, but I careen back and laugh.

Farrow raises a hand in surrender. "You're not going in the water, *only* because of that." He points at the phone, referring to my fracturing heart. "He text you back yet?"

"Yeah." I show him the text. "What time can I stop by tomorrow?" I chose the penthouse as the meeting place.

"Pick anytime, Oliveira. The door is always open." He tilts his head back and forth, reconsidering. "More like, partially *ajar* for you."

"Aw, fuck you," I say in a grin and text Jack.

Morning. 8 a.m.

I press send, hoping it didn't sound too curt. But I can't exactly attach a bunch of heart emojis. He's giving me enough mixed signals to power the sun, and I don't want to add to that.

I set my phone aside on the gray stone.

"I think it goes up like this. Oh, wait, fuck, no the other way," Sulli says in the water, setting up a pool volleyball net with Luna and Jane.

Banks and Akara jump in the water to help them. Akara's hair has grown a little longer this summer, the black strands wisp over his ears and brush his neck.

All of SFO is on the rooftop hanging out together. The pent-house is a mega-upgrade from the 900-square-foot Rittenhouse-Fitler townhouse that burned down. We're not all cramped together, for one. For another, it's a fucking *penthouse*. 33rd floor. Philly skyline views.

And three floors below, Akara, Banks, Donnelly, and Quinn moved in together. Fucking expensive, but Kitsuwon Securities pays for housing, and I'm sure our pay-cut helps afford my Hell's Kitchen studio and the 30th floor apartment.

Whenever I'm off-duty, I like coming here.

Just to be with the people I'm missing.

Thatcher Moretti is grilling burgers and sausages, the smell making my stomach growl, and my gaze drifts over to my baby brother.

Quinn has been doing sit-ups and planks. Thank the Lord he hasn't wanted to rip my head off the past couple of weeks. Just what I need, a war with my brother while all this other shit is happening.

"Horses are walked," Donnelly calls, coming through the sliding doors and unclipping leashes on the two Newfoundland *puppies.*

"Thanks!" Luna shouts from the pool. Orion is her hyper dog, and he's chasing his tail in a circle. I reach for my two paperbacks that I'm in the middle of reading and notice Farrow looking bummed at the sliding glass door.

Donnelly isn't who he wanted to see.

I laugh into a grin.

"Shut the fuck up," he says into his swig of beer. "Weren't you just sending cry-face emojis to Jack?"

I'm still grinning. "Says the cry-face emoji next to me. Don't worry, Redford, the Husband will be back. He didn't drown in the toilet. He knows how to swim out of shit."

Farrow shakes his head but he's laughing. "You're one of the wittiest fuckers I know." I have a quip for that, but his features turn more serious in a beat, and he tells me, "I'm almost *mad* at him. You deserve so much better than the mind games he's making you play."

"I don't think it's intentional," I defend. "It's *Jack.* When has he ever been cruel to anyone?"

Farrow nods a couple times.

I nod back, understanding that he's looking out for me exactly how I'd look out for him. Farrow and I don't have to dive into the weeds in order to get deep. With few words, we reach that place, and we both drink our beers and bathe in the hot summer sun.

I'm glad to have good friends that'll be with me when I crash and burn.

Besides my job in security, it's about the only thing I have going for me right now.

I decide between my paperbacks I've read countless times: *The Grapes of Wrath* by John Steinbeck and Laura Esquivel's *Like Water For Chocolate.* Choosing the former, I find the dog-eared spot, and I don't get far before Farrow and I talk about our clients.

How Maximoff and Charlie seemed more like actual fist-bumping *friends* at the lake house last week. They sat on the dock talking for about an hour. All of us on SFO theorized about what:

"Religion," Banks guessed.

"Sports," Thatcher said.

Akara nodded. "Sports."

"Dingle-berries," Donnelly said.

Everyone laughed.

"Plato, probably," Farrow threw out.

"Ditto, add in Confucius," I said.

"Who's Confucius?" Quinn asked.

My baby brother. *He should've gone to college.* I bit my tongue from saying that one because *that* definitely would've ignited an Oliveira Civil War.

At the rooftop pool, I say to Farrow, "Remember the tour bus days when they were in each other's face?" *Feels like eons ago.* It's been over a year.

"If you mean Charlie getting in Maximoff's face, then yeah, I remember that."

It's not complete revisionist history.

I don't always defend Charlie—he provokes on purpose, especially Farrow's husband which puts me and my friend in hard spots. But back then, I know Maximoff's short-fuse didn't help. Being Charlie's bodyguard lets me see his perspective better than most ever could.

"Speaking of the Husband," I say as Maximoff enters with a volleyball and his sixth-month-old propped on his waist. Ripley has a happy-go-lucky smile in his papa's arms, sun hat shading his fair Irish skin. We all celebrated Ripley's adoption at the lake house last week, and I've never seen the Hales, Meadows, and Cobalt parents cry so much at once.

Joy is a feeling I live for, and my joyful ass cried too.

Farrow smiles wider. "Miss me, wolf scout?"

"Who?" Maximoff feigns confusion, tossing the volleyball to Sulli, then stepping into the pool with the baby. His tattoo on his bicep is in full view. *Farrow's name*. He got Farrow's name tattooed on his arm. Almost couldn't believe it when I saw it. But then again, yeah I can. He's really in love with my best friend.

"Hey, Hale," I cut in before they launch into five-minute flirty insults. "Did Charlie tell you the reason he wants a docuseries filmed about his life?" Now that they're chit-chatting around bodies of water without one pushing the other in, maybe my client could've dropped a hint to his cousin.

"Other than what you said—how Charlie's setting you and Jack up to kill the Oslie rumor—no," Maximoff tells me while Ripley slaps the water ecstatically.

When I told Maximoff about the "set up", I made sure to leave out the part about Charlie calling me *lonely*.

"But honest-to-God," Maximoff continues, "I think it's more than that. I know my cousin, and this colossal undertaking—being filmed day-to-day for who knows how long—doesn't sound like something he'd do just to squash a rumor."

"Oui," Jane Cobalt says, swimming closer since she overheard us talking about her brother. Cat-eye sunglasses cover her blue eyes, and she adjusts the straps of her pastel purple tankini. "Charlie has other motives, most surely."

"As Charlie's bodyguard, I agree with that assessment," I say with the sip of my beer.

Farrow makes an uncertain face. "He could just be 5D chess-ing this show into his version of *The Bachelor*."

"It is his favorite show," Jane muses.

Charlie is a bunch of contradictions. Whatever moves he is making, they'll be what he said: selfish and selfless. Oxymorons to the tenth degree.

My phone buzzes, and my pulse jolts with too much fucking excitement. I grab my phone.

"Da-da," Ripley giggles, trying to swim to Farrow who plays peek-a-boo, using his inked hand to shield his face. Maximoff has their son loosely in his hold, but the baby can already float too well.

I read the text.

K. See you tomorrow at 8 am. — Highland

Curt.

To the point. No compliments or ego boosts. Definitely *not* Jack. But I'm not dumb enough to think he had his friend or little brother message me on his behalf. He's just responding in the same cold tone.

I stifle a dismal groan.

Estou morrendo de saudade.

"He's *reupholstering* the limo, Moffy," Jane says, more hushed but audible. "He just replaced the interior last year. I'm telling you my dad knows that Thatcher and I had sex in the backseat."

Cobalt drama is like a Cool Ranch Dorito. It makes me happy inside, and I'll gladly take anything right now. Especially Thatcher, my lead, fucking his fiancée in his future father-in-law's limo. Look, I'd pay good money to see Connor Cobalt's reaction.

"Your dad can't know that, Janie," Maximoff refutes. "He wasn't there, and none of us would've said a damn thing."

"Hey guys," Sulli calls over, breaking up some good harmless drama. "You all wanna play?"

I sit out.

Not feeling the "team sports" spirit today.

And I crack open my book while Quinn, Luna, and Maximoff face off Akara, Sulli, and Banks. I place a bet with Donnelly and put a twenty on Sulli's team.

Music pumps, an "SFO" playlist. We all added songs, and right now, Cher's "Believe" blasts which is causing Farrow to grimace.

Cher was my addition.

I grin.

And ten minutes through, I look up and slowly turn a page.

"I got it," Sulli calls out, competitive because the volleyball is soaring towards six-foot-seven *Banks*. He spikes the ball as she slams into his chest. "Oh, fuck—sorry, sorry."

"It's alright." He combs back his wet hair. Her eyes fall down Moretti's body, and the volleyball sails back on their side. Somehow poor, *poor* Sullivan Meadows ends up elbowing Akara in the abs. He buckles, and she apologies profusely.

"I'm okay, Sul."

I watch the dumpster fire for another *five* minutes. Sulli keeps running into Banks and Akara's wet bare chests, bodies and limbs colliding left and right, and the more they do, the more flustered she's becoming. Her breath looks shortened, and I'd bet a crisp hundred it's not from physical activity.

"You see that?" I ask Farrow beside me; his son is on his lap, playing with his silver rings. But even though Farrow has been watching the volleyball match, his eyes are more glued to his husband.

"Who?"

I explain and he shakes his head, "Not my business."

"I don't know how you do it, bro." It's not my business either, but it's in my face and I see it. So give me the popcorn.

We watch as Sulli climbs out of the pool, dripping water, after her team loses the game 4 to 21. She darts to the platter of grilled food, avoiding Akara and Banks still in the pool.

From a lounge chair, Donnelly makes a cha-ching motion to me. He's been eating a burger.

Not upset I lost a bet, I'm about to return to *The Grapes of Wrath* when Akara reaches for his phone and asks, "Hey, everyone, is it okay if I invite Jack over for lunch?"

I solidify.

Kitsuwon. He cannot do this to me right now. His friendship with Jack is going to fucking kill me. I imagine Jack strutting in and smiling that hundred-watt smile as he says, *"Beautiful people"* to everyone—and I can't.

Not today.

Not now. Not when I'm setting boundaries tomorrow.

"We love Jack; of course you can invite him," Jane says, sitting across Thatcher's lap on a chair.

My head dizzies, and I skate a hand down my mouth.

I feel Farrow and Donnelly eyeing the living fuck out of me.

Come on, Oliveira. I go to speak, but breath is tight in my chest.

"Nah," Donnelly says coolly. "There's not enough food."

"There's plenty here," my brother pipes in with knotted brows.

Farrow opens his mouth, about to slingshot another excuse, but I locate my vocal cords. Loudly, I declare to everyone, "I'd rather not see Highland right now."

The rooftop deadens, except for Ripley babbling in his dad's arms and the music speakers blaring "Chega" by DUDA BEAT, Mateus Carrilho, and Jaloo. Another of my song additions.

"Did something happen?" Akara questions, actually concerned.

Absolutely love Kitsuwon as my boss. I'd move mountains for Akara. He cares and would put his ass over hot coals for my ass, so I'd do it for him. Not all men I've worked under in security were like that.

Did something happen?

I bake under embarrassment and the sun. "Yeah." I pick myself off the patio. "I made a mistake and asked to kiss a straight guy."

The Moretti brothers, plus *my* little brother, and Akara stare dumbfounded and shocked.

Way too many people know now about the rejection.

But there's no turning back.

"Look, you can invite Jack," I tell everyone. "I don't mind, but just give me a warning beforehand. Because I'm leaving if you do."

Akara is quick to say, "We don't have to invite him, Oscar."

I nod once.

So deep in my feelings, that I tell them I'm going to use the bathroom. But I take my two books and just head inside to cool off.

14

Jack Highland

"I JUST DON'T GET why you live in a closet," Jesse complains over the phone, his choice of words icing me over, even if he's just referring to the size of my apartment. "My surfboard can barely fit next to yours."

I ride the elevator up thirty-three floors to the penthouse. My camera hangs at my hip, the strap across my chest, and I remind myself to *breathe*. In, out.

Ride the swell.

"I don't know why you brought your board, Jess," I tell my little brother. "You're my PA, when do you think you'll have time to drive an hour and a half to New Jersey and surf?"

"After doing PA stuff." He pauses. "I'll have some breaks *di ba?*" *Di ba* means *right?*

I'll have some breaks, right?

I smile and stay quiet, letting him sweat it out.

"There are labor laws, Kuya," Jesse says, sounding more worried.

"You'll get breaks," I smile more, pressing the phone firmer to my ear. "But you didn't come out here for a vacation. I need your help, remember. And you need this on your resume."

Since Ali and Ambrose said *no* to my pitch yesterday, I decided rather than hire a stranger, I'd hire someone I trust with secrets.

My brother.

Jesse flew in on a red-eye last night, and now he's finishing summer school online.

Over the phone, he mutters under his breath, and the elevator doors glide open. I land in the empty private foyer facing the penthouse's front door.

"Ano?" I ask *what?* to Jesse.

"I get why Mama's worried about you now. She doesn't want you to turn out like them, working super long hours. That's actually why she let me come out here, you know. Maybe *I'll* be a good influence on you, she said."

I smile. "Mama did not say that."

"She implied it."

She's more understanding of me working hard than Jesse slacking, which is probably why she let him come out to Philly. For the opportunity.

Can't pass it up.

I pull the phone down to check the time: 7:54 a.m.—I'm supposed to meet Oscar at 8. "I have to go," I tell Jesse. Even though I'm early, I feel late. "Make yourself at home. Pantry is stocked—oh and my neighbors were hijacking my WiFi and slowing the internet, so I had to change the password since the last time you were here. The new one is *LeChatRouge0502.*"

"How do you spell it?"

I spell out *le chat rouge* and describe the capitalization.

"Why 0502? Don't you usually go for 1118 in passwords?" 11/18 is my birthday. November 18th.

May 2nd is Oscar's birthday.

And I didn't think anything of the password when I created it, other than having Paris and Oscar on the brain. Didn't seem like a big deal.

But hearing Jesse ask, I feel tilted sideways. Switching my phone to my left ear like I'm trying to balance, I tell him, "It's the birthday of Charlie's bodyguard. You'll meet him during filming."

"Sweet." He sounds distracted like he's typing in the password. "You know I'm amped to be here. I get to flex my camera skills, hang with my big brother, travel wherever Charlie Cobalt flies off to. It's gonna be a gnarly summer."

I smile, one that vanishes fast.

This summer has been a cyclone of feelings and missed opportunities for me. It's already been gnarly, but not completely in the positive way Jesse used the word.

Still in the empty foyer with the elevator behind me, I thank Jesse again for flying out so fast, and we say our goodbyes.

"Talk later, Kuya."

We hang up, and I rap a fist on the penthouse door.

Two seconds and it swings open to a six-foot brunette. Sulli towers, her biceps cut and abs visible in a bikini, towel bunched in her hand. It doesn't feel that long ago that we sat down together at Superheroes & Scones and had her first production meeting. It was really *our* first introduction to each other too.

A Secret about Sullivan Meadows: at 13, a swim coach told her that she needed to shave around her bikini line better. It was one of the only things she feared telling her protective dad, who she tells everything to.

"Oh hey, Jack." She motions behind her shoulder. "Oscar's in the library."

I tense. *She knows I'm here for him?*

Off my confusion, Sulli frowns. "You have a meeting with him, right? Fuck, did I get that wrong?"

"No, no." I shake the thoughts from my head. *I'm an idiot.* "Yeah, that's right. That's why I'm here." I recover with a wide smile. "So I heard about your speed climb. First place. Congrats."

"Thanks." She twists her hair in a bun with one hand. "It was a fun event. But I think that's probably the last speed-climb for a while, oh *cumfuck*—"

A fluffy dog and calico cat scamper towards us. I slip through the door and quickly shut it behind me as the pets skid to a halt.

Sulli bends down, rubbing behind the dog's ears, while the calico cat prances off. "Orion, you know fucking better," Sulli says, and then tells me, "Luna says her dog is trying to commune with his star people and that's why he tries to leave."

I laugh. "Yeah, what's Carpenter's excuse?"

"He's a little shit-stirrer." Sulli smiles.

As she stands up, I ask, "Why no more speed-climbs?"

"It's getting fucking boring, honestly. I've already won what I set out to win. There's not much left, it feels like."

My smile weakens as I mull over her words.

I have no clue what it truly *feels* like to reach the pinnacle of my goals. I'm close, but I'm still climbing. Talking to Sulli over the last couple of years, I realize now how empty it must feel once you're there.

How lost.

She keeps tacking on new goals to fill an unfillable void.

It scares the shit out of me. Because I lived my life in that competitive lane, and ever since Sulli joined the docuseries, it's been like staring into a mirror that reflects the future. *This is what you could be.* And how strange that a twenty-one-year-old Olympian's life could be *my* future that I fear.

In the end, I'm invested in all the famous one's happiness. Because I care about them. But for me, Sulli's happiness is different.

Maybe if she turns out okay, it's a sign of good things to come for me. That people like us aren't destined to always be yearning and searching and wanting. That we can succeed and that can be enough.

Just thinking those words heavies a weird weight on my chest. Like I know there's a lie there somewhere.

"So if you're done speed-climbing, what's next?" I ask her.

"I'm contemplating a few things...hey, if you're free sometime this week, you should come by for a swim."

I smile brightly. "Definitely. I would never turn down the chance to swim against an Olympian."

"I—" Sulli starts to reply when Orion barks up at her. "Alright, I'll find your mom. Sit, *sit.*" He plants his ass on the ground, tail swishing back and forth. She nods towards the stairs. "You remember where the library is?"

The meeting. I realize I'm hard-core stalling, and my chest knots. "Yeah." I already know this is going to end badly.

Because I didn't bring Oscar's clothes with me.

Not sure why I purposefully left them at my apartment. I'm still trying to work through that in my head.

And I have about twenty seconds to figure it out.

Fantastic, dude.

Here we go.

Heading to the library, two more of Jane & Thatcher's cats dart at my ankles. They figure-eight between my legs, and I try not to trip. As soon as I reach the door—like they know this is a big deal for me—they scamper away quickly.

I enter.

Mahogany floor-to-ceiling bookshelves line the walls, reminiscent of stately, old collegiate libraries like Oxford. Plush chairs are pushed into a long wooden reading table. Green stained-glass lamps sit on the surface, and so does Oscar Oliveira.

Yale tee loose with gym shorts, his hair is damp like he spent 7 a.m. doing chin-ups and arm curls. *Would've joined him.* Not that he's invited me often to work out, but I just thought maybe…

What did you think, dude?

That you were friends?

No.

That's not it, and I boil up in multiple ways, especially as I graze his beautiful features, his masculinity that's been fueling raw, untamed desire inside me.

Oscar looks up from his cell and his eyes sweep me from head-to-toe quickly. His brows furrow. "You forget something, Long Beach?"

His clothes.

I lock gazes, not shying away. "You said you wanted to talk," I remind him, skirting over his question.

He nods towards the door. "Close that."

I nudge it closed with my palm.

Oscar sets the cell beside him, giving me his full attention. "We need to talk about Paris," he says plainly.

I want to ask him *which part?* On the plane—when he saw my hard-on after I woke up from a sex dream about him? The time where he was hit on in front of me at the museum? Or when Charlie stripped down to his underwear in public?

Instead of asking, I just nod and let out a simple, "Sure."

His brows knit together. "You're not at all concerned that Charlie wants to set us up?"

That.

I lean back, resting my shoulder blades against the door, and I thread my arms loosely. I hoped we'd talk about *us*, but now that it's here, I feel more unbalanced. Nerves flame my body. The only way to combat the feeling is to act cool. Calm. *Chill* like I'm on the beach ready to hit the water.

My chin moves from left to right. "Not really."

He steeples his fingers at the bridge of his nose in frustration. "Of course, you wouldn't," he says gruffly. "*This* doesn't really affect you, does it?"

I stiffen. "What is that supposed to mean?" I feel very affected by the prospect of a romantic set-up with Oscar. I've barely slept in the past *two* weeks! I keep thinking about him.

I can't *stop* thinking about him.

He waves a hand at me. "Nothing changes for you, bro," he says angrily. "You're just happily riding this fucked-up train where I'm being set-up with the guy who rejected me. I mean—what in the ever-loving *hell?*"

My chest rises and falls heavily. Pressure mounting. "You think I'm happy right now?"

"You're not exactly upset," he counters.

"I'm not upset," I admit. "Okay. I'm not. But I'm…" My tongue grows thick in my mouth.

"Willing to do whatever for this show," Oscars says, thinking he's finished my thought.

"No...yes..." I feel lost in my own head. I hold up a hand. "Can we rewind for one second?"

Oscar hops off the table. "Look, you're a good guy, Highland. I'm willing to go ahead and put myself in an uncomfortable situation for your goals, but I just need you to know I'm not going to be playing into your flirting—or whatever you want to fucking call it—anymore." His stride is strong as he approaches the door, the one I'm leaning against. "This is strictly professional between us." He stops inches from me. "And I want my goddamn clothes back."

My heart is beating out of my fucking ribcage. A scorch swallows me whole like he just set the library on fire. His jaw. It tightens. Clenches down. I crave to feel the sharp angle against my palm.

I crave so much with him that I never thought I would or *could*.

"Are you going to move?" he growls.

I don't move, except for my fingers that weave through my hair. And my hand stays rooted on my head.

"*Jack.*" His eyes redden, almost glass with emotion and frustration that I'm causing. He tries to reach around me to the doorknob.

I sidestep and block him, and Oscar stops and shakes his head, looking as torn up as I feel. "*Jack.* Did you hear what I said? I can't do *this* anymor—"

"Stop!" My two hands are on my head.

"I can't stop!" His voice is anguished. "I need out!"

"I like you!" I yell from my gut, from my heart. "I like you, Oscar!"

He careens back like I shoved him.

I'm combusting into a million little pieces, but I push forward from the door. "You're *right*, I'm not upset by the set-up. Because I *like you*." I speak from the core of my being that I never reached until recently. Until I was twenty-seven and fell for him. Maybe I've been falling for even longer. I just couldn't piece it all together.

He shakes his head slowly.

I take another step forward. "I like you so fucking much that the idea of losing what we have makes me sick. I don't want to shut the door on possibly the *greatest* opportunity of my life, and it's right here—it's you."

I never considered being in love, falling in love, *finding* love a sky-high opportunity that I should chase. But I guess I just never found someone worth chasing.

I extend my arms and let them drop hard at my sides. I'm breathing like I'm running marathons around the library.

And Oscar is hardly breathing at all. "You said you're straight."

"I did say that," I inhale, exhale. "But I don't really know….I don't know what I am other than really, *really* attracted to you." My eyes well up with emotion that stings. "I can't fight or change what I feel." I add, "I think about you all the time—I think about what it'd be like to kiss you. I've *imagined* kissing you, and more—way further."

My body blazes, but I stand my ground. So he knows I'm serious and not just stringing him along.

He keeps walking backwards until his ass hits the reading table. Leaning against the edge, he clutches the sides with a tight grip. His eyes plant on the floor.

I shift my weight. *God, what I'd give to be in his head right now.* "Oscar, I'm sorry," I tell him, breath caught short. "I'm sorry about Anacapri—"

"Stop," he says roughly.

It almost pummels me.

And then he says, "You don't have anything to apologize for." His gaze lifts to mine.

I swallow down a rock, trying to muster a smile but it's weak. "I've been less than fair to you, dude." I run my hand back and forth across my head, then down my jaw. "It's my fault for not explaining this sooner. So many times, I could've told you I was confused, and I didn't."

He rubs his mouth, looking me over like he's seeing me clearer. "No, you didn't owe me that, Highland. You have a right to sort through things on your own and on your own time."

I nod slowly, more to myself. "I'm actually still trying to sort through some shit." I focus on his brown eyes, and with a small warm smile, I throw out a life raft, "You want to help me?"

"Help you...?"

I'm drowning here. "I just—I don't have anyone to talk to about this. I don't know if I'm gay or bi or pansexual or something else or nothing at all, and then on top of the labels, I've never been physically *intimate* with a guy before."

Oscar processes. "You don't have any friends that could help?"

I run my tongue over my teeth as I shake my head. "No. No one I'd want to confide in other than you." I find myself beginning to smile at him.

His eyes trace my lips, his clutch loosening on the table. He starts to grin, and he shakes his head, a groan caught between his teeth. "Highland."

I think he needs a stronger pitch, so I keep going, "My friends aren't like yours. I don't have one that can shit on my lawn and we laugh about it a whole ten-years later. Not even my fraternity brothers—"

"You were in a frat," he realizes with wide eyes.

"Yeah. All four years at Penn." I study his reaction. Shit. My chest caves. "You hate frats, I take it."

"I've just never been into a frat bro before..." He nods to me. "Sorry I cut you off."

Lungs on fire, I speak up. "I was just saying that none of my friendships were deep. The ones now are I-scratch-your-back, you-scratch-mine. People call me up because they need something from me down the road: a connection to a producer, a director. All I am is a useful contact, and I'm just as guilty of forming surface-friendships." I take a breath. "And I think Akara is one of the few genuine friendships I do have, but even then, there's topics we won't touch because he's security, I'm production."

Sulli.

She's off-limits, and I understand he's protective of her.

"I'm security," Oscar reminds me.

I'm fumbling left and right around him. "You're *the only* one I want to talk to about this, Oscar. I don't even know how'd I go about telling Akara. Do I say the truth? That there's this extraordinarily hot guy who I've pictured sucking me off until my eyes roll back—who I'd drop to my knees for, and I'd love to find out what it's like to take him in my mouth today, tomorrow, weeks from now."

Oscar shifts at my words. His hand drops, splaying over his lap like he's hiding a semi. But he's so confident and casual about the arousal that it literally stirs my own dick into action.

Successful pitch.

"Eyes up here." Oscar points to his face, and I follow the guidance with a smile. Damp pieces of his hair fall to his lashes, and he shoves them back. "You haven't been attracted to any other guy besides me?"

I shake my head, contemplating. "I think I was so set on being with a woman that I didn't even consider I could be attracted to a man. And then you came along. So are you the first guy I've been attracted to and acknowledged it? Yeah."

He lets out a noise.

My pulse jackhammers. "Is that bad?"

"No, of course not. It's just…" He pushes aside a worn hardback on the table. "Jack, you're like a literal wet dream. Do you know how many motherfuckers wish the straight guy they're crushing on could say what you're saying to me?"

I skim him, up and down, smiling. "So it's good?"

"It's complicated," he rephrases. "You and I are complicated. You're still figuring things out, and that's fair. But I don't want you to get hurt. And I don't want to get hurt."

"I won't hurt you," I say, adamant. Even thinking I could starts churning my stomach. "I genuinely like you, and I just want to see where this goes."

Oscar stands off the table. "I'll help you." My smile brightens, and he explains, "I've been where you are. It's confusing, and I didn't really have anyone to talk to until college. I wish those people were there sooner."

I nod and walk closer. At first, I plan to touch him, but as soon as we're in distance, I bail and pick up the thick, worn hardback next to his phone. *War and Peace.*

Tension stretches at our closeness. I examine the spine of the book, and his voice sounds huskier as he tells me, "You can ask me questions, and if you want, I can ask you questions too."

I slip a smile over to him. "You can ask me anything."

His grin edges. "Don't tempt me, Long Beach. I have a laundry list when it comes to you."

So close, the warmth of his skin radiates off the swelter of mine. I'm *radiating* heat because of him, and the more strides we're making, the faster I want to run towards Oscar. Even if a lot is new to me, he's experienced. *He'll show me*, and Jesus, I want him to. The thought alone sends shockwaves.

"I'd want to go through your laundry list," I tell Oscar. "Consider yourself tempted."

Our grins are matched.

"Alright," he says. "Before we go there, we should agree to something."

I rest part of my ass on the table and hold my camera. "What is it?"

"We shouldn't fuck each other." He drops the gavel. "No sex."

Sex.

I'm over here willing to explore new territories that I've never seen. I'm *wanting* to, and I crack a dying, disappointed smile.

I wanted to fuck Oscar—or for Oscar to fuck me? FYI: I know physically where a dick goes, but would he be on top...or would I? The exploration with him is just as enticing as the actual act, and he's saying, *no.*

"Why?" I ask him, my eyes flashing to another hardback on the table. *Brave New World.* I wonder if he pulled out these books before I arrived.

"Because sex is complicated, and this is already on another level of complicated. We don't need to be fucking." His resoluteness is *sexy,* even when this decision feels a lot like the Grinch coming down and stealing a bunch of toys.

It also feels like he's Velcroing elbow-pads and kneepads in case of a fall. "You know," I say gently, "that I wouldn't just fuck you and chuck you."

His face hardens, and his throat bobs as he says, "I don't know that yet. And I can get sex anywhere, Highland. That's not what I'm looking for. So if you need to date around to figure shit out, then I'll help you out with a Grindr profile or go with you to a gay bar. Maybe if I'm still single in a few years, you can come hit me up then."

That stings.

It shouldn't, because he's being incredibly nice right now. Generally, when I'm into someone, I've never eliminated *sex*. Not since I was a teenager and a virgin.

But why would I play the field when I've already found the guy who's captured my entire interest?

I only want him.

Oscar isn't the hypothesis in an experiment where if I dislike the result after I test it out, I'll trash the whole thing. But I can understand him thinking I might. He doesn't want to be used, and I don't want to use him like he's just a hard dick.

"We don't have to have sex," I agree to the stipulation, and in a pause, I add, "I hope after a while you'll realize you can trust me."

Oscar brushes his hand over his unshaven jaw, his gaze drawing hot tracks down my body. "I might be open to other things."

Other things. "Are you talking hand jobs? Blow jobs?"

He's about to answer when his phone lets out an angry buzz beside me. I stand off the table, and my eyes peel to Oscar as he grabs the cell and clicks into a text.

"Charlie?" I ask.

He nods. "He's leaving for New York, and I need to pick him up before he takes off in an Uber."

"He told you where he's going?" I say, surprised.

"He does that sometimes." Oscar gathers a couple books. *Those were his hardbacks.* "Charlie likes to be inconsistent." His eyes fall to my camera still strapped around my body. "You coming?"

"Yeah." I smile. "It is my job to come."

His nose flares, latching onto the innuendo, and then he laughs while fitting a comms earpiece in his ear. "This is gonna be fun. Just try not to come too hard on me, Long Beach. I've still got a Cobalt to protect."

"What a coincidence, I've got a Cobalt to film." I lift up my camera.

He opens his mouth, but his phone buzzes again. "Fuck," he curses at the text, seriousness overtaking him. "We've got to go."

I animate fast and follow him out of the penthouse and to the elevator. The unanswered question about "other things" hangs in the air.

Bad timing—I have a feeling Oscar and I might be magnetically attached to it.

15

Oscar Oliveira

WE WAIT IN THE FOYER for the elevator, and I could laugh at myself.

First off, *Grindr*. I offered to make Jack a dating profile, and immediately, I thought about how I'd need to upload the absolute ugliest ass photos of Jack Highland so no one would tap on him. But let's be honest, an unattractive pic of this guy doesn't exist.

And he's not straight.

He's been questioning his sexuality.

He's been thinking about kissing me. Blowing me. Me blowing him. He likes *me*.

Holy shit.

I smother a smile. Not going to lie, I feel vindicated. I've been going out of my mind thinking Jack's been coming onto me, and every time I confronted it, the door would slam in my face. It's nice to know that I was right all along.

While we're waiting, I grip my two hardbacks in one hand, and I reclip my radio to the waistband of my gym shorts with the other. I check him out on my left.

Jack keeps running his fingers through his dark, *dark* brown hair. Six-four and ripped, he's breathing like he's winded, like we've already fucked on the floor.

Take it easy with this one, Oliveira.

I grin more.

Jack catches sight of my curving mouth. "What'd I miss?"

"Just thinking about how excited you are." I adjust the volume on comms.

His smile grows, eyes flitting to the ticking numbers outside the elevator as it comes to pick us up for a descent. Still in the foyer. Still lingering with a swarm of quickly amassing fervor and warmth. Jack stares back at me with a hotter look. "How excited are you?"

"I'm a solid 12." I hold his gaze. "You?"

"Rock-hard 12." He coasts into the innuendo but breathes a shallow breath, then shifts, and an aroused knot rises in my throat.

I could give myself fifteen gold medals for just laying down groundwork for *no sex*. I feel my age. Thirty-fucking-two. I realize he's younger than me, and for the first time, I'm in this responsible position that I've never been in before. Maybe this is why I've always dated people older than me.

The elevator finally reaches us. We saunter into the empty space that suffocates with our body heat, and I stand against the wall. He stands right next to me, and we stare ahead at the elevator doors, watching them slowly, slowly glide closed.

Even with thick tension and confession of feelings, I expect nothing to happen.

Jack glances over at me. I lock eyes with the pretty boy, and he leaves his spot, shortening the space between us. Oxygen is imprisoned in my lungs.

Nothing is going to happen.

Jack faces me.

Nothing is happening.

He braces a forearm to the elevator wall beside my jawline. His chest lifts and lowers in coveting breath against my taut body.

Nothing...is...

Our mouths are achingly close, his knee edges near my groin as he leans in, and our eyes peruse each other so fucking quickly, I can hardly keep up with Highland.

He's in pursuit of me with rapt fervor. "Ask me again."

Nothing is happening?

Damn am I wrong.

Heart rate spiked, my gaze consumes him, seeing if this is real.

Jack presses closer, uneasiness flashing in his eyes, like maybe I'll reject him. "Oscar…"

I hesitate to touch him, my muscles on fire. "Don't fuck with me—"

"I'm not," he chokes out. "I'm *not.*" We're not touching, but it feels like we're already clinging to each other for dear fucking life. "*I promise.*"

Our foreheads nearly brush, his lips ghosting over mine, and in a husky breath, I whisper, "Can I kiss—"

His mouth presses to mine, the tension of *this is happening, this is happening, this is happening* stretches tendons in our necks and arms and bodies—and when it sinks in, we snap fully together. We collide into each other with breakneck desire, our lips crushing and teasing open.

I drop my hardbacks.

Barely hearing them clatter at our feet, my freed hand clutches the back of his skull, and he fists my Yale tee and claws at the hard edge of my face. Lip-locked, I feel his curiosity. His hand that strokes the roughness of my jaw. His waist that arches against my pelvis. The outline of his erection brushes against my hard length. Fully-clothed, he can feel me.

I can feel him and the twitch of his dick as he craves more. I'm burning the fuck up, and his tongue slides against mine with effortless skill that welds me to him with molten steel. *Fuck.*

I grind forward into him. He pushes back, still trapping me against the elevator wall. His breath hitches against my mouth, maybe overwhelmed at the newness of being with a man. Like he's been starving for this his whole life and wants to drink his entire fill in one go.

Thirty-three floors.

We have to descend thirty-three floors together before the elevator reaches the ground.

His hand curves around my neck, my traps, feeling my muscles. A groan is trapped in my throat. *Holy fuck.* Making out with Jack is like strapping into a carnival ride and whirling at high speeds. Dizzying, adrenaline-fueled.

Muscles flexed, I thread my fingers through his hair and deepen a teasing, playful kiss, my grin against his mouth, his smile against mine.

I squeeze his ass.

"*Fuck*," he groans roughly when our lips break, his forehead pressing to the wall beside my jaw with a staggered breath. His hand is still on my jaw. Our eyes are open, and I watch his head turn and his attention draw to our bodies. We're two men pushed chest-to-chest, pelvis-to-pelvis, and it's taking everything in me not to palm him. To feel him against my hand.

And then Jack drags his hand back and forth over his length that bears hard against his jeans. "I'm so hard, dude," he breathes. "It's killing me." His gaze lingers on my mouth.

Christ.

Blood cracking another thousand degrees, I glance over his shoulder at the numbers ticking downward. *Floor 3*. He follows my gaze and sees too. We pull apart. Lit up to an indescribable degree.

I grab the hardbacks, still set to broil. He faces the elevator doors, his hands on his head and breath coming hard.

He seems relaxed. Like he's basking in the aftermath of a good fuck, even if all we did was kiss. *He made the first move.* This time, at least. I almost can't believe it. But then again, his blood cells might as well be named Charisma and Confidence, swimming around in his veins.

As I near him, I notice Jack has a single freckle by his temple. The randomness makes it even more beautiful. Makes him beautiful.

Call me a poet.

D-rated, probably, but hell, I'm a poet after kissing this guy.

Books in my grasp, I stand beside Jack. His gorgeous honey-brown eyes pool against mine, and then he smiles, still catching breath.

I grin. "Guess I don't need to ask if you're alright, Highland."

He drops his hands off his head with a soft laugh. "I'm better than alright. That was…" He zones into the elevator number. *Ground floor.*

Our stop.

I want to hear what he has to say, but I'm on-duty, and protecting Charlie has to take priority. "This conversation isn't over," I tell him with a wider grin while we exit the elevator. "Just on ice for a second."

"Good, because I need to cool off before we see Charlie." He adjusts his package and walks with me to the parking deck.

Charlie. That little bastard hooked me up with Highland, and somehow, it worked.

I UNLOCK MY HELL'S KITCHEN STUDIO APARTMENT as the time closes in on 4 a.m. And that's exactly what happens when you have to chase after Charlie's shadow all day.

Say hello to the never-ending job. Home to sleep-deprived, hungry motherfuckers, which is why I remember to bring *snacks*. Or else I'd accidentally drop twenty pounds.

I complain a lot, but I love it. Being a bodyguard.

My life didn't make sense before security, and it doesn't make sense without it.

Today was typical, but not with Jack in tow. What started as a trip to the Morgan Library, ended up being another visit to NYPL, a pitstop at the hospital to donate blood, drinks and dinner at The Purple Room, and a handoff of cash for entrance into a private garden after-hours.

Somewhere between the beginning and end, we also dropped off his bloody button-down to his assistant. Parker's going to package and ship the shirt off to the eBay winner tomorrow.

Stranger than that, I'm not coming home alone. Or with a one-night stand. Or with a bad night's worth of baggage.

But I don't know how to classify what Jack and I are, and I don't need a definition.

As long as he's not messing with me.

Jack is so alluring, he could sell me the heart already in my chest, and I know he said I can trust him—but I'm a bodyguard. Being cautious is second nature.

And right now, I am actually carrying baggage. In the form of a black camera bag. "What the hell do you have in here?" I ask. "A small child?"

It weighs at least forty-five pounds. Nothing I can't carry, but when I'm on-duty, I can't carry shit for him. He has to tote all his equipment himself, and honestly, I'm concerned for Highland. Prep is over; this was the first time he's actually *tried* to film Charlie all day. And not to bruise his ego too much, it went...less than *stellar.*

Jack shuts the apartment door, yawning out, "No small children. Just a boom kit, lighting kit, batteries, clamps, quick releases, a gimbal and slider..." He pats the blue backpack he slips off his shoulder. "This has three lenses and two cameras." I watch him rub the corner of his eye tiredly as he says, "I'm banking on it being easier with a two-man crew."

"With your brother, you mean?" He told me Jesse is in Philly.

Jack nods. "Being a solo shooter is harder when the subject keeps changing locations." He yawns again. "I have to fix that quick release plate. The screw came loose a dozen times, and I kept having to stop shooting and retighten it."

My concern is on him as I place his camera bag on a barstool.

For years, I've been around *We Are Calloway* crew as they did their thing, but I never realized how much went into it. Equipment malfunctions, not having the right accessories, sound issues, lighting issues, all while they're trying to make art.

I study his sinking posture. "Is there any way to leave behind an extra lens or something to keep the weight down?"

He shakes his head, smearing a hand down his face a few times. Exhaustion drags his limbs. He's six-four and hunching. He's the "make-the-best-first-and-last-impression" guy. He doesn't hunch.

Christ. "You won't have a subject to film, if you can't keep up with his pace, Highland. I almost left you in the dust after The Purple Room, and you're not that slow."

His smile tries to fight fatigue. "I appreciate the compliment. Taking a page from my handbook?"

"No," I say with a small grin. "I always compliment guys I like."

Jack shifts, his breath shallow before he lets out a larger yawn.

Fuck. Now I'm yawning.

I flip on the dim lights over a bookcase, and a warm glow casts on the dark wood of the luxury apartment.

We haven't mentioned the kiss in the elevator yet. His first kiss with a guy. Our first kiss together. Hell, as far as Charlie knows, we're still just co-workers. We're both serious about our work, so we fell into keeping it professional.

Work is now done, and I want to take the conversation off ice. But he's clearly spent.

"Thanks for letting me keep my equipment here," Jack says while fumbling dazedly in his pockets. "It'll save me time to pick-up and go."

Because Charlie lives in New York. And I'm in New York.

"Yeah, no problem," I say, but my light tone is hijacked by serious-ness. Good Lord, he looks like he's about to pass out.

Elbow on the edge of my kitchen bar, Jack digs in his back pocket again. Finally, he finds…a set of car keys.

I frown. No fucking way. "You're not driving."

Wrinkles crease his forehead. "It's only a couple hours."

"*Only* a couple hours," I say. "Bro, you look like you're two *minutes* away from collapsing on the floor."

Jack laughs exhaustedly into a wide smile. "Some of my best work is done on the floor."

Instantly, I picture fucking him on the floor.

Fuck me, flirting while fatigued should be a crime. Someone needs to come restrain Highland. And I'll be the first volunteer.

I'm the only one handling this guy tonight.

I walk closer. "How about the couch? You can crash here."

He tries to stand fully upright. "Are you sure?"

"You're not driving to Philly tonight, and a two-hour Uber ride is too expensive. So either you spend the night at my place or I'll drive you home."

He mumbles something about it not being that pricey but he's nodding. "I'll stay." He pockets his keys, a smile in his eyes. "You put all the guys you like on the couch?"

"Honestly? Usually they're in the bed with me."

His smile is gone. "Yeah?" He's nodding a lot, too much, and my muscles constrict. *Didn't mean to hurt him.* But fucking *ugh*, I can't lie, and I don't want to rush into sex with Jack.

The bed seems like a danger zone.

I nod back. "You know I can take the couch and you can take the—"

"The couch is perfect," Jack says, hunching again. He winces as he tries to straighten up, and he explains before I ask, "My back is so tight, dude. I should've stretched this morning before handling equipment."

His choice of words drops my eyes.

Drops *his* eyes.

I recall the feeling of his erection brushing against mine in the elevator. "You handle equipment often?" I joke.

Jack wears a forty-watt, *tired* smile. "Yeah. When can I handle yours?" He knows the double-meaning of all his words as he says them, and it makes me think all the times he's joked with me, like about "top" and "bottom" Jenga pieces at Farrow's bachelor party—he wasn't that innocent.

"When you aren't falling over."

He stretches his arms behind his back.

"You still feeling strain?"

"Mmmh, yeah. Right here." He taps his upper back.

"You want me to crack it?" I ask.

"You know how?"

I nod. "I studied Kinesiology. Sports medicine. It's actually how I met Farrow. We had some classes together at Yale since the sciences overlap."

Jack quickly agrees to let me help him out, and I tell him to rotate. His back to me, he faces the kitchen, and I come behind his lopsided stance. "Stand straight. Cross your arms over your chest," I instruct.

He crosses them.

I never considered cracking someone's back an intimate affair. But as I press my chest up against his shoulder blades, my jaw teasingly near his jaw—I'm distinctly in tune with how my breath warms his skin and how I can hear and *feel* the beat of our hearts. Heavy, loud.

Proud.

His smile is going to ruin me. *Frat bro.* Repeating that isn't making my cock soft like I thought it would, so at this point, I doubt anything about him will.

I wrap my arms around Jack, holding each of his sculpted biceps. Like I'm hugging him from behind. "Breathe in," I tell him.

He inhales.

"And out." I lean back with him in my grip as he exhales. The cracking sound comes, then his sigh of relief.

When I draw away, my arm skates against his bicep, and his gaze descends my muscular build from head…to toe.

My chest rises, blood sweltering. I can feel myself resisting the pull towards Jack. I'm just afraid of where this ends.

It has short-term fling written all over it.

Normally I wouldn't even give a shit. But I just wanted more for myself.

I detach from his attractive sphere and start to chuck off leather sofa cushions.

Jack stops me. "Don't pull out the sofa bed. I can just sleep on it."

I hesitate because he clearly has muscle aches. But he's yawning again, too tired to have a full-on debate.

Fine.

I toss them back on the couch, and Jack takes a slouching seat with another sigh. "This is a good place to be stuck, I guess."

"You guess?" I give him a look. "You fail Geometry in high school, Long Beach? Your place is *half* the size of mine."

"Mmmhmm, true." His eyelids weigh heavy. They close, then open. He's even more exhausted than I realized. Evidence: he's still wearing Allbirds. I don't remember a time Jack has ever kept his shoes on past the doormat.

I kneel in front of the couch. My fingers gingerly unlace the sneakers. When I shift off his left shoe, he glances down at me.

I meet his eyes as I untie the right laces. "You know you don't have to follow Charlie the whole time. You can grab a couple hours of footage and call it a night."

"I want to make sure I have everything," Jack replies softly. "I haven't figured out the narrative structure of the pilot yet...and I figure...more footage will make that easier on me in the long-run."

I know next to nothing about filming a documentary. And Jack only has one person to rely on. His seventeen-year-old brother.

I feel badly I've made it harder on him by requesting a small crew. But then I remember how annoying it is to have five people shoving around me with cameras and booms and I'm less upset by this outcome.

I pull off Jack's right shoe. "You should get some sleep—"

"Wait," he cuts in. "Just..." He sits up more on the couch, legs spread open. "Can we talk?"

About the kiss.

I ask, "Yeah, we can talk if you don't fall asleep on me."

His lip quirks. "I won't. I'm really stoked—" He tries to catch another yawn.

I decide not to point it out. "Not shocked you're *stoked*. You are Mr. McCheerful."

He laughs quietly. "You're Mr. McDreamy then?"

"Oh no, I'm Mr. McSnacky." I grin. "And you've been eating my heart out." My friends would be giving me such shit for that line, but I'm too confident to care.

Jack leans forward, elbows on his knees. Still fighting exhaustion. "Yeah? Let me take a bite." He playfully fists my Yale tee, and I grab his wrist.

Heavy breath expels from us, but I cut it off first. Dropping my hold of him, I take a firmer seat on the *floor* and back up from the couch.

He has to release his grip of my shirt.

The show.

We should talk about Charlie.

Jack battles the umpteenth yawn.

And in the quiet of my apartment, I tell him, "If you're going to be following Charlie all day just like today, you need to start listening to my advice." I rest my forearms on my bent knees, his shoe still in my hand. "When I tell you to take a nap in the car, you should actually take a nap."

Grid-locked in traffic on the way to the library was the best time for Jack to catch up on sleep.

"I was trying to fix my quick release practically all day," he explains. "And I never saw you nap."

"Because I'm used to this." I absentmindedly pass his shoe between my hands. "You need to also eat when you can. Even if you're not hungry. When you are hungry, you might not actually have time to eat."

He nods, looking deeper in me for answers to his bottomless pool of questions. He's a filmmaker. He sees the subtext.

I care about your health, Highland.

I actually really care about you.

Why else would I be flinging pro-tips at him? I don't personally benefit from Jack eating a granola bar.

But I must still be wary to put my heart on the line. Because I add, "I don't need a casualty on my hands. And that's what's going to happen if your scrawny ass keeps forgetting to eat."

"You keep saying that." His lip rises as he leans back. "But I'm not scrawny." He eyes the shoe in my hands, and I set it on the floor. "What were you like in high school?" he shoots out, and off my confusion, he adds, "Did you fail Geometry?"

"No, never failed a class. Never *skipped* class. I tried hard." I laugh at myself. "I was a try-hard."

"How come?" he wonders. "Did your parents pressure you or was it self-motivated?"

I muse playfully, "Highland asking all the interesting questions."

"Comes with the—"

"Job," I finish, "I knew that day one, bro. But it's also a little part of you at this point, isn't it?"

He runs his fingers through his hair, slowly and languidly. "Yeah, I can't turn it off." He smiles more at me.

"It was self-motivated," I answer him. "The studying, the extra insurance I make it in an Ivy League and get an academic scholarship. I didn't think boxing would really pan out for me, and I wanted something more mentally stimulating."

Jack frowns. "But you went pro?"

"And I quit at eighteen. I wasn't very good. Not like my little brother." I stare off at the ground. "Thinking back, I just wish my parents had pushed Quinn and Joana towards school. But my parents—my dad most especially—value *physical* prowess over mental aptitude. It was one of the reasons my brother randomly took up field hockey in high school just to get him off his back. My dad's largely unimpressed by academic achievements, but if you have a nasty uppercut, he'd gift-bag you a dozen mortadella sandwiches, coxinhas, and invite you over for dinner like you're family. And my mom's coxinhas are *heavenly*."

Jack lets out a breath, his smile flickering in and out. "I have so many questions. What's a coxinha?"

His pronunciation of *coxinha* isn't perfect in this cute way, and it makes me grin. "It's fried dough in a teardrop shape with shredded chicken inside. Quinn likes it with jackfruit instead of chicken. He's—"

"Vegetarian," Jack finishes. "I remember." *Right.* "Mortadella? Isn't that Italian sausage?"

"It is, but I grew up eating a lot of mortadella sandwiches in Philly. You take the meat—lots and lots of meat, add provolone, mayo, Dijon, all on sourdough." Damn, my stomach is practically growling—I need to stop painting portraits of food. "They're popular in São Paulo." I think Jack knows it's where my family is from, based on my tattoo.

The motto of São Paulo is inscribed in Latin across my collarbone. *I am not led, I lead.*

"Did your parents eat them in Brazil?" Jack asks.

"No, they immigrated to America when they were both babies. Their families made them mortadella sandwiches growing up too."

Jack looks confused. "I thought your grandparents still lived in Brazil. So...how'd your mom and dad come over here alone as babies?"

"They didn't. My dad's parents are still in Philly, and my mom's uncle was already here. Her aunt was bringing her over to live with them." I watch him nod, but I can tell something else is on his mind. "So my mom's parents are the ones still in Brazil, along with her two brothers and more cousins." I want to ask about his family.

But he lets out, "Back to what you said before about *physical prowess*..."

"Yeah?" I cock my head, wondering where this is going.

"I don't have a nasty uppercut." He tries to smile, but it levels-out again. *Is he nervous?* "To tell you the truth, I don't have *any* kind of uppercut. I've never been in a fight or punched anyone before..." He trails off at the sight of my grin. He smiles back. "You knew."

"I figured you'd hug it out before punching it out." *Not a surprise.*

Jack massages his hand, still seeming uncertain or...again, *nervous*. Maybe, though, he's still just in a war with fatigue. "So your parents don't care that you went to Yale?"

"My mom brags to family and friends, but they bragged harder when I was a pro-boxer." I add, "And they let my brother skip school all the fucking time for fights." I shrug. "My siblings never really *cared* about an education the way that I did. So I went to Yale, and they both ended up in the ring."

Jack leans forward again, arms on his thighs. He always sits like a jock holding a football between his spread knees. Only instead of a football, he's usually gripping a camera.

You're way too into him, Oliveira.

Yeah.

I should go to bed too, but this feels like the most comfortable place to be. Awake, talking to him.

"I don't understand why Quinn followed you," Jack says. "To security, I mean. If he was so good at boxing, why not stay?"

I shake my head. "All he's ever really said is that he wanted something different. He knew security work existed, so he left boxing behind. Our dad would've fucking blown a gasket, but Jo was and *is* really good. She's the new protégé." I push some curls off my forehead. "*My* biggest pet peeve with Quinn is that he didn't even look at colleges. This career takes more than it gives, and there's so many other paths he could've taken."

Jack rubs his tired eyes. "I get what that's like. Jesse wants to follow my path and do camera work—photography, mainly, but I guess it's a bit different from your situation." He explains, "My brother wants to go to college. My alma mater."

University of Pennsylvania, located in Philly. "Were your parents happy about you going to UPenn?"

"I just call it Penn," he says with a smile. "And *no*. Not at all. It was all the way across the country. My mama and dad kept saying, *why not Standford?* Jesse begged me to stay in California, but I liked Penn's swim team." His lips downturn. "I broke his heart that day. But it got better the more I FaceTimed and called."

"Can relate," I nod. "On some level, I guess. My brother *hated* when I went to Connecticut for college." Here we are eighteen/nineteen and our brothers are just little eight/nine-year-olds, and we're tearing away from them. Jack went through that too. "I think he felt like I wouldn't ever come back to Philly. Like I'd never see him again." I shake my head at myself. "I didn't do a good job staying in touch. I barely ever saw my family while I was at Yale, barely ever came home. But I always told myself I'd end up with them anyway, so the four years would go by and we'd be together again." I meet his eyes. "You know I studied sports medicine with the idea that I'd come home and help boxers my dad trains—like my brother and sister. I'd help them after bad blows and intense trainings. Ice baths, stretches, PT."

"I didn't know that," Jack says softly. "How come that changed?"

I scrape a hand over my tensed, unshaven jaw. "Once I graduated, I started realizing that I didn't want a full-time career around boxing. My family trains at Akara's gym, and Akara is the one who introduced me to security work. So I ended up here. And eventually, I did try to be with Quinn more. I tried to train him in boxing while I was a bodyguard. To reconnect. But it went down like a grenade. I don't think he ever got over me leaving." My muscles strain. "Looks like you're *What To Do* and I'm *What Not To Do* when it comes to college and little brothers."

"No," Jack tells me. "I just got dealt a different set of cards, Oscar. Probably the easier set."

I'm not quite sure that's true. But I ingest Highland's sunny outlook anyway. Our conversation has roused him awake more, and I feel badly about fucking with his beauty sleep.

I go to stand. "You should get some rest." Once on my feet, I press a hand to his broad shoulder to ease him back against the leather couch.

He grabs my forearm with one hand, and we both go still, our breaths heavying. Our eyes descending and exploring.

This can't be happening. But damn, how many times am I going to be surprised in a day? *Until it sinks in for good.* That he's into me. That he's not playing me.

He scoots forward on the leather couch. I stay standing like a brick wall, and his other hand—his other hand settles on my waist, fingers edging towards the elastic band of my gym shorts.

"Jack," I breathe.

He stares up at me from beneath long lashes. "I've been thinking about this all day...ever since we kissed. You said we could do other things, right? I don't know if I'll be any good, but can I..." His chest rises and falls like he's mid-marathon again. "Can I suck you off?"

Fuck.

My cock swells in response. *Yes. Fuck yes.* We're already in a perfect position. I'm standing between his spread legs while he's seated on the couch.

It was like our bodies agreed before our brains.

"You've never had a dick in your mouth?" I question, just to be sure. Of goddamn course I remember him saying he's never been physically intimate with a guy before.

"You'd be the first," he smiles. "Like I said, I might not be any good, so if you tell me to stop—"

"I wouldn't," I cut him off. "Sexual affection isn't about being perfect, Long Beach. If you're about to bite off my dick, I'll tell you, *less teeth, open your mouth wider.* Half the fun of fucking is the discovery. What works for you and me together..."

Those last words hit strange.

Like a left hook that thumps too softly on a bag. Too tenderly.

It feels good, but it won't knockout an opponent. It's not right for the situation. Because we're not sleeping together, him and me.

Jack searches my face. "Have you changed your mind about the agreement?"

"No," I say. "No sex. It still stands."

He nods once. "But we can do this?" He begins to draw my shorts downward. Our shallow breaths fill the quiet.

"Yeah," I answer, and I go ahead and drop them to my ankles. Stepping out of my shorts, I thumb the elastic band of my Calvin Klein boxer-briefs.

His gaze glues to the length of my cock, which presses hard against the navy-blue fabric.

I don't know how I feel about being his first. It could mean I'm just gearing him up to be more confident to journey off into the land of dick. But at least I know I'll treat him right. How he should be treated for a first time, and the thought of Jack being in damaging hands— being hurt or emotionally wrecked—is enough to lower my guards. I know I want this now.

With him.

Especially with him.

Jack begins to tug down my boxer-briefs, and I let him pull the fabric down my ass. My hard length is freed from its confines and stands at attention. I watch his chest collapse in raw arousal. The sentiment coats his gaze the longer he stares and stares and *stares.*

Blood pumps down into my groin. I harden more.

Fuck.

16

Jack Highland

I'M WIDE AWAKE, muscles tightening in blood-rushing, mouth-watering, *scorching* desire, and I'm staring at a hard cock. *His cock.*

Oscar is bigger than me, and I'm pretty well-endowed. Did not expect him to outsize me, and I'm not bruised by it. But I'm simultaneously more aroused and more nervous of taking him in my mouth.

My left hand clutches his muscular waist, and I let my palm trail to his back. Down to his ass, and I grip him.

His abs flex.

Jesus fuck, a grunt tangles in my lungs, and we're not even doing much yet. I shift on the couch. Wanting closer, I edge forward. He stands between my knees like a confident fortress, and I'm used to foreplay with more delicate and soft things.

But I like this too.

A lot.

"Remember how we were talking about stopping?" Oscar asks. "You know you can stop at any time too?"

"Yeah, I know," I nod. But my breath is jagged. Ragged. Torn up like I'm being plowed with feelings—physical and emotional peaks that I've never met. I'm starting to wonder if this is what it's like to really be with someone after amassing so much untouched desire and deep interest over so many years.

He's not someone I saw on a college campus *one time* and then met up with for a date.

It wasn't quick and simple.

While I drink in his arousal, I rub my palm over my jeans, feeling the strain that begs for firmer grip and touch, and then I take that hand to do to him what I'd do to myself.

I fist him. I stroke him once and study his expression. Oscar is staring down at me, watching me as intently as I am him.

Nerves swarm with a strong pulse of *need*. I question whether Oscar has been with someone who couldn't take him in their mouth.

Maybe I'll be the first that can't do it—*fuck that thought, dude.* I've never failed at the things I've set out to do, and it might take me longer to reach some goals, but in the end, I always reach them.

And I hang onto his words about guiding me if I struggle. I could've picked a worse man to blow. A complete bastard.

Oscar isn't that.

I trust him, and I tug him a couple more times before I slide him in between my lips. Nerves begin to wash away, replaced with instinctual want and craving.

Heat gathers, my dick begging for the back-and-forth friction that I'm giving Oscar. I know how this feels. To have a mouth run back and forth along my shaft. The pressure. The lit nerve-endings. And doing it to someone else, it's…unlike anything.

My fingers dig into his ass.

A gruff noise splits apart his lips. "*Fuck.*"

We're in an inferno. Sweat building on us both while I sit and he stands. While I give and he receives. I'm trying to take more of him, but it's not easy.

"Breathe through your nose," Oscar instructs.

I didn't realize—but yeah, I'm not breathing. I intake a lungful and keep working him over with my mouth. His muscles contract, and another noise rumbles through him. So unlike the high-pitched cries I'm used to hearing.

Deeper. Throatier.

The sounds almost make me come in my fucking pants. *Hold it together.*

"Jack," Oscar says my name in a husky whisper.

My dick responds, enjoying that.

I pop him from my mouth to breathe better, and remembering what's been done to me—what I've liked in the past—I slide my tongue down his shaft. Oscar's head almost lolls back, tendons taut in his neck, and I realize how much I'm watching his reactions.

How much his grunts and body twitches light me on fire. I like making people feel good, but making *him* feel good turns me on in more extreme ways.

Oscar bows his hips, and he fills my mouth again. I'm about to ease back for friction, but he grips the back of my head and leans more forward. He even presses a knee to the couch. Deepening...I think I'm coming a little.

Fuck.

Fuuuuuck.

His shaft slowly sinks further between my lips. "Hold still," he tells me, and I wonder if he can see how attracted I am to *this*.

Because he pumps his hips. I'm watching as he does the work and guides his length between my lips back and forth. Pleasure wraps me in a vice. My arousal is a live-wire he's toying with, and Oscar disappears inside my mouth. He hits the back of my throat, and I gag a little.

He slows, careful not to hurt me, but thankfully, he continues satiating us. I've never been this hard. He thrusts.

I clutch his waist and his ass, feeling him flex forward.

I'm about to burst, and I just want...*friction*. Ravenously, quickly, I unbutton and unzip myself. His heavy breaths are noises I'll go to bed dreaming of tonight. His movements are faster with a starved pace that I feel. His hand tightens on my head, fingers clenched in my hair, and I dip my hand under my boxer-briefs.

With him in my mouth, I stroke my swollen erection just once, and we both release *hard*.

"*Fuck*," Oscar groans.

He tastes bitter and salty, and I have no trouble swallowing it down.

Oscar eases out of my mouth, and I breathe harder, especially as he notices I came in my palm. I'm about to ask if he has a cum rag, but he already says, "Here." He leaves for the kitchen and returns in seconds with a dishtowel.

I wipe myself up.

We're both on a euphoric come-down. Oscar lowers with a satisfied breath on the couch next to me. He leans in and presses a warm kiss to my cheek.

It instantly makes me smile. I turn my head more to him, and our mouths instinctively meet. I deepen the kiss, and when our lips break, he plants kisses at the base of my jaw and says gruffly, "Christ, Highland." He cups the back of my head in affection before standing up. "Next time, wait a bit and I'll do that." He nods to my unzipped jeans. "I feel like I missed out on something."

I don't mention how I probably would've erupted in my jeans seeing and feeling him come, even if I didn't touch myself.

The thought of Oscar fisting my cock though—that almost makes me hard again. I hang onto his words: *next time*. There'll be a next time...

I smile and zip my jeans. "Looking forward to it."

He grins back and pulls up his boxer-briefs, then his shorts. He takes my cum towel and saunters to the nearby laundry room with the confidence of a king. "You'll get some sleep now?" he asks over his shoulder.

I watch him throw the towel in a hamper. "Can I ask you a question first?"

He comes back and takes a seat on the coffee table. "Go ahead."

It dawns on me in this moment that I'm used to discussing other people's sex lives. *Sex* is such an intrinsic topic of *We Are Calloway*. From Lily Calloway's sex addiction to Rose Calloway's sex tapes and all the way to how those have affected the people closest to them. Their sister Daisy. And their children.

Jane struggled with guys assuming she liked BDSM like her parents, so she often talked about that to me. I listened and recorded the interviews that later would air.

Moffy always said *no*, whenever I asked if he wanted to talk about sex. *What's it like to be the son of a sex addict?* Really, I was happy that he didn't feel like he had to voice this truth to the world. Maybe this part of his life wasn't bothering him, then.

But there's only one person I want to talk to right now. I feel more like a viewer, wishing and hoping to relate to some aspect of another person's life. And I know that person is Oscar sitting across from me.

"When did you know?" I ask. "I mean, when did you know you were into guys?"

Seriousness draws across his face.

Shit. I scoot forward. "You don't have to answer if you don't feel comfortable—"

"That's not it." He shakes his head. "I'm fine answering anything you want. It's just I'm thinking maybe we should have talked about this…before *this*…" He motions from me to him.

"We didn't have penetrative sex," I remind him. "Our agreement is still intact."

He laughs, one that fades in a softer grin. "I like how you included the word *penetrative*."

I smile, leaning back. "Thought it'd help."

"I'm pretty sure I just penetrated your mouth, Highland."

Fuck. I take a shallow breath. "No anal sex then?"

"Yeah, but to be entirely clear here, oral sex is still sex. But when I said no sex, I meant anal." He grimaces at himself. "Sorry, I should've been clearer upfront—"

"No, it's okay," I assure. "I assumed that anyway." I summon a brighter smile.

He still looks upset, like he shouldn't have relied on assumption. "I'm not used to being with someone where this is *all* new to them.

So it's good if you ask questions because I might forget that you don't have the answers." He snaps his fingers. "Penetration."

Why the hell am I so nervous? I feel like I'm sweating. Like he's a heartbeat away from calling this off between us, and I'm scared it'll screech to a halt too fast. "What about it?"

"We don't have to have it—anal sex. It's not the end-all, be-all. So if that's something you never want to try out, that's cool."

I haven't considered that before. Maybe I'm adventurous because the idea of never exploring anal sex bums me out.

But I don't tell Oscar that. What if he's saying he'd rather not ever go there with me? I rest my elbow on my knee, my eyes roaming him. "Do you not like it?"

"I love it, but I'd never pressure someone for anal or make it essential." He scratches his eyebrow. "Alright, honestly, I've never been in a relationship *without* it, but Farrow has."

"With Moffy?"

Again, Maximoff doesn't talk about his *sex life*, but I'm realizing that Oscar knows because of Farrow, and now I feel like a *prying* fan. Quickly, I add, "Don't answer that."

I really don't need to know.

Oscar nods once, then says, "When did I realize I was into guys?" He repeats my earlier question.

"Yeah."

"I was fourteen. Every summer, I went to this boxing camp in Upstate New York. There was this guy a year older who I couldn't get over." Oscar stares off with a grin and a laugh in remembrance. "We hooked up in Cabin 3 on the last day of camp." His eyes focus on mine as he clarifies, "We blew each other, nothing further. And ever since then, it was apparent for me that I was attracted to guys. It took me roughly another year to figure out that I was still attracted to girls too."

A knot is in my chest. "Do you think it's strange that I'm twenty-seven and just going through that? What you went through at fourteen?"

"No," he says with raw conviction. "Everyone has their own timeline, Highland. Yours just happens to be now and not back then."

I ingest his words like liquid courage.

"And if anyone gives you hell for it in your lifetime or invalidates your feelings because they knew their sexuality for longer—don't listen to them. They can't tell you who you are. The fact that they're trying to says more about them than about you."

I breathe that in. "Were you nervous about coming out to your family?"

He scrunches up his face, almost to say, *sort of.* "I was more nervous about coming out to friends. I didn't really think my parents would have a problem since they were adamant about joining the LGBTQ-friendly church. So I came out to them when I was sixteen and asked this boy out from high school—my first boyfriend."

I nod, but my stomach cramps in a way I didn't expect. I try to hold onto his assurance about *no timelines*, but I feel behind. Maybe the overachiever in me is recoiling. "Were they happy?" I wonder.

"Oh yeah, my mom loved Ryan Kruger. He ended up being a D1 football player, then got drafted to the NFL."

Ryan Kruger. I bite down hard to keep jealousy at bay.

"My dad loved him too," Oscar continues, staring off in thought. "But like I said, *physical prowess* means more to my family. It doesn't matter what gender you are. They only have an issue if you're too delicate and can't lift a fifty-pound weight. My dad wants all his children with athletes who can take a hit."

I try to expel a breath. I am an athlete. But I'm not sure if I can take a hit.

What are you worried about, dude? It's not like Oscar wants me to meet his parents. But yeah, I'd want to be liked by them. Accepted. Welcomed.

When he first brought up his parents valuing physical over mental skill, I was fucking *nervous.* I just kept thinking, *they won't like me.* I attended an Ivy League. I'm a documentary filmmaker. A producer. I can't punch worth shit. All my trophies are for art, not athletics.

Though, again, I was a college athlete.

It seems like my only *in* into the Oliveira family. Then again, swimming is a non-contact sport.

Oscar is studying me too much, so I ask, "How'd your friends take it? You said you were most nervous about them knowing you're bisexual."

He rubs his knuckles. "Yeah, all my close friends in high school were straight. I was afraid they'd treat me differently. Some did. I wasn't invited to hang out with *the guys* anymore; if I brought up dating, they were suddenly not interested. Other friends stayed the exact same." His mouth curves upward. "Those are the best. They still make the same crass jokes, still ask about who I'm with—even if it's a dude."

I smile off his smile.

He holds my gaze. "You know it wasn't until I went to college that I had friends who weren't straight. I joined LGBTQ clubs, learned more about gay culture, and I also learned something important."

"What's that?"

"Some people will tell you you're not 'gay enough' or 'bi enough' or 'this enough'—that you don't do X, Y, and Z—and even when you think you're around the most inclusive people, someone will try to set requirements and a checklist that you feel like you need to complete to be accepted."

I recall what he said earlier, *They can't tell you who you are. The fact that they're trying to says more about them than about you.*

"That happened to you?" I ask him.

"I definitely felt pressure to *belong* my Freshman year of college. I overcompensated at first. My dorm room had rainbow flags, rainbow coasters, rainbow pillows—don't get me wrong, I love rainbow, but not when it looks like a Care Bear took a shit in my dorm." We laugh together, and he adds, "I still love drag shows. A lot of slang like *realness* and *throwing shade* originates from the drag community in the 80s. Especially from trans women of color."

I nod, actually knowing this because of a documentary about New York's ballroom scenes. "I've seen *Paris Is Burning*. It's one of my favorite documentaries."

Oscar grins. "You have good taste, Long Beach." He collects his thoughts. "What I'm trying to get at—you don't need to have a dozen rainbow flags or attend drag shows. It doesn't make you any less into men. We're all human, and humans have different interests. You do you."

It sets me more at ease knowing it's okay if I don't fit a "mold" of the perfect gay guy or bi guy or whatever-label-I-choose guy. That the label I pick isn't just one type of person. All it defines is my sexuality. Not everything about who I am.

I inhale a bigger breath, and I think about coming out. To my family. And Jesse. And so I ask Oscar, "How'd your brother take you coming out?"

"He was only six," he reminds me, "and Jo was even younger, so they've really always just known me as liking boys and girls."

I nod again, my gaze falling to my hands.

"You nervous about coming out?" he asks me.

I start to shake my head, then shrug. "I don't know. Changing the status quo on them feels like a big deal." I take a pause. "I had always imagined my future with a wife, but my parents painted that picture with vivid colors. Especially my dad. He loved whenever I brought a girlfriend along to family trips."

Oscar nods with understanding.

So I keep going. "My ex-girlfriend always hung out with my mom. She was another woman to talk to when my Lola wasn't around. So it might not be easy for them to just burn my old future into the trash and replace it with a new one." I let out a laugh. "It's not like it's been easy for me. So can I really expect it to be easy for them?"

"Yeah, they may need time," Oscar says. "But hopefully they'll adjust and love whatever new picture you paint. Just do what you do best and stay positive, Highland."

I smile.

He studies my features. "What about your brother?"

"I doubt Jesse will care, but he might ask a lot of questions."

"Runs in the family, huh?"

We both laugh. But mine fades as I realize, "I might just hold off until I'm ready."

"Take your time," Oscar says strongly. "No rush."

I frown. "You're okay with not telling anyone about you and me?"

"Yeah." He takes a beat. "Look, I didn't expect to go shouting to all my friends that I kissed you. Otherwise, that forces you to come out and I'm not doing that to you."

My lip rises, eyes stinging. "Thanks." I wish I could give him a definite time, not this ambiguity of *just when I'm ready, Oscar*. I'm a secret he's about to keep, and as a long-time keeper of peoples' secrets, I know it's not always easy. It can take a toll.

Oscar just nods in reply, especially since I yawn into my bicep. He stands up. "It's almost 6, and I've fucked with your sleep enough." He grabs me a pillow and blanket from the closet. Tossing them to me, he says, "See you in the morning, Highland."

I watch him climb up the stairs to the loft. "See you in the morning," I call out. Even though I'm yawning up a storm, I don't know how I'm going to fall asleep tonight.

He's all I'm thinking about.

17

Jack Highland

"JESSE, CONCENTRATE." I try to catch my brother's wandering eyes while we separate our equipment. *I trust him, I trust him, I trust him*—that's why he's here among the famous ones and not some random friend of a friend camera operator.

He's taking in our current location: Camp Calloway. Which he's only ever seen on the docuseries or social media posts. The woodsy camp in the Poconos is fit for a Charity Fun Run today, hosted by H.M.C. Philanthropies.

Charlie Cobalt is on the board of the charity that Maximoff Hale created, but he's wasted no opportunity to tell me that he's unemployed. He has *no* job. I have way too much footage of that response, even during a spontaneous interview I did at a café yesterday.

Thank God I remembered my portable lights. Setting up a key light and secondary light for interviews makes the quality of the shot infinitely better, and I had to rig it all in a matter of minutes, like my life depended on the speed. Any longer and Charlie could've just stood up out of boredom and bolted.

Anyway, I remember his response at the café when I pressed him further about H.M.C. Philanthropies.

He said, "That's not a job. It's an obligation."

Well, today I'm filming Charlie at an HMC event, and I'm curious to see how he'll handle being at one. If it really is just an obligation to him.

Jesse rifles through his camera bag on the grass. "I'm concentrating, Kuya, but it'd be easier if security kicked out the dildos over there."

I have no clue who he's calling a dildo.

But I glance around the packed campgrounds. Security are posted at various spots like knights in the woods, and I stop myself from searching for Oscar among them.

Dude.

You're the one who needs to concentrate.

One breath out, I focus.

The famous families are congregating in their respective friendship groups, and the runners who bought tickets to attend the Fun Run are stretching at the starting line or still registering at a check-in desk near the mess hall.

Refreshment tents are off to the left and largely unoccupied right now. The cluster of camp cabins are also pretty barren, except for a banner that reads, *Medical.* Good thing no one is hurt, looks like.

Oscar already gave me a map of the Fun Run this morning, and the trail is supposed to lead down a hill, then wrap around the glittering lake. No one has left yet.

So I have to ask, "Who's a dildo?"

Jesse looks up and around. "They must've left somewhere." He explains, "Some guys who look my age were being crude towards the families." He doesn't specify towards who.

"It happens a lot." I squeeze his shoulder. "It's good to empathize, but don't let it distract you."

His shaggy hair shifts with the shake of his head. "This is their charity event. Shouldn't their bodyguards send them packing?"

"We're production," I remind him. "We don't do security's job for them, and they don't do ours." We have to respect that boundary or else we'll both start trying to walk all over each other. "And anyway, if security tried to remove every person that made a transgression against the families, there'd be like five people here, Jess."

He sighs. "That blows."

I lift my camera. "We film the shit that blows. With the small hope that it makes a difference when people see it. *Empathy*, Utoy. Don't lose it. Use it."

Jesse smiles. "Always, Kuya. You're so petmalu." It means *amazing* in Tagalog slang. He nudges my arm lovingly. "Lodi."

I can't believe I know that *lodi* is *idol*. It's also slang, and it's *idol* spelled backwards. Stuff he picked up from our cousins on social media.

I smile brighter and mess his hair. "You're grabbing B-roll today."

"Sweet, I'll use the telephoto lens."

I also hand him an ultra-wide lens. "Use your walkie-talkie if you need me."

"Got it." He's in charge of B-roll, basically extra footage (landscape, wide shots, etc.) that's used in the show.

"Who are you not allowed to film?" I ask him while we both fit on our lenses and adjust our camera settings.

"Winona Meadows." His eyes flash briefly over to the Meadows girls. Sulli and Winona stretch under an oak tree together. "Also, Beckett Cobalt and Vada Abbey."

"Yep." Those are the only three that are more private and haven't signed waivers to be on *We Are Calloway* or in the background of *Born into Fame*, the working title of the docuseries.

We stand up. I hand him the backpack with his extra lens. "Boom kit is also in there if you need it, but you shouldn't have to mess with sound too much." I plan to leave the heavier camera bag at cabins with medical.

Jesse slips on the backpack and clutches his Canon, ready to go.

"Now go get me some B-roll." I make the *hang loose* gesture. "Shaka brah, *brah*." I smile.

He smiles back on his way to the lake. "Talk later, Kuya!"

A minute later, I drop off the camera bag and regroup beside Charlie. I'm gripping two handlebars on either side of a Canon. The gimbal helps steady the camera and avoid shaky shots. Sometimes I'll use a Steadicam, which is harnessed to my chest, but both are hard to operate and ache my muscles after a full day shooting.

I can already tell my forearms are going to kill me.

Beauty is pain, and I'm searching for that beautiful up-close frame. The one where I push closer, that feels personal, like the viewer is almost uncomfortable at the intimacy. Feeling like they're a voyeur to Charlie's life.

I am.

I am one, and it's something that I know has to be translated well or else it's all for nothing.

Right now, I capture footage of Charlie waiting for a woman behind the registration table. She reaches out and hands him a bib number.

I feel Oscar nearby.

He's off to the side. To my left and a little further back. He's surveying the crowds, but as I risk a glance, our eyes catch for the briefest second before we return to our jobs.

My breath hitches.

Focus, dude.

That's how it's been for the past three days.

All work.

We haven't done anything since the night I slept over—not for lack of interest—just lack of time. It's July 31st. *We Are Calloway* production starts tomorrow, and when Oscar is off-duty, he's been in security meetings for the Fun Run. We're both swamped outside of Charlie's show.

And still, Oscar has occupied almost 80% of my mind.

I just keep replaying everything over and over and anticipate it happening again. We've texted a little, but not enough to distract us from our professions. My nighttime dreams of him and me do that enough.

I angle my camera more on Charlie. *Focusing.* "Are you excited for the race?" I ask him.

"Overjoyed," he says dryly.

"Excuse me, excuse me." A business-casual man in a pair of gold-rimmed aviators shoves his way to the front of the line, next to Charlie. Oscar sidesteps to let him through, and a second passes before I place his face and affiliation to the families.

Ernest Mangold.

CEO of H.M.C. Philanthropies.

He's the same board member who exercised a coup and overthrew Maximoff from the position. I step back to capture him.

Ernest's salt-and-pepper hair flies with a gust of wind. He lays his sights on Charlie, but Charlie ignores him by slowly sticking his bib number to his mesh tank top.

Unfortunately, Ernest whips to me. "Shut that off—"

"No," Charlie says flatly. "It stays on. He's filming me."

Ernest says words like *lawyer* and *sue* and *not authorized* before reaching for the camera, and that's when I have no choice but to stop rolling.

"It's off," I ensure, pulling away from him.

He makes me show him that I'm not recording.

Out of the corner of my eye, I notice Oscar shooting daggers at Ernest like he almost seized *my baby* from me.

I begin to smile. I'm not used to a bodyguard being on my side. Usually they'd be cheering Ernest on. *Take the camera down.* Makes their job easier.

Now that Ernest has disabled camera footage, he closes in on Charlie. "You said he wouldn't be here," he whisper-hisses.

"Who?" Charlie asks.

"*You know who.*" After an agonizing beat, Ernest says, "Maximoff."

I glance over at the open field where most are gathered before the race. Maximoff is extending his arm over his chest, leading a group stretch with his uncles and dad.

"He's a Hale," Charlie tells Ernest. "Last time I checked, H.M.C. Philanthropies stood for Hale, Meadows, Cobalt. You're an idiot if you think he wouldn't be here."

Ernest's eyes darken. "Watch yourself, Charlie." His voice lowers. "I own the board. I could remove you tomorrow if I wanted."

"You do already want that," he says flatly. "But you won't. You know why?" Charlie tilts his head, avoiding a ray of sun. "Because I'm the son of Connor Cobalt. And the only reason this company hasn't dissolved is because I'm still a part of it. I will concede—you do own the board, Ernest. I have no control over them. But you don't own me."

He walks off towards the west side of the woods, completely avoiding the entrance to the trail.

Jesus, shit.

I jog after him. Following close as we leave behind everyone at an alarming rate. Oscar keeps the same pace on the other side of my subject. "What was that?" I ask Charlie.

"A prick." He dips his head underneath a branch and enters the dense part of the woods. People are fading behind us. Tall evergreens landscape the area.

"Can't get rid of him," Charlie says, stepping over a boulder. "Just have to withstand him. Story of my life."

Muscles burning, I keep a steady shot. "What do you mean?"

"Hey, let me get out front, Charlie," Oscar tells his client.

"You don't know where I'm going," he refutes.

"Do *you* know where you're going?" Oscar counters.

Charlie grins and glances back at both of us. "Do I?" His brows rise. "Maybe? Maybe not. Isn't that the fun of it?" He continues his pace and answers my earlier question. "Story of my life is being surrounded by people who aggravate the fuck out of me."

"Is your family among that group?" I wonder.

"Sometimes. But they usually aggravate me the least. Especially Beckett." He takes a sharp right into a thicker area. But he's skinnier than Oscar and me, able to slip between trees and branches easier.

Plus, I'm busy looking through a *camera*.

I stumble over a rock, and my heart jettisons, mostly fearing my equipment will be crushed underneath my weight. And I'm not referring to my dick.

Oscar extends an arm and grabs my waist. Keeping me from enduring a massive face-plant. I balance better, two hands on the handlebars of my gimbal, and Charlie's pace quickens.

My fuck-up puts us behind him.

"Shit," I curse, watching him disappear behind a larger oak.

Oscar follows my gaze. "We'll catch back up." He pushes a branch away from my face, and I duck and move with him. "What do you want to ask him so badly anyway?"

Am I that obviously eager to interview him? "I don't understand why he's a part of the board, if he hates Ernest so much."

Oscar's face softens.

"You know?"

He nods. "For a lot of people, Charlie's a mystery. But I've already solved parts of him a while ago." His lip hoists. "And I didn't need to interview the hell out of him to do it."

I can't help but smile. "You rely on your talents; I'll rely on mine."

Oscar grins. "After you." He waves me on. But really, we squeeze closer together as we journey ahead. Not much room to shift between trees. Our arms brush, our hands skim, and I almost feel him catch onto my fingers.

To hold my hand.

But he retracts fast—so fast that my pulse skips. *He doesn't want to force you to come out.* I hope that's it, and it's not Oscar being scared I'll bail on him.

As we battle through the thick brush, my heartbeat rises to my throat. We keep glancing at each other, and the inability to talk or touch with Charlie so close is adding unnecessary strain.

We're working.

That fact slams against us as we find Charlie in a small cloverfield clearing. *He knew where he was going.* I focus my shot on him. He leans against a mossy boulder, book in one hand and a blunt between his other fingers. He doesn't glance up at us as we arrive.

"Getting lost in the woods together—one of my favorite romance tropes," he muses and sticks the blunt in his mouth.

Oscar and I share a tense look.

Fuck.

Charlie hasn't let go of this "set-up" even after confessing his intentions. I guess he wouldn't. The more I'm understanding Charlie, the more I'm realizing he's more of an open book than people would believe, but his pages are written in an ancient language.

"Hilarious," Oscar tells his client, then presses a hand to his earpiece. Listening to comms.

My walkie-talkie beeps in my own surveillance earpiece. "10-2," Jesse calls. "I'm a mile from camp. Can I go in the woods?"

10-2 is code for *I need to take a number 2.*

A shit.

I stifle a smile and detach my walkie, pressing the button and speaking low. "You can't take a 10-2 in the woods. You're a professional."

He grunts like he's running with gear. "10-4, over and out." *10-4* means he's received the message.

Oscar watches me attach my walkie, and surprisingly, he tells me under his breath, "Donnelly made a joke about Wawa catering the event on comms."

We draw closer together. Quietly, I tell him, "My brother needed to take a shit in the woods."

He laughs hard.

Which causes me to laugh, and Charlie eyes us from his perch on the boulder. Like we're being discovered, the noise slowly fades from our mouths.

Back to business.

I hoist my Canon. Camera rolling.

Oscar scans our surroundings.

"I have a question," I tell Charlie.

"And the sky is blue." Charlie flips the page of his book, smiling at something he's reading. I can't make out the title of the paperback. It looks like he—or someone else—scratched off the letters with a knife.

I prod further. "If you hate Ernest, why don't you just quit the board?"

"It's not a job. It's an obligation," Charlie tells me for the umpteenth time.

It hits me now.

"You can quit a job," I realize. "You can't quit an obligation."

Charlie flips another page. "I suppose I could quit an obligation, but it'd have far reaching consequences."

"The company would dissolve?"

Charlie nods. "My parents, my aunts, and uncles would pull their money out. Something Maximoff built from the ground up would be destroyed overnight." His yellow-green eyes flit up to me. "I don't love being the life support, but it's where I'm at."

He sinks into his book and his blunt, and while my subject is stationary, I change lenses and focus on wide shots. Oscar chats with security, and I try not to bother him.

An hour later, we walk the same densely wooded area back to the open field with the starting line and registration. Charlie doesn't try to lose us this time. Maybe giving up on the whole "romance lost in the woods" act.

We breach the thick, tall trees, and I'm surprised no crowds are here. The only runners who've completed the 5k loop are Sullivan, Ryke, and Maximoff.

Sweat barely stains their tees, water bottles half-empty, and they loosely stretch on the grass like they just jogged one-lap around a block.

Oscar, Charlie, and I walk closer to the registration tables.

Something...itches...

I scratch my shoulder. Grimacing, I try to relieve the irritation a few more times, but the itch only grows. "Hey, Oscar," I say. "Is something on my back?"

He walks around and scratches at his own bicep. He zones in on my shoulder that peeks out of a sleeveless tee. "Highland..."

My eyes fall to his arm. Small dark bumps dot his brown skin. *Oscar.* "What'd we walk through in the woods?"

He itches his bicep again. "Let's go to the cabins."

Medical is located in the camp cabins.

Shit.

18

Oscar Oliveira

CHARLIE IS SCRATCHING his neck, so I tell him to seek medical with me and Jack, and on our way to the cabins, I'm resisting the urge to maul the inflamed patches on my bicep.

Poison ivy, that's my best guess.

We frolicked through motherfucking poison ivy.

I could grumble over comms, but A.) Jack is beside me and I don't want to be *that* petulant in front of him. I have to show some class.

And B.) drama strikes.

"Fight at the refreshment tents!" an Epsilon temp shouts over comms, using the main frequency for the event. Every bodyguard is on the same channel. "I need backup!" His voice pitches in my ear. "I need backup!"

I narrow my focus on the white tents as we cross the open field. A bunch of teenagers are crowding the table with water jugs and cups. And two teenage boys are yelling at each other while the stocky temp tries to pull them apart.

They shrug off the bodyguard and keep shouting. Can't piece apart the words from here.

I strain my eyes, making out dark-brown shaggy hair and a camera in his hands. Holy fucking shit, that's Jesse Highland. Alarm triggers in my body, and I don't think. Just react.

"Charlie stay here for a sec," I tell him.

His brows knit together, but he stops mid-walk.

Jack hears the commotion under the shady white tents, and he takes off with me as I sprint towards the fight. "Jesse!" he yells at his brother, camera gripped tight. "JESSE!"

I click my mic and speak as I run. "Oscar to Security, I'm handling the fight—don't send anyone else." Last thing Jack needs is to have security all over his little brother's ass.

A douchebro shoves Jesse in the chest, and Jesse shoves him back. They push each other and yell a few more times, and right when we reach the tent, both boys thrust each other into the table. Water jugs fall and spill, paper cups litter the ground. The crowd cheers on the douchebro, and the teenagers wrestle on the grass. Neither throws a punch, and I grip the douchebro beneath the armpits and wrench him off Jesse.

I growl out, "Come on—"

"Grow a fucking funny bone, bitch!" He's still yelling at Jesse, even as I drag him back.

"Grow a *fucking* brain, ass-clown!" Jesse shouts hotly, trying to charge forward. Jack puts a hand on his chest and restrains him.

"Cool off, breathe," Jack coaches. "Hey—*Jesse.*" He forces him from rushing at the douchebro, and I'm doing the same to the other teenager.

"I need everyone to exit the tent!" I shout at the gawking teenagers. "Now!"

"He started it!" a few yell and point at Jesse.

"Exit the tent," I say with threat and force. "*Now.* I'm not fucking around." Intimidation on point, the teens take the hint and shuffle out, leaving a broken plastic table and litter in their wake.

While Jack talks to his brother under his breath, I interrogate the other teenager.

"What's your name?" I ask the douchebro and release my tight grip on him.

"Tyson."

"Last name too."

He rolls his eyes and then glares at Jesse. "This is all *his* fault!"

Look, I don't know Jack's little bro that well, but Jesse seems like he has a good heart. And Jack calls him a free spirit. Not a devil or a dickhead.

"Lay off him," I growl at the teenager. "What's your last name? I'm not playing around, bro."

Charges won't be pressed for a schoolyard shove-fest. I just need to log this down for security, and you bet your ass that I'm remembering his full name so he never invades Jesse's space again.

"Why aren't you giving him the third-degree?" Tyson gapes. "I'm telling you, *he* started it! This isn't fucking fair!"

Jesse huffs and shakes off his older brother's hold, just to pick up his camera that fell on the grass. He says nothing.

Jack reaches out a consoling hand. "Jesse—"

"I have more B-roll to grab." He hoists his backpack on his shoulder. "Sorry, Kuya." Apologies flash in his eyes to his brother before he exits. Not saying what happened.

Jack is about to run after Jesse, but when he reaches the flaps of the tent, an imposing man blocks him.

Aw, *shit*.

Bad timing has crept upon us again.

The Epsilon lead is here, hands on his radio and hip. A surly soldier, Korean-American, mid-forties and one of the longest-lasting bodyguards—I've known Jon Sinclair since I first joined security *years* ago, and his beef with me has annoyingly endured.

"What in the goddamn *fuck* is going on?" His glare nails onto me, then the douchebro.

"Tyson was just telling me his last name." My deep voice is all severity. "He was in a fight with another teenager. It's done and diffused." I leave out Jesse.

I'm playing favorites.

Is it fair? Yeah, *no*. Life isn't fair, and I have intense feelings for the pretty boy with the camera. And if his little brother is in a pickle, I'm going to help get him out.

Without the details of the fight, I might not be on the right side of morality, but I don't always need to be.

"It was that kid named Jesse," Tyson complains. "Not me."

Sinclair spins onto Jack. "Your brother Jesse?"

Jack tucks his camera under his arm. "It was a misunderstanding—"

"Did I mishear the part where *production* is starting fights at a charity event?" Sinclair cuts him off.

The Epsilon lead cutting off one of his bodyguards, *fine*. Him cutting off Jack Highland, *not fine*. Not at all.

"It's *diffused*, Sinclair," I rebut and tell him lowly, "we should leave this area before more runners pass the finish line and need water."

He's stewing more than the douchebro.

But Tyson blurts out, "I was *joking*. That guy Jesse can't take a *joke*."

"What happened?" Sinclair questions.

"I was fake-humping the table, and Jesse got bent-out-of-shape over it because another person—not me—said that's how I should ride Winona Meadows."

My jaw hardens, eyes narrow, head cocks because I'm *used* to these aggravating comments. No one likes this kind of peanut gallery, but they can't shut up when it comes to the famous ones.

Jack looks exasperated, also too used to hecklers. "Your friends can't talk like that here, man, and they shouldn't talk like that anywhere—"

"Let security deal with security issues," Sinclair cuts in before reiterating the same shit to the teenager. "That's no way to talk to any woman or any person."

Tyson scratches a pink bumpy patch on his fair skin, and what do you know—I think I gave the douchebro poison ivy.

I'd laugh about it, but I'm busy watching Jack back away from the situation. I only want to follow close before he disappears on me. And also, I left my vanishing client *alone*.

It'll be a miracle if Charlie is still waiting for me.

Sinclair surveys the mess of water and cups on the grass. "Clean this up," he orders the temp guard. "More runners are about to come in."

Jack exits the tent, but not before casting a glance back. Our eyes catch in a beat that says, *we're on the same side.*

Not necessarily as production and security.

But just as myself and him.

As Oscar and Jack.

I'm really falling for this guy, aren't I?

He disappears.

It pounds my pulse. Aches my joints and muscles, almost pushing me to go after him. *Run after him.* With one more professional exchange to Sinclair and a short talk with Akara over comms, I sprint out of the tent.

Jack is already gone.

Charlie….is also gone.

My muscles are on fire, breath caged as I click my mic. "Oscar to Farrow, is Charlie in the med cabins?" Farrow has been off-duty for security and on-duty for the med team.

Right now, my desire to chase after Charlie has been replaced with a full-fledged desire to chase after Jack.

Comms crackle. "Farrow to Oscar, that's a *yes.*"

I exhale.

If Charlie is safe there, then I can go find Highland. And so I text him and wait for his answer.

JACK AND I MEET-UP IN AN EMPTY CABIN CALLED

Blue Daisy, just four bunks here, a rustic bench, and a blue trunk.

Farrow left us a tube of corticosteroid cream to treat our poison ivy, which he diagnosed after looking at Charlie. I must've had the plant oils on my clothes and that's how Tyson got the rash, otherwise it's not really contagious person-to-person.

I'm officially off-duty while I treat this shit.

My arms, my legs, my neck—it all burns and itches like I've been dipped in a vat of fire ants. I shed my shirt and unbutton my pants.

Jack places his camera on a top bunk, the mattress thin and flimsy.

"You think Charlie knew he was leading us into poison ivy?" He pulls his tee over his head. "Just to get you and me naked together?"

I let out a laugh. "Now *that* would be some 5D-chess." I step out of my pants.

"It is working," Jack notes, standing in only gray boxer-briefs. But he's itching his neck to hell and back.

"Stop scratching, Highland." I catch his wrist.

His chest rises, his eyes drop down my half-naked build. I'm only wearing dark blue boxer-briefs, and a part of me is screaming to kiss him. To clutch his jaw and pull him closer. But we're both in slight pain right now, and a lot just happened with his little brother.

I slide my hand down his wrist and into his palm.

I hold his hand.

Jack sweeps my features with questions that I don't understand. It makes me nervous. Does he like this? Does he not?

I glance down at our interlaced fingers. "You have a good grip, Long Beach."

He smiles that dazzlingly smile.

A heady feeling washes over me. *Butterflies.* I'm thirty-two and still getting butterflies from a handhold, and we've already run some bases together.

Jack squeezes. "Not too tight for you?"

"Never too tight for me," I grin.

We take a seat side-by-side on a bottom bunkbed. The camp cabin creaks with a heavy gust of summer wind, and we inspect each other's rashes. His worst is along his neck, flaming his light-brown skin.

Mine is crawling up my arm and shoulder.

Jack unscrews the ointment. "Charlie ran through the poison ivy too, so if he did it on purpose, he's knowingly making himself suffer."

"Yeah." I nod slowly. "He doesn't have much *care* for his own life."

But the more Charlie doesn't care, the more I just want to ensure he's still standing at the end of the day.

Jack looks troubled.

"What's wrong?" I ask.

"The ethics of this show, but…that's not even at the forefront right now." His smile is sadder. "My brother." He tips his head to me, the light in his honey-brown eyes almost fading. "Did I make a mistake attaching him to this project—to these families?"

I shake my head. "He'll learn that you can't fight fire with fire. You and me—we're *jaded*. We've seen it all, been through it all, and when you bring a soul in here who hasn't experienced the ridicule and hatred, it's going to hit them differently."

"I don't want this to change him," Jack confesses. "I don't want him to be bitter or for him to lose his innocence too fast."

I think about Quinn.

When my brother first joined security, he was naïve, not realizing how much unwarranted shit is thrown at the families, and I know he's more hard-edged now than before.

"He's seventeen," I tell Jack. "Our brothers are gonna grow up whether we like it or not. The good thing is he's here with you, and you're with him." I hang my head with a coarse breath. "But let's be honest, I'm probably the *last* person who should be giving brotherly advice."

Jack slips me a smile. "No, you're the *first* person who should. At least for me. You've already been twenty-seven with a seventeen-year-old brother, and not that many people can say that."

I grin and scrunch my brows. "Are you calling me old, Highland?"

"Would you be flattered if I did?"

"No."

"Then no."

We laugh.

Jack smiles more at me. "Turn around, I'll get your back."

"I'll do you first."

He shifts at my choice of words, his nose flaring. Heat blankets me, and I search his eyes for more understanding but…

I can't read him that well.

Sadly.

Gladly? I don't know, it's definitely adding *something* between us. Can't say it's all bad. But a few bricks mortar around my heart.

Don't get hurt, Oliveira.

He angles his head back, giving me more access to the nape of his neck. I squirt cream on my fingers, dab the patchy spot, and rub small circles with my thumb.

I hear his breath in the quiet. Ragged, winded.

The noise seeps pleasure in my throbbing veins. Alone in a camp cabin, a palpable current of intimacy is strung between me and Jack.

"Is this what it was like?" he asks me. "Back when you were fourteen and had a sexual awakening at summer camp?"

I laugh, a soft breathy one that feels gentle. "Are you feeling sexually awakened, Long Beach?"

He rests a hand on his head, fingers woven in his hair. "I'm feeling something." *Me too,* but I can't say the words, he's already telling me, "I keep replaying our conversation at your apartment that one night."

That one night.

Can't forget any second of his sleepy ass, the blow job from heaven, and me opening up about my family. I gush forth way too much to Jack all the damn time, but I can never find a lever or wrench to help me *stop.*

I finish coating his poison ivy splotches, and Jack rotates to face me. Bunkbed's springs squeak beneath his weight. His legs are spread, and his knee knocks into my knee.

We're bare-chested. Only one piece of fabric away from being buck-ass naked.

My eyes want to track down the ridges and valleys of his muscles. But I hang onto a slat of the bunkbed above us. Like I'm headed for a collision and need to brace myself.

Jack takes the ointment and smears the cream over my bicep. "You said half the fun of fucking is the discovery. I have questions."

"No surprise there," I joke.

A charismatic smile spreads across his face. "But after you said that, I realized I'd rather your body answer all the questions, not your words."

My blood cranks to a detrimental high.

His smile falters, more uncertain. Probably because I'm not saying a thing.

Come on, Oliveira.

I intake a tight breath. "Is that wise? Look, I know what I said, but you've never been with a guy before. Maybe we should talk it out first and not after the fact. Basically what we didn't do last time."

"I liked last time," he says confidently, setting the cream aside. "I'm more adventurous than timid, if you haven't figured that out by now."

I give the frat bro a once-over. "Oh, I have. Trust me." I let go of the slat above my head. "But I'm probably *stronger* than any woman you've ever been with, Highland. The power dynamics are different. Even if I try to be gentle with you, I'm not soft. I'm going to feel rough and hard."

He bows forward, forearms on his thighs, breath hitched. *He's aroused?* His eyes flit over to me, then to the closed cabin door. "I'd do anything to feel you right now, Oscar, and usually, I can flash a smile and get my way but that works only 50% of the time with you. So I'd honestly grovel if that's what it takes—"

"Don't grovel," I cut in and lean in, cupping the back of his head. We breathe hard, and my mouth is a teasing inch from his lips.

His hand skates up my abs in exploration.

"You want to know what I like to do?" I whisper against his mouth.

A jagged groan scrapes his throat. "Yeah, *yeah*, I want to know."

I kiss him hard, bringing his chest against my chest, and I lift him up on the bunkbed further and bear my body down on his athletic build. His shoulders and back press into the flimsy mattress. I barely break the passionate, sweltering kiss, and his lips split apart to curse out a pleasured, "*Jesus fuck.*" His hands fly to his head.

He keeps doing that.

It's actually really fucking cute.

I grind into him and clasp his thigh, stretching his leg around my hip. Jack clutches my bicep, his eyes open as he drinks in our bodies and the friction. He hardens against me, and blood boils down south.

I kiss him again. And again. His fingers grip my hair, and our foreheads press together. Hot, electric breath sparking between us.

Jack chokes out between breaths, "You prefer it rough?"

I try not to laugh. "You think this is rough?"

He puts a hand on my abs, telling me to take a pause. I do.

I hover over him, palms on either side of his head. My lips stinging. *Camp4Ever!* is written in green sharpie on the bunk's wooden post.

Jack struggles to catch his breath. "What was that to you then"—he pants—"if it wasn't rough?"

I skim *him* for answers and to ensure he's okay. "Did you enjoy it?"

His smile bursts forth. "Yeah." He wets his lips. "I definitely did."

I'm grinning. "I'd call that me being more aggressive, not necessarily rough. I'm not yanking your hair, Long Beach. I'm just in control."

His eyes sink into me. "You like to top?"

I lean closer and whisper against his ear, "What happened to letting my body show you?"

His body flexes, practically arching up into me. "*Fuck.*" He reaches down and palms his shaft, still constricted behind boxer-briefs. "You're killing me, Os."

Os?

I sit up off Jack in a jolt.

He has another hand on his head, face frozen in too many emotions. "I, uh...sorry." He straightens up too, breath knotted. "It just came out." He tries to smile. "You don't like nicknames?"

I love them. I'd give him a hundred corny, sappy nicknames if I could. But I listen to the signs that read:

Danger!

Warning!

Going too fucking far, Oliveira!

I can't lie to the guy though. "Just don't call me Ozzy."

"Why not?"

"My college boyfriend wore that one down."

"Noted." He stiffens, and we both slide further back on the bunk-bed, leaning against the wall. Our legs are scrunched up towards our chests. Knees bent.

I cut through an awkward tension by wrapping an arm around his shoulders.

He smiles weakly over at me. "I thought I fucked that up between us."

"No." I shake my head at him. "Just so you're aware, being a top or bottom has nothing to do with being dominant or submissive. Dominant bottoms exist."

He nods with another smile. "Good to know." He tracks a hand from my kneecap down to my thigh, breathes in, and then retracts, like the intensity and swelling feelings are too much. My skin is still tingling from the touch, and I listen as he explains, "I can't say what I'm into yet...being a top or bottom, I guess I won't figure it out until I have sex."

I push back curly strands out of my eyes.

I want to tell Highland right here that I do prefer to top. That the last time I bottomed was over ten-years ago. I want to tell him that I'll take care of him if he's nervous, and I'd never pressure him to do anything he's not ready to do.

But I'm a coward and too afraid of his reaction to those words. So I don't utter a single one. He could either run scared because he doesn't think we're sexually compatible. Or worse, he could believe we are.

And then what? We have mind-blowing sex, the best sex of my life? We find out we're *too good* together in every aspect. Too perfect for each other, a match orchestrated by a twenty-one-year-old genius named Charlie Cobalt and maybe even a higher power.

Fate.

The stars in the sky.

Aligning for him and me.

And then Jack could call this a stepping-stone. *Short-term fling.* Maybe that's all I'm good for while I'm in security.

Insecurities are such assholes, and I know I'm riding this one hard and dry.

So I swallow the pit in my throat, and I hug him closer and kiss the freckle on his temple. His lip rises at me.

He places his large hand back on my thigh.

"So," I say, "when exactly did you know you were into me, Highland?"

He chokes on a sound that I think was supposed to be a laugh. "When I met you."

I rock back, my skull touching the wall. "That was...*five years* ago."

His fingers rake through his thick hair. "I didn't know what it meant—my feelings for you. I couldn't process them beyond the fact that they were so different than anything I'd felt before." His Adam's apple bobs.

My mind races back to that time and place. I met him around the same time I became Charlie's bodyguard.

Jack Highland was just twenty-two and a production assistant for *We Are Calloway*.

I was near the top in security.

It wasn't until he became an exec-producer at twenty-five that his world started a head-on collision with mine. He was heading meetings with security during filming days, and we've had our fair share of flare-ups concerning Charlie and WAC shoots. But it was always professional.

Until the tour bus.

Until the FanCon.

And then...gloves off, I guess. His compliments became flirty, and I just gave in. Because why not? It was fun for a while. When I didn't *yearn* and long for more. And then he rejected me, but now he's embracing me, and he's saying he's felt a connection early, early on.

Jack holds my gaze. "When I talk to people, I love making them feel good, but with you...I never wanted it to stop. I wanted to come back for more, even when my work said, *focus on your subject*. I just wished that my subject was you."

My chest rises.

I am in…way too deep.

And I don't want to swim back out.

"Why do you think that is?" I ask him.

"I thought you probably just had what I had." He flashes a smile. "*Charm.*"

I grin. "I do have that, Long Beach."

He laughs. "Yeah, but it's something else too. It's more." His gaze drifts and he rests his head against the wall next to mine. "How could I miss something this monumental about myself for so long? Twenty-seven-years, dude. It feels like fog is shifting and everything is so clear, and I just wish I had that clarity sooner."

I would've asked him out.

No doubt, Highland would be my boyfriend by now, if he was comfortable with his sexuality way back then. That is, if he still liked me as much as he does in this second.

This moment.

The *what if* game hurts, and look at me, still playing that game.

Against the defenses around my heart, I turn to Jack and say, "I'm glad you're finding clarity now. You can figure out your new path—a new life plan."

The cabin creaks before he can respond, and a knock raps the door. Jane Cobalt asks if we're okay. She's been with Charlie in another med cabin.

"Yeah!" I call out. "We're heading out in a sec!"

Jack is already scooting off the bed. He grabs his clothes in a heap and starts dressing. I follow suit, and when he buttons his jeans, he tells me, "I'm not planning out my future anymore. I'm just going to see where the ride takes me." He makes a *wave* motion with his hand.

I laugh weakly. "How California of you."

He smiles. "It is my favorite place on Earth."

"The longer you're with me, the more likely that'll change to *Philly.*"

Jack tugs his shirt over his head with a brighter laugh.

It floods my chest, but I end up shying away so he doesn't see my hint of unease. I realize that I just wanted brick-solid assurance that he's here for me. I shouldn't even ask for that when we haven't *defined* what we are.

We like each other.

I'm helping him through the clouds.

That has to be enough right now.

19

Oscar Oliveira

RED VELVETEEN BOXED seats at an ornate operatic theatre, home to one of the most prestigious New York ballet companies—it's fit for royalty, so no one should be surprised a Cobalt would be here.

Least of all *me*. The man guarding one.

I adjust my earpiece, the chair hard under my ass despite it looking soft. Only four seats occupy the box, and my client is sprawled out across the front two.

Charlie is sleeping, the program for *Romeo & Juliet* splayed over his eyes. He rarely looks tired. Rarely, if ever, yawns because he finds random and opportune times to catch sleep.

A good distance from my client, Jack and I are seated behind him. Giving Charlie and us space.

With the dimmed theatre lighting and the orchestra playing sweeping songs from one of the most classic, tragic love stories, I'm lured into the sensuality and romance of the ballet. Especially with Jack sitting next to me.

We wear well-tailored black tuxes. Like we're the kings for the night.

Our eyes keep snagging, holding a beat too long, and I've edged closer to Highland. My arm wants to splay over his chair like we're on a date.

Nothing has felt more like a *first date* than this moment with him. And I'm on-duty—how nuts is that?

My gaze melts over his neck. No more angry patches mar his skin from poison ivy. The Charity Fun Run is a couple days in the past.

And right now, Jack sucks on a lime sucker, the ball pushed against the inside of his mouth. It's driving me mother-effing wild. I run my fingers across my jaw, and his glittering eyes smile more than his lips. While he watches the ballerinas, he whispers to me, "Would you attend the ballet if it weren't for Charlie?"

I hadn't given it too much thought. "Probably not." My voice is hushed next to his ear. "I appreciate the ballet, but it's not something that completely interests me." I look him up and down. "What about you, Highland?"

"Probably *yes.*" He tilts his head to me. "I really love art."

He is a filmmaker, and I start wondering if his family approves of his profession. "Are your parents pro-arts?"

He shifts the sucker with his tongue. "I'd say they're more pro-business. They respect what I do, especially after I've succeeded, but they would've preferred I went into some sort of finance sector."

Finance?

I don't crunch numbers all day. I chose a career that outwardly showcases brawn more than intelligence, and not everyone can see how much common sense, strategy, and brains it takes to be a damn good bodyguard.

What if his parents envisioned him with a business-minded entrepreneur?

That's not you, Oliveira.

My chest tightens. What do I care? It's not like we're a couple, and I might never meet his parents. But I do know Jack's family means a lot to him, and naturally, I don't just want to be on their good side or best side, but rather their *favorite* side.

He lowers his voice to explain, "My parents weren't always as business savvy as they are now. My dad—Jack Sr. served in the Navy. During a mission in the Philippines he met the love of his life, Eleonor Loanzon."

"Your mom?" I whisper.

"Yeah." He has a softer smile when he talks about his family. Like he's cradling all the loving memories. "Anyway, she studied nursing at the University of Santo Tomas in Manila. Their ambitions started out practical, but she quit nursing after they got married. His service ended, and they both wound up in my dad's hometown."

"Long Beach?" I ask.

"Long Beach," he confirms with a nod. "They chose a new path together and went all-in on real estate, and it panned out." I can't ask more; he's too quick with a question. "Would your parents hate the ballet?"

I nod strongly. "Oh yeah. Without a doubt." We stare ahead as a ballerina playing Juliet floats across the stage, and I add, "Though, my mom will enjoy anything the first and hundredth time. She really relishes in the experience."

Speaking of my mom.

My phone vibrates in my fist. I silence the fifth call from her tonight and text: I'm on-duty.

The biggest meltdown on the Oliveira crisis line yesterday was a fictional death on a Brazilian novela. My mom rehashed the entire episode over the phone to me before I had to cut her off, and I expect today's catastrophe to be similar.

But damn am I wrong.

Please call Jo. She's saying she's moving to Alaska! — Mom

I try not to roll my head back in frustration, and I text: I'll call her later. I have to put my family on hold in order to stay on-duty. I'm lucky I even have this time with Highland.

I pocket my phone in my black slacks.

"Everything okay?" he asks quietly.

"Yeah, just family drama." I check on Charlie with a quick glance, then zone in on Jack.

He's tinkering with an ancient camcorder on his lap. Reminding me that he's also working tonight, but I can't imagine that equipment is for

Charlie's show. Honest: I haven't seen a video camera that old since I was in high school.

And Jack has told me that he'll pay top price for the best quality cameras and lenses so they'll hold up. Even Jesse's Canon looked like it cost a fortune. His little brother isn't at the ballet shooting B-roll. Jack said he's organizing equipment at his Philly apartment.

We both open our mouths like we have too much to say in so little time, but the orchestra pumps up the tempo. Our gazes veer to the stage again.

A dirty-blond-haired Romeo serenades a thin, brunette Juliet from her balcony. I lean into Jack to whisper, "We don't like him."

"Romeo?"

"The guy who plays Romeo."

He nods, understanding. "Leo Valavanis. Beckett's rival in the company." He smiles more as he asks, "Who is we? You, Donnelly, and Farrow?"

"No, no, no." I hold up a hand. "At least not Farrow. Donnelly, yeah. *We* encompasses anyone who's Team Cobalt, and Farrow has always been Team Hale, even before the Husband." I tease, "Choose your sides wisely, Highland."

He leans back in his chair. "Production can't pick a side. I'm Team Everyone."

A grin edges across my mouth. "That's way too diplomatic. I hate it."

He forces back a laugh, then wets his lips. We watch the ballet for another five minutes before he whispers, "You know, if I had to pick a side, I'd just choose yours."

My chest swells, then knots. On guard.

Not wanting to be, and maybe his lines aren't manufactured for just anyone. Deep down, I know they're genuine and made specifically for me.

I have a lot of responses:

Wise, Long Beach.

I'd choose your side too.

We can make our own side.

But I land on the worst one.

"I'm not famous." My voice sounds too curt.

Jack stops tinkering with the camcorder. He looks from me to the stage and back again, and when I catch his gaze, I nod to him like, *we're alright.*

I wish I could just show affection. Touch is my favorite love language, and I can't wrap an arm around him like I did in the camp cabin.

More tensely, we watch the ballet, and I worry my cautious ass ruined our first non-date that feels like a first date.

Romeo leaps lithely across the stage. Have no idea the correct ballet terms, *at all.* I honestly think Donnelly knows more than me from attending so many of Beckett's rehearsals and practices.

And Beckett should have landed the lead role, but he lost out when he was stuck in Scotland with the rest of us.

He's still in *Romeo & Juliet.* Just as Mercutio.

Jack slides a panel off the camcorder. He brought a little toolkit with his camera bag, and he sets aside the tiniest screwdriver. Once he captures my attention, he whispers, "How often does Charlie come here?"

"At least once a week. Sometimes more. Can't say he stays awake for every one."

Charlie bought out the box for a whole year...for the past four years. Same box. Same chairs. My ass probably has a permanent imprint in this one. And I explain how Charlie and Jane made a bet to see who can attend the most performances to watch Beckett dance.

Some months, Jane wins. Other months, Charlie does.

Jack curses under his breath as he messes with the camcorder.

Now I've got to ask. "What is that?"

He pops out the battery. "I thought you'd know." Genuine confusion arches his brows. "Farrow gave it to me. He said the camcorder belonged to security, and he asked if I could fix it without damaging the footage."

Huh? "That's...odd." Usually I'd keep this uneasy feeling to myself since it's *security*, but I'm destroying all kinds of boundaries with Jack Highland.

His hand freezes on the camcorder. "What do you mean?"

"I haven't heard anyone in security using a camcorder or needing one, and I stay pretty in-tune on comms when I can." I shrug. "I guess I could've missed something during one of the flights around the world."

"Farrow probably has a reason," Jack says quietly, jotting something down in a spiral notebook. "It seemed important to him."

Weird.

Farrow likes to do shit himself when he can. He doesn't ask for favors that often. I skim him as he finishes note-taking and slips the pen behind his ear. "What'd you write down?" I whisper.

"The type of battery." He places the camcorder in a camera bag at his feet. "I need to order a new one before I can do anything else."

Our focus returns to the stage.

Beckett Cobalt is in a sword fight, his nimble movements like silk as he dances and thrashes a blade against another. The audience sucks in a collective breath as he staggers back, wounded. He plays a pompous character and acts as though he's fine.

But he stumbles in his quest towards his foe, stumbles more, and fights one last time. All the while, he glides, as weightless as a human can be without actually flying.

Effortless beauty and grace with the ferocity of a lion. Charlie read that review to me after Beckett's first season as a principal dancer. He smiled at his twin brother's success, and no matter how many hundred times I'm here seeing Beckett jump and twirl, I think of that quote.

And how it's the pretty sheen of the Cobalt Empire, the romantic one, but underneath it all, there are cracks. But like so many people, the romanticism is needed on heavy days, and sometimes I even try to let it help carry me through.

Jack watches, enthralled. Gaze lit up. As Mercutio perishes, the dancers and their emotion reflect off his glassy eyes. And our gazes catch every few seconds in sensual, hot beats. We both drink in more than just the beauty on stage.

His reverence drapes a fantasy over us. A moment so full of make-believe romance found mostly in medieval fairytales. I've wanted *this* type of heart-stopping moment for so fucking long that I almost can't believe it's real.

Watch me accidentally blow it all up.

My confidence has been shot to hell with Jack, but I clearly like a guy who humbles me.

He edges closer, our thighs touching, his sandalwood beachy cologne filling my nostrils like a drug. I inhale for more.

Jack tenses, and then he stretches his arm over my shoulders. My pulse is on a rollercoaster while my heart is playing bumper cars with my ribs.

We're in the dark. No one can really see or snap photos. More private than public, still working and on-duty, but blame the ballet, I'm sitting here trying to bask in the fantasy of him and me.

For tonight, we are the kings.

He grows more comfortable, his arm loose across me, but I hear his shallow breath in the pit of my ear. I sense the rise and fall of his chest.

Juliet is distraught on stage. Lovesick and in mourning.

I sink a hand onto Highland's thigh. He shifts in his chair...closer. We steal hotter glimpses of one another. Tension stretches, and while we pretend to watch the ballet, he lets his arm fall off my shoulder and grazes his hand on *my* thigh.

Fuck...I don't shift like him. But I'm rigid, breath caught. I caress his thigh upwards, and his hand ascends up mine.

I want to experiment with Jack like I would any new partner, but I don't want to be *an* experiment. Squashing the thought, I let pleasure guide me.

My fingers slide against his hardened bulge, and his palm rubs over mine. Muscles constricting, I ignite on fire, doing everything in my power not to initiate a kiss here.

Ballet. Semi-public.

I want to give that choice to him.

His gaze caresses over the tension in my neck when he kneads me. *Fucking* ah, Christ. I shut my eyes in a long, aroused blink.

I thumb the sensitive spot around his tip, and he swallows hard, his other hand flying to the back of his head. *Got him.*

Jack bites down on the sucker stick to force back a noise.

And then Charlie stirs, the program falling off his face. We both go rigid and retract our hands. Charlie is...still sleeping. Eyes shut.

I touch my earpiece. *Working.* I'm working. Shouldn't have fallen into that so easily. "Sorry, Highland," I breathe.

"Don't be sorry." He pops out the sucker stick, pent-up tension in his flexed shoulders. "I should get back to this too." He unpacks his Canon to take more footage for the show.

No one has ever been that understanding when I have to prioritize work. Hell, I've never been able to have a date on-duty—or a non-date. Whatever the fuck we're doing.

On occasion, his job can even be more grueling than mine, and I respect his tireless work ethic. But I'm just thinking about *after*. When I'm off-duty tonight. He's put away his camera. I don't really care what time it is or how long we've been awake. And considering he fought exhaustion before just to talk to me, I don't think he'll care either.

So I whisper, "Highland?"

"Hm?"

"It'll probably be another late-night. You can stay at my place, if you don't want to drive back."

He smiles. "I'd like that."

20

Jack Highland

OSCAR SWITCHES ON A PHILLIES game and passes me a beer bottle. The leather couch bobs as he sinks down beside me. We undo our black bowties and pop a few constricting buttons of our white shirts. After the ballet, coming back to his studio apartment feels like the hottest romantic invite I've ever been extended.

So I took it.

There is no denying how attracted I am to him, or how badly I'd like things to progress *upstairs*. To his loft. His bed.

But I can't tell if that's where this is going.

Not yet, anyway.

"Try these." I pass him a bag of corn nuts, which I packed in my camera bag for him.

Oscar reads the label. "Boy Bawang Cornick. Chili cheese flavored." He grins as he rips open the snack-sized bag. "Are these your favorite, Highland?"

"They're up there, as far as Filipino snacks go."

He tosses a corn nut in his mouth, crunches, and my smile widens while he *assesses*. He blows out a breath and swigs his beer.

"Too spicy?" I laugh and grab a different snack.

"Should've warned you, I'm a baby when it comes to food that makes me breathe fire." He takes another hearty swig. "And then you have my sister Jo who carries around a bottle of *molho picante*." He explains, "Brazilian hot sauce."

I take the Cornick from him. "Looks like me and your sister are two peas in a pod."

Oscar gives me a look. "If all it takes is spicy corn nuts to get in the same pod as you, then hand them back." He reaches for the bag, and I put a hand to his chest.

We both flex, heat pulsing my veins, and I raise another snack bag. "Clover Chips. Plain cheese flavored." I chuck them lightly, and he catches.

While he tears the bag, I cut the taut silence. "Jesse loves the garlic flavored Cornick. Next time I see you, I'll bring some."

His mouth lifts, almost grinning. *Almost* because he seems to stare off for half-a-second while he digs into the cheesy, melt-in-your-mouth chips. It's not surprising since Oscar has been hot and cold towards me.

But it is alarming.

Fuck, my leg nearly bounces. That hasn't happened in a while. When I was ten, eleven, my leg would jostle, I'd break out in a sweat, my throat would close up—all because a teacher called on me to answer a question or I'd need to recite a poem in front of the class.

I look at myself in the past five years—speaking to network heads, interviewing celebrities—and I feel like a different person. My parents paid for a tutor to help me with public speaking when I was younger, and after a while, my anxiety retreated.

I learned to breathe.

Inhale. Exhale.

I learned to believe that *I can*. Even when it feels like I can't.

Breath and confidence have guided me without a stumble for years, but with WAC filming starting, plus the stress of Charlie's show, and the newness of what's happening between me and Oscar—my anxiety has made a slow but mighty return.

I exhale.

My leg stays stationary. "Verdict?" I ask him.

He pops a chip in his mouth, and a satisfied noise rumbles out. "So good," he expresses as he shovels a handful between his lips.

I smile in a sip of beer. We eat Clover Chips, drink, and talk about the Phillies. After Oscar groans when the Braves hit a homerun, bases loaded, I ask him, "Baseball is your favorite sport?"

"To watch, yeah. What about you?" He washes down chips with beer.

I hang my arm on my leg, beer loose between my fingers. "To be honest, I've never really liked watching baseball."

His face drops. "Fuck, bro. I can change the channel." He reaches forward for the remote.

I clutch his shoulder. "No, keep it on. I'll watch it now."

"Why?" Oscar slowly leans back.

"Basta ikaw," I say in Tagalog and translate casually, "as long as I'm with you, because it's you." I swig my beer. "Baseball isn't so bad in your company."

Oscar grins, one that feels as overwhelming as the smile on my face. We're in the *hot* phase of hot-and-cold, and I love it here.

"Soccer," I tell him, reaching into the Clover Chip bag that's in his hand. "That's my favorite sport to watch."

He nods a few times. "My mom and sister are big into soccer. They'll go all out for the World Cup and wear jerseys for Brazil and America, even if the teams get knocked out of the bracket early."

"Your sister likes soccer too?" I swallow more beer with a bright smile. "She's already becoming my new best friend."

I expect Oscar to make a light joke about me and best friends. But he's rigid, his arm splayed tensely over the back of the couch behind me.

He takes a tight sip of beer, brown eyes plastered to the TV.

I have too many questions. My head is spinning. But before I can ask a single one, he turns to me and speaks.

"This pea pod you're with my baby sis—"

"It's a figure of speech, Os," I say with a frown.

He goes quiet when I call him *Os*. We stare deeper, our edged breaths timed together.

Oscar rests the bottom of his beer bottle on his thigh. "Look, I just have to ask…are you interested in Joana?"

My brows shoot up. "She's *nineteen*. She's your *sister*."

He groans at himself. "I know. I know." He rubs a hand down his face. "I'm just reexamining this"—he motions between us—"way too much."

He's reexamining us?

I set my beer on the coffee table and stand up. I'm wading in a rougher ocean with him, and maybe I need to offer better reassurance. "If Joana asked me to spend the night with her after the ballet, I would've politely declined."

I could be asleep in a bed right now, but Oscar is the only person I want keeping me awake.

He nods repeatedly, rising to his feet. "I can't lie, I have reservations and hesitations right now—"

"Why?" I question, breathing harder.

"Because you're Jack Highland!" he shouts in frustration. "You're too captivating, too hopeful, too sexy, too determined and bold. You're the total package—you're a *knockout*, bro, and maybe I'm afraid you're going to knock me out."

Pulse racing, I step closer. "You think I'm not scared too? I'm running at a half-open window that you *almost* keep closing!"

He chokes on emotion. "What do you have to lose?"

"You!" I yell from my core, eyes stinging. "I could lose you!"

His face twists with raw feelings.

Please fucking believe me.

Oscar seizes my gaze and moves closer like a bullet of desire. He cups the back of my neck, and my fingers dig into his traps as our legs thread. As our firm chests weld together—and we're kissing. Starved, aching kisses that feel as *raw* as our sudden declarations.

We rip apart each other's white button-downs. Opening them to touch skin on skin, his body warm and heartbeat fast.

I want to know Oscar more intimately. What he likes in bed. I want to feel the answers until they shatter me.

He walks backwards while I slide my tongue against his, but he's the one coaxing a groan out of me. "*Oscar*," I breathe, winded against his lips.

Our eyes connect with deeper longing. "We're going upstairs, Long Beach."

I've leveled up. I'm too hooked on him to say the line. Right behind him, I follow Oscar up to the loft. The ceiling is lower here, and I feel like I need to duck.

While we're no longer kissing, our bodies no longer touching, we watch one another yank off our black slacks and nerves bubble up. Along with excitement, which I try to grip more strongly.

Oscar studies my face. "You sure you don't want to talk first?"

Am I sure?

Yeah.

But he makes me stop and question myself. "Do you usually have in-depth talks before getting into bed with a guy?" I wait to strip down since he's taken a pause, his dark-gray boxer-briefs mold his length and ass. The more I stare, the more my dick pulses.

Blood pumps harder.

Pulse speeds faster.

"Not really," Oscar admits. "But I've also mostly been the less experienced one. You're like a vulnerable, delicate little hatchling, and I'm trying not to squash you."

I think he's vulnerable too, just in a different way. And I ease more with the cemented knowledge that Oscar cares about me. About whether I'm ready and okay to do more and explore.

"You won't squash me," I say strongly, a smile edging. "I know I've never thrown a punch, but I can hold my own." I tug off my boxer-briefs, and his eyes trace the cut of my muscles on my waist, the V-line that leads to my hardened cock, *begging* for friction.

I'm breathless already, just seeing Oscar devour my body from four feet away. His nose flares, and swiftly, he sheds his boxer-briefs and closes the distance between us.

His mouth crashes against mine, shooting adrenaline and pleasure in my veins. I grip his curls and he leads me to the bed. My ass hits the mattress, and his knee sinks next to me. Oscar clutches my waist and lifts me further up the bed.

God. I choke on a groan. My head meets a soft feather pillow, and he spreads my legs further apart with his knees so he can fit between them. I'm not used to anyone *lifting* me like he did. I grip the back of his neck. Wanting him closer and closer.

I have extreme difficulty catching my breath around him. In bed together, it's even worse. I'm suffocating under the intensity as we kiss, as our hands roam. My palm travels over the dark hair along his firm chest, and I feel the hair on his legs as our limbs tangle. He grinds against me, our erections rubbing together with the movement.

God, fuck. "Oscar," I groan, water cresting the corners of my eyes. I squeeze his ass that flexes beneath my palm, and he sucks the nape of my neck.

We're not having sex, but nothing has ever felt this intimate to me. His hand glides up the back of my head. Arousal pools in hot waves. We're muscle on muscle, and I watch as his palm dives south between our abs. He wraps his fingers around my cock and creates mind-numbing friction. Up and down, up and down. Lighting up the sensitive places.

"Fuck," I choke.

The more amped I feel, the more I realize I'm not *giving* enough. But the thought fades as he digs forward, our kisses hungered, his biceps flexed near my jaw. I run my hands up and down his bare ass. Our muscular thighs slick with sweat.

Oscar grunts against my mouth, "*Christ.*"

A hand soars to my head. *Dude.* I cannot, for the life of me, catch my fucking breath.

And our lips are finding each other again. Tongues wrestling. His facial hair scratches against my jaw, brewing more heat. I buck up, and he pushes me back down with his build.

That felt too good. I tear our mouths apart. "I can't," I choke.

He freezes.

Shit.

No. "No," I pant. "I meant…" He's already sitting up off my chest. "Don't stop, Os."

"What was that?" Oscar asks, his lips swollen. Abs flexed. "You said *I can't.*"

We're both still painfully erect and *wanting.* I lick my lips into a smile. "It was just a lot. It was *good.*"

He studies me, then his mouth curves upward. "You gave me a heart attack, Long Beach. I thought I broke you."

I let out a soft laugh. "I'm not that easy to break." At least I sincerely hope I'm not. I trace our positions over and over, and there is a question I can't contain. "Do you have lube?"

He stiffens. "We're not having sex—"

"I understand that, but if one of us is eventually taking a cock in the ass, shouldn't we work up to it?" I've Google-searched prepping before anal, and I was able to figure out douching on my own. So I don't bring that up unless he does.

We texted each other not long ago our recent screenings at the clinic. *Negative. No STDs.* But I only took our agreement to get checked out as both of us being careful and responsible in case something did happen between us.

It wasn't a guarantee.

It's still not.

Which is why I'm on pins and needles as Oscar processes.

And then he pulls away and stretches his body to a nightstand. His hand stays on my thigh like he's telling me to stay put. I watch as he pulls a black bottle of lube from the drawer.

He waves the bottle. "Pick your poison: you want my fingers in you or your fingers in me?"

Choices.

My muscles strain. "You choose."

"You might not like my choice."

"I'll tell you to stop if I don't," I assure. "All I know is I'd try both."

Oscar leans back down, and I fall back off my arms. We kiss again, and the swelter reignites as we sink into a sensual mood.

His hand descends between our bodies, and he jerks me off better than anyone ever has. *Fuck.* I force myself not to blow a load before we enter a new territory.

The anticipation of *who* he chooses to give and receive is annihilating me. And our eyes are on each other as he takes the bottle and lubes his fingers.

This is happening.

I picture the moment, his fingers in me, and I shift my legs, my dick aching. I tug myself, and Oscar's whole body tightens in arousal. We're both straining and in need of a powerful release.

My eyes trace his beautiful build. Curves and cuts and sinewy angles.

Curly hair brushes his eyelashes. His nose ring makes him even sexier. Faint scars dot his chest and knuckles, and his nose was probably reset a few times after punches.

Beautiful.

I don't want him to be with anyone else.

No one.

Just me.

I slide my hand back against his neck and bring his mouth on mine. We kiss for another minute before he whispers, "Turn on your chest."

I roll onto my forearms, exposing my back and ass to Oscar. Questions prick my gaze, wondering if this is right. My pulse is skipping, and I ease when he shifts my legs for me. Spreading them apart. He grips my waist.

"Do your California best and chill some more," Oscar says.

It makes me smile. "Am I not relaxed?"

"I don't want to hurt you."

That wells up inside me. Even though he's said it before, it feels more like a commitment and promise.

He kisses my bicep, my neck and lips one more time before pressing his body up against me. Pleasure steals my breath, and anticipation descends in rapid headiness.

I imagine him thrusting against me, and I feel weak at the knees and I'm basically lying down on all-fours. I look over my shoulder. Meeting his serious eyes that reassure and calm anxieties.

His cold finger circles my entry, and his other arm wraps around my waist. He strokes me with one hand and enters me with his other fingers, slight pressure nuzzling me—I stiffen.

He lets go of my shaft and trails his free hand up my abs, creating firm waves that leave fiery wakes. So many sensations melt my brain, and I *chill* inside the moment.

A second later, he slides his finger in me. My eyes snap shut, overwhelmed for a beat. I bear down on my teeth, breathing aching breath through my nose. He makes a come-hither motion and finds a spot that jerks my limbs in intense bliss.

Fuck.

He thrusts his hips with the movement of his finger. A primal noise rumbles out of him and out of me, our groans the best music in the air. His hard body rocks on top of mine, against mine, with mine—pressure.

Pressure.

I reach back and try to grab onto Oscar, but his hips and thighs and body are firm muscle that my hand slides off. I almost give up, but then I feel his palm slip into mine. Fingers interlacing and squeezing tight.

Jesus fuck.

I bury my head into the pillow as he starts moving his finger deeper and faster. Another groan strangles me. "Os," I choke out his name like a wounded animal. Like I'm pleading for that pressure to turn into a release.

And the way he's riding me…

It's too good.

I try to shrug off his hand from mine—so that I can touch myself.

"Nonono, shhh." He holds tighter to my palm and kisses the back of my shoulder. "Hold out a little more. Trust me."

Trust him. There is no question. No uncertainty. He has all my trust. I've gift wrapped it and delivered it to his door.

Emotions spill over pleasured shockwaves. My breathing comes out hoarse and ragged, and Oscar keeps whispering in my ear. His gruff voice turns me on just as much as how he works me over. When he hits my prostate, lights dance in my vision. It happens again. And again. "*Os*," I cry out. Everything else that leaves my lips are noises and grunts and heavy breaths.

But my head is one giant chant. *Os. Os. Os. Os.*

A climax annihilates me, and it takes me a second to realize I released in his palm. With all the confidence in the world, Oscar grabs a towel and wipes off my cum. He kisses the edge of my lips, and I fall onto my shoulder blades, both hands on my head.

He grins. "Not gonna lie, you enjoyed that *way* more than I expected."

I laugh in a pant. "Am I your biggest surprise?"

"Oh yeah, every fucking day, Highland."

I eye his erection. "I can—"

"Just catch your breath." Oscar stands near the foot of the bed, and he strokes himself a couple times. I heat up, and I watch this gorgeous guy *come* with another firm tug. His muscles flex, and he grits down on his teeth, eyes almost rolling.

I only wish his orgasm was closer to me and from my body or hands. "Now *I* feel like I've missed out on something."

He uses the same towel to clean up, his grin rising again. "Maybe next time, Highland."

Next time. I want the hot-and-cold just to be boiling hot between us. I want to reassure Oscar so the window flies fully open and I can climb all the way through. But I'm not sure how to do that without a major declaration.

One that could change my entire life.

Am even ready to tell my parents I'm not straight? To tell Jesse? To tell all of Oscar's friends and everyone else we know?

My throat closes.

Inhale. Exhale.

I breathe out and let those concerns go for tonight.

Oscar comes back to bed. Lying next to me, he reaches over my chest to pull the cord to a lamp. "It's five a.m.," he says. "You should get some sleep."

We both should.

But we're awake another hour. We lie on our sides, hug each other's frames, and whisper about his job, my job—the top-secret aspects that we can't really share with other people. Details about the famous families. If we discuss sex, we might actually do more, so we make a concerted effort not to bring up what just occurred.

We talk until we put the moon to bed and wake the sun. Bright rays cast over the loft, the bed, *us*. Sleep catches up. Sleep that I don't want but my body demands.

And finally, our eyes begin to shut.

21

Oscar Oliveira

THIS MOTHERFUCKER.

I stare with a strained wince at Gabe Montgomery in the Studio 9 Boxing & MMA Gym. The new temp I'm training acts like his head was screwed on ass-backwards.

"But like…" He rubs his temple. "If I'm in front of the client in a crowd, how do I *see* them?"

Leaning a hip against a boxing bag, my Cheeto freezes halfway to my mouth. "You can glance over your shoulder, Gabe."

He shakes his head, wavy blonde locks falling across his pale white forehead. "But wouldn't it just be like easier to walk *behind* the clients?"

I slowly chew and take out my aggravation on my Cheeto. "Then how are they going to make it to the door?" I ask. "They can't push through paparazzi and crowds like you can."

Gabe's delts are the size of honey baked hams. This kid is only twenty-two, same age as Quinn, and he's built like a bulldozer. Security doesn't usually hire guys this built because their endurance tends to be in the gutter, but Gabe passed all the entry-level tests.

Too bad he's an idiot.

"Huh," Gabe ponders all of this. "So…I make the path?"

I nod slowly and pop another Cheeto in my mouth. Kitsuwon Securities needs a good batch of temps to run efficiently, which means all of us on Omega have to clock in time training new guys. So while

I'm here teaching Tweedledum, Charlie Cobalt is in New York with another temp on his detail.

I just hope Gabe can retain some of the shit I'm throwing at him. He can't be such a lost cause if Thatcher Moretti referred him to Kitsuwon Securities. Apparently, he's fresh out of the Navy and friend of a friend of a family member. If you ask me, we're scraping the bottom of the barrel these days.

I glance at my watch. We've been working through basics for the past three hours while Studio 9 is closed to *security only*. We're the only ones here right now.

"Give me twenty laps around the gym," I tell Gabe. "And we'll call it a night."

"Right on." He darts off. I watch him sprint. Alright, the kid is fast for being that big. I'll give him that.

The gym door blows open, and I hear a cascade of shouting and squealing. "MAXIMOFF! FARROW! MAXIMOFF!" and "MARROW FOREVER!"

I yearn for a forever-in-love stable relationship like Farrow has with Maximoff, but damn do I not want that cacophony and headache brought by the media. The Oslie rumors are bad enough.

Farrow is grinning at his husband as they stroll in. The Hale prince looks high-key irritated at whatever Farrow said or did.

Where's the popcorn?

I dig into my Cheetos.

"Can you wipe your memory?" Maximoff asks the guy with a near-perfect photographic memory. "Scrub the last two minutes and tack on another century. Except don't erase all the parts where I remind you that I'm smarter and hotter."

"You mean the parts where you lie?"

I laugh, and it draws half of their attention to me while they approach.

Maximoff growls out his frustration. "Seriously, you didn't hear what I said."

"I heard a fan outside ask who your celebrity crush is," Farrow grins wider, "and I definitely heard you answer, *my husband.*"

"Aww," I pile on the teasing with the bat of my lashes.

Maximoff is bright red. He looks to Farrow. "It's like you want me to shove you in a gym locker or something."

"Or something," Farrow laughs.

I have a theory that no one taught Maximoff Hale how to flirt. He literally does the kindergarten sandbox "I hate you" maneuver with Farrow, and largely, it's probably because he's never *needed* to flirt to get cock or pussy. He's a fucking celebrity.

They kick off their shoes to walk on the gym mats. Coming closer, they weave through the hanging boxing bags.

I pop a Cheeto in my mouth. Trying not to let bitterness replace good-natured humor. Maximoff is balancing Ripley on his waist, and while Farrow takes earplugs out of their son's ears, I hear Maximoff say more quietly, "I just want our son to know I love you. When he sees media footage, I don't want him to think I don't care about you."

Must be why he answered the paparazzi too honestly and not jokingly. Farrow whispers something softly, his hand on the back of Maximoff's skull, and then their lips meet in a tender kiss.

A pang thumps against my chest.

I'm not a bitter guy, and I hate wading in these shitty emotions for even half-a-second.

I'm about 99% positive it's what Charlie has felt ever since Maximoff got a boyfriend. Seeing the cousin he hates receive the love he wants has caused more jealousy. But I'm not a twenty-one-year-old genius who can't control my base impulses. And I *never* want to be bitter at the sight of someone else's happiness or love. Especially a friend's.

I look around the gym.

And I just wish Charlie were next to me so Highland would be here too. I'd turn my head and see his focus behind a camera. He'd notice me and smile that hundred-watt smile, and maybe he'd even redirect his lens my way.

"Oliveira," Farrow says, snapping me out of a bad daze.

"Yeah?"

Our heads turn when Ripley drops his stuffed pirate parrot. I pick up the toy that I bought him and rattle it. "No doubt, you love Uncle Oscar the best."

Ripley hugs onto the toy with a giggle. He's a cute baby.

"Thanks," Maximoff says to me, his sincerity soulful. "You know where my brother might've left his phone?"

My brows knot. "Xander left his phone at the gym?"

Farrow explains, "After a boxing lesson this morning. I didn't want to announce that shit over comms." Yeah because Donnelly would be reamed out by the boss for that security mistake. Xander Hale is his client, and a missing phone is a heartbeat from a security leak.

Donnelly isn't usually that careless.

"I haven't seen it," I tell them, "but I'd check the lockers."

Holding Ripley, Maximoff leaves the mats and searches the wall of lockers.

Farrow sticks around me. "You okay?"

"Why wouldn't I be?"

"You tell me," he says, concern in his pierced brows.

All I've really expressed lately to Farrow is that Jack and I are better. We're cool. No more awkwardness. *Pretty true.* But I can't explain anything further without telling him Jack's not straight.

I already promised I wouldn't do that to Jack.

"I'm good," I nod a few times. "When's the *Out Loud* magazine photoshoot? I heard it's soon."

"Next week." He skims my eyes.

I hang onto a feeling I love.

Pride.

I'm proud of my best friend for agreeing to be on the cover of *Out Loud.* It took him a while to say *yes.* And now here I am, unable to talk about the guy I'm kissing and falling for.

Unable to even hug him in public.

I don't love it, but I have to be okay with it.

For me, pride is best felt embracing the people I love. And I just wish I could embrace Highland.

I'm so fucking far gone.

I don't even know what I'm doing anymore. I wish I could ask Farrow for advice. He's the "relationship guy"—the one who establishes boundaries up front before hopping into bed. He won't even sleep with someone unless there is potential for an *actual* relationship.

And look at me with this flimsy "no sex" declaration. I already jumped way past first base with the guy.

Don't beat yourself up, Oliveira.

I exhale a rougher breath.

Jack is complicated. He started off questioning. This was never going to be *simple*. And I want to believe that he's willing to be in a relationship, but it can't be easy for him to rewrite the story he envisioned for so long.

He's used to sticking to his life's script. And that's it.

"You still want to do Woody's for dinner?" Farrow asks me, thankfully not giving me a hard time even though he can tell something's up. "Donnelly said he'd meet us."

"Yeah, for sure." I'm too in my feelings, so I focus on downing the rest of the Cheeto dust, and I tell Gabe to go home.

The trainee ends the run with sweat streaming down his jaw. "Really?" he pants, out of breath. "I can go another ten."

I take it back. Tweedledum isn't so bad.

"Go home," I say again. "I'll see you again tomorrow morning." I'm squeezing in a comms lesson before the start of the day.

"Thanks, Oscar." He heads towards the showers.

"He's huge," Farrow says.

"But fast."

Farrow whistles and looks back at Gabe "No shit."

Maximoff makes a face at Farrow like he just cat-called another guy. I laugh.

"Shit," Farrow says between his teeth, but he's smiling. They're both territorial motherfuckers.

I elbow his arm. "Wanna bet that Kitsuwon's going to fight over the temp for Sulli's detail?" Akara always puts the best temps on her whenever Banks is unavailable.

"No. Because I don't want to lose a bet."

Smart, Redford.

"Found it!" Maximoff calls out, showing us his brother's phone. Ripley reaches up for the cell.

Before we leave the gym, Farrow says to me, "We have to drop off the phone, and then we're grabbing the furball before we head out to Woody's." *The furball* is their weird Newfoundland puppy. Arkham thinks a pint-sized bird is a pterodactyl.

"Sounds good." I sling my gym bag on my shoulder. "See you there."

We split apart, and I forget to ask Farrow about the ancient camcorder he gave Jack.

I end up at the cheesesteak restaurant alone and climb up the rickety wooden deck. Chipped, old red paint on a plank overhead reads *Woody's.* The place is mostly outdoors with picnic tables along the deck, and the order-at-the-counter station is inside. The mouth-watering scent of grilled meat floods my senses.

God, I'm hungry.

The downside: Woody's is packed tonight. People spill onto the street, and since I have to order first, then hunt down a table, I just wait on the deck for Farrow, Maximoff, and Donnelly.

I rest my arms on the wood railing, phone in my hand.

Alone.

I'm ignoring the few glances as people try to place my face. *Bodyguard to the famous ones. Security Force Omega hottie.*

I suddenly remember my conversation with Jack about cheesesteaks. Without much thought, I pop up his number on my phone. But I think he's in New York right now. He was shooting some footage of Charlie this afternoon.

I hesitate.

Fuck it. I text: Wanna grab an actually good cheesesteak? Meet me here. I drop him a pin of my location. My stomach twists for a solid minute. I expect him to tell me he's not in Philly, but my phone pings.

Cool. Be there in ten. — Highland

My smile hurts my face.

"Someone looks like they got dicked down real nice." Donnelly appears behind me with a lopsided grin. He fists a slender can of a Lightning Bolt! energy drink. "You wanna spill?" He leans into my shoulder to try and read the text.

I press the phone-lock fast, the screen now black. "Good dick is good."

"Poetry," Donnelly smirks.

"I am a poet these days, bro." I almost grin back, but our banter makes me miss him with me in New York.

He pulls a cigarette out from behind his ear. "You still into Jack?"

An image of the other night pops up. Where we fell asleep in each other's arms as the sun rose.

Yeah.

"I'm working on it." I pocket my phone and retie my rolled bandana. "You into anyone lately?"

He shrugs, then sips his energy drink. "A gentleman never kisses and tells."

I glance past him. "Where's the gentleman?"

Donnelly laughs. "He's one." He points to his dick. "And he's in need of some nice warm love."

"Rub harder next time."

"My hand is nothin' compared to a…" He mimes a blow job with his hand and tongue against the inside of his cheek.

A lady shoots Donnelly a scathing glare from a picnic table. "There are kids here," she sneers, a hand covering her daughter's eyes.

"Nah, really?" Donnelly lights a cigarette even with a can in his hand. "I just thought that was a mini adult."

Her aghast noise is drowned by the click-click of cameras and screech of paparazzi. "Redford's here," I say.

Though, I can't see yet. Hot sun begins to set, and I shield the shine with my hand.

But sure enough, cameramen trip over themselves as Farrow and Maximoff saunter down the sidewalk side-by-side. Donnelly and I watch as an on-duty Farrow blocks cameramen from crowding his son and husband. Ripley wiggles his legs in a tactical vest on his chest, and Maximoff is actually *carrying* Arkham. The puppy acts like a scared, furry baby.

At this point, their son braves the paparazzi better than their dog.

Donnelly and I laugh, and we rib Farrow while we try to hop in line. Too many motherfuckers are just clustered together waiting for their order to be called.

Thankfully, paparazzi aren't allowed on the deck, but we're pushed further back towards the railing while fans approach Maximoff and ask for selfies. I'm off-duty and still surveying the area.

It's a good habit. Considering a famous one is in our company.

We stand in a jagged ass line, and we could shoulder our way further in, but doing that would piss off too many people and stoke bad press.

"Is that Jack Highland?" Donnelly asks, bouncing on his feet.

Nearly in unison, our heads turn, and we all gaze over the deck railing.

Jack's—kid, you not—longboarding down the sidewalk like he's back on the west coast. His biceps look even more sculpted in a blue-and-green tie-dye tank. Not in a million years did I think I'd fall for some California guy.

A smile lifts my lips. "Yeah, I invited him," I say and leave it at that.

Farrow nods and begins to grin. "You're hopeless."

"I'd like a six-pack of the best beer when my heart breaks."

"Nice try, one beer. Warm. Not even chilled."

I laugh, and looking down to the street, I stare at my guy.

"How's it going, beautiful people?" Jack calls up to us from the curb.

Better now that you're here. Maybe my eyes reflect that. His smile looks more overwhelmed, and he has to shift his gaze.

"Pretty good," Maximoff calls back. "It's nice seeing you, man."

Understatement.

"You too, Moffy." Jack grabs the long skateboard off the ground and begins squeezing through the crowded stairs.

"Thought you didn't want us calling you *Moffy* as a nickname?" Donnelly questions.

Farrow raises his brows at Maximoff.

"Jack is different," he explains, leash in hand. He already put Arkham down, and the puppy drinks from a communal water bowl. Dogs allowed here.

I chime in, "Meaning, Jack is production." I almost add, *I'd give him special privileges too.* My eyes never leave Highland as he pushes through the masses, coming onto the deck.

He reaches us, and I have to restrain myself from greeting him with a hug. A kiss. Especially as his glittering honey-brown eyes graze over mine, and his lips rise in an even stronger smile.

"You're just waiting?" Jack asks everyone.

"And dreaming of a wiz steak with onions." Donnelly sips Lightning Bolt! from the same hand that has his cigarette pinched between his fingers. "Been wondering why we're here, though. Better ones are in South Philly."

Jack glows, his grin blinding. "Someone told me they're better here."

"Who?" Donnelly barks.

"Me."

Donnelly shoots me a look and then points to me with his can/ cigarette hand. "Sustained."

Farrow and I share a look. "What the fuck," I say into a laugh.

"When did Donnelly go to law school?" Farrow banters, his smile stretching. "Not a good one either."

Donnelly blows a middle-finger kiss. "Xander's been watching a bunch of Law & Order."

We move up the line and pass through the opened double-doors. The counter and overhang menu come into view.

My arm brushes against Jack's, and his fingers slip lightly along mine. I'm caging breath, and he's breathing hard. The story of our lives.

Donnelly suddenly pats his pockets. "You know what. I'm not that hungry. Later." He pats Farrow's back and my back, then shoulders his way *out* of the restaurant. It happens so quickly—I'm still trying to detach from Jack Highland's mesmeric aura.

"What the hell was that?" Farrow asks me.

"He didn't have money," I realize. "Fuck."

We all start heading backwards through the opened doors, and instinctively, I reach and clasp Jack's hand. So he'll follow.

We're not a couple.

I drop it immediately.

He's not even out.

Fuckfuckfuck.

Our eyes catch, and apologies ring in mine.

He mouths, *it's alright.* And he pushes my back lightly, encouraging me to keep chasing after my friend.

Okay.

Okay.

Outside on the deck, I quickly see two exits: the stairs or the railing. The stairs are jam-packed, and so without stopping, I hurdle the railing and land softly on the sidewalk below.

Farrow has to take the stairs, strapped with a baby and on-duty.

I survey the congested street and squint in the setting sun. Rush-hour traffic, cars honk loudly, and there's no fucking sign of Donnelly.

I even jog down the sidewalk and glance along the alleyways.

Pulse thrashed, I pull out my cell and speed-dial his number. Pressing it to my ear, I growl out, "Pick up, you motherfucker."

Farrow, Maximoff, and Jack reach the curb where I'm walking and redialing my friend.

"No answer?" Farrow asks.

"He's in trouble, bro."

Farrow combs a hand through his bleach-white hair. "I don't know how to fucking help if he keeps pushing us away."

I don't either.

It scares me.

Jack drops his longboard and kicks off next to me. "Could he have just forgotten his wallet?"

"He would've asked us to cover him," I say as we reroute and walk back to Woody's. "This has to be about what he did..." I trail off. Everyone's eyes fall to Ripley against Farrow's chest.

We lower our voices and stop on the curb as paparazzi sprint toward us.

"If he's giving Scottie money in prison," Maximoff says, "I can pay Donnelly back—"

"He won't accept it, Hale. We're all a bunch of prideful idiots." Farrow wipes a hand down the side of his face. "Shit."

Yeah.

Shit.

We can't do anything. Our friend is going to continue down whatever path he's carved out for himself.

"Chances are he's headed back to his apartment," I tell them, shoving my phone in my pocket.

Farrow nods. "Let's grab food, and I'll bring him back a cheesesteak."

"Sounds like a plan."

Paparazzi follow Maximoff and Farrow as they head towards the wooden stairs and crowds. Strung multi-colored bulbs suddenly switch-on along Woody's deck, the sun nearly disappeared.

I can't help but focus on how Maximoff wraps an arm around his husband's shoulders. How they cave into one another and talk quietly.

A pang returns to my chest.

"You okay?" Jack rolls up beside me. Stepping off the longboard, he keeps a foot on the top so it won't slide down the sidewalk.

I glance back one more time at my best friend. His husband. Baby. And puppy.

I shouldn't feel *alone* with Jack standing right here. But air separates us. Distance. An unbearable ache that we're both struggling to close.

As soon as I look back at Highland, I realize he's not bright and sunny. He shifts, takes a sharp breath, a hand resting on his tensed neck.

"Are you?" I ask him.

He goes to speak but chokes on a word.

Be with me.

I shut my eyes tightly. He is with me, and I can't pressure him for more. When I open my eyes, the torment in his gaze is exactly what I feel. We're in the same ball-pit of anguish. Flailing around.

He inhales a big breath.

As he exhales, he asks, "Can you promise me something, Os?"

"Anything."

"Anything?"

I nod, confident that I'd do just about *anything* in the world for Jack motherfucking Highland.

His soft laugh sounds breathless. "Okay, promise me that whatever happens next, you won't shut the window on me. Promise that it's wide open and I'm on the other side with you—that it's you and me and anyone who tries to come in, you'll help me keep out?"

Emotion pricks my eyes.

Strongly, undoubtedly, I tell him, "I promise. It's Oscar and Jack take on Philly, New York, California, the world—you and me, Long Beach." I point from my chest to his chest, tears threatening to well.

One already slides down his jaw.

He suddenly, mightily, resoundingly bridges the gap—and his lips are on mine. Time freezes. The world recedes, and we clasp each other's face and kiss and *kiss* with soul-bearing passion. Hanging on. Like we're spinning on an axis and headed for the sky.

Agony vanishes. And a feeling I've met once or twice in my life washes over me more powerfully than ever before.

Our foreheads touch as our lips break, arms around one another's shoulders, and we're not escaping our embrace yet. He's smiling brighter. I'm grinning stronger. My heart beats outside my ribcage, and I breathe, "You just kissed me in public, Highland."

In the middle of a sidewalk.

In front of a packed cheesesteak restaurant.

In front of my friends.

In front of paparazzi.

He kissed me.

"You kissed me back," he says in a smile, as if that'd even be a doubt. "So we can officially say that we're dating, right?"

I'm so fucking happy.

"Come on, dude," he breathes, his eyes sparkling with the light that I feel illuminate inside me.

"Oh yeah, I'm dating the hell out of you."

His heart thumps fast against my chest. I must glance down because he laughs, "You feel that?" His hand rises into my curls.

I nod. I can't tell if Jack is scared or nervous or… "You regret—?"

"No," he cuts me off quickly. "I've never wanted something this badly in my life, Oscar, and I've wanted a lot. I've gotten a lot. I just haven't had you."

I made a promise, and I'm a hundred-percent committed. Window wide open for him. "You have me now," I murmur strongly, and we're about to bring our lips together again when something sails at us—too late to see or catch.

A cold, wet liquid splashes my cheek.

Jack…Jack's covered in strawberry milkshake. Pink liquid drenches his hair and drips down his temple, his jaw, stains his tie-dye tank and soaks the longboard at his feet.

I shield Highland, swiftly stepping out in front, keeping a protective hand on his chest. I'm not tensing up, not solidifying—too conditioned to stay alert in mayhem, to not freeze in shock. But *bodyguard instinct*—where was that when he got hit with a fucking *milkshake*? How did I let that happen?

I drill a harsh glare at the crowd of cameramen, fans, hecklers, and just baffled people trying to order a fucking cheesesteak.

"Homewrecker!" a teenage girl, no older than thirteen, yells behind gathering tears. Her finger is pointed at *Jack*. A Woody's cup in her grip, remnants of strawberry milkshake drizzling out.

My head is whirling. My eyes are narrowing. Blood is boiling.

"Oliveira!" Farrow calls, pushing closer with Maximoff to help defend Jack.

No. Not good. As much as I love Farrow, he comes with paparazzi, and tactically, I need to get Highland out of here before another teenager chucks their milkshake at him.

"Redford!" I shout back and raise my arm high, then point down the street.

He understands, and he takes off with his family in the other direction. Paparazzi always trail after the most famous people in the room. In this case, on the street. And every cameraman races after Maximoff's heels.

Leaving us with this.

"You're a HOMEWRECKER!" the girl screams the word with every fiber of her being and shrieks a shrill decibel that twitches my face.

Her friend films on a cellphone, also in tears. "Oscar is with Charlie Cobalt! What are you doing with him?!"

The moment the milkshake girl's hatred aimed solely on Jack, I figured out where their emotions stemmed from.

Oslie.

Oscar + Charlie.

The bane of my fucking love life. And their deep attachment to Charlie Cobalt is now coming at Jack's expense.

Highland grabs his soaked longboard, and I catch his hand in mine.

"Let go of him!" the milkshake girl cries. "You're hurting Oscar!"

I thought I was largely desensitized to emotional outbursts, but this one is kicking my frustrated ass into *rage* territory. "*I'm* holding his hand," I growl hotly. "Charlie is my client. We're not together!"

"Stop lying!" she cries.

I'm not lying!

I make an aggravated noise through my clenched teeth.

Jack fists the back of my shirt, pulling me away.

She tosses the empty cup at him, and I smack it aside. "Back off!"

"What did you just tell my daughter?" Her mom emerges from the restaurant with a to-go container. She pushes the girl behind her back. "You're grown men. You should know better than to be talking to a thirteen-year-old in the middle of the night on the *street.*"

I hear Donnelly in my head. *Miss, we're on the sidewalk.*

He'd make it worse, but fuck I miss the laugh.

"I'm not trying to fight with a teenager," I tell her. "And I'm also not the one who threw a milkshake on another person."

Her eyes ping down to her daughter. "Claire?"

That's my exit.

I spin around and walk alongside Jack towards…? "Did you park around here?" I ask.

"Yeah, two blocks down." He tries to mop up the milkshake with his dirtied tank.

"Here." I grip the back of my tee and pull the fabric over my head. I toss him the shirt. "You take all my clothes anyway, Highland."

His lips rise. "You might not see this one again." He wipes off pink liquid from his hair. "It's a Summer Fest tee, right?" He inspects the festival logo while I study his reaction to *everything* that just happened.

Jack…Highland…

He senses my silence as we walk. "What's wrong?"

His plea to me. Before the kiss. He said, *it's you and me and anyone who tries to come in, you'll help me keep out?*

You'll help me *keep out.*

"You knew," I realize. "You knew that if we kissed in public, in front of cameras, you weren't just coming out. You knew you'd be confronting the Oslie rumors. You knew you'd be 'the other man' to Oscar + Charlie."

Jack smiles softly. "Understanding public perception is part of my job. And the types of fans who pair you and Charlie are intense. So yeah…I had a good hunch it'd all blow up in my face."

"And still, you kissed me?" He knew the cost of being with me was astronomically high, and I had no clue.

We stop next to a Mazda parked on the street.

He breathes in. "I would've regretted *not* kissing you. Like I've regretted rejecting you in Anacapri." He swallows hard, rests a hand on his head. "Not to beat around the bush, I'm scared."

His fast heartrate. The one I felt after we just kissed in public. It wasn't regret. It was fear. "About what?" I hold his longboard for him.

"Of having millions of enemies," Jack says with reddened eyes, digging in his pocket for car keys. "It overwhelms me when I consider the hatred I've seen and filmed for so long is about to be directed at me."

It's crushing me knowing he's probably right. He's about to face a tidal wave of negativity. And what can I do?

"I'm trained for this. I'm going to protect you the absolute best I can." *I'm in for the long-haul, Highland.* We edge closer, our legs threading as we hug. I press a kiss to his temple, tasting a hint of strawberry.

His fingers stay in mine for another minute before he lets go and unlocks his car. "Coming out tonight actually makes me feel better. Because at least *that* fear is largely gone…and I'm not in this alone."

He has me.

Undoubtedly.

I nod, my mouth curving up. "I'm proud of you."

Highland smiles, a more emotional one, and we hug again, this one tighter and longer.

When we break apart, he asks me, "Where'd you park? I can drop you off at your car. I'll be at your place tomorrow morning, and we can start early." He means for the show.

Work might be his distraction technique from emotional bombs.

"The other direction." I point back towards Woody's and stare at his hair, matted with dried milkshake. "Let me drive you home. I'll get my sister to come pick up my car." I'll owe Joana one, or twenty, for the favor, but it'll be worth it.

I just don't want Jack to be alone tonight.

"Another second with Oscar Oliveira—why not?" He smiles and tosses me the keys, and when I climb into the driver's seat, I realize I actually have regrets about how this all went down.

I wish I screamed louder and harder back at Woody's that I don't like Charlie. I wish I yelled that I like Jack.

I'm dating Jack Highland.

I'm with Jack Highland.

Every phrase in every dictionary that means, *he's it for me.*

22

Jack Highland

THE HUM OF THE CAR'S air conditioning is a familiar, pleasant sound. Back when I lived in SoCal, the sun would beat down on my Mazda, and sometimes I'd just shut off the music as I sat in bumper-to-bumper traffic on the PCH. Windows rolled down. Fresh wind off the coast cooling me as much as the air from the vents.

Being in my car tonight is a little different. No ocean in view. City noises surround me as Philly twinkles in the early night. Honking. Shouting as people smoke outside bars and gather with friends. And my phone is a mess of texts from people I haven't even spoken to in years.

> Hey, man! Long time no chat, just saw the news! You're really with Charlie's bodyguard?

> Congrats on the new beau! Is it true???

> I had no clue you're into guys. Good for you, dude.

> Didn't know you were gay. Why didn't you tell me?

And then my little brother…

> KUYA! Wtf?!? — Utoy

He's tried to FaceTime and call *fourteen* times, and I already texted: I promise I'll call. Just give me a sec. Love you.

With sticky milkshake coating my skin, my tank suctioning awkwardly to my chest, I shift tensely in the passenger seat and keep scrolling through social media. Who is Jack Highland? has been trending, along with #homerwrecker and #OslieSurvives

I replay a video on mute of my kiss with Oscar outside the cheesesteak restaurant. Our strong hands are on each other's face, our builds fused together, our grip tightening in urgent yearning, and our lips beckon the other one closer—a powerful breath floods me.

That feeling is why I decided to catapult my life in the air with no idea where it'll land. That feeling with him would be too devastating to lose.

He's what I cling to as everything else *spirals*. My parents—God, my parents are calling me for the fifth time, and I let it ring out and text: I'll call later. Everything's okay.

My phone pings.

Is this a publicity stunt? — Dad

Ouch.

I rock back with a heavy breath.

"You alright?" Oscar asks, glancing at me for the umpteenth time. His clutch strengthens on the steering wheel. Like if I asked him to go anywhere, he'd whip the car and reroute in a millisecond.

"My dad just asked if the kiss was a publicity stunt." I unsnap my seatbelt. Too uncomfortable, I pull the milkshake-soaked tank off my body. "I can't fault him for going there—even though, I'd like to believe he'd think better of me. That I'm not the kind of person who'd *pretend* to be into dudes as a PR ploy. But he's not in my head. We all have different perspectives."

"My perspective isn't as accommodating as yours, bro." His glare blazes the road, then the rearview mirror. "That's shitty of your dad to text you that. He could've led with anything else."

"He's not that bad," I say, but I smile at how Oscar is defending me. Wadding up the dirtied tank, I throw the thing in the backseat where my longboard rests and reply to my dad.

I text: not a stunt. I'm dating Oscar. I'll call you & mama later.

Oscar switches lanes. "I'll try not to judge too harshly until I meet him."

Meeting the parents. I buckle my seatbelt.

Will they like Oscar? He's a Yale grad, but he's a *bodyguard.* Predictably, my dad will ask me, *what's his goal in life? What is he striving towards?*

I'm not sure "protecting a celebrity" is going to cut it.

My dad served in the Navy. He could've gone into a private security sector later on, but he chose a more lucrative career. High risk, high reward.

Oscar's job is high risk, no reward. I respect that, but I can't foresee whether they will.

Stressed out, I roll my linebacker-like shoulders, stretch my arms up and then extend one over Oscar's headrest.

"Is your body sore?" Oscar asks, considering I've been hoisting heavy equipment.

"I'm stressed out, man," I confess.

I catch myself off guard whenever I say *man.* I said "dude" a lot more when I lived in California, and it reminds me I've been in Philly since I was eighteen.

Fuck…almost *ten* years.

Where has time gone?

Chasing a dream. Searching for higher ground. That thought reminds me of a song, of music, and I almost fiddle with the radio.

Oscar's concern is on me. "Meu raio de sol, let me give you some positive affirmations."

What'd he call me in Portuguese? My lips rise and I look him over. "Isn't positive affirmation-giving my job?"

"I don't just dig for compliments, Long Beach. I know how to give them."

I smile more. He's boosted me up far higher than anyone ever has. "That's true." I keep my arm over the headrest.

"Ready?" he asks.

"Yeah."

He catches my eyes for a beat. "Your phone might be on diarrhea-mode right now, but it's fleeting. And this stressful moment in time will pass."

I like that one.

Inhale. Exhale.

I breathe out and try not to look at my phone that's definitely taking steaming piles of shit.

"How was that?" Oscar wonders.

"You're a solid A+ in my book."

"Appreciate the praise." Oscar slides me a serious look. "But I really meant, *how are you now?*"

I nod a couple times. "Adjusting better."

I'm dreading the moment where we arrive at my apartment. Not because I have to see Jesse, but because I'll be saying goodbye to Oscar. He's my central core of comfort right now, and to leave that behind sounds agonizing.

"You know what'd be better?" I say with the start of a soft smile.

"Food."

I laugh. We left Woody's without ordering cheesesteaks. "Yeah, and it'd be even better if you spent the night with me." I feel smooth in my come-on, despite the stress of tonight. Which I delight in since I've been more rattled around Oscar lately.

"I wish I could…" His voice is strained, lips downturned, and his deep-brown eyes return to the road.

My pulse plummets. Fuck.

"Charlie's temp told me he's back home," Oscar explains fast. "It's early for him, which means he'll probably be awake at the crack of dawn. I need to be in New York."

No lie. That hurts a little.

I swallow down a lump in my throat and press my skull to the headrest. Right as I drop my arm off his seat, he tells me, "Come stay at my place tonight."

My head lazily rolls to the side to meet his eyes. He glances from me to the road, then to me with apprehension. I start to smile.

He sees it. "That a yes?"

"Yeah," I say. "That's a yeah."

He matches my grin. "Good." He takes a hand off the wheel just to clasp mine. I thread our fingers, and his chest rises. He adds, "I'll stop by The Walnut so you can grab your things at your apartment."

"No need." I have to let go of his hand as I rotate, the seatbelt cinching over my bare chest. I wrench my backpack from the backseat and drop it on my lap. "I have everything right here. Even a toothbrush and a suit. I heard around town that Oscar Oliveira gives good advice, so I thought I'd listen."

"Sounds like I'm dating a smart guy." He checks his rearview as an SUV rides our ass. "And I'm legitimately surprised you packed clothes."

I thought about purposefully forgetting just to steal yours. "I surprised myself too," I smile, but as I shove the backpack to the ground, pressure that I haven't felt in a while sits on my chest.

"You have that look again," Oscar says, worry hardening his face. "What's bothering you, bro?"

I rake both hands through my hair, leaving them on my head and leaning back. "I really haven't given a lot of thought to *what* I'm supposed to tell my family or the public." I clarify, "About my sexuality. And I honestly haven't had time to mull over a label. People are going to ask what I identify as, and I don't have an answer."

"Just say that."

"Without one, I'm afraid I'll keep getting asked, *are you sure?* over and over. Or people will think it's a phase."

"They could think that even if you say you're bi," Oscar tells me.

I nod. *Also true.* "You know, if I really sat down with my feelings for longer than a few minutes, I think I'd know that I'm attracted to people. Flat-out. No matter the sex or gender. It's probably always been like that, but I cut myself off to anything outside of my narrowed frame of what I thought my life *would* look like." I let my hands fall to my thighs, expelling a breath. "I'm trying to hold onto what you told me about my sexuality having nothing to do with where I've been or what I've done. It's just who I'm attracted to. But sometimes I feel like if I call myself pansexual, I'd just be a fraud. Like I don't serve the label well enough. I'm twenty-seven. I'm too late to the party."

Oscar's face breaks. "You aren't too late. Do what you feel without letting judgment cast you aside. So whatever label you choose—or don't choose, you don't have to have one—don't let anyone take that from you. Live your truth. And if someone tries to check you on it, I'm going to check them back in the fucking mouth." His grip tightens on the wheel, veins spindling in his biceps.

I can't look away from him. He's hot as hell when he's defending me. "You're Team Jack Highland?"

"Let's put it this way—whatever president was sitting at the top of the Jack Highland fan club has been dethroned by me."

My heart swells. "What a coincidence. The Oscar Oliveira fan club president was usurped by me."

We're both grinning.

I roll down the window. Letting the summer night rush into the car, and I expel another deep breath, pocketing my phone for right now.

Oscar notices. "Is there something that helps you stay on the bright side?" He must be concerned about me since the onslaught of negativity is just beginning.

"Confidence, breathing, sometimes surfing."

"And when that fails?"

I stare at the cord to my car's entertainment system. Plugging in my phone, I tap into Spotify. "Blaring music." I pause before clicking into the song. "I'm about to be *painfully* California, but this is my dad's favorite band and I grew up listening to them."

"They're your favorite too?" he asks, not knowing who it is yet.

"I know basically every lyric to every song, and they have over ten albums."

"So that's a *fuck yes*," Oscar laughs. "Play it, Highland."

I put on *"Higher Ground"* by Red Hot Chili Peppers, originally sung by Stevie Wonder, and I immediately start singing the lyrics and bobbing my head to the beat.

Oscar surprisingly joins me. He knows the chorus, and with an arm out the window, I tap my hand to the hood of the car.

We sing to each other, and I thought I had a good voice, one that melts like butter on a hot day. But Oscar sings the fuck out of this song. His voice is deeper and richer and smoother, belonging in the air like a current of wind.

And his hand slips back into mine. We coast and sing, and I let his affection and the melodies calm the outside noise that fights its way in.

Don't let it in.

"DID I SAY OR DO SOMETHING TO WHERE YOU thought you couldn't tell me?" Jesse wonders, his face shadowed in the dark over FaceTime. I can barely tell he's in bed, head on a pillow.

Oscar just left to pick up take-out and give me some time to call my family. So I cup my phone, sitting on a kitchen barstool with a towel around my waist. Thanks to a hot shower, I no longer smell like strawberries and cream.

"It wasn't you; it was me, Jess," I explain. "I've been confused, and I wasn't ready to tell anyone until now." Quickly, I add, "And before you ask, I'm still attracted to women. I feel like gender and sex aren't really factors in who I'm romantically or sexually attracted to at all."

"Okay, okay." Jesse lets this sink in, his grin erupting. "I mean, as far as people go, you really landed an ace in the set. Oscar is sick. At least, from what I know while I've been on this project with you. He boxes, protects celebrities, speaks multiple languages, cracks funny jokes—ah wait, question." Jesse sits up for this one, and I relax forward, happy my brother is cool with the news. "So are you giving or receiving, Kuya?"

My face feels hot. This is all so new. Including this question from my brother. "I'll let you know when I've figured it out. Only if you don't mind me asking you the same questions."

Jesse smiles. "That's totally fair. I have a more important question. The *most* important question."

I stiffen. Don't know where this one's going.

"Does he surf?"

My lip quirks. "Not that I know of."

"When are you going to teach him? We should go to the beach tomorrow. Jesus, *Kuya*, does he even know the difference between a paddleboard and a longboard?" He goes off on a tangent and I listen with a laugh. I only stop Jesse when he begins to plan a surfing trip to New Jersey tomorrow morning.

"Postpone that, wild child. We have *jobs*."

He sighs. "Shit, the dreaded J.O.B." He grows quieter, then asks, "So how long have you and Oscar been dating?"

Officially? Today. Though, I've been skirting around my feelings for years.

I end up telling him, "Not that long. It's new."

"I like new." His encouragement means a lot, and I express that, then tell him he has the apartment to himself tonight. Now he's *really* amped on me dating Oscar because he has more room.

"No parties," I decree.

"Who would I invite, Kuya? My only friends in Philly are my surfboard and laptop."

"I thought you exchanged numbers with Winona after the Fun Run?"

"I thought so too, but she gave me the number to some Wildlife Conservation fund." He lies back down, not expressing much defeat in that rejection.

We talk more about shoots for the *Born into Fame* docuseries before we say our goodbyes. "Talk later, Kuya," he says before the screen goes black.

Now for the harder call.

I phone my dad, and FaceTime pops up. Bottles of red wine in wooden slots fill the screen. *My parent's wine cellar.* "Dad, flip to front-facing camera."

"Dammit, sorry." He swears casually often. Once the camera flips, I'm staring at a sun-tanned face that could grace classic western movies. But he can't act for shit. He warned me too, and still, I asked him for help on an amateur film project about skateboarding.

He sounded like a robot.

And he almost broke his ass on cement after trying to ollie.

I love him a lot.

"I was just grabbing a 1934 Merlot." Creases line his forehead. Only a few grays in his brown hair—he was young when I was born. "So…? You're okay with the press? You're safe there?"

I nod. "Yeah. Is Mama around too?" I'd rather talk to them both at the same time.

"She went to bed, but I'll let her know what's going on. She's very proud, you know. She wants to meet him." He inspects the label of the Merlot.

"What about you?"

He sets the bottle down. He offers a lot of supportive words of me being with a man, as much as I expected. He says he loves me, and then the questions arrive.

When did you know you liked guys? Are you bisexual? What's Oscar like? Is he good to you?

I answer honestly to each one.

And then he asks, "What's his goals? He doesn't want to be a bodyguard forever, right?"

"I think so."

He makes a *hmm* noise.

"It's a good profession."

"No it's not. I have a friend in private security, and it pays nothing. It's fucking dangerous. Plus, his back will be shot by fifty."

"My back will be shot before then."

"*You* need to stop doing camerawork. Take care of your body now before you become old like me." He pauses for a second. The air strains like he's thinking back to the serious topics.

"What's wrong?" I ask.

"I'll be honest, it's taking me a longer time—longer than your mama—to get used to the idea of you with a guy. I keep thinking that if you marry a man, I'm going to have a *son*-in-law." He lets out a breath. "Just never pictured that."

My muscles tighten, even though I knew this might be coming. That future picture. The one so vividly painted. "I get it," I say, but my heartbeat pounds loud in my ears. "But just think it's just as good of a picture because it's what I want. And I'd be happy in it."

His smile is warm. "I know that. Whatever you choose, you know I'll be happy for you, too."

I nod, and I do believe that.

He doesn't press about Oscar as we talk more. He hikes out of the wine cellar and ends up on the private dock, his boat rocking with glittering water in Naples Canal.

Seeing my childhood house makes me miss Long Beach.

After I finish the calls, Oscar comes back about ten minutes later. I catch him up and leave out the part where my dad hates his career choice.

We eat New York cheesesteaks which Oscar said aren't like Philly's. And then we end up in his bed together. We both crash, falling into hard sleep with our legs and arms tangled.

I'm not sure I would've been able to fall asleep that well without him. The weight of his limbs, the warmth of his body, the beat of his heart—it's music quelling my fears.

I wake before him.

And I skulk down the loft's stairs to the kitchen. I left my phone plugged in on the bar counter, and my head whirls at all the missed texts.

I read them while I make breakfast. Warming a frying pan, I untwist a bag of pandesal and cut a soft roll in half. I brought the bread in my backpack for Oscar to try. Did not think I'd be toasting pandesal while my life is imploding.

Jesus, shit, these emails.

The other exec producers on *We Are Calloway* are asking me about my relationship with a bodyguard, and whether that will affect the integrity of the docuseries.

It's fine.

It's fine.

I can charm my way through this one. I click into texts. Ali said her and Ambrose have my back if the other execs ask questions.

Ambrose texted, welcome to the fam.

My lips rise, and while I place the bread on the pan, I click on a group chat thread with Jane, Maximoff, and Sulli.

We love you & support you 100%!! If we can do anything to curb the bad press, let us know. — Jane

Here for u. Whatever u need. Call us and we'll be there — Moffy

So sorry this is fucking happening to you. Swim & donuts one day you're free? — Sulli

I reread those ones.

For years, I've been there for Moffy and Jane when they needed a friend or a helping hand in a crisis, more recently Sulli too. They understand the heat of the spotlight and punch-to-the-gut rumors. I've been with them during too many, and really, I've never been in a position where I needed them just as severely.

I do now, I realize.

Feeling lighter, I text back: I might need to chat. I'll call you when I'm free. Thanks xo.

And out of habit, I open social media notifications, tweets sent to me. Pressure returns, pulse ramping.

You're a homewrecker

Why couldn't you leave Charlie and Oscar alone

Oslie was perfect until you

What's wrong with you?

Fuck you, Jack Highland, you no name loser

You're irrelevant for a reason. Go away

"What's burning?" Oscar races down the loft stairs.

"Shit," I curse, spinning around to the blackened pandesal on the frying pan. I shut the burner, and Oscar wafts the smoke with a towel. I shake my frazzled head. "Sorry, I have more." I grab the bread bag.

Oscar isn't blinking. He stares at the bread, then to me.

"It's Filipino bread."

"You were making me toast?" He says it like I got down on a knee.

I smile. "Yeah, it's likely the only thing I cook well." I chuck the burnt bun in the trash. "Usually."

He nods slowly and rubs a hand at the back of his neck. Orange halos shine on the wall as the sun begins to rise. "Can I help?"

"I got it. You paid for dinner last night." I cut another piece of pandesal. "Akara texted me."

Oscar grabs protein powder and a bottle. "Me too. He said, *congrats. Good choice in bros.* He knew you were a frat bro, didn't he?"

I laugh. "Yeah. He's met some of my frat brothers."

Oscar shakes his water bottle with mix. "Where was I?"

"Working or flirting with me." I eye his washboard abs, and our arms begin to slide around each other's cut waists when a loud noise emits from my phone.

"Can I look?" Oscar asks me.

"Have at it."

He checks the notifications. His glare goes from a low simmer to angry boil, but he tries to rationalize the future. "I'm not with Charlie.

It's a fucking lie. They can't believe it for long. I'm just a bodyguard—I'm not even that famous."

I plate the hot pandesal. "It's so much easier creating perception than to change it, Os. When people believe a lie, they will cling to it with all their fucking might. You know why?" I turn to him, wiping my hands on my sweatpants. "Because if they admit it was a lie, it means they were wrong." I laugh bitterly. "People don't want to be wrong."

My phone lets out another angry buzz in his hand and he powers it off and slides it across the counter. "Yeah, well, they're all fucking WRONG!" He yells at the phone.

I just start laughing.

His lips lift. "Stop," he tells me. "Because I really need to scream at these motherfuckers, and I can't do it on the job."

"No, I needed that." I wave him on. "You look hot when you're angry and trying to defend me."

His lips hoist. "I'm always hot, Highland." He walks over and puts his hands on my cheeks. "Being with me is complicated."

My pulse ricochets every which way. "Do not shut the window—"

"I'm not," he forces

"You sure?"

"For sure," Oscar says strongly. "Just giving you the opportunity to crawl back out of my open window." He swallows harder, choked at the thought. "You can still back out. This is day one. You're not in that deep."

I laugh like he has no idea. "Yeah I am." My feelings...can't walk away from those. And he's the safe place right now. He must see this answer in my gaze that sinks into him.

Something heady passes between us, and Oscar presses a kiss against my lips, one that brings our bodies so much closer. My nerve-endings prick—and then we're cut off by a new noise.

His phone buzzes, and when he peeks at the caller ID, his concern jacks up. Switching on speaker-phone, the first thing I hear is a fire alarm and the muffled sound of Charlie's voice.

23

Oscar Oliveira

"I CAN'T HEAR YOU, Charlie!" I yell at my cell. He hangs up. Jack and I don't even put shirts on before we're down the hall in a flash.

Gold *2166* number on the door, I bang hard. *Just what we need this morning.* Surliness is a look that I wear pretty fucking well from time to time.

Catastrophes are commonplace among the Cobalts, but I wasn't looking forward to one so soon after a media shit storm rained down on Jack.

And he made me toast.

Alright, the guy *burned* the toast first, but damn if that didn't get to me more. Jack isn't a flawless person, and I had this idea of the perfect guy who'd be obsessed with the Phillies, cook a perfect breakfast, and never attend a frat in his life.

Who I thought I'd end up with has been swept aside to leave a more beautiful reality of the man I'm falling for.

And now that we're officially dating, I'm dying to give my all to Jack. For the fucking crap he's getting online, he deserves my attention, effort, and protection. It feels like Day 1 together, the start of something more serious, and look at me now, leaving the guy behind.

Not entirely true, Oliveira.

Highland is right next to me. Jack knocks on the door too, his shoulders straightened with the same urgency and concern. He loves these families. He has a little brother. *He understands.*

Thoughts zip out fast as Charlie swings the door open. Blocking me from entering, he slides out and shuts the door behind his back. "I have it handled," he says. "But we have a problem."

"You have that handled?" I wave towards his apartment. "What's with the fire alarm?"

"There's smoke," he says like it's obvious.

No *duh,* Sherlock. I want to draw a big red circle around a glaring fact: WE JUST HAD A TOWNHOUSE BURN DOWN.

Smoke = fire = let me the fuck in. I'm not about to slip past this.

"*Charlie*, please let me in." Typically, he'll bar me from helping with the aftermath of debauchery in his place.

"You're not coming inside."

"Why?" Jack asks, resting a hand on the doorframe above Charlie's head. His athletic body flexes with the stance. *Jack Highland,* everyone. Doesn't matter if we're in a flirt-ationship, non-friendship, or actual relationship—he's a distraction with a giant D.

I tear my eyes off him.

Charlie is looking right at me "Oscar knows why."

"I get it," I say, not missing a beat. "You don't want me to clean your messes. You think this isn't a part of my security duties—"

"It's not. You shouldn't have to sweep up glass—"

"There's glass?" Jack frowns.

I'm so close to barging in like this destructive American god is my baby bro.

"Minimal glass," Charlie emphasizes. "Not as much as before."

As before.

Wasn't allowed in for that one.

Jack reasons, "What if we just check it out and see if we can help? If we can't, you won't even know we've been here." His tactic: trying to gain permission inside by staying friendly.

Like hell that'll work with my client, but I commend Highland for the effort.

"No," Charlie says like an endnote.

"Look, we're here, Charlie," I say more forcefully. "No one else is but me and Jack." *And we care.* "So *please* let us in. Would you really rather deal with a fucking apartment fire on your own?"

He hesitates one more second.

"I'm offering, bro. Take it."

With a sigh, he pushes the door wider. "Be my guest."

Jack and I share a cautious look before we follow him inside. Vaulted ceilings, dark woods, leather, and industrial lighting—the apartment is a lot like my studio down the hall.

Just bigger.

A luxury bachelor pad that must've been on fire.

Smoke sputters from a couch, the armrest singed, and a single gust plumes towards the fire alarm. Knives are stuck in the walls, and someone played darts with a Van Gogh, the painting tilted and torn. Shards of glass litter the floorboards under the broken frame.

Pewter goblets scatter the kitchen counter, red liquid dried on leather barstools, the aftermath of some party last night I'm sure.

A party.

The single word slowly simmers my blood. What's *actually* in my job description: vet all guests in a house party.

It'd be nice to even know about the party. But I wasn't even given that. *No one told me.* Charlie had a temp on his detail yesterday, so that info should've been passed from his temp guard to me.

Didn't happen.

Better yet, though, Eliot, Tom, and Beckett's bodyguards could've called me up, texted, slid a motherfucking note under my door to alert me that there was a party here.

I'm literally down the hall from Epsilon's apartment where the Wreath brothers and O'Malley live. So the further I stride into Charlie's place, the angrier I start getting, but then I catch Jack's dazzling eyes in a quick glance and his lip quirks.

I begin to grin back.

Can't believe I'm fucking grinning right now. He has the power to vanquish my surly ass mood. And Jack Highland isn't fazed by the mischief of the Cobalt Empire.

Even as we walk into the aftermath. Tom Cobalt is perched on a shirtless six-foot-four Eliot Cobalt's shoulders and unscrews the fire alarm from the ceiling.

"Oscar," Eliot says with a nod. "Did Charlie tell you?"

I'm on guard, my eyes pinging to the windows. To the doors to their bedrooms. Entrances, exits.

"I was about to." Charlie rubs his temple and cinches his eyes closed as the fire alarm continues to wail. "For the love of God, shut the thing off."

The noise dies.

"Got it," Tom says.

Charlie looks to me. "My brothers threw a party last night and didn't think to tell their guests to stay out of my fucking room." He shoots Eliot a glare.

"I did tell them," Eliot rebuts, helping Tom off his shoulders. "Your door was locked, Charlie. How was I supposed to know he could pick locks?"

"I don't know," Charlie says dryly. "Because people lie, Eliot. You could've let your bodyguards into the party to keep an eye on the guests."

That idea—I like. "Did your temp know there was a party?" I ask Charlie.

"No. He dropped me off here and left before it started."

I shake my head. "You didn't think to text me about it?"

His yellow-greens pierce me. "I did *actually* think about it, but you had your hands full last night." He glances at Jack. "Congratulations. You were trending for a solid hour there. Homewrecker Highland." His sardonic tone is noted. He skims a hand through his hair, messing the strands. "I hate people."

"They could be calling me a lot worse, you know," Jack says. "Homewrecker Highland has a ring to it." His smile dims and weakens.

It tanks my pulse. He's either trying to keep positive for himself or for Charlie.

I reach out and clasp his hand in mine. His carriage lifts at the touch, and while we lace our fingers, I say, "Yeah, it has a shrill ring. I'm gonna put a *mute* on that one."

Jack smiles more. "Come on, it's catchy. Homewr—"

I cup my hand over his mouth. "Muted, meu raio de sol." I love my dramatic-ass nickname that is too damn accurate for Jack.

He laughs against my palm, and the air lightens when we return back to the remnants of the party.

"How many people were here?" I ask, watching as Jack lets go of my hand to check his phone. He mouths, *Jesse.*

I nod, and he leaves to take his brother's call in the hallway.

"Four people," Tom answers, collapsing on the singed couch. "*Barely* even a party."

Charlie snorts. "Four is the most Beckett and I would let you invite."

I stroll around the place, inspecting nooks and crannies where a smart "guest" would've planted hidden cameras. "Where is Beckett?"

"He stayed at our parent's place," Tom explains.

"Because he knew he'd wake to this." Charlie lights a cigarette. "And *this* isn't even the problem." He looks back to me. "Luna's fanfic was swiped."

I roll to a halt by the bookcase. "What?"

"It was stolen, robbed, *pilfered*," he clarifies.

Thank you, not.

"I know what *swiped* means."

Charlie skips over that. "I need to retrieve it, but I don't have the last name of the guy who stole the manuscript."

This is a major fucking problem.

"Ian or Vance should know," I rebut. Tom and Eliot's bodyguards aren't completely incompetent, and even though they're Epsilon, I've worked with them long enough that they'll supply me a name.

Something's still not adding up. I look to Charlie. "If you weren't home last night, where were you?"

"I was on the roof."

Of course he was. Because *why not?*

Eliot starts buttoning up a black button-down. "We're coming with you."

"No you aren't," Charlie says, cigarette smoke billowing from his lips with the words.

"Luna's our best friend, if something of hers was stolen, we're going to help retrieve it." Eliot tucks his shirt into black slacks. "It's our duty."

I really need my radio.

"*No*," Charlie tells him. "You both have done *enough*. You're staying here and cleaning this fucking place so that Beckett doesn't lose his shit. And I will go find the fanfic with Oscar and Jack. Understood?"

Tom and Eliot exchange a look, before Tom says, "As you were."

Eliot nods. "We'll concede. This time."

Charlie rolls his eyes, then snuffs out his cigarette on the singed couch.

I'm already heading to the door. Leading the way.

RADIO ATTACHED, COMMS ON, GUN HOLSTERED, and the thieving bastard's name in my possession, I leave the Hell's Kitchen apartment building without socking the Wreath brothers in the face.

Call me mature. An adult.

Still can't believe they iced me out of the party, but at least they gave me the thief's home address. Saved me time tracing it myself.

I drive a security SUV. Charlie is gazing out the window in the backseat, and Jack is messing with the air conditioner in the passenger seat. It's a sauna in here.

I switch lanes, trying to shake off a paparazzi van on my ass. Glancing at Jack, I realize how strange it is to see him without a camera. He's here for me. For Charlie.

Not for *Born into Fame.*

Traipsing around New York for a stolen manuscript isn't his job, but I can't tell him to *go home.* I like Highland too much in my company, even more when clouds start shielding his sunshine. Because I just want to cheer him up somehow. Make him feel better. Take his mind off the negativity, and I can't do that if we're split apart.

Jack shuts off the A/C. "It must be broken. It's only blowing heat."

"You have Banks Moretti's number?"

"Yeah." He unpockets his cell.

"Will you text him and let him know it needs fixed?" Banks is the resident mechanic, and Akara has been trying to save money for the new firm wherever he can.

"Sure. How will he know which car?"

"SFO calls this one the Black Widow."

He smiles while he types.

My phone lets out a ping. It's already docked on the dashboard, but I can see a notification for a few missed texts from Farrow and Donnelly. I reach over and click into them, and I'm careful to keep my eyes on the road as I read quickly.

You and Highland. Cute. Didn't expect it, but super happy for you, Oliveira. Don't listen to the negativity. We've got your back. — Farrow

Get that ass! And fuck the haters. You're fire. Jack is fire. Together, you're a big ball of fire — Donnelly

I can't help but smile at my friends' reactions. Their steady, loyal friendship is the best I've ever had, and I'm glad they're here for me.

I glance over as Jack says, "Kumusta ka?" He's on the phone. After a couple minutes, he hangs up.

"Did you just say *how are you* in Tagalog?" I ask in shock.

"Yeah?" he says in slight surprise. "How'd you know?"

"Como está?" I say in Portuguese. "They sound a lot alike."

We share a bigger smile, and Jack explains how many words in Tagalog sound or are derived from Spanish, and I know a lot of words are similar between Spanish and Portuguese.

When I'm a few minutes from the thieving bastard's house, Jack asks, "What if Clifford Flannagan isn't home? What's the plan then?"

Charlie messes a hand through his hair. "Go to his work. He's a gaffer at the theatre where Eliot performs." He lets out an annoyed breath. "I cancelled my trip to Prague yesterday."

I look at him through the rearview mirror. "I heard about that." The temp did alert me that they no longer were headed to the airport.

Jack glances over his shoulder. "Any particular reason you stayed in New York?"

"My brothers." Charlie slouches. "I had a feeling they were going to pull something." He'd been hoping Maximoff and Jane would move to New York to deal with his brothers, but in the end, he told them to stay in Philly.

He knew he'd have to play babysitter. And he's sticking around New York a lot more lately. I can only assume he's feeling a greater responsibility to protect them and clean up after their mistakes.

Jack nods, rotating back in his seat. "Intuitive."

"No, they're just predictable." Charlie flips his phone in his palm. "Speaking of predictability, I see my set-up had the intended effect."

"No," I say, trying to shut this convo down before it starts.

"No?" Charlie bows forward more between our seats. "So you two didn't kiss last night? Was that a deepfake then?"

"We kissed," Jack and I say in unison. It causes both of us to smile. And I add, "But not because *you* set us up." I don't care if he put us in the right orbit together; I don't need Charlie meddling in my life.

Ever again.

"Of course not." Charlie leans back again. "You two would have definitely hooked up had I not orchestrated it. I'm sure you would have found a way to spend all this time together without me."

I grit down so I don't grin at his sarcasm. *I'm not a buddy-guard.* Not. A. Buddy. Guard.

Jack rakes a hand through his hair, his smile rising.

Charlie taps the window. "It didn't fully work though, did it?"

"What do you mean?" Jack asks, his face falling. Eyes darting to me. Like I told Charlie something about *us* and left him out. No way.

I shake my head tensely at Highland.

"It was supposed to *end* the Oslie rumors," Charlie explains, "not make people loathe you because of them." He expels a frustrated noise. "It's all a fucking mess."

"Story of our lives, bro." I switch lanes and pull into a parking garage.

"Yeah." Charlie nods slowly. "So it goes."

I park, and we reach Clifford's apartment complex with relative ease. No paparazzi. No screaming fans. It's almost too easy. So it's not a surprise when Clifford isn't home.

Next stop, the theatre. We find another parking spot, and when we climb out and walk towards the theatre building, it's clear this is…a shit show.

Girls and guys hoist posters and stake out the front of the old 1900s structure. Theatre security pushes them back, and a couple paparazzi vans hug the curb with parking meters.

"They're always here early," I explain to Jack and adjust my earpiece. "Eliot has an afternoon performance in a couple hours." We approach from the side, not spotted yet.

"Eliot's fans are my favorite," Charlie says. "They're mostly theatre nerds who send him Shakespeare love letters and dead ravens."

"CHARLIE KEATING COBALT!" That shrill piercing scream comes from a girl holding a giant pink poster board that reads ELIOT ALICE, CAN I BE YOUR CORPSE BRIDE?

Jack takes it all in with interest, and I almost clasp his hand—about five times—like I'm strolling down the street with a boyfriend.

I'm working.

I'm on-duty.

Here to protect *Charlie*. I playback the words in my head to stay sharp. Alert.

Charlie waves a nonchalant hand at the crowd—more like he's brushing away a gnat than greeting them, and they all respond with an awed noise as though he just proposed.

He's unaffected.

Don't like that we're exposed.

"Back door," I instruct and step quickly in that direction. It's too late though. Someone spots Jack.

"Homewrecker!" she screams.

Charlie stops in his tracks and turns around. I fist his shirt before he charges away from me. "I'm straight!" he yells at them. "There is no Oslie!"

"It's okay, Charlie," a girl pipes in. "We know you want it to be a secret. We know you're not ready ye—"

"Fuck you," he sneers.

"Oh my God, Charlie, can you say that to me too?!" someone jumps up and down.

"Charlie, please fuck me!" A chorus of requests pitches the air.

Charlie just turns around and meets my eyes. "Go."

I begin to lead him into the theatre when I detect a projectile sailing at Jack. *A shoe.* An ugly rubber sandal—and I smack that shit out of his way.

What is so unlike me while on-duty—I nearly lunge and backtalk.

"Stop." Jack curves an arm around my waist. He guides me away from the source of my frustration and rage. I hated Oslie stans before, but now that they're physically attacking the guy who has my heart, I almost can't even withstand them.

We're in the theatre and Jack cups the crook of my neck. "Hey, I'm fine."

I nod, cooling off, my chest rising and falling heavily. I almost kiss him. *On-duty, Oliveira.* And this is why you don't bring your boyfriend to your dangerous-as-fuck workplace.

We pull apart.

Shit.

Charlie has already darted away.

I grind down on my molars and shoot to action. Picking up my pace, I jog out in front of Charlie. Hurriedly, we make it backstage where a white guy with a short mohawk balances on a ladder, fixing the large stage lights. Beside him, the stage is empty.

"Hey!" Charlie yells. "Clifford Flannagan!"

Clifford glances down.

My muscles strain, on edge, but I see what Charlie is about to do before he even moves. Being tactical means being five steps ahead, and even though I'm a single foot ahead of Charlie now, I don't stop him.

I don't want to.

It's not really my job to.

So I skid to a complete halt, and Jack just gives me a thunderstruck look.

Charlie rams his right foot into the ladder like he's shoving an enemy off a cliff. It careens, and the metal ladder and Clifford plummet to the stage with a loud *crack!*

"Fuck," he groans, holding onto his knee. His eyes flash murderously to Charlie. "You psychopath!"

Charlie skirts around him and squats down a foot away. "And so the psychopath says to the thief," he says coldly, "you have something of mine, and I want it back."

Clifford's nose flares. "I don't know what you're talking about." His gaze cuts to me and my cold glare. Fear bubbles in his eyes. "Uh…"

"You have thirty seconds," I tell him.

Clifford shakes his head. "Fuck you both." He looks to Charlie. "I'm selling your writing to the nearest buyer and for how weird and disgusting it is, I'm getting my money's worth."

Charlie blinks. "Final answer?"

Clifford breathes heavy, still clutching his knee.

"Think quickly here, Clifford," Charlie says, lighting a cigarette. "You're running out of time, and this psychopath is so easily bored." He blows smoke in his direction.

Clifford lets out a breath. "It's underneath the prop table. In the basket."

Jack jogs there and digs through the basket of props.

Charlie's not done. "You won't speak to Eliot ever again. Keep away from my brother, or I will ruin you." He flicks his cigarette at Clifford before standing up.

Jack returns with the manuscript, and I lead Charlie towards a rear backdoor. As soon as we're out of view from Clifford, Charlie starts limping and lets out a frustrated, pained wince.

"Charlie—" I start.

"I'm fine," he says casually. "You have it." He looks to Jack, already knowing it's in his possession. Their eyes meet for a beat. "Wishing you had your camera?"

Jack shakes his head. "No, not really." We stop next to the stage's exit. "That's not something I'd show."

"Why not?" Charlie asks. "It's who I am."

24

Oscar Oliveira

YOU STILL AWAKE? I TEXT Jack on a Wednesday night after a security meeting. Drinking stale-ass coffee at the Independent billiards & darts bar in Philly—typical. But I'm not single anymore.

I have such *little* free time, and right when I finally find myself off-duty, I'm called to a late-night security chitchat.

"Why the long face?" Farrow asks me as he pops a bubble gum bubble.

"Did Jack thumbs-down your dick pic?" Donnelly asks, half-concentrated on drawing cherries in his sketchbook.

"Only you send dick pics, bro." I flip my phone over on the booth table.

Security meeting is officially over. With a capital O.

Yet, I'm still here at the local bar with the rest of Omega. From the booth, I can see Thatcher, Banks, Quinn, and Akara playing a round of pool and also drinking stale-ass coffees. No one wants to drink alcohol tonight since Alpha and Epsilon bodyguards are *also* here and not drinking. If there happens to be an emergency, whoever is drunk can't actually go save the day.

We all want to be the heroes. And I'm all for one-upping Price's Triple Shield.

I check the time. *Late.*

My ass would be high-tailing it back to New York with my client, if it weren't for the fact that it's Wednesday with a capital W.

The weekly Cobalt Wednesday Night Dinner is something Charlie tries his absolute best not to miss. Whatever goes down on Wednesdays drives him back to Philly like an obsession. No clue what actually happens. No one but the Cobalts and Thatcher Moretti are invited. Already tried to get that lucky bastard to spill details, but he wouldn't break.

Charlie being safe-and-sound in a gated neighborhood means that I'm off-duty and enjoying rare free time. Unless I'm called in for security meetings or temp trainings.

I look across the table.

Farrow raises his brows. "You have Jack when you didn't think you would, so what's with the angst?"

"I'm a solid catch," I say with a nod, "but you know what, I'm not even sure *I'd* date myself right now. I have Wednesday night off and then *bam!* I'm called for a meeting." I throw up a hand. "Tell me, bro, would you date me?"

"No," Farrow says slowly, "because I'm married to Maximoff Hale."

I clap, almost grinning.

Donnelly claps too.

Farrow rolls his eyes. "Man, if Jack had a problem with your work, I doubt he would've kissed you in the first place. He knew what he was getting into."

That is true.

I ease back, sitting on the same side as Donnelly. He takes off his reading glasses. "Maybe you should send him a dick pic."

I laugh with Farrow.

"Let him know you're thinkin' about him," Donnelly finishes.

"And that's why you don't take dating advice from Paul Donnelly," I say and flip over my phone. No new text.

He must be sleeping.

But damn I wish he were awake and wanted to hang out. Even if it was a five-minute, *hey there, looking good, Highland,* kind of convo.

"Call him," Farrow suggests.

"I shouldn't wake him up." I stare at my blank phone screen. "He had a horrible time trying to film Charlie this afternoon. Couldn't ask him a single question since every time he opened his mouth, paparazzi shouted at him."

Farrow chews gum slowly. "About your kiss?"

"Yeah."

Silence eats at our booth, and the sound of billiards balls clinking seems louder.

"It's annoying as fuck," Farrow finally says. "Paparazzi, the hate online, but some weeks are better than others."

I flip my phone again, realizing how much frustration I've been feeling. "The hate towards Jack is nuts, bro. These fans of mine, who are obsessed with the imaginary mother-effing romance between me and Charlie, will not *stop*. One told him to *go choke* and *die* the other day." I've heard this kind of fandom language before and hardly blinked, but now that it's directed at someone I have feelings for…

It stings.

I'd rather be the one they're playing target practice with.

"They're not fans," Donnelly says. "They're stans, but most likely antis."

"An *anti*?" Farrow arches his brows.

"I'm with Redford. What the hell is that?" I know what a stan is—in short, an overly passionate fan. But I'm not as deeply involved in fandom culture like Donnelly. Though, I do keep up with it better than Farrow.

"Anti-fans, anti-shippers," Donnelly explains. "They root hardcore against a couple. Like hate-watching a TV show, but real life, man. It's my least favorite part of a fandom. No love, all hate."

Fuck. "Now we're dealing with anti-shippers? It's my fault," I continue, "what's happening to Jack is on me. You date me, I come with baggage."

Farrow leans forward. "See, that's not what we're doing here is blaming yourself. You didn't create Oslie, and you can't get rid of online bullshit and anti-fuckers. But you're going to find a way to protect Jack because you're Oscar Oliveira."

I nod slowly.

Yeah.

I have to find a way. Because that's the only avenue where I come out feeling like I'm worthy of being in a relationship.

"How much are you charging me for that advice, Redford?" I ask lightly, the mood lifting with my words.

"Eh, it's free. I'm writing it up under, *I couldn't look at your face anymore*." Donnelly laughs.

"Aw, fuck you." I flip Farrow off, and we're all grinning. For a moment, I start forgetting that Jack hasn't texted me back.

SFO finishes their pool game, and Thatcher, Akara, Banks, and my little brother slide into our booth. We shoot the shit about the Phillies, Thatcher's upcoming wedding, and Epsilon who keeps eyeing us to death.

Jealous motherfuckers.

"Get outta Philly!" a couple drunk guys yell from the bar.

I clamp a hand on Donnelly's shoulder as he pops up. He shuts his mouth as his ass hits the seat. I'm sure he was about to yell, *"We're from Philly!"*

Heard it before.

Inciting jeers happen at this bar too regularly now, ever since SFO gained some fame. Locals can't stand us even if this has always been our local spot.

We refuse to be kicked out.

Akara gives him a friendly look. "Hey, don't give Epsilon a reason to say they're better than us."

Donnelly nods, but Thatcher is glaring at the bar.

South Philly guys pop off so easily when their city pride is at stake. Love Philly to death, it's been my home, but I'm not feeding into local hecklers.

We go back to our conversation, everyone grimacing at the cold coffees, and after another fifteen minutes, Farrow stands up on his seat—he's wedged against the wall because everyone filled the booth. And instead of asking Thatcher, Akara, and Banks to move their asses, he literally walks across the table and jumps off.

Donnelly and I applaud mockingly.

Farrow just lifts a couple fingers in goodbye. "I'm out. See you boys later." He walks casually to the exit.

"And there he goes," I quip.

"Gone so soon. RIP," Donnelly says.

We all laugh, but my smile fades as I glance at my phone. Knowing, for sure, that he has to be asleep. *I'll see him tomorrow.*

I hang onto that, at least.

25

Jack Highland

GREENLAND.

Colorful houses in bright reds, yellows, greens, and blues landscape steep mossy mountains that plunge down into a fjord, a deep inlet of water between cliffs. Icebergs jut out of the teal water, and while whales breach the sea, the sound of playful seals fills the chilly air.

The location is so *stunning* that it seems fabricated. Like some pitch I've embellished as a location scout seeking to shoot in the Arctic Circle.

It's real, though.

On the deck of a bright blue house, I fix my camera on a tripod. Aches and pains flare up as I move around my equipment. Underneath my winter jacket, bruises decorate my body. All over my *elbows*. Down my hips. I have a big welt on my thigh and knee.

These past five days trying to film Charlie *and* push back paparazzi has been taxing. Physically, sometimes mentally. A little emotionally.

They shove their cameras in my face and yell, *"Jack! Jack! Did you know about Oscar & Charlie before you kissed the bodyguard?!"* It's irony, right? I have a camera. I'm there to *film* Charlie, and the paparazzi are filming me while I film him.

But Charlie gave me permission to prod into his life. And I'd say I'm nowhere near as aggressive or caustic as most paparazzi. They make me look like a *butterfly* gingerly capturing footage and not actually weighed down with fifty-pound equipment.

I have a high threshold for uncomfortable situations. I make the best, do my best. But I almost reached my limit while on a WAC shoot filming Jane, Sullivan, and Luna at a pub together. Not only did another cameraman ram an elbow in my back, but he ruined all my footage by screaming questions at *me*.

I had to scrap everything.

Charlie is even over the outrage. He actually gave me and Oscar a whole day's notice before booking a flight to Greenland. A private plane and shuttle ride later, we arrived.

He literally flew to the *Arctic* to escape it all.

I position my lens towards panoramic views of Disko Bay's endless teal water and picturesque icebergs. It's peaceful and calm outside. A stark contrast to what we left.

But I find myself eyeing a prettier view. Oscar rests his forearms on the deck's railing, leaning in a nonchalant lunge, with a paperback in hand. His winter gear is worn well, a total pro at harsh climates, and as my smile rises, I shift my camera. Until he's completely in frame.

I zoom in on his face. His curly hair warms his ears, and his eyes drift over towards the yellow cabin to the right of ours.

Charlie lounges on a porch chaise and reads a book, bundled in an outdoor blanket.

If I didn't understand Oscar's job, maybe it'd aggravate me that he keeps glancing over there. I've been no better with my focus on taking footage of the scenery.

Anyway, his concentration on Charlie is letting me capture Oscar in all his glory. I watch him through the camera, my smile widening. He runs a couple fingers back and forth across his unshaven jaw before flipping a page in his book.

We're dating. My pulse skips in anticipation of where that'll lead us, practically giddy. The more I'm around Oscar, the more *enchanted* I feel—and with my work becoming a giant stressor, I hold stronger onto these feelings.

I zoom more.

Oscar turns his head back to me. A grin edges across his mouth, his eyes on me, then right into the camera. "Are you filming me, Long Beach?"

"You're in my frame," I smile more and tilt up the camera to capture the light in his brown eyes. "Prettiest part of the setting so far. What do you have to say, Oscar Oliveira?"

He rotates fully towards me, elbows resting back on the railing. Paperback loose in his hand. "That it's not possible to be the prettiest part of the setting when I'm looking at the prettiest thing here."

His eyes never abandon mine.

Something luminous brims inside my body. "How's flirting with the cameraman going for you?"

He mimes checking a watch that he's not wearing. "Too early to tell, but so far, so good. I'll let you know more when I have him naked and in my arms."

Breath staggers in my throat. Jesus *fuck*. Do I want to fool around with Oscar? *Is that even a fucking question, dude.* The more we're drowned in work, the less time we've been able to explore further, and there is no other exploration that sounds as enticing as letting him discover my turn-ons and me discovering his.

"Keep me updated," I banter with a smile. A cool gust blowing through, I shiver and zip up my outer-layer of the winter jacket and fix the baseball cap on my head.

Oscar kicks off from the railing, fitting his paperback in a back pocket. "Still can't believe you packed *that* hat and not a beanie."

"I wasn't thinking." I shake my head, remembering. "Something distracted me when I was packing." I see his confusion as he approaches, so I come clean. "The other execs heard that I had *no* footage of the girls at the pub, and they asked me what happened."

"You tell them paparazzi encroached your space?" He tugs down the zipper of his jacket and unspools a scarf around his neck.

"No." I tense. "I *lied*." I run a hand through my hair four or five times.

"You lied?" Oscar looks shocked. "Have you ever lied to them before?"

"Never," I say strongly. "But I knew if I told them the truth, they might limit my involvement in shoots, and it's important to me to be the camera operator for Jane, Sulli, and Moffy."

"Why?"

"They trust me," I explain. "We're all friends, and if I had to sit out, it feels like a loss for them and me. And maybe it's pride too." I crack a dying smile. "I've never been kicked off a project. So I lied and said the equipment malfunctioned."

Oscar nods a few times. "I probably would've done the same thing." That actually makes me feel a bit better, but his face is serious. "So they're off your ass?"

"Yeah."

He's still tense like me. "I hate that being with me is affecting your job this fucking terribly. It wasn't supposed to be like this—"

"It's okay, Os." I rest my hands on my head, really on the blue baseball hat. "The *pros* outweigh the *cons*." I flash a smile at him. "You're my pro."

He grins. "I am a pro at many things." He slowly twists his scarf around my exposed neck. "Like keeping you warm, Long Beach."

I blaze inside, our eyes trailing hot tracks over each other. I drop my arms to his shoulders, and he spins the brim of my hat backwards. Just to lean in and kiss me.

Our mouths meet with a slow build-up of prickling heat. My fingers slip up into his soft hair, our bodies singing with primal pleasure against each other. Every kiss feels like we're spinning in 360-degrees. Blood rushes out of my head, dizzying. Exhilarating.

And then he clutches my jaw too hard. Where a bruise formed.

I wince between my teeth.

Oscar breaks a kiss. "Sorry."

I breathe hard.

His concern tightens on me. "Was that…here?" His thumb brushes the tender skin along my jawline. A Canon made impact with my chin. *Paparazzi hazard.*

"Yeah." I try to catch my breath. Partly in need of oxygen because I'm too attracted to this guy. Partly because of the media mess we left behind. Hot, I unravel the scarf and let the ends hang against my chest.

He glares at the deck, then at the icebergs. "I'm not sure I can protect you and Charlie at the same time, and it's driving me nuts."

"You've done enough." He's caught more than one projectile headed for me.

His eyes return to the bruise on my jaw. "Let's go count your bruises, Highland."

I let out a weak laugh. "I'm not *delicate* like you think. This is now a casualty of *my* job, and I'm choosing to stick it out." I grip his shoulders. "I'm not going to pretend to be a bodyguard. I'm not one. I probably can't hit a man to save my life, but your job is to protect *Charlie*. Just let me film."

He nods, then grins, "Did I just get a Jack Highland pep talk?"

I begin to smile. "Did you like it?"

"I didn't like the part where you put yourself down," he admits. "If you need to hit a man to save your life, I know you could save yourself, Highland." He turns my hat straight but lifts up the brim. "But I'll be your hottest back-up."

I believe that.

He reaches for my hand. "Come here, I want to show you something." He brings me to the edge of the deck, our elbows meeting the railing. The sun hovers just above the horizon, casting an orange glow on the sea. "Check the time."

I pull out my cell and click into the local time.

No?

"That can't be right," I whisper.

"It is." His mouth curves. "Midnight." He leans a hip against the railing. "It's called a midnight sun. It only happens during the summer in places around the Arctic and Antarctic Circles."

Wow.

My eyes try to paint the portrait in front of me. The sun coasting along the teal iceberg-scattered sea. A whale splashes in the distance, spraying water overhead.

"It's beautiful," I murmur.

"Charlie asked me where I wanted to go," he breathes. "I wanted you to see this."

My lips part in surprise.

He takes a deep breath. "It reminds me of you."

A noise between a shocked breath and an overcome laugh escapes me. My stinging eyes are on him. No one has ever made me feel like the focal point. The center of attention. I'm never the subject.

He doesn't just *see* me. He acts like I should be the lead of not just one movie but every movie, and fuck if that doesn't feel good—I don't know what else could.

I take another glimpse of the midnight sun. "The brightest light shining during the darkest hour," I smile. "That's pretty good."

"I'm only doing my best work with you, Long Beach."

I smile, but my lips fall gradually. "What happens when the light dims? You'll still be interested then?"

"Oh yeah." Oscar nods. "I'm every star circling around you. You need a spark, I'm there." He says it like a promise.

It wells up in me. My eyes redden, my smile more overcome. I'm always a positive force for others, and to have someone be mine is everything and more.

Oscar grabs the ends of the scarf and draws me in. Our lips collide in a hungered kiss. We pull and grip for more contact. And our eyes speak the same passionate need, *just you and me now.*

Gathering my camera equipment, my dick strains against my pants. Oscar types out a text with one hand and holds the door open to our blue house for me. He explains, "I'm letting Charlie know that he needs to call me if he goes into town or hears anything outside."

My lips lift. "You're off-duty then?"

"Yeah, for now." He shuts the door behind us. "You have me all to yourself, Highland."

Our eyes devour. And I put my camera shit away as fast as possible. When I told Jesse about the travel plans, he pleaded with me to stay back in Philly to edit footage. Really, I think he knew this was his chance to freely surf, and the Arctic is the last place he wants to be.

So it really just is me and Oscar.

The quaint mountainside house is outfitted with a full-sized bed, fuzzy blankets, knitted pillows, and a woven rug in front of a wood-burning fireplace.

Romance is alive in Greenland.

We shed layers upon layers. Until we're down to boxer-briefs and Oscar kisses me up against a distressed blue-painted armoire. Lips stinging, head spinning, my shoulders dig into the wood but my hips flex towards him. Rock-hard, I'm aching for his hand and skill.

I curse and bang my head back for breath.

He grinds forward, causing a deeper noise from both of us. The roughness of his jaw brushes against the light stubble of mine as he whispers, "How badly do you want my cock inside you tonight, Highland?"

I'm so fucking hard. His words almost make me explode. We're dating, committed. The *no sex* agreement has flown out the window. I keep drinking him in, head to toe. Oscar has the physique of a pro-boxer, even if he's not one anymore.

I wonder how he'll feel inside of me. How close I'll feel to him, how his weight and strength will be up against my body. It'd be a first for me, and firsts are always slightly nail-biting—but that adds to the appeal.

How badly do I want his cock inside of me tonight?

"More than you know," I say in shallow, wanting breath.

He palms my hard-on. "Think I have a pretty good idea." His playful grin usually coaxes mine out.

I'm too waist-deep in pleasure to smile. Too enamored with Oscar's confident, caring hands that feed my need. He yanks the elastic of my boxer-briefs down my muscular waist. His hand grazes burning trails down my thighs as he lowers to his knees.

I stand at solid attention. My hand cradles the back of his head, and I watch his eyes trace every dip and cut of my body. His gaze softens on the bruises and welts.

"You like to do this often?" I wonder since he hasn't given me head yet. This is a first. A guy blowing me—Oscar blowing me, or at least, he's about to, and I might be leaning partially against an armoire, but I feel like I'm on the edge of my seat.

"More than you know," Oscar grins, using my words. "You've just kept coming too fast for me to even try."

I let out a low laugh. "I promise I usually last longer, dude. You just have a perfect grip and touch." He could wrap his palm around my length, stroke twice, and I'd shoot my load.

"I do know how to handle a dick, Long Beach." Oscar rubs me before taking me between his lips with expert ease. *Oh...my...fuck.* A groan rakes against my throat.

I arch my hips further, wanting deeper.

He moves in-out in his mouth, the pressure lighting up nerve-endings. Sending shockwaves throughout my entire body. My muscles burn, my hand sliding down his unshaven jaw. Pleasure tightens my balls, and like he knows, he squeezes them with just the right force.

My other hand flies to my head.

He eases my dick out of his mouth with a grin, skates his tongue across the length, then goes back in for more. I'm basking in this moment.

So caught up in us and what he's doing to me that my body climbs to the peak faster and faster. Racing to the top, and as soon as he quickens his pace, I jerk forward. Head rolling to the side with a knotted groan escaping my parted lips. "*Oscar.*"

I'm spinning.

He swallows, rises to his feet, and milks my climax with a couple more strokes. I flinch against him, that pleasure rippling out of me. We're eye-locked. Lips ghosting lips.

"That was...the best head I've ever been given." I'm still shaking in ecstasy. "No lie."

Another grin toys at his lips. "It makes it easy when I love the cock I'm sucking. And the guy."

I smile more. Is he saying he loves me? *Probably not.* But I'll always pocket Oscar's praises, just like I know he won't throw away mine.

He backs up, strips off his boxer-briefs, and walks naked to the bed. I'm so interested in what the hell he's doing, I don't follow his footsteps.

Oscar throws pillows onto the woven rug. When he glances back, he must see a shiver skate through my limbs. "You're cold?"

I rub my biceps. "Yeah. I need your heat apparently."

He laughs. "Weak California blood." He kneels at the wood-burning fireplace and throws on a couple logs.

I use the bathroom, and when I come back out, Oscar has his forearms on his knees, sitting on the woven rug and watching the fire crackle.

Buck-naked, I take a seat next to him. Warming my palms, I turn my head. He kisses me; I kiss back just as strongly, and we're about to sink into something I desire.

I put a hand to his chest, pausing the moment.

His body tightens. "You alright, Jack?"

Jack. Whenever he uses my first name, he sounds serious. It sets me more on edge.

"Let's talk," Oscar urges. "Screw this *no talking* beforehand bullshit, I'm through with that."

I exhale. "Okay. Let's talk." I want to make this clear. "I'm dying to have sex with you, Os. I've *been* dying to have sex with you, so that's not where I'm leading you."

"What then?" He pushes curls off his forehead. "You'd rather give, not receive? You're afraid of it hurting?"

I tilt my head. "You're not that far off."

Oscar rubs his eyes. "You'd rather top?"

I smile because I've known for a while that Oscar prefers to top. No one would ask me things like, *how badly do you want my cock inside you?* without wanting to go there. I could fuck with him, but that'd almost hurt my soul a little.

"I'd rather try bottoming," I say honestly.

His hand falls to my knee, confusion lining his forehead. "Alright, now I'm at a complete loss of where you're taking me, Highland."

Figured.

I smile. "I was just wondering if there's something I can give you first. I haven't tried to finger you or anything. You haven't really asked, and I didn't know if it's because you thought I was afraid to try or if you didn't want it."

Realization washes over his features. "I didn't think you were scared. I just like being the one fingering."

I look him over. "So have you ever been fingered or bottomed before?"

"Yeah." He nods. "But it's been a while. My first time receiving anal was nineteen. College. And I haven't done it *since* college."

"How come?"

"I just get off more being in you than you in me."

I smile, about to joke about how he hasn't been inside me yet, but Oscar beats me to the punch and says, "I'm not talking about another guy's asshole when I just want yours, bro."

I'm hard again.

His erection is already begging for touch, and we're drawing closer. "If you do want to top one day, I'd bottom for you," Oscar breathes. "But truthfully, I can't promise I'd be into doing it every time we have sex."

I appreciate him being upfront.

"I think that'll be okay," I say quietly, fire warming my skin. Warming us. Embers crackle, and flames cast shadows on our bare bodies. "How bad does it hurt the first time?"

"I'll work you up enough that it shouldn't." He kisses my jaw, then my lips, and I drag a hand down his abs to his length. While I stroke him, he bears his weight against me. Guiding my back against the woven rug, and my neck and head meet a pillow.

We kiss deep, rougher as our legs intertwine. My waist bucks up. He keeps bearing down, his palms planted on either side of my deltoids.

I glide my hands along his ass, and I lose myself to the sensation. How my legs spread on either side of his hips. His erection teases against my entry, but he eases me more with a finger, then a lubed plug. The pressure overwhelms me, contracts my calves, my abs, every single tendon of muscle.

I breathe hard.

The physicality of being intimate with Oscar is mind-blowing: his muscled body, his strength and control. His hand that grips my jaw as he kisses me—that alone just lights me on *fire*.

But it'd be nothing without his all-consuming gaze that reads my reactions, my muscle spasms, that dives deeper and deeper, as though wanting to hold onto my core. My essence while we ride a wave together.

I cup his jaw, my hand rising up to his hair, and my thumb traces the scar above his brow. Small but not as faint as the others.

His nose flares in emotion. "You ready?"

"Yeah." Nerves prick me, and I inhale, exhale. He gently eases out the plug, and my cock twitches, wishing for that fullness again. "Should I...?" I'm about to turn around.

"No." Oscar catches my knee. "Stay there." He positions a pillow under my lower back.

I lean back and hold onto his ass again. Our chests and erections brush lightly while he leans down to kiss me. I edge his lips further open, tongues wrestling, and he grunts out an aroused noise as he pulls away to grab a condom.

He tears the packet, sheaths himself, then lubes his length.

I arch up. My body more impatient than my mind.

Oscar rubs my thigh. "If I'm hurting you, you tell me to stop."

I nod, anticipation wound up.

He grips himself and at the same time, crushes his mouth to mine in a levitating kiss. I feel him guide his veined cock into me. Pain pinches at first, and my legs shift.

He stretches one higher, kisses deeper. I'm the recipient of pure, raw pleasure. It takes me aback. How much he's *giving* me. How little I'm actually worried about his need.

Oscar pushes in further—my breath catches.

He waits.

"Fuck, *fuck*." I grip his ass. "Go deeper, Os."

He eases in more.

Pain is gone. He's bigger than the plug, but lube helps with the friction. Making the experience a blistering, head-spinning one. He thrusts.

He's thrusting.

Jesus holy...

His dominant hand strokes pleasure from my hardness between our chests, and he pumps and pumps. Our eyes stay locked when we're not sharing primal kisses.

I will let him fuck me again.

He can tomorrow, even.

And the next day.

He works his hips. "Highland," he groans against my mouth. We're heavy grunts, sweat, and earnestness—feelings that carry us further and further.

The friction inside me is unlike anything I've ever felt. He reaches my prostate, and I gasp on a noise I've never even made before now. "Os, *Os*."

Pleasure mounts all around me, and I close my eyes to stop myself from saying his full name. Hand to the back of his head, I tangle my fingers in his curls, then drop them back to his ass.

The pace kills my senses as I feel him rock into me.

His ass flexes against my palms. I squeeze his ass cheeks, and a husky, pleasured noise rumbles out of him.

I slap his ass.

He grins back at me while thrusting.

I smile until a groan tears out of me. "Fuck," I grit down. *That feels amazing.* Sweat builds on us, and he quickens and deepens his pace.

Reaching the spot again.

And again.

Holy—

And I come so hard, I almost black-out.

"*Fucking ah,*" Oscar groans, thrusts one more time, two more times as he ekes out a climax, and his hand is still wrapped around me.

I breathe too hard and glance down at our chests. Cum—my cum— is slick between our abs. My lips begin to lift.

Oscar laughs out a heavy pant. "God, that was seriously A+++."

"I'd give you another plus." I'm still scrounging for oxygen.

"Don't. Let me aspire to something," Oscar grins, and gently, he pulls out and falls back next to me. I stretch my legs, our ankles hooking.

We hold each other a little and talk about it.

How much we enjoyed that, and the truth is, I'm starting to understand why I'm so caught up in the moment with Oscar. Why I come too easily when I never did in the past.

It's not that he has a "perfect touch"—though it feels like it—I'm just used to concentrating on someone else's pleasure in bed. To feed their orgasm. To help them reach that place.

Having sex with Oscar, I feel…selfish.

My tongue weighs heavy when I consider bringing up my *feelings*. I'd much rather not ruin the moment. Sex on the floor in front of a fire in Greenland.

With Oscar Oliveira.

I couldn't have written the script any better.

Before we sleep, Oscar tells me, "Set your alarm for 5 a.m.; we're getting our asses up early."

"What for?"

"You'll see."

I almost mention that Charlie is rubbing off on him with the lack of details, but exhaustion takes hold, and I fall asleep.

26

Oscar Oliveira

"BEST IDEA YOU'VE ever had," Jack says in an aching sigh of relief.

He lowers across from me into the steaming cedar hot tub. We're out on the side-deck. Privacy walls and an overhead trellis block any potential onlookers, but we still have the same views of the iceberg-dotted sea out front.

I skim his bruises and welts from afar.

Ugh, that's hurting my heart. I'm used to seeing men beat to hell after fights in a ring. And I might be too scarily desensitized to that, but when it comes to Jack, I'm not unfeeling.

I flinched the first time I saw the welt on his thigh.

I cringed at the one on his jaw like someone took a right-hook to my face.

And I wished I brought lotion to Greenland for him. Looks like I'm gonna have to start packing extra crap for Highland. He can't remember to bring anything he really needs—besides his camera equipment.

I think he'd leave a *tooth* behind before his ultra-wide lens.

"That's what they call me," I banter. "The idea machine."

Jack flashes a smile as he leans back, arms spreading over the circular wood edge. Biceps sculpted and on display. "Yeah? They call me something too."

I give him a look. "Don't say it."

"Homewrecker—"

I dash over to Jack in the water, cupping a hand across his mouth. "Love nicknames for you. Hate that one."

His smile softens against my palm. Cold nips my skin as I stand over him, submerged only waist-down, and his honey-brown eyes roam over my hard, bare chest. And lower.

We're naked, and I'm two seconds from reaching into the water and gripping him.

A noise swerves my head.

My phone buzzes on a high-table, one that I pushed against the hot tub. Just in case Charlie wakes up and calls.

Fuck.

I drift away from him.

"Charlie is already awake?" Jack asks, and I hear his faint sound of disappointment.

Damn, I feel cheated from the moment I created. "I thought he wouldn't get up before 7."

He glances at the sky. "The sun is up. That could've changed his mind."

Reaching out, I seize my phone. And the verdict is…

"Not Charlie," I tell him. "Akara texted a date and time for Omega's next security meeting." I read more. "It's prep for the huge charity golf tournament that all the families are attending."

Jack nods. "Yeah, I got the WAC production schedule for that event. I'm supposed to be shooting Moffy and Jane more than anyone. Which is an issue since Moffy's not around Charlie that much, and I was hoping to get some footage for *Born into Fame.*"

I take a seat across from him again. "Why can't you just go follow Charlie and say it's for *We Are Calloway* but use it for the side project?"

"Because the other execs will know that's what I'm doing. Moffy and Jane's life largely makes air, so it's worth the time and money to follow them. Charlie's one-word responses and non-answers aren't, and he's been opening up more but there's still content I can't even use."

Like the theatre, I realize.

Where Charlie knocked a bastard off a ladder.

I slouch to dunk my shoulders in the warm water. "He might not even go to the charity golf thing."

"He went to the Fun Run," Jack says, "and several other H.M.C. Philanthropies events. He said it's an obligation."

"He's been known to skip that obligation a lot."

Jack sighs. "I hope he goes. It'd be good footage." He stares off in producer La La Land, then shakes his head. "Anyway…" His eyes glitter on me. "I have a question about you."

And I definitely want to hear this. "Shoot."

"How'd the giant age-gap happen between you and your other siblings? Did your parents plan you?"

"Oh yeah," I nod. "I was the firstborn love of their lives."

"Seriously?"

"Seriously," I grin. "They had me a few years after their marriage, during the height of my dad's boxing career. He learned to box from a family friend, since my uncles are more trained in jiu-jitsu. But because my parents traveled a lot for fights, they just had me." I explain that my mom's a personal trainer, but not in boxing. More cardio and weights. And then I add, "Once my dad retired and became a trainer, they decided to have more kids. Then came along the baby bro and sis." I nod to him. "What about you?" My chest elevates, loving that I can volley the question back to Highland.

That he has the same ten-year age-gap.

I also ask, "Did they plan you?"

"No," he laughs. "I was a complete surprise. My mom had me when she was twenty, and if it were up to my parents, they would've waited until thirty like they did with the kid they *did* plan." *Jesse.*

I lean back. "You were a surprise to me too, Highland."

He smiles a ninety-watt smile. "Well, I love surprising you." He gestures me forward with a couple fingers.

Call accepted.

I come over.

Our mouths crash together with slow, sensual speed. Pulse thumping, I draw out the languid temp with my touch. My hand sinks down his abs beneath the water, and I wrap my fingers around his hardening length.

Jack groans out a, "fuck," against my lips.

I eat him up. His ragged breath, his hand that returns to his head, his body that flexes up in need of more. He's *too* much. My cock rouses, a firm ache contracting around me.

Yeah, I want to fuck him, even more after being inside him last night. The idea of having sex with Jack is high-tier. The actual reality shot the idea out of the fucking atmosphere.

"Oscar." He holds my face, his chest heaving for oxygen. So I figure he needs to catch his breath. He squeezes my ass. A gruff aroused noise stirring in my lungs, and I resist jerking him off more.

What I've learned about Highland: he's a mix of playful and passionate. A combo I'm starting to enjoy and need like a daily dose of Vitamin D.

He wets his lips. "You want to fuck me?"

My muscles constrict. "No doubt, Long Beach." I kiss his jaw and then grin seeing his rising smile. "Wait here." I climb out of the hot tub, cold biting my flesh, but I go inside to grab a condom and lube. Not like I thought he'd want to hook up so soon after his first time.

I must've fucked him *really* good.

Confetti might as well be raining down on me knowing just how much he enjoyed last night. And when I walk back outside on the side-deck, I come up on a beautiful picture.

Jack has his strong arms folded over the cedar edge, leaning forward and overlooking the teal sea. Steam skates across the water in the hot tub, cocooning him in a field of vapor.

Being a bodyguard has awarded me this trip and luxury with Jack. I'm a thankful fucker right now. That he's in production. That he can be *here* with me while I'm working and he's working.

His smile brightens on me. He's about to spin around as I walk around the hot tub, but I say, "Don't move. Stay like that."

Arousal parts his lips, and his broad shoulders tighten. The tension could either be from nerves or desire. Admittedly, I have trouble gauging which.

So I ask, "You alright with that?"

He nods, and his eyes glue to my body as I easily sheath my erection with a condom and lube myself. He asks, "You're implying that you're about to take me from behind, right?"

"Yep."

His nose flares, *definitely desire*. "Let's go there."

His ass is definitely adventurous. I grin at the words in my head. Heat has already bathed me before I even return to the water.

But I'm stepping back into the hot tub now, more warmth ascending my legs, my waist, my abs. I come up behind Jack, my chest melding to his toned back, and when he turns his head slightly, we catch each other's lips in a sweltering kiss.

Muscles burning, my cock is a torturous distance from his ass, and I force myself not to take him so fucking fast.

I use the moment to tease him open with my finger. His breath hitches, breaking a kiss.

"You alright?" I ask against his lips.

He nods once. "That felt amazing." His voice is choked like he's already on the brink. He faces Disko Bay. He's about to put a hand on his head, and as fucking sexy as that habit of Highland's is, I lie my arm over his folded arms. Keeping them on the cedar edge of the hot tub.

We're closer, braced stronger together, even more so when I edge my way carefully into Jack. His body contracts, and I hold off for a second, kissing his deltoid.

He's breathing hard. "Can I do anything for you?" he asks.

I begin pumping my hips. "Just enjoy the ride." I enter further, my cock disappearing inside Jack—the sensation electrifies every sensitive nerve, and he responds with a sharp pleasured noise that bows him forward. I hold him tighter to my chest.

My body takes over on instinct, doing what feels best, and I thrust in a hypnotic rhythm up against him. Inside him. Rocking causes the water to ripple. Creating waves around us, and my jaw brushes his jaw as I flex further.

Christ.

Jack groans, "*Os.*"

I stroke his mouth-watering erection beneath the water, and I tilt my head to try and see him better. His eyes are shut in pure euphoria. Jagged breaths emit between his parted lips, and I clench my teeth as a groan barrels through me.

Attraction is a hot torch fusing us together.

He opens his eyes onto me, and we kiss once before the pleasured sounds leave us both. I circle my hips a little, then pound his ass faster.

"*Uh, fuck*," he gasps.

Shit. I slow.

He looks up out at the sea, then back at me, nodding. *He's alright.* We kiss, and I return to my quickened pace. Each thrust forward, water splashes over the lip of the hot tub.

I rub him and give his balls a squeeze.

He makes a surprised, heavenly noise like he's met an angel.

"*Jack*," I groan huskily, lowly. Being inside him is lighting me up, but so is being this close. My chest against his back, my arm around his arms. Thrusting and bringing him with the movement. We are on a ride together, and I might be at the helm but it'd be nothing without him.

I climb up the highest peak. On the edge. Three more deeper thrusts along with my hand feeding Jack more pleasure, and we hit a climax.

His orgasm shatters him forward. I hold tighter, feeling his muscles spasm and ripple against my build. *Fuck.*

Fuck.

I imprison breath, black spots in my vision. On instinct, I pump to milk that last bit of pleasure left, and I take my arm off his arms.

"God," Jack chokes, resting his forehead on his folded arms—he takes a hot second to come down. All the strain and ache in his sore muscles look gone. "I could get used to that after long shoots." He clarifies, "Not the hot tub."

"Hear that, cock," I say as I slowly pull out of Jack, "you outrank a hot tub."

"Not just your cock," Jack breathes, running his fingers through his hair, wetting the strands. "All of you, Os."

My chest rises. Sure, Highland always knows just what to say to flatter me, but there is sincerity in his deep words and brightening smile. One that actually fades.

He exhales a breath, his eyes dripping down me with a look I can't decipher. I'm not a motherfucking archeologist. As much as I wish I could excavate Jack Highland in a second-flat, we're just now crossing into something new for him. And it's new for me to do it *with* him.

He faces me fully and tries to smile, and that one vanishes even faster in a heavy silence.

What the fuck.

My internal organs have just fled my body. I cannot leave my fucking heart in Greenland. "Something's wrong," I realize out loud.

"Nothing's wrong," he says lightly. *Sounds like the truth.*

"Something's bothering you then," I rephrase and hold his waist.

He shudders from a chill in the air. To stay warm, we sink deeper in the center of the hot tub. Water rises up to our chests.

Jack clutches my ass cheeks with both palms. Which is making me not freak the fuck out. He's touching my ass, he can't be regretting what just happened. Don't care if that logic is a stretch, I'm stretching this shit between multiple continents.

He finds the words. "We just had sex again. And *again*, I did nothing to help you. I feel like a jackass with how much of a selfish partner I'm being."

"Selfish?" I extend a hand towards the lip of the hot tub where we just made serious love. "You let me *inside* of you, which sounds like a fucking self*less* act to me."

He shakes his head. "I didn't think of it like that."

"How'd you think of it?"

"From my perspective, I'm barely focused on your need."

I nod. "Probably because you know I'm going to get mine. I'm in control, so you're not wrapped up in trying to get me off. You don't need to."

He holds my gaze. "I've only slept with women. Until now..." We both begin to smile. "And back then," he continues, "I spent a lot of time ensuring they reached an O."

"To satisfy them?"

"Yeah."

"Well, I'm satisfied and satiated, Highland," I assure. "You're not a selfish partner. What we have is just a different dynamic than what you're used to. The better question is, did you like it?"

His smile explodes. "Like water in a desert."

I grin back and use my *best* pick-up line. "Keep quenching your thirst with me."

He squeezes my ass under the water. We laugh against each other's lips, about to kiss, and then I hear the crunch of a sole on land right in front of our deck.

My head whips forward.

"Good morning." Charlie sips an espresso shot, fully dressed in a thick peacoat like he's about to hightail his ass to town. And I'm in a mother-effing hot tub with Jack. Naked.

We're naked.

Shit.

Fuck.

Shit.

We both hurry out of the tub. Wrapping towels around our waists so my client doesn't see our packages—but he knows I just had sex.

He's a genius, and it doesn't take his extreme IQ to put the pieces together.

"Are you leaving? Why didn't you call first?" I ask seriously.

"Yes, and I thought I'd surprise you." He flashes a wry smile. "I know how much you love surprises."

I'm never surprised, I want to sling back, but Charlie and Jack are the only two who consistently keep me on my toes. "Call *first*," I emphasize.

Jack already jogs into the blue house. It'll take him ten times longer to pack a camera bag than for me to just put on clothes. No radio needed when I'm the sole bodyguard in Greenland.

"You usually like the surprise," Charlie says in a sip of espresso. "What's changed?" His lip rises like a little wiseass. And his eyes ping to the condom wrapper and bottle of lube on the high-table.

I'm a professional bodyguard.

I'd even dare to say I'm among the *most* professional in Omega. Jokes and fun times aside, I keep it well-mannered and appropriate with my client.

He wants to talk about uncouth—this is uncouth.

This morning has dinged my reputation. I'm just glad Omega isn't here to see it. Unless I open my big mouth to my friends in a haze of vodka and bourbon, I'll bury this.

"Nothing's changed," I force out. "Stay there." I head to the door.

He calls back, "If I wait for you, then something has changed!"

I know, Charlie. I don't acknowledge him as I enter the house. I start getting dressed. Jack is already shrugging on a winter jacket and trying to gather his camera equipment.

"I'll meet you there," he says. "Just text me."

I have to catch up to Charlie. Leaving Jack behind isn't easy. My muscles almost shriek and try to rip me back towards him. At least we're not in Philly or New York where he'd be pelted with caustic words and projectiles. It makes Jack doing his job and me doing mine easier.

With a quick kiss on his lips and squeeze of his hand, I run out.

Charlie didn't wait for me.

My mouth curves higher as I race after him.

27

Oscar Oliveira

BACK IN THE STATES, back to a grimmer reality.

"Hey, hey, hey." I get as close to Jack as I can as his face shatters a thousand different ways, his reddened eyes on his phone. "Don't look at it. Disable your notifications."

"You don't understand." His voice lowers, stress puncturing his features. "This isn't the usual *fuck you* condemnation, Oscar." He grips his camera at his side.

Our feet sink unevenly in hot sand. We're on a beach in *California*. Seal Beach, to be exact. No cloud in the sky, the salty ocean laps against the shore.

And I shift my gaze off Jack for half-a-second. Even a fucking millisecond feels like a betrayal to him right now. He's upset about some type of *Oslie* shit online, and look at me, glancing over at *Charlie*.

Fucking Charlie.

My duty, my job at every waking second of every waking minute of every fucking day. I'm fifteen feet away from him. He lounges under a blue umbrella, eyes shaded with green-tinted sunglasses.

Nearby, Jesse Highland uses Jack's short pause from filming to shake out his arms. Jesse has been holding a heavy boom mic. Since we're at the beach, the waves were apparently causing noise interference, so they popped out a boom kit.

Charlie is safe.

He's fine.

But not too far away on his right side, four sun-bathing college girls keep ogling him from their pink Zeta Beta Zeta towels.

Please don't be a problem.

Not right now, not when I want to be here for Jack. Attention back on him, his face is more torn up. "No, no…"

"What is it?" I ask.

He looks sick as he scrolls.

It's tearing *me* up.

"*Jack*," I say forcefully.

He shoves his phone in my chest. "They're all over my Instagram comments."

"They've already been all over your comments." And he's largely pushed past the vitriol

"Not like this." His jaw tics. "They're also on *We Are Calloway's* Facebook Page, the docuseries' Instagram account."

I look at the comment section.

Stop filming the Cobalts! Quit NOW!

You should be fired!

Youre disgusting. Put ur camera down.

Homewrecker! Quit filming Charlie!

We wont watch We Are Calloway until ur gone!!!

#FireJackHighland

#FireJackHighland

#FireJackHighland

They're trying to get him fired.

It's a hard kick to my gut, and this has to be a hundred times more painful for Jack. This is his career. The dream he's been chasing, the ladder he's been climbing, his life. It's starting to crumble around him.

Around us.

I glare at the hashtag. "I'll post on my Instagram account again," I tell him. I already re-downloaded the app I deleted, and I've been sharing cute couple photos of us. But week-old pics. I use the account *tactically*, and I don't want anyone to know our location in real-time.

Jack rubs his pained eyes. He's better versed in public perception than me, and he must know it's a weak attempt. His hand drops with a tight breath. "They're calling for my *termination*. They could be emailing the other producers, Oscar."

"Would they really fire you over some hostile stans with hurt feelings?"

Jack shrugs tensely, then grabs his phone out of my hand. "It's *terrible* publicity, and firing me could be an easy way to wipe their hands clean of the mess." He blinks back this tortured look.

I can't even wrap an arm around him right now. "The Hales, the Meadows, the fucking Cobalt *Empire* won't let that happen to you, Highland."

He shakes his head, his chest taut like weight is bearing on him. "You don't know that for certain, Os."

I'm about to offer greater reassurance—all that I have—when movement catches my eye.

Fuck my job.

I don't know how to live with it. Definitely don't know how to live without it. I slip Jack an apologetic look before I run towards a sorority girl in a striped bikini.

She's left her friend group to approach Charlie.

I glance back at Jack.

He's lifted up his camera to film my client—returning to work too—but so much tension lines his muscles. He keeps shifting his weight like he can't get comfortable.

Rip out your earpiece, Oliveira.

Go off-duty, go comfort him.

I can't.

Like everyone on SFO, I made an oath the day I signed up to be a bodyguard. To put someone else above Charlie's safety breaks that soul-bound promise.

So I keep my pace and roll to a stop in front of the sorority girl. "Sorry," I say cordially. "You can't approach him."

Her face falls. "He knows me."

I've heard that one a thousand times, but she's right. Charlie does sort of know this sorority girl. Her face is familiar from one night in the past, but her name isn't hitting me. "You still can't approach."

She lifts her sunglasses up to her blonde hair. "What if I wanted to give him something?" She plucks an envelope out of her straw beach bag.

Charlie Keating Cobalt is written neatly in black ink.

"He needs to read this." She waves the envelope in my face. I follow her gaze that darts to another bodyguard.

More security in California is why I have a radio.

Gabe Montgomery, the short stocky blond-haired temp I trained, loiters around Jack Highland. Arms crossed, permanent scowl, his intimidation is on point, so the sorority girl isn't considering negotiating with him over me.

Eliminates that potential headache.

I explain, "I can give Charlie the envelope if nothing hazardous is in there, but you can't approach him or talk to him." Truth: Charlie doesn't open his fan mail. He throws it away.

Her friends start packing their towels, books, and beach bags.

They better be leaving and not coming over here.

"Can't you just ask him?" she snaps.

"I already have."

I did the second we reached the beach. I reestablished his wishes, and he said, *no one talks to me.*

She bristles. "Really?"

"Really." I have no creative retort.

The #FireJackHighland tidal wave that just pummeled Jack—it's still crashing against me and ramping up my impatience, and I'm proud of myself for not raising my voice. For keeping my fucking cool.

De-escalation is the name of the best bodyguard game.

"Give this to him then." She hands me the envelope. "Make sure he gets it. You probably don't remember me, but I spent the night with Charlie once. So it's *that* kind of important."

She's implying that she's pregnant.

I don't even bat an eyelash.

For one, I know way too much about Charlie's sex life. He's told me countless times, "I *cum* on women. Not in them." I never talk about *my* sex life with him—Greenland was the first jolt of that between us—but Charlie will tread into TMI territory about his own.

I didn't ask for more details, but he told me he helps clean them up afterwards, so if anyone claims he's the father of their kid—it's probably a trash bin declaration.

For another, the one and only time he's met up with this sorority girl was too long ago for her to be pregnant with *his* child.

"Daniella!" her friend calls, trekking towards the parking lot with the other Zeta Beta Zeta girls. *They're leaving.*

Daniella jogs after them, teetering in the sand.

I survey the area, lingering for a half-a-second on Jack—who should be my entire attention. He still films Charlie lounging on a chair sunken in the sand.

The fact that we're both working should make me feel better, but it doesn't. My job impedes us more. Between security meetings, temp training, and actually protecting Charlie, it pulls me in a hundred directions.

And in the past week, we haven't found time together to have sex. Not since *Greenland.* And sure, sex isn't everything in a relationship. But it's something in ours.

I just keep hearing my failed short-term flings that I thought would last longer.

"You're never around, Oscar."

"You dipped out of *seven* dates early."

"What's the point in continuing this if you're hardly available?!"

I'm waiting for Highland to realize he deserves more time and emotional support than I can give. And then the axe will fall, and we'll be done when we've just started.

I trudge closer to Charlie and hawk-eye his surroundings again. Most people stay back from my client and snap photos of him on their cells, all at a distance. I already approached a crowd of college students in UCLA tees and told them to keep a twenty-foot perimeter. They were kind enough to comply with that, and they haven't pushed it.

Once the sorority girls disappear out of sight, I tear open the envelope.

Protocol: check Charlie's mail, even if he trashes it.

Charlie, we met at that thing back in June and hooked up. I'm pregnant. I would love to have you in this baby's life. I can't imagine you not being by my side during this time. I don't need money. I just need you.

Please contact me any way you can.

She left her full name, phone number, home address, Instagram and Twitter handle, and her TikTok account.

I hope in time Charlie can find someone who won't manipulate their way into his life. But today is not that day.

Needing to give him the letter, I have to stay an aching distance from Jack. I realize Jesse is packing up the boom, and Jack is back on his phone.

Put the phone down, Highland.

I'm a foot from Charlie.

"Gabe to Oscar," the new temp says over comms. "I've got a group of male beach volleyball players approaching."

I click my mic, noticing the same thing. Two of the guys are also holding expensive professional-looking cameras, ones often used by paparazzi. I speak in comms. "Don't let them near him."

When I say *him*, I mean Jack.

Coming home from Greenland, I knew the best way to physically protect Jack, when I can't, would be to hire a temp bodyguard.

Gabe has been assigned to his detail, and it's been going well. Considering it's only been seven days, I'm cautiously optimistic. Jack hasn't had a head-on collision with paparazzi. Gabe's even intercepted any and all projectiles. The Fizz Life soda can that was meant for Jack ended up bouncing off Gabe's iron-man chest like the aluminum was air.

"Copy," Gabe answers.

I focus on my client.

"Trash it," Charlie tells me before I even offer the envelope.

"Read this one," I advise. Just in case he somehow Houdini-ed into her pants without me realizing.

Charlie sighs, then plucks the envelope from my fingers.

My gaze veers back to Jack.

He's pocketed his phone, camera in his anxious grip, and he asks his brother, "Can you grab some B-roll of the coast before we leave?"

Jesse looks longingly at the ocean. He must've thought he was finished working so he could go surf. But he nods to his brother. "For sure. You want aerial shots? I can go grab the drone?"

Jack rubs his forehead, only partially present. My chest knots, my gaze cutting between Jack and Charlie.

"Kuya?"

He snaps into focus. "You know what, I'll get it. You've done a lot already. Go surf."

"You sure?" He hesitates. "I don't really mind—"

"Yeah. I have this." He lifts up his camera. It seems heavier in his hands somehow.

"Thanks, Kuya." Jesse bumps his brother's fist and finishes packing up the boom kit. His eyes rest on his older brother for a beat longer. Like he can tell something's up too.

"This is so fucking annoying," Charlie mutters with an agitated breath. Balling up the letter, he tells me, "It's a lie. We slept together in October, almost a year ago. I haven't seen her since, definitely not at 'a thing' in June." He uses air-quotes.

I nod, concluding as much.

Charlie catches me checking on Jack, who fits on a new camera lens. I expect some sort of wiseass comment from my client, but he pushes the green-tinted sunglasses to his head and tells me, "You can put Gabe on my detail and go off-duty. Did Jack not want to teach you how to surf?"

Yeah.

That was before the bad news, and Jack said that as a generalization. We didn't think we'd have leisure time to splash in the fucking ocean together today.

Hearing Charlie's words, Jack looks up from his camera at me. He still seems nauseous, and my stomach roils. With a breath, Jack says, "As much as I'd love to teach Oscar how to surf today, I have to grab this B-roll." He finishes attaching the new lens.

I want to convince Jack to put the camera down. For one second. But who am I to talk? I can't even utter the words, *I'm going off-duty. Gabe, take my detail.*

I sweep the beach with a quick glance. "I thought you were retired from being cupid," I tell Charlie. "And aren't you here for a fashion show?" We flew to California this morning specifically for some pop-up show he wanted to attend.

It's grossly overpriced if anyone asks me.

Nobody needs to pay a fucking grand for a ripped T-shirt. But it's not my money. Charlie can do what he wants.

"I am here for that." Charlie shades his eyes with the sunglasses again. "But I can achieve multiple things at one time."

Like your docuseries, I almost shoot back. He has *multiple* reasons for wanting a show centered around his life, and I still have zero clue his main motive for being filmed.

With angry Oslie stans demanding Jack be fired from *We Are Calloway*, I don't love the fact that a hanging question mark is hovering over this other project. A project which means *so much* to him.

Charlie's reasoning could have the potential to ruin the show. A show that Jack is working his ass off to make happen.

I'm just on an edge, and I'm afraid Jack is stepping even further off this cliff and I should be the one to catch his hand and pull him back.

Me.

Oscar motherfucking Oliveira.

What happens if Jack falls because I'm too busy chasing Charlie?

In that case, I should be single forever.

My mind is reeling, and even though I'm still on-duty, I can find moments with Jack. And I manage to capture one while he's at the shoreline filming surfers who wait for the perfect wave.

Water laps over his bare feet, and I come up next to him, angled so I have a good view of Charlie too.

Jack is quiet.

"I'm sorry this is happening," I say, voice husky and riddled with his pain that I feel.

"It's not your fault—"

"Ah, no. This isn't Jack Highland Makes Me Feel Better hour. I'm here for *you*, bro."

His eyes well up as our gazes embrace in ways that our bodies can't right now. "I've never been knocked back before. Not this hard. I've believed that I'm capable of anything, so I could power through to the top, and now it feels like *everything* I've ever strived for in my career is about to be ripped away."

"It's not," I say strongly. "If you can believe you're capable of anything, then *believe* I won't let everything fall apart right now. You chose me, didn't you, Long Beach? You risked it all for a guy who's gonna be the glue keeping the pieces together."

He inhales a bigger breath, then nods. His smile tries to fight through. "You give good pep talks."

I'm about to reply when Gabe jogs over, a trickle of sweat running down his temple. "I, uh…just had a thought, Oscar."

Imagine that. "Yeah?"

Jack zooms the camera on his little brother paddling out in the ocean.

"I thought maybe you could convince Akara to let me join the 24/7 roster." That'd officially make Gabe an Omega bodyguard and no longer a temp. He adds fast, "I already talked to him. He said I can't go onto the roster now because they don't have the budget for it. Then… you know, I asked why I'm working all these long hours compared to other temps. He said that I am being paid more, but by you, so I thought maybe you could convince him to just let me join the main roster, you know."

Jack spins on me, his camera instantly hanging at his side. "Wait a sec, you're *paying* for Gabe?"

"You needed the security."

"I thought the firm would cover the cost because it's related to Charlie…" He lets out a hurt noise. "I'm a fucking idiot—"

"Hey—"

"I should've known they don't have the money for *periphery* security. Akara is squeezed tight as it is." He rubs a hand down his face. "How much are you paying?"

Half my paycheck. Probably the first grossly large expense I've made at a time when I should be saving more. What I would've called a bad financial decision in the past, but damn is it worth every penny.

"I have you covered," I tell him.

"*Oscar.*"

"*I have you covered,*" I emphasize.

"I have the money," he says under his breath. "Just let me pay—"

"No—"

"Why not?"

"Because you're my *boyfriend,*" I say with utter fucking conviction. "You're my boyfriend, Jack, and if I can't physically be there for you, then I'm going to hire someone who can be." I pause. "Which I did." I jab a thumb towards Gabe, who stands an awkward distance from our argument.

Our first fight, I realize.

It's small.

And it simmers down almost immediately. A surprised breath leaves him, his lips ascending. Until he's smiling more heartwarmingly. "So what, we're mag jowa now?" His eyes fall down my build.

I begin to grin, just seeing his playful happiness make a powerful return. No clue what he said in Tagalog. So I ask, "Mag jowa?"

"Boyfriends," Jack translates.

I laugh with a nod. We've been dating, but we haven't outright called each other "boyfriends" yet.

'Bout time, Oliveira.

"Yeah"—I keep nodding—"you're my frat bro, happy-go-lucky boyfriend."

"Maybe cross out the lucky part." Our fingers toy with catching hold of each other's hand.

I shake my head. "At the *very* least, when all else fails, you're lucky that you have me."

Jack laughs, a lighter sound, but the noise fades. "I'm grateful you hired Gabe, you know, but if you're not willing to let me pay everything, then let's just split the cost. It'll make me feel better."

I only agree because of that last declaration.

28

Jack Highland

"WALKIE-CHECK," a PA says over the walkie-talkie.

I click mine. "Good check."

Every single *We Are Calloway* crew member is on site tonight, plus some extra grips, and I'm hauling ass across the golf course in the dark, a Steadicam harnessed to my chest.

A big charity event with the famous families means a big shoot. All the Hales, Meadows, and Cobalts are in attendance. Including their bodyguards. Add in family friends, donors, and plus-ones, and bodies are moving everywhere.

I prefer one-on-one shoots, but I love the huge group ones too. More than anything, I'm hanging onto tonight. This could be my last shoot with *We Are Calloway*.

I'm still an exec producer, but after this charity event, I'm scheduled for a serious meeting at the WAC offices. A sit-down with the other execs.

To talk about "my future" with the docuseries.

Anxiety is a four-thousand-pound seal on my chest. Heavier than the Steadicam. But I inhale, exhale—trying to breathe the animal *off*.

The bright side is Oscar. He said he'd drive me to the meeting. I actually look forward to the car ride alone with my boyfriend.

He's not getting off-duty tonight, dude. That thought blows, but I'm trying to lower my expectations. Mitigate my hopes so I'm not crushed or disappointed when he says, *I can't anymore. I have to follow Charlie.*

Oscar assured me, "I'm going with you to the meeting—I'll be there," but he also sounded like he was trying to convince himself.

Anyway, I have more pressing matters in the *present* than worrying about a few hours from now. I keep jogging across Hole 5. That thought almost makes me laugh.

Dangling twinkle lights brighten the first nine holes. The H.M.C. Philanthropies annual charity golf tournament has turned into a charity golf *soiree*.

Men in suits. Women in ballgowns. Fancy tables and pop-up bars dot the course, and golf carts decorated in green garland leisurely ride from one stop to the next.

Oscar told me Banks Moretti called it, "Bougie bar-hopping." That was before Oscar and I split apart—not stoked about that but we're both busy working.

I sprint up to a golf cart, familiar faces in the front seat. Akara slows to a stop for me, and next to him, Sullivan balances her bare feet on the dash.

"Hey," I greet with a pant. "Have you seen Charlie anywhere? I need to get some footage of him quickly." *Before it looks like I'm favoring the Born into Fame pilot.*

I also add, "And apparently some boss of some badass security company pulled Oscar onto Hole 3 for paparazzi control. So I can't even ask my boyfriend for Charlie's location."

Oscar isn't around Charlie right now.

Akara smiles. "That's because your boyfriend is one of the most senior security guys among both firms. I had to shift him and then put temps on Charlie. Paparazzi were invading the course from the bushes."

"It was fucking creepy," Sulli says.

I bump her fist, then Akara's in more of a greeting.

A Secret about Akara Kitsuwon: my college-friend raved about Akara for four weeks after they hooked up. He restrained her to a headboard with rope and made her come five times.

Akara confirmed her retelling. He made me swear not to gossip to production.

Of course I kept the secret.

"I can find Charlie," Akara tells me. "Hold on."

I wait while he switches a knob on his radio, attached to his slacks. Bodyguards are in designer suits to *blend* among guests, so he literally looks like a million-dollars, and I'm sweating over here in workout clothes.

Production can't blend with camera equipment.

Since Sulli also wears formalwear—a green sequined romper—the two of them almost look like a couple next to each other. I've always thought Akara was into her, but he's adamantly said, *no*.

Lately, from what I've seen, they're slightly awkward together. Sulli slips him a look now, then he slips her one. She whips her head away, staring up at the stars.

He keeps his eyes on her while he speaks in comms. "Akara to Security, anyone have eyes on Charlie?" He waits for a response, his gaze back on me. He laughs at the walkie in my hand. "Is that little dinky thing not working for you, Jack?"

Security ribbing production. *One status quo still intact.*

I dangle the walkie by the antennae. "This little dinky thing is doing just fine."

He laughs again, the noise more in his chest.

I smile back, but my lips downturn.

Because I actually could ask the PAs on the walkie if they've seen Charlie. Thing is, I'd rather not advertise to the crew that I'm hunting for Charlie specifically. Do *not* need them thinking my priorities are set on this side project.

Which is why I need to move fast. Sweat drips down my temples, and I wipe my face with my wrist.

"Thank you. Roger that." Akara eyes me. "He's at Hole 2."

Jesus, shit.

That's a far run.

"Hop on," Sulli gestures to the backseat. "We can take you there."

I immediately seize the offer. "Thanks, Sulli." I climb onto the backseat, a little stiffly with the Steadicam, and Akara presses on the gas, swerving the electric golf cart towards Hole 2.

"Where's your brother?" Akara wonders.

"I told him to go grab as much footage as possible. So he's around here somewhere." *I trust Jesse.* He's been doing excellent work. My brother is talented with a camera and landscape shots.

We bump along the course, and Sulli starts twisting her hair in a high-bun—Akara hits the brake. "Sulli, down!"

"What? Kits?"

He pulls her down over his lap.

A golf ball flies at the cart and I lean back. It *dings* the frame and bounces off. My pulse skids. A few inches lower and that would've hit Sulli in the face.

"What the…fuck?" Sulli lifts her head slowly, cautiously. Hair falling out of a half-done bun. She's staring at Akara's lap.

I mean, her face was in his crotch.

I could laugh. I *almost* laugh, but her face is beet red. His chest collapses in a strange breathing pattern. He looks her over, then whips his head towards three drunk men with golf clubs.

"Sorry!" they laugh.

"FOUR!" one chuckles.

Akara is fuming. "Stay here, Sul." He hops off the cart. "Hey! No one is playing golf tonight!"

Bougie bar-hop.

I can't wait around for Akara.

"See you, Sulli."

"Yeah…" She's in a daze watching Akara confront the drunks.

I'm off running.

And I reach Hole 2 dripping sweat and trying to catch my breath. No one wants to hear me cough up a lung on footage.

Charlie loiters at the edge of a dark pond in the night. Temps stand off to the side, not interfering. I focus my camera on him.

He sips champagne, the bottom of his wrinkled shirt untucked from his dress pants. His gaze turns away. "Trying to upstage me?" he asks.

I back up about to capture the other person he's speaking to.

Fuck.

It's his twin brother. Dressed in a crisp suit, dark hair artfully styled, Beckett Cobalt saunters up to Charlie. I turn off my camera.

Can't record Beckett.

Still, it took me forever to reach Charlie, so I might as well wait out this interaction.

"Believe me, everyone I've run into today has asked for *you*," Beckett says into a smile. "You were cursed by the fucking devil at birth, I swear."

Charlie smiles bitterly. "The one who wants to be alone is always wanted." He finishes off his champagne. "Too bad I can't be wanted by someone interesting."

Beckett slides over that comment and acknowledges me with a nod. "How's it going, Jack?"

"It's going." My shoulders ache under the Steadicam. "Charlie's been a great audience. I actually prefer to socialize with him over the guests."

And I do mean that.

The ladies and men who laugh in their clustered groups all appear glossed over with false bravados. Even Connor Cobalt, Charlie's dad has put on an air of charm that has a layer of deception underneath its sincerity.

Charlie might be "a pain in the ass" as Oscar puts it, but he's always himself.

"Charlie's said the same about you," Beckett says casually.

That surprises me—that Charlie would talk about me in private to his twin brother. Then again, I have been following him for weeks. I guess, I've become a part of his life in a way that I never have before.

A Secret about Charlie Cobalt: He told me that he's the one who introduced Beckett to cocaine, and he's regretted it ever since.

Charlie plucks another champagne flute off of a passing server's tray.

"Jack!"

I turn at the sound of Oscar's nineteen-year-old sister Joana.

Oh no.

I shoot Beckett a quick look that Oscar would nail-gun in his brain. *Leave Joana Oliveira alone.*

She jogs over, her silver dress hiked up with one hand, and her curls bounce with each footfall to the pond. She's wearing a pair of Vans instead of heels, and she makes a concerted effort to avoid Charlie and Beckett as she stops in front of me. "Have you seen my brother?"

I shift to block Beckett. "Which one?" I ask.

"The one you're dating," she says. "Obviously."

"Hole three."

She's about to leave, when Beckett glides around me and says, "Hi to you, too."

Joana stiffens and then turns her gaze on him.

I tense.

FYI: I have never been in this position. This is my boyfriend's baby sister. Yes, *baby* sister. I have seen her name in Oscar's phone and heard him call her "baby sis" way too many times. I know he considers her almost like a daughter, and the fact that he hates—no, he *loathes*—the idea of Beckett and Joana together has my pulse on an adrenaline rush.

When it comes to these families, I'm used to not intervening on anyone's behalf. I let security take sides.

I'm a filmmaker. I watch. I record. I stay back and let things play out. Oscar's the one who'd fling himself between them.

My camera is off, and ethically, I have to keep it off for Beckett.

Instead of being Oscar's fill-in, I decide to do what I'd do if his sister were my brother. I observe like an adult chaperone at a high school dance. Threatening.

And ready to intervene when necessary.

Joana starts looking around Beckett, stepping close like she's trying to find something. She pretends to search behind him.

Beckett frowns and gracefully one-eighties to face her. "What are you doing?" He has that iconic *what the fuck* face that has been meme'd to death on Reddit.

"Oh sorry," Joana says like she's not sorry at all. "I was looking for the mattress that's always attached to your back."

Charlie chokes on his champagne.

I stop breathing.

Beckett's brows rise at Joana. He looks her up and down. "I'd say the same for you, but you seem like the kind of girl who loves getting pounded from behind."

She snorts. "Classy."

What the fuck am I watching?

He raises his glass. "Toujours." *Always.*

She lifts the edge of her dress, so she can jog again. "With that"— she looks to me—"I'm going to go find my brother."

"Good idea," I agree.

I probably shouldn't be a chaperone at a high school dance ever. Oscar is going to flip. I turn to Beckett. "Don't go there again," I say. "All of SFO have warned you. So now I'm warning you."

"She instigated that one." Beckett grabs a pastry off a server's tray, a smile toying at his lips. "Plus, she basically called me a slut."

Charlie says something in quick French to Beckett, and my walkie crackles, "Ethan for Jack."

I hit the button. "What's up?"

"We need you on Jane in the clubhouse."

Come on.

I hesitate to comply and leave my subject. But I say, "On it." And then a large crash echoes from up the green. Near hole three.

Oscar.

Clubhouse or Oscar?

We Are Calloway or my boyfriend? He has a lot of people on his side, a lot of bodyguards there to help whatever just happened, but the crash was loud. Fear and worry propel me in his direction.

I take off running to hole three. With adrenaline pumping, the Steadicam suddenly feels lighter than air.

29

Oscar Oliveira

"OSCAR TO SECURITY, I need a medic. I need a medic." I repeat twice and add my location so everyone knows, despite my controlled voice, that shit is bad.

A golf cart just capsized and rolled.

My vigilant ass is set on hot coals. I'm running with all I have over to the slope that the golf cart just tumbled down. Twinkle lights *barely* illuminate the area. It's dim, and I'm only nearest the crash-site having just dealt with paparazzi.

A couple Alpha guards are still restraining cameramen who snuck in the event.

"Is anyone hurt?!" I yell, racing in a quick descent to the flipped cart. "Luna?! Tom?! Eliot!?" I saw all three on the golf cart before they crashed.

Just what I never wanted to see happen again. I don't care if it's in fucking golf-cart-sized form. I never wanted to come up on another crash.

That was one of the worst days of my life.

And I'd bet a solid grand most in Alpha, Epsilon, and Omega would say the same.

An extreme amount of adrenaline keeps me focused as I squat down to the cart. "Can you hear me?!" *Motherfuck, someone answer me.* I need to lift the golf cart off them in case they're being crushed.

"Uh…" Tom suddenly rolls woozily out from underneath the frame. Grass stains his white shirt, and a trickle of blood runs from a forehead cut.

"Eliot! Luna!" I call out.

"I'm pinned," Eliot grunts.

"Ow, ow," Luna winces.

It's hard to see them in the dark.

Quickly, I widen my stance and grip the golf cart. Quinn appears at my side before I lift. He's out of breath like he jogged over, and he grabs the other end.

"One, two, three," I count, and we heave the golf cart up together. We hold it steady.

Eliot elbow-crawls out, but not before ensuring Luna can follow. She pushes herself with her legs, cradling her arm against her glittery jumpsuit.

My muscles burn while I keep a firm grip.

Eliot looks okay, but Luna's bone is one-hundred-percent fucked. Radius, ulna—her forearm is painfully bent. Once they're clear of the golf cart, my baby bro and I right it on its wheels.

"Luna!" Maximoff is running towards his little sister in a full-on sprint down the slope. The Hale prince is out-running Farrow, who's a few feet behind, a med bag strapped to his shoulder. Ripley's not with them, so I assume someone in Maximoff's family must be holding the baby.

"Her arm, Redford."

His focused eyes ping to me as he passes by, a small, serious acknowledgement that this was too close to what we both experienced together. Thank God it's not nearly as bad.

While Farrow does a medical assessment and Maximoff checks on his family, I do a quick sweep of our surroundings. My pulse still at a peak.

Onlookers exist, watching from the clubhouse's deck, but not many guests are around Hole 3. Besides paparazzi, it's been vacant since the non-alcoholic bar is posted here.

Maximoff's concern is replaced quickly by anger. "What the fuck?" he growls at them. "Who was driving? Why were you doing donuts?"

Did not see the troublemakers doing donuts.

Comms blow up in my ear. Epsilon and Omega. I pick apart Akara's voice. "Akara to Quinn, did you see Luna, Tom, and Eliot steal a golf cart and a case of champagne earlier?"

Quinn isn't responding.

"Hey." I nudge his arm. "Akara just radioed you, little bro."

Quinn rolls his eyes at me, then clicks his mic. "Yeah."

I hate narking on a client, but my brother should've called that one in. Akara wouldn't have ratted them out to the parents. They're all adults.

And at least we'd all know they were drinking and taking a joy-ride.

Quinn glares at me. "What?"

I'm disappointed in him, and I can't hide that from my face.

"Oh—fuck," Eliot curses, causing us to look back. His gaze is latched to the clubhouse's deck where their parents are descending in a fury.

"Is that Mom?" Tom squints and holds a hand above his eyes.

"Brother, see you in the afterlife," Eliot says. He taps knuckles with Tom, but they don't leave Luna. They stay while Farrow speaks softly to her and helps her to her feet.

She needs X-rays.

"Can you talk to Dad?" Luna pleads with a pained wince to Maximoff.

He caves. "Yeah."

"Akara to Quinn, why am I just now hearing about your client on a golf cart when it's already flipped?"

Quinn clicks his mic. "It wasn't important."

The line dies, and I can feel Akara halfway across the golf course cursing the night sky with frustration and anger. Our mistakes are his mistakes.

My brother drops his mic cord. "What?" he growls at me again.

"I didn't say anything." I catch the sight of Jack—my Jack—running towards us, a heavy Steadicam strapped to his chest.

I read his lips from a distance. He mouths, *are you okay?*

His concern shouldn't surprise me. Hell, his appearance shouldn't either, but both do. Probably because I just thought…he's filming.

He's working. How is he making time for me? Especially when my ass struggles to make more for him.

My chest rises, longing for Highland to keep his pace towards me. And I nod to him. *I'm okay.* But I could use a Jack Highland hug.

A kiss. Three kisses. Endless amounts.

Fuck, I'm greedy.

"You didn't have to say anything, Oscar—you had that look," Quinn snaps.

My gaze tears back to my little brother. I hold up my hands. "I'm just standing here, bro."

He scratches his jaw, his gaze pierced with venom. The scar under his eye—I wasn't there when he was KO'd in the ring. A hard punch split the skin on his cheekbone.

"You need to say something to me?" I ask very gently, not trying to set him off.

I am *genuinely* confused on why he's so heated off so little. And I want to know.

"You're the one who's not talking," Quinn retorts. "You're just *staring* at me like I flushed your Doritos down the drain."

I crack a grin. "Good analogy, bro."

He glowers. "Fuck you."

What the hell? "Quinn—"

"Just say it!" He gets in my face. "You think I should've called it in. You think I should update Akara on every *little* movement I make because I can't do my job—"

"I never said that you can't do your job." My eyes narrow in confusion, hurt. "Do I think you should've called this one in? Yeah. Do I wish you did? Yeah."

He groans into a frustrated growl.

"I never said you're a bad bodyguard."

"You didn't have to!"

"Is that what this is about?" I question.

"Fuck off," he growls, shoving me back with two hands to my chest.

I rock from the force and step back on my own accord. Giving us space. "Just talk to me, bro." *Please.*

He's stewing. Glaring.

I snap. "This feud is in your fucking head, Quinn!" I point an angry finger at my temple.

"In my head?!" He rams his hands at my chest, and I stumble back against the golf cart we up-righted together. We draw attention, but if I even look away from Quinn, it feels like the whole golf course will explode.

"Quinn." I come forward.

He grabs the collar of my shirt like he's trying to shake me. There's so much fucking pain in his face that I don't understand.

Voices pitch all around us, but the cacophony bleeds away.

It's just me and my twenty-two-year-old brother.

Talk to me.

He takes a swing.

I duck—he knew I'd duck.

His right hook slams into my ribcage. Wind knocks out of me. I heave for breath. We honestly don't physically fight like this a lot. I've been hit plenty of times in my life, but the worst ones always come from my brother.

He comes back, and we grip each other. Wrestling upright, trying to get a strong hold, and we draw each other further away from the golf cart.

His fist connects with my gut again.

Fuck.

He rams me into a sand pit. Little spotlights illuminate the pit, and I see better. I sock him in the jaw—just to keep Quinn from landing a harder blow.

His lip is split—I split his lip.

What the fuck am I doing? I feel sick, and I grapple trying to stand up in the sand. But we're both taught to fight, not flee.

We grew up learning to solve issues with our *fists*.

Fight it out.

I've never wanted to fight my brother.

He socks my face, the blow so hard that I land on my ass. Blood fills my mouth; I wipe it with my hand while a groan rips through me. Another blow.

And I hold my throbbing cheek. Stars in my eyes. I feel his anger seep into me, and he's barely using force anymore.

He's kneeling and pounding a light fist into my arm. Breathing like he's on the verge of crying.

So raw and painful that I can't for a second believe I didn't do something to cause it.

I'm sorry.

I don't know what the fuck I did, but I'm so sorry.

Arms pull at my shoulders and then drop to my waist, tugging me, and the voices around me suddenly come into focus. Like someone finally turned up the volume to the television.

"STOP IT!" Jo is shrieking the loudest. She's pulling at Quinn while I realize Farrow and Jack are dragging me away from the fight.

"Oscar." Jack's voice draws my focus. He's the one directly behind me. He's the one who's holding me around the waist and trying to tug me backwards. I realize, he has no Steadicam on anymore. He must've snapped it off his chest.

My blood-stained palm slides on top of his hand that's pressed against my abs. We're still in the sand pit. My head is whirling. I turn more to Jack, my arm slipping around him.

"Does it hurt?" he asks, wincing at my swollen cheek.

"No." I glance over at my brother who slowly rises to his feet. *That hurts.*

Jack laces our fingers. It almost brings tears to my fucking eyes. Thank God he's here right now. I suck in a sharp breath.

"What's wrong with you two?!" Jo screams at us as she holds onto Quinn's bicep. He doesn't dare try and fight against her. He spits a wad of blood into the sand.

Thatcher and Akara jog towards us, and I sweep the green. Shit. *Fuck me.* We're the center of attention. Guests have crowded the clubhouse's deck in the distance. Watching us. And it has nothing to do with the golf cart crash.

I can barely think straight right now. It barely registers when Akara says, "Get the fuck out of the sand pit."

Over comms I hear the Alpha lead say, "Kitsuwon, get a fucking lid on your men."

The air tenses.

Heat expels from Akara like an inferno of anger. This is a bad look. Kitsuwon Securities is a new company with a low margin for error, and there's always an undercurrent of acknowledgement that we're competing in reputation with Price's Triple Shield.

All of us shuffle onto the green, leaving the bloody sand behind. We head towards the stolen golf cart and smashed bottles of champagne. "Akara—" I start.

"Give me one reason I shouldn't fire both of you right now," he spits, glancing between me and my brother. "One fucking reason!"

Quinn and I are both quiet.

He should really fire us.

There's no excuse for brawling at a charity event. But what is my life without security? It's been a perfect fit from the start like nothing else.

Jack disentangles our hands. "Akara." He steps closer to my boss. "You can't fire him." He sounds like he's negotiating a contract. Which would probably work for Highland, but this is security.

This is SFO.

He's an interloper.

Still, I have to applaud my boyfriend, he has some guts.

Akara's glare detours to Jack. "Don't you dare. Don't you *fucking* dare use our friendship right here."

Jack looks hurt. "I can't ask you for a favor, Akara? Really?"

"*Really*," Akara forces. "Not about this. You dating Oscar is great—I approve. Wonderful. But the second it interferes with my men and security, that's where I have a fucking problem, Jack. I can't do you a solid by giving partial treatment to Oscar. If he fucks up, there are repercussions."

Jack nods. "I understand and respect that, so throw out us talking friend-to-friend. How about just rational person to rational person? You can't fire Oscar. Because you won't find someone else who can be Charlie's bodyguard. Not like him."

Mic drop.

My mouth curves upward.

Highland is good. He knows as long as I'm Charlie's bodyguard, I might as well be tenured in the position.

Akara cools off somewhat, not disagreeing with Jack.

I nod to my boyfriend in appreciation, and he nods back with a rising forty-watt smile—but we celebrate too soon.

"Mandatory Omega security meeting right after the charity event ends, for all of SFO," Akara decrees. "Meet up in security's bus. Temps will escort your clients home."

Right after the event?

No, no, no.

I'm supposed to drive Jack to *his* meeting with the docuseries execs. The make-or-break meeting—the one where he might come out with zero job. His whole world blown to smithereens, and I need to be there for my boyfriend. I need to be his shoulder to cry on. His pick-me-up. His pep talk and biggest fan.

I can't be stuck in a security meeting.

My mind is a Tilt-A-Whirl, barely registering Akara's next words.

"Oscar and Quinn, you're off-duty immediately. The SFO meeting is still *mandatory*, so you'll have to stick around the event until it's over."

I'm in no position to move the meeting to another day, but I try anyway. For Jack.

Because he did so much more for me tonight.

And what the hell am I even doing for him? "I have to be in Center City right after this," I tell Akara.

"I don't care," he snaps. "You fought in front of the fucking *families*. In front of guests. In front of Alpha and Epsilon. You're so lucky I haven't already fired you."

I know.

Jack shrugs his shoulders in a way that punctures my heart. "It's okay, Os."

It's not. I shake my head.

"I'll call you."

"Right after," I make him promise.

"Yeah. Right after."

THE EXTRA-WIDE SECURITY VAN HAS AN AISLE

and four rows of black leather seats. We're parked outside the golf course's clubhouse. Six of seven SFO bodyguards are present. Everyone except Farrow. Not shocked. Just annoyed.

Adjusting the icepack to my cheek, I check the time on my phone.

I'm going to kill Redford. This shit can't start without him.

"Pringle?" Donnelly offers the slender can of BBQ Pringles to me. He's in the row in front of mine, and we sit sideways, our heads against the tinted window, and I see a sliver of his face, the rest obstructed by the seat.

"No thanks." I can't even stress eat right now.

My baby bro is in the very first row near the driver's seat. He's had his earbuds in, staring out the window. The Moretti brothers and Akara are in a convo at the very back, so hushed that I can't distinguish anything. Bet they're discussing my brother's fate in security.

I'm irreplaceable, but Quinn can be let go.

It weighs on me.

Feeling choked, I pop a couple more buttons on my button-down. Most of the guys have shed the tailored suit jackets and undone ties. We look like a sober bachelor party that ended in a fistfight.

It did end in a fistfight, Oliveira.

I blow out a coarser breath.

"How many times did it roll?" Donnelly asks more quietly. He means the golf cart.

"I couldn't tell." Alright, I do steal a Pringle.

Sweet, heavenly *food.*

Donnelly crunches on a chip. "Been sayin' all along Cobalts are invincible. Eliot and Tom have what—a cut? And Luna's arm is probably broken."

"It is broken," I whisper. "No fucking doubt about that, bro."

Donnelly sighs. He hates seeing the families hurt. We all do, but I'm gonna take solace in the fact that no one was gravely injured tonight.

He stacks five Pringles together. "Bad luck crew." He stuffs his mouth full, and I know he's referring to the Hale family. He mumbles something about "Cobalts never die" with reverence.

If Jack weren't alone right now when I should be with him—I'd be grinning. I lick the barbeque seasoning off my thumb.

And if Farrow were on time, he'd butt in with, *"Technically, Charlie got hurt in the car crash last year. So did Ben. They're not invincible."*

But he's not here to knock the Cobalt Empire down a few pegs. And we delight in the armored romanticism of our favorite famous family.

I check the time again.

Come on, Redford.

"You'll make it, man," Donnelly reassures. "Jack might be in the production meeting for a whole two hours."

True. I could catch him right as he leaves.

If Farrow would hurry the fuck up.

Three minutes pass.

Then five more. "Kitsuwon," I call to the back.

"Yeah?"

"Can we just say Farrow is med team tonight and not SFO and start without him?"

"I'll catch him up," Donnelly pipes in. "I can take notes." He's about to put on reading glasses.

"We're waiting for Farrow," Akara decrees, his no-nonsense, strict perimeters part of my punishment, I think. "He's SFO as much as he's med team."

Fucking, *ugh*.

The clock keeps moving.

Ten more minutes, then another twenty. Three more Pringles cans dusted off. And finally, Farrow dips into the van. He barely reaches the first row, and I can't bite my tongue.

"Where the fuck have you been?"

He stops in the aisle, meeting my harsh glare with confusion. "At the hospital." He throws his med bag on a vacant seat.

Yeah…I feel like a dick.

"Is Luna alright?" Quinn asks about his client.

Salt meet wound. *Biggest jackass award goes to me.*

"She needed X-rays," Farrow explains. "She'll be okay." That's all he can really reveal under doctor-patient confidentiality. He takes a seat across the aisle from mine and shakes his head at me like *what the fuck is wrong?*

I haven't had time to talk to him about Jack's meeting. So Farrow didn't know the importance of getting the fuck out of here ASAP.

"Tell you later," I mutter, our eyes veering as Akara heads to the front. Standing, our boss starts the meeting.

Let's go.

I'm ready to end this thing.

Akara snaps his fingers to his palm. "We all know what happened tonight is grounds for termination. I want to make this absolutely clear, if we were all still employed by Triple Shield, I wouldn't have the power to keep you two around." He looks from Quinn to me. "You'd be *fired.*" He addresses everyone now. "We don't all have to be best friends, but if we're going at it—the families should never know. We should appear like an unbreakable fortress, and if we show our asses, we've failed.

They need to have unwavering faith in our ability to protect them at all fucking times."

The bus is quiet.

We all respect Akara, and I take his words to heart.

I fucked up royally tonight.

"Oscar, Quinn." Akara speaks to us directly. "If you can't work together, then you both can't stay."

I've thought about this moment. I knew it'd come, and I choose my words carefully. "If you fire him," I tell our boss, "I'm quitting."

Farrow chews gum slowly with a look at me like *what the fuck are you doing now?*

Donnelly pipes in, "Oscar quits, I quit."

Farrow shakes his head and rolls his eyes like we're dumbasses.

I hear Banks say something about "the Yale boys" to Thatcher in the back.

Both of my friends' reactions are intrinsically *them*, and I can't help but grin. Before tonight, I would've probably given anything for my little bro to be sacked. Leave security behind and apply to college. Get an experience he missed out on.

But Quinn's pain is still so fresh in my mind. I can feel it against my swollen cheek. I can feel it writhing around in me. And I don't want him to lose anything.

Quinn turns slightly in his seat, earbud cord hanging around his neck. His expression breaks on me, but I still can't see the gnarled roots under the oak tree.

"You're really putting me in this position?" Akara asks, staring at me like I'm a ghost of a person.

"He's my brother," I say.

Akara looks between me and Quinn. "You both want your job? You want to stay on SFO? Then you have two month's pay-cut and mandatory therapy together. Once a week."

Quinn barely even looks my way. How is therapy going to work if he can't meet my eyes?

I'll try anything, though.

We go over a few more security matters. Like scheduling for training temps. And I'm biting my nails watching time slip by.

Meeting ends, and I bolt out of the van. I'm going to drive another security vehicle, the Black Widow, and I'm halfway to the SUV when my phone rings.

No, no, no.

If he's calling, then that means his meeting is over. His fate has been decided, and I wasn't there. I'm not there.

Don't be Jack.

Don't be Jack.

I dig for my pocket and glance at the screen.

Caller ID: *Highland.*

My stomach sinks. I missed it.

Why in the ever-loving hell would anyone want to be with me?

30

Oscar Oliveira

JACK DROVE BACK TO New York to be with me after his meeting. He's still in limbo. He said they're still "evaluating" the situation, but Maximoff and Jane have been putting pressure on the execs to keep Jack on in the same role. Like I thought they would. They really care about Jack.

My boyfriend was a wreck last night. Not in a typical meltdown fashion. There were no tears. His leg kept jostling while we hung out on the couch. He hardly ate the takeout dessert, which I brought home as an *I'm sorry*.

His career is in purgatory, and that's stressing him out more. If they'd given him a direct final answer, I wonder if he'd be this anxious.

"Sorry, I'm such a buzzkill right now," he told me, trying to swallow the cake with a knot in his throat.

That hurt my heart. "Do you think I expect you to do cartwheels and throw glitter around me?" I asked him seriously. "You had a bad night. We both had a bad night. Let's wallow together and eat cake."

Light touched his eyes.

I slipped a strong arm around his waist.

He slouched back, his smile slowly ascending. After a minute or two, he asked, "You want to kiss it out?"

Yeah, we did a lot more than kiss. It was a freeing cap on an emotional night. And waking up to a new day is like waking with a massive hangover.

It's already the afternoon, and mentally, I'm scrolling through the charity golf event with a nauseous cringe.

Kitsuwon Securities 1 – Triple Shield 1.

Alpha and Epsilon bodyguards have been boasting all day about our face-in-the-mud failure. How they cleaned up Omega's mess. It's a far fall from our high when SFO found the girl squad in Anacapri.

I'd put myself near the top of Omega, at the risk of being an arrogant ass. Mistakes and I aren't friends. We're not even acquaintances. I'm the bodyguard who has the brilliant ploys, who has the correct reads on threats, who sneaks around chaos before chaos catches my ass—and now I'm the bodyguard who cost Omega a win.

We're not losers yet, but I didn't think I'd be the first one to tarnish the firm's reputation. Almost guiltily, I'm glad I screwed up because of my brother and not because of my relationship with Jack.

I don't want anyone believing I'm unable to be a good bodyguard with a boyfriend. If I'm only successful at this job being *single…*

Yeah, I'm not going to sit on that tragic thought for long.

At the moment I'm preoccupied. And I'm on my knees in the loft—sadly, not to blow Jack Highland and see him come.

I'm unpacking my sister's suitcase.

While I fold her jeans into a drawer, she's on the edge of the bed next to Jack and showing off her music playlist. "You should add Emicida and Ludmilla to your joint playlist with Oscar. He probably just put a ton of pop and axé in there."

My baby sis taking shots at my favorite music genres, and she's been living with me for half-a-second. She just really loves funk.

Jack grins back at me. "What's axé?"

He's unaware he's listened to it already on the playlist we made together. We keep adding songs for the two-hour rides between New York and Philly. "Axé sounds a little like reggae and calypso," I explain.

"It has African origins." I look to Joana. "And I take offense to the attitude towards *pop*. Everyone loves Lady Gaga."

"Hmm." Joana squints with mock consideration. "Don't think that's true."

I outstretch a hand towards Jack for back-up.

He smiles while he wets his lips, his sparkling eyes say he loves me more than Lady Gaga, which is why he tells Jo, "I like Lady Gaga. 'Stupid Love' is a cool track." It's the only song of hers he won't skip halfway through.

When Jo focuses on her phone, Jack mouths to me knowing I can read lips, *two peas in a pod.* He motions to me and him. Not because we like the same music—we don't always—but because he'll join my lonely pea pod.

What the fuck, I sound like a twelve-year-old dork with a crush.

My mouth curves upward.

More and more every single day, I love the foundation of our relationship. Built on encouragement and love and support. Knowing that he'll be my biggest fan and I'll be his is a beautiful fucking thing.

Jack smiles a brighter smile.

Igniting my lungs.

If only Oslie stans could see *this*—maybe they'd get it. #FireJackHighland is still a hashtag they love to spread, but I'm hoping the longer I'm with Jack—the longer we're seen out together in public— the more they'll realize this isn't short-term or a publicity stunt.

We're here to stay.

I have to believe that too. Even when I'm screwing up left and fucking right.

"You'll love this one," Joana says, clicking into a new song. She plays "Levanta e Anda" by Emicida, a Brazilian rapper.

They bounce their head to the rhythm.

"You know who else would love this?" Jack says midway through. "Akara."

I groan at the mention of the boss I fucked over.

Jack winces. "Still a sore subject?"

I push curls out of my lashes. "I still feel like the biggest jackass. Especially since Kitsuwon Securities is footing the therapy bill for me and Quinn." Akara didn't have to do that. "I need to send him about fifteen *I'm so fucking sorry* gift baskets. I won't even eat the cookies out of them this time."

Jack laughs.

But Joana shuts off the music too suddenly. "How was therapy this morning?" Her seriousness causes me to sit up straighter, one of her workout tees halfway folded in my hand. She eyes the welt on my cheekbone.

I've already told Jack the truth: therapy feels important, but it was ineffective today. Quinn stayed silent for the entire sixty-minutes. If a professional can't help us resolve this, I'm starting to lose hope we'll ever reach better ground.

It's day one. Maybe everything is still too raw from last night's fight.

"It went well," I say, stretching the truth…a lot.

"Really?" She sounds hopeful.

I nod and take her inhaler out of a suitcase pocket. "Yeah."

"So maybe you don't need me to move in after all," Joana says.

She finally agreed to live with me because she pitied my ass after the fistfight with Quinn. And to be perfectly clear, I purposefully made myself look *pitiful*. Best strategy I could think of.

And it worked.

I have no guilt over the tactic. Her next plan was to couch-surf on random sofas, and I'd much rather her be safe here. Even at the cost of being down the hall from Beckett.

Jack rehashed my sister's run-in with Beckett Cobalt at the golf course, and I considered penning Beckett a letter entitled:

Flirting Etiquette 101:

Stop Flirting with Joana Oliveira

He keeps seeking her out when she wants to be a hundred-feet away from him, so I have a big issue. But I know my sister can hold her own too.

"I need you here, Jo." I give her a look. "And you're already unpacked."

"Halfway, but you're doing a great job." She adds, "And I'm not going anywhere."

Good.

I'm about to return to her suitcase.

I stop and assess them on the bed and me on the floor. "You're over there sharing music with my boyfriend while I'm folding your tops. What's wrong with this picture?"

"You should be hanging up the tops, not folding them," Jo quips.

I clap loudly.

She applauds herself too. "Thanks for helping me with my things, really." Her lips rise. "I like that I get to spend more time with Jack." She tells him, "Oscar never brought home his college boyfriend, so I never got to grill him."

Jack looks shocked, his hand runs through his dark hair and stops on his head for a long, long beat.

Shit.

My chest tightens at his reaction and at the mention of an *ex*. I glance at Joana. "Like you're grilling Jack right now? You're closer to calling him your BFF."

"I already knew Jack before you two started dating. It's different. I never met Darrien."

"Darrien?" Jack repeats.

Look at that, she gave him the *name* of my ex. "Yeah." I imprison a breath, our eyes locked. Wondering what he's thinking.

His knee bounces. "Why didn't you bring him home? Were you scared your parents wouldn't like—?"

"No." I shake my head stiffly. "I just didn't come home a lot, so I didn't bring him to Philly when I did."

"Oscar was married to Yale," Joana explains. "She was the other woman stealing my brother from the family."

Jack shifts his gaze to my sister. "College will do that." He slips me a furtive smile like, *I understand.*

I can't regret Yale, not for a single second. The experience opened my world and changed my life forever. I am who I am because I left home and discovered myself without any familial pressures attached. It was a freeing time of my life.

It's also a personal, introspective take on the situation. If I shared this with my brother and sister, they'd be upset thinking I valued being alone over being with them.

To me, that's *not* it.

I didn't love college because I never saw them, but being on my own did help me figure out what I wanted for myself.

Jack glances anxiously at his phone, his fingers racing back through his hair. He's still waiting for the execs to email an actual verdict.

I stand up.

"So if I'm taking the *bed*," Joana says, hand on the gray comforter, "and *your* brother lives with you too…?" She eyes Jack. "Then, how are you both going to…?" She glances between us.

Good fucking God. My nineteen-year-old sister is asking where me and Jack are going to fuck.

Highland has his knuckles to his mouth, his smile rising. I love that not much fazes him.

"Ah, ah, ha." I wave a finger at Jo. "That's off-limits."

Boundaries, I have them when it comes to my nosy family and who I date.

She throws up her hands. "It's an honest question, Oscar. There is no door! We're in a fucking *studio*."

Jack tips his head like, *she has a point.* He stands off the bed. "I'm a filmmaker," he tells Jo. "I know how to get creative."

My muscles contract. He might've given my sister way too much info, but fuck is he hot.

Joana nods, impressed. "I respect that."

He slings a messenger bag across his chest. "I should head out. I'm supposed to be teaching Jesse a new editing software." They have enough footage to begin piecing together some of the pilot, and Jesse is only going to be in Philly on the weekends soon. Jack said his brother's senior year is about to start. Which also means Highland and I won't have to "get creative" for that long.

I come up to my boyfriend before he goes, and then a knock sounds on the door.

"Oscar!"

"Joana!"

"Mom and Dad are here?" Jo asks me at the sound of their voices.

"Yeah." They just showed up unannounced. Also, not shocked. I'm sure they just want to help Joana get settled in. "Can you get the door, Jo?"

"You bet."

While my sister descends the loft's stairs to answer the door, Jack stops cold a foot from me. "Am I about to meet your parents?"

"Unless I toss you out the window, but we're in a high-rise, so…"

Stress lines his face. "Fuck."

I catch his hand in mine. "Hey, you're a people-person, Highland. You've got this."

"I want your parents to like me, Os." He rubs his forehead. "After the execs told me I'm a 'liability' to the docuseries last night—I feel more like crawling into a hole and crying into a baby blanket than putting on a happy face."

"Why cry in a baby blanket when you have me?"

His laughter dies too fast. He lets go of my hand just to place his palms on either side of his waist. Like he's on a cool-down after a marathon.

His confidence is on a hiatus, and I'm about to bring it back. "You are legitimately the most endearing motherfucker on a first meeting. You could make polar icecaps melt."

He cracks a dim smile.

"You could make all the stars in the sky fall for the sun."

Jack looks deeper into me. He takes a huge breath and hangs his arms over my shoulders like a casual slow-dance. "Tell me a secret that you've never told anyone else."

We have a short window of time. Joana is at the door, but I take advantage of every single second. Holding his waist, I lean in and whisper, "Estou apaixonado por voçê." I translate, "I'm in love with you."

His smile spreads across his face. Eyes full of vivid emotion.

I feel it in my chest.

"Oscar Felipe Oliveira," my mom calls from the kitchen. "Why are your cupboards full of junk food?" She curses in Portuguese. "How do you expect your sister to eat?"

I focus more on Jack.

He's radiating, his smile unable to wane. He clasps my hand, and he's the one leading us as we descend the stairs to the bottom floor.

How do I expect Jo to eat? I answer my mom, "With the mountain of arroz e feijão you brought over, that's how." She has containers upon containers of homecooked food stacked on the counter.

A perk to inviting Joana to live with me.

"And thank God I did," my mom says, finding space in the fridge. Her curly hair is styled in frizz-less ringlets. She carries herself like a famous soap star, and when she spins on me, she sighs at the welt on my cheek and goes on about how Quinn and I should be banded together as brothers.

Get that.

Want that.

Do not have that with the baby bro right now.

They see our brotherly relationship as a work-in-progress with highs and lows.

I kiss my mom's cheeks and introduce Jack. "This is my boyfriend."

She hugs Jack before he can even say, *hi.* "I remember seeing you at some family events." She gives him a tighter squeeze, and she means the Hale, Meadows, and Cobalt families. She backs up. "You're usually carrying a camera around." Her hand touches her heart. "You have such a beautiful smile."

Jack is smiling that hundred-watt smile. For sure, I'm taking partial credit for summoning it. "You're the gorgeous one, Mrs. Oliveira," he says warmly. "Casting directors would hire you for beauty shots on the spot, and I'd probably be put on a waitlist."

Yeah, right. I almost laugh.

My mom looks beyond flattered by Highland, as I knew she'd be. "Call me Sônia. Oscar's father is Rodrigo."

Right now, my dad is more preoccupied with Jo and boxing. He holds up his palms and calls out combinations. She punches lighter than she would if he wore pads.

"Come on, faster," he coaches.

She smiles, then fakes left but misses the uppercut he requests.

"*Jo,*" he frowns. "Listen." He taps her temple.

"I did," she snaps.

Our mom sends Jo a disapproving look for backtalking.

I cut into that fast. "Dad, this is Jack, my boyfriend. He has to head out soon, but I wanted you to meet him before he leaves."

Jack steps forward and shakes his hand. "It's nice to finally meet you."

My dad scowls so well, he could scare the hair off a fucking grizzly bear.

I rake a hand across my unshaven jaw.

Jack tries to hold eye-contact, but *Rodrigo* is shaking his hand for two beats longer than normal.

I'm thirty-two. My dad shouldn't be treating meeting a boyfriend like a job interview into the family.

Jack Highland is qualified to be with me because I say so. "Dad," I interject, "is this a staring contest or are you going to talk to him?"

He gives me an annoyed look, then tells Jack, "I read about you online, of what Oscar didn't tell me."

I catch a rough noise in my throat.

"All good things?" Jack asks with a charismatic smile.

"Eh." He lifts a shoulder, then walks away.

Jack looks baffled, his face slowly dropping.

I wrap an arm around Highland. "It's not you. He's just playing around."

"Rodrigo," Mom chastises.

"Dad," Jo snaps.

He spins back then tells Jack, "You have a good handshake." He eyes Jack's six-four height. "Collegiate swimmer? I saw an article about your high school championship. You must work hard."

Jack nods, ejecting a tense breath. "It wasn't easy."

My dad nods back, eyes shifting to me. "He's a good fit." His lip rises, just slightly, but that might as well be a million-watt smile from Rodrigo.

I excuse myself from my family to say goodbye to Jack. In the hallway alone together, he combs a hand through his hair. "I almost shit myself."

I laugh, and he keeps breathing out in relief until he laughs with me. Our eyes fasten, and the noise tapers off, replaced with something sweeter.

"I have a question," Jack breathes in. "How long have you been keeping that secret?"

"That I'm in love with you?"

"Yeah." He nods.

My pulse speeds. "A while." I pause. "You don't have to say it back if it's…" I taper off, and I grin at his emerging smile. "What's so hilarious, Long Beach?"

"You really think I don't love you?" Jack says with a laugh. "Oscar." He shakes his head, and then his face contorts in seriously *bad* emotions. Ones that've been plaguing him lately. "Your love is one of the only things keeping me afloat right now. I feel like I'm…" He sighs out heavy tension.

"Hey." I curve an arm around his shoulders. We hug tight and sway to the tempo of our breath and pulse. A minute passes, and I start singing to him. Not a slow sensual song, but something upbeat and fun.

"Faith" by George Michael.

He instantly laughs. Jack snaps his fingers and joins me in hallway karaoke. He sings, "baby," against my mouth, and our lips meet in playful passion.

We're smiling in a deeper kiss, our chests welded, legs threaded, hands roaming—it's a perfect moment, one for the *Oscar Oliveira* history books.

I almost wish he'd have his camera out.

Film us.

Our genuine feel-good love.

It's worthy of the spotlight. He's not background. Neither am I. And we should be the favorite ship online. Fans should be making cupcakes with our mother-effing names and hoisting up posters that say, *Oscar & Jack for All Time.*

All time.

Not for a short time, not a long time. But for all fucking time.

That's going to be us. If we can get through the tough parts. I'd bet on it.

Before Jack goes, he stops midway in the hall. He twirls a pen between his fingers, something he does absentmindedly. "I have to tell you something."

I watch him walk back to me. "You have my attention."

"I've been meaning to tell you, but—"

And then my radio buzzes. I'm off-duty today, but I kept comms on. The earpiece dangles on my shoulder, radio chatter echoing in the hall.

"Quinn to Akara." My brother's voice freezes my blood. "Luna is heading to the Hell's Kitchen apartment. She's spending the night with Tom and Eliot. I'm requesting permission to sleep at a hotel."

At a hotel.

Jack frowns.

The alternative is for Quinn to stay in my studio. SFO is supposed to crash here when their clients end up at the Cobalt brothers' apartment. Akara and the rest of Omega already okayed Joana living here, knowing there'll be less space for times like this.

Akara answers, "That's not protocol. You need to stay at the security apartment in the same building as Luna."

I wait for Quinn to argue, but a second later, he just says, "Fine."

I understand what Akara is doing. If Quinn and I can't work together like any other guy on the team, then we shouldn't be here. But our fight is so fresh, and I see my brother *trying* not to start shit. I don't want tonight to ruin our progress on day one.

"If Quinn is sleeping here, I might go somewhere else for the night," I tell Jack and explain my feelings.

"You can stay with me, but you'd be 2-hours from Charlie if something happens."

That is a risk.

Before I figure out my plans, I ask, "What is it you wanted to tell me?"

He shakes his head. "It's not a big deal." His uneasiness says otherwise, but I don't want to prod past comfort. He's been dealing with so much shit, and if I can be one less thorn, then I'm going to be that silky smooth petal for him.

DIDN'T THINK I'D END UP HERE TONIGHT. I'M ON the pull-out couch of SFO's Philly apartment. The one located three-floors below Farrow's penthouse. And I'm with Jack. He's under the thin sheet next to me, barely able to sleep on the uneven springs.

How we ended up here is classic what-the-fuckery. It began with a text.

Since Quinnie is staying at your place, you think it's against policy to rent out his room for the night? — Donnelly

I was driving to Philly when I got that text. I talked into my phone. "Bro, why do you need to rent the room? Send."

Because it's an empty room. What if I rent out the couch too? Thoughts? — Donnelly

My thought was, *he's nearing broke.*

I told him that I knew someone who'd rent out the couch. He didn't ask for a name. Just an email address so he could send an invoice to the "couch renter"—and since Donnelly knows my email, I reached out to my boyfriend.

Jack sent the money to Donnelly. And when we showed up to crash on the couch tonight, he was pissed in the way that Donnelly gets pissed at friends.

He sighed really hard. And then he let it go. He even offered Jack a beer.

Standing ovation for my ingenuity.

We should be sleeping easy knowing Donnelly has some money, at least. But the pull-out couch is uncomfortable, and we end up whispering most of the night.

"When was the exact moment?" Jack murmurs, lying on our sides. My arm is draped around his waist, and I listen to him clarify, "Where you were like, *yeah, I'm into him. I could fuck that guy.*"

I grin. "I was thinking more like, *I could hit that.*"

"When?" His smile inches up.

"The same day you joined the FanCon tour. It was that night after everyone finally left the hotel room in LA." Crowd control was terrible. The Hot Bodyguard video just leaked. My life was upending for a moment, and there came Jack Highland with a bag of supplies to get everyone through.

His levity was a breath of fresh air on a suffocating day. And he started flirting with me. Like *really* flirting with me that night.

I whisper all of this to Jack.

And I add, "You're also hot, so yeah, I could hit that."

He smiles more. His hand has been comfortably chilling on my ass. "I was so into you that night, and I think I knew it was attraction. I just wasn't sure what kind. But I wanted to hang around you the whole time."

"Why?"

He thinks for a second, then his lips quirk. "Basta ikaw," he says in Tagalog, and translates again, "Because it's you, as long as I'm with you."

My chest swells, and we start to kiss. Quietly, gently. Our muscular legs tangle up under the sheet, and then I hear the squeak of floorboards.

I sit up, eyes narrowed in the dark.

A body wanders into the kitchen and bangs into the wall.

"Fuck," I curse, throwing sheets off my legs. I jog into the kitchen.

"What's going on?" Jack whispers, following me.

I flip on the lights, and he sees Donnelly sleepwalking. My best friend is running into the wall, his eyes are open but not focused. He turns towards the microwave, his chestnut hair askew and boxer-briefs low on his waist.

"He's done this before?" Jack whispers, watching me carefully try to guide my friend back to his bedroom.

"Yeah, sometimes. Not all the time."

Donnelly mumbles, "Mmahmm…"

I'm trying not to scare him awake. "This way, bro."

"Mmah…Lun…Luna…"

Jack and I exchange a confused look. Why is my best friend muttering Luna Hale's name in his sleepwalking haze?

He lowers his voice. "They're just friends, right?"

I whisper back even softer since Akara and Banks are asleep in this apartment right now. "Loosely. The kind of friend you'd see in group settings and catch up with." He has offered her condoms before, but as a wingman—not for his dick.

"…Lun…yeah…lemme help you, babe." He's about to run into the pull-out couch. I try to block him. He bumps me, then turns back towards the hall. "…best pussy…"

Motherfucker.

Jack frowns and mouths, *they hooked up?*

I shrug.

Seems like it. Unless it's just his fantasy. Either way, all signs point to *bad.* So fucking bad. Luna Hale's dad is a recovering addict.

Donnelly's entire family are meth *addicts.* No way will Loren Hale ever want him involved with his daughter.

Too late.

"I'm going to pry for answers tomorrow," I whisper to Jack, "when he's actually coherent—"

A phone rings too loudly.

Donnelly suddenly startles awake.

"*Fuck.* Sorry." Jack runs to the pull-out and searches for his cell twisted in the sheets.

"Donnelly. *Donnelly.* You're safe, bro."

He slips and falls on his ass.

"You were sleepwalking."

"Huh?" He squints at the light.

I take a quick glance at my boyfriend. Wondering if the other execs are calling him about his job. But it's 5 a.m.—early for a business phone call.

Jack puts his cell to his ear and races out of the apartment. Taking the call in the hallway, I'm assuming. My chest is on fire, but if he wanted me to follow him, he would've motioned me.

So I trust Jack not to pull a Charlie and disappear on me without details or warning.

I focus on my friend and squat down to Donnelly. "You need a water?"

"Nah." He rests his forearms on his knees. "How's the couch? Worth the price?"

"It's worth 0 cents." I sit down on the floor. "1-star rating."

"1-star is better than no stars." He massages his knuckles, reading my tensed features. "What?"

"Luna Hale?"

His face drops. "Farrow told you?"

I choke on surprise. "Farrow knew?"

"Shit." He shuts one eye, then opens it. "So it's a long story. But I'm not doin' anything with Luna now."

"But you did?"

"Once." He glances towards the hall and then whispers so quietly I have to strain my ears. "I ate her out. That was it."

I get most of the story and learn that only Farrow, Maximoff, Jane, and Thatcher know. Now me and Jack. *Let's keep it that way.*

I'm still reeling. Going out of my ever-loving mind trying to process this. Donnelly and Luna.

Luna and Donnelly.

A science experiment?

I can't believe he crossed that line. Mostly because Luna is Maximoff's little sister. Maximoff was Farrow's fiancé at the time. And Donnelly is loyal to Farrow. It's a crossed friendship line.

"Do you still like her?" I ask.

"She's cool," he says nonchalantly.

Normally, I'd be grabbing a bucket of popcorn, but I have bad feelings. And Donnelly is going through enough, so I'm not going to dig into it tonight.

I stand back up, helping Donnelly to his feet, and he heads to bed. Jack hasn't returned. I reach the door.

Please still be there.

Please be in the hall.

I open the door, and I glance down the cavernous hallway. And I realize it's empty.

My phone pings.

Had to go to my apartment. Sorry. Call later — Highland

This isn't like him. Worry morphs into instinct to *go*. I grab my keys, put on pants, and I head out to chase after my boyfriend.

31

Jack Highland

I'M FRAZZLED. The amount of attention on me is too new. Jesse is usually the one in trouble—and I'm not "in trouble" the way that a seventeen-year-old would be.

I'm not breaking a curfew, but to my parents, one of the worst life paths is possible career implosion. If I imploded it myself, that's fine. My mom changed-up her nursing career. But if someone else is doing it—not cool.

So apparently, they flew here like I'm in need of saving. It had something to do with Jesse telling them my status as exec producer is on the line.

As soon as they called me, saying they arrived at my place in Philly, yelling, "Where are you?!"—like I'd already been sacrificed to the career gods—I didn't think, I just left SFO's apartment.

I left Oscar.

And I drove to The Walnut.

Immediately, I wanted to turn back around and tell him where I was headed. Ask him if he wants to join. But I couldn't waste time knowing my parents were upset in my apartment. Back-tracking would make me feel worse. And staying the course didn't make me feel any better.

I could text him. I couldn't figure out how to formulate a specific reply, so I was vague.

I hated that I was vague.

I'm torn in so many directions that I'm being swallowed.

Ride the swell.

Dude.

I'm drowning. "Mama, I'm fine. Sit down, please."

She won't sit. "You're a good person. You wouldn't hurt anyone." She's in tears, wiping the wet streaks beneath her thin-framed glasses. "What they're saying about you online, it's horrible, Jun-Jun." She uses a nickname for me.

"We were talking about you filing a defamation lawsuit," my dad says on the couch next to Jesse. The Murphy bed is pulled down like Jesse just woke up.

"No," I tell them, and I hug my mom. "It's more of a headache going through that, and for what?"

"Your reputation." She rubs her face. "The truth."

Jesse gets her a box of tissues.

"You know the truth, Mama," I remind her. "Jesse knows. Dad knows. I'm not a homewrecker. I said what I could. This is how the media plays out." I let go of her when she dabs her eyes with a tissue.

The kitchen is a mess. That sticks out to me. Annoys me in ways that it usually wouldn't. I go over there to clean. I haven't been here as often as Jesse. Rice is stuck to a pot on a stove. Bits of hot dog are in the sink with remains of banana ketchup.

I scrape the food into the trash.

"Dammit," my dad says hotly under his breath and the shake of his head. "You're really saying that there's nothing we can do to help? There has to be something."

I wish, more than anyone, that I could snap my fingers and make everyone see what I see. Just for a moment. I've always known there are so many lenses and filters and views.

Even the docuseries that I film can be interpreted a thousand different ways by a thousand different set of eyes.

"It'll take time for public perception to shift, if it does," I explain, washing dirty dishes. "The best thing to do is to just wait it out."

"Susmaryosep," my mom exclaims with a hand to her forehead. She basically said *Jesus, Mary, and Joseph.*

I wipe my hands on a dish towel. "I'm okay, Mama."

She hugs me. "I love you, Jun-Jun. We love you so, so much."

Her maternal warmth is something I didn't realize I needed. My chest floods, and I hug back. I thought, initially, that they were here to fight for my job.

But it feels more like they're here just for me.

Jesse comes over to help clean. He grabs the walis, a Filipino broom, and sweeps up coffee grounds on the floor. I have a suspicion my brother could tell I've been overwhelmed. So he called in reinforcements.

The Highland family. We might not be famous, but we're tight.

When my mom finally sits, sinking down next to my dad, he hugs her to his side. She says, "I liked you working with those families, but now I don't know anymore."

"Is that why you haven't touched the water?" I point to the PuraFons water bottles I gave my parents when I first got here. PuraFons is a Fizzle product like how Dasani is to Coca-Cola.

And Fizzle is essentially what connects all the famous families together.

My dad opens his hands like he's being peaceful, but his words are heated. "We don't feel the need to support them if they're not helping *you.*"

"They are helping," I say with a strained breath. "Moffy and Jane are doing *everything* they can so the execs don't fire me, and I can't even tell you how many of them have posted pics and stories of me and Oscar on their Instagram."

My mom sniffs, then takes both water bottles. Giving one to my dad.

"Why isn't it working then?" he asks, unscrewing his water bottle. "Why the vitriol towards you?"

"Because," I tell him, "sometimes people grip so hard onto the concept of *hate* that they can't let go for two seconds to even try to *love.*" They want to hate something.

Someone.

I am that someone right now.

Those are words I've said before. I've said them to Maximoff Hale. Trying to ease his hot-temper and frustration. Therapy with Jack Highland.

I crack a smile at the memory because it's a good one. He got what I said because he felt that already. Understanding is powerful. Feeling understood. Feeling heard.

We hugged at the end, and I felt closer to someone. Looking back, I think I needed those deep, powerful connections just as much as Moffy and Jane did.

Standing among my loving family, thinking about loving friends that I'm certain now that I have, and picturing the guy I've fallen in love with—that helps ease some of the pressure.

Hang onto the love.

I reach for my phone. "I need to call Osc—" A knock raps the door. I just have a feeling it's him. Who else would be here this early?

I whip open the door to see Oscar's deep, urgent concern on the other side.

A Secret about Oscar Oliveira: He's in love with me.

"Are you alright?" he asks the same time I say, "I'm sorry."

We're suddenly hugging in the doorway.

I explain what happened in a soft breath against his ear.

He cups the back of my head. I wipe leaking emotion from my eyes. *Spent.* Fuck, I'm so spent. We kiss, and I tell him, "I'll introduce you."

Shutting the door behind us, I motion to my parents who stand up. "Mama, Dad, this is Oscar."

He goes to my mom first. "I'm glad I can finally meet you two. Sorry, I'm not…wearing a shirt, Mrs. Highland. I ran out."

He ran out for me.

That fast.

Partly, I feel badly that I caused him distress, but mostly, I'm just grateful I have Oscar. Even if the online hate and calls for my termination derive from being with him, I'd still do it all again.

"Just call me Tita Len," she says, then hugs him. I hear her tell Oscar, "Protect him, will you?"

I feel myself smiling. This is new. I'm so used to my mom telling *me* to protect whoever I'm dating, and I did not think she'd switch that up.

"No doubt, always," he promises.

I grin wider, and I watch my dad shake my boyfriend's hand next. "We were just talking about ways to help Jack with the hate he's getting. You're in security. You have any ideas?"

"Nothing we haven't tried already, sadly." He upnods to Jesse in greeting, and Jesse makes the hang-loose gesture, putting aside the walis.

Oscar's radio goes off.

The air could snap as he touches his earpiece. We're all quiet, but for different reasons. They're curious about his job, and I'm thinking, *he's gone, dude.*

Charlie is on the move, and I can't follow with a camera for *Born into Fame*. Not right now. I need to stay with my parents.

Oscar wears his sadness, then apologizes to my parents, says quick goodbyes, but before he leaves, we wrap our strong arms around each other and hold tight for an extended beat.

He kisses my temple, my forehead, my jaw, my lips, and against my ear, he whispers, "I'm sorry I can't stay longer."

"You don't need to. This was enough." It meant everything that Oscar even showed up. He could've been pissed that I left like I did.

He never even brought it up. Like it was insignificant. All that mattered were my actual feelings and what I was dealing with.

That's...sexy. I'm attracted to emotional maturity in people, I guess.

Once he's gone, I shut the door and I face my parents. "What'd you think? Mama? I know he had to leave fast, but..." I trail off with a smile.

My mom has tears in her eyes. Different kind. Better kind. She nods a lot, choked up. *Approval granted.*

I expect my dad to go off about Oscar's occupation. "You two make a good match." He clears his throat, happy for me. I see that clearly. "He's not what I expected for you, but I can see you love him."

Love. I feel it, but I also need to tell Oscar something. I tried to tell him earlier before bad timing reared its ugly head again. It may not even be a big deal—or maybe that's just my optimism soaring in. But the longer I keep it from him, the more it's growing into one giant secret.

32

Jack Highland

JACK: WEDDING DRESS shoot with Jane and family

The note was posted in the Google spreadsheet that's shared with my WAC crew. My production manager did a last-minute switch, and I'm one of three camera operators filming the famous ones in the Calloway Couture boutique.

Wedding dresses, RSVPs, bridal jubilation.

Let the good times roll, right?

Except the day I don't have to attend *another* wedding, will be all too soon. Hell, I foolishly believed I was past wedding season.

No more weddings for Jack Highland this year. I've had my fill. I hit a max.

Being face-to-face with another one is like watching an embarrassing home video, even knowing the good outcome—me and Oscar together—exists.

It reminds me of Anacapri where I flubbed an opportunity to kiss Oscar.

It reminds me of Ali & Troy's wedding and Ambrose & Cody's where I wandered around alone and thwarted the "who's your plus-one" question a hundred times.

Then my RSVP came in the mail, along with a photo of Thatcher & Jane on a pastel blue couch, seven cats strewn on their laps.

And I knew I'd make room for this wedding. In my heart and my mind. November 1ˢᵗ, I'll be there. Might even be filming (if I still have a job) or I could be hand-in-hand with an actual plus-one this time.

Every day feels good being with Oscar.

Anyway, tabloids were shockingly sweet to Jane with articles like, *Re-create Thatcher & Jane's Quirky Cute RSVP!*

Out of the famous ones, she's one of the least likely to elicit a positive response from the media. And as someone whose relationship is attacked and dissected daily by Oslie stans, I'm glad the media is celebrating her upcoming wedding and not tearing it down.

Jane Cobalt deserves that.

What do you deserve, dude?

My job, for one. No question. No hesitation.

I've worked too hard to lose it all.

But my role as exec producer is still in "evaluation"—and the irresolution of it all is the worst part. The feeling of *incompletion.* Every project, every goal around me is halfway done, and no matter how much effort I put forth, it might never be finished.

I've always finished what I've started and carved out a path to a bright future, and knowing that I could be on no path…

That has taken a toll on me. Mentally.

It's made more than just my work feel incomplete. Little things like not having time to fill up my Mazda with gas. A quarter tank shouldn't feel like a tsunami is about to sweep me under.

And I confess, it didn't used to.

I miss being able to walk through my days like a sunny breeze. I told that to Oscar, and he asked me if I've ever seen a therapist. I have, when I was younger. I used to take medication for anxiety, and when I stopped having to take meds, I was stoked. Proud, even. Like I was stronger now.

I know I was wrong.

I'm not weak for needing help. It's not a badge of shame. It's a tool to take my life back, and I feel that today. After seeing a new therapist, after taking anxiety meds this morning, that overwhelming sense of incompletion has been hushed.

And finally, I can focus on my work without drowning.

I mill around the boutique (store closed to the public today) while the Calloway sisters and their daughters chitchat on chaises and cream-colored couches. Everyone waits for Jane and her mom to exit the dressing room.

Red-headed, blue-eyed Audrey Cobalt spits a strawberry petit four in a napkin and looks directly into my camera. Like she was caught stealing.

Won't air that. She'd probably request to keep it on the cutting room floor.

I smile from behind the Canon and make the hang-loose gesture.

She blushes.

I try not to laugh.

Out of everyone in the families, I thought Jane's fourteen-year-old sister would be the most upset that Oscar Oliveira is no longer single. She had an enormous crush on him, but she was one of the first to post her support on social media.

Giselle, a camera operator, is assigned to Jane while she's in the dressing room.

So I walk over to a refreshment table and film Maximoff.

He fills up a glass of ice water from a pitcher and sees me more than the camera. "Jack Highland survives another day."

"I'm hanging on," I say lightly, shifting so no mirrors catch sight of me in footage.

"Have you heard from the other producers?" In the lens, I see his sharp cheekbones and forest-green eyes simultaneously toughen and soften.

"Not yet." I stop recording for a sec. "Whatever they decide, I think it'll come down to the integrity of the docuseries." I explain how beyond the public outrage, they're still saying I'm too close to the subjects and too much a part of the narrative.

I've also considered how this is changing *Born into Fame*. What story am I telling if I leave out the Oslie rumors and my involvement? Both are a part of Charlie's life.

Maximoff stares off, thinking for a long beat. "If there's anything else I can do, I'm here."

"Thanks, Moffy."

"Have you told Oscar yet about what you told me?"

That. "Not yet." It was easier letting out my secret to Maximoff, Jane, and Sulli. I knew they could relate in a way. I'm not sure about Oscar's reaction. I shake out my arm that's been flexed holding the gimbal. "You see on YouTube Kingly almost broke Phelps' record for 200m freestyle? It was *sweet.*"

"Yeah. He has to be part fish or secretly Aquaman."

I smile more and catch sight of another camera operator giving me a stink-eye. I'm in a cutthroat field. Jealousy is behind-the-back, not to the face. A lot is directed at me because I'm young and in a high-ranking position. And now I'm shooting the shit with a subject.

Fantastic. *Give them more reason to fire you, dude.*

"Rolling," I tell Maximoff as I switch the camera back on. I pan over the dessert spread, petit fours and chocolate turtles; I capture some of the women waiting for the bride-to-be, then zoom back on Moffy. "How do you feel about being Jane's man of honor?"

He's the only guy from the famous families invited today.

And his lips slowly lift into a wide, heartfelt smile. Before he can answer me, a collection of awed noises erupts from the couches.

I focus the frame on Jane.

She shuffles out in a mint-green dress, pink fabric flowers embroidered in the bust. Rose Calloway trails behind Jane with a determined, focused gaze and helps her daughter step onto a circular podium.

Audrey places a hand to her heart. "Oh Jane, you look positively lovely."

Family members shout praises and opinions. Talking over each other so much that I lose track of who says what. After ten minutes, the consensus comes in: too green, even though Jane requested *no white dress.*

Rose purses her lips. "I can change the color, if you like the style."

Jane slides her hands down the fabric. "I think…maybe let's try another one? It needs more tulle."

"Then more tulle is what you'll get." Rose whisks her daughter back to the dressing room. Giselle follows with her Canon.

I turn back to Moffy since he's nearest. "Did Jane's mom design all the dresses?"

He nods. "All ten options."

We're only on option 3.

I struggle not to glance at my watch. Dejection, I feel it. As much as I enjoy being around Jane and being a part of a milestone in her life, I've been having trouble grabbing solid footage of Charlie. Ever since *We Are Calloway* filming started, I've been pulled in other directions.

Born into Fame doesn't have a shot in hell if I don't have material to make a good show, but focusing on a side project is exponentially risky now. I should be 100% focused on *We Are Calloway* and not pissing anyone off.

But…

I can't deny that being around Charlie means I'm around Oscar.

Working on the pilot does put us back in alignment, and what can I say? I like feeling balanced.

Just today, I've missed the way he looks at me like I'm distracting him. That stern and sexy *I'm working* face. Which is sometimes followed by Oscar offering his snacks to me. How he looks put-off whenever I aim the camera on him.

"I'm not your subject, Highland."

Yet, he'll just watch me watch him through the lens. I also revel in the hectic days and the exhausted nights curled up in his arms.

Where we're fighting sleep just to talk one second longer.

Before Jane returns in dress option 4, I type out a quick message on my phone. Hey, if you're off-duty tonight, you want to meet me at WAC Offices for some fun?

I just hit send.

Reading it again, it sounds like I'm asking for sex. Don't care. I do want to fuck him. As well as talk to him. And stare at him. Jesus fuck, I'd take standing in the same room as him. Being in Oscar's presence isn't even a want at this point. It's a need.

I need him.

My phone beeps a second later.

Pick a time, Long Beach. I'll be there. — Oscar

IT'S LATE.

Too late for anyone to be at the production offices, so I'm not even a little concerned when Oscar and I stumble into my office, lip-locked since the elevator.

Blinds drawn shut, Oscar sightlessly pats around the wall for the lights. As he turns to flick them on, I hip thrust against his ass playfully.

He grins back at me. "Perfect form, Highland."

"You're not that bad yourself." I grip the back of my tee and pull it over my head. "I'd let you fuck me."

"Oh yeah?" Oscar rotates and catches my waist, drawing me closer. Pieces of his curly hair fall over a yellow rolled banana. "I'd do you."

I kick off my shoes, and my muscles contract at the look in his eye. The one that's eating me whole. "What does 'do you' entail?" I ask with an edging smile.

"Me inside you."

Heat ascends, like flames lick the middle of my office.

"Where?" I ask.

"Against the desk. The floor. The wall. Anywhere…everywhere."

My chest caves in a breathing pattern reminiscent of bad endurance athletes in high altitude. Consistently, unsurprisingly, Oscar makes me feel like we're at 8,000 feet above sea level.

I let out a breathless laugh.

Fuck.

You're attracted to him. How was that ever a doubt? It seems so obvious, so clear now.

"Any more questions, Mr. Filmmaker?" Oscar asks, tugging off his Yale tee, tossing it aside, and his attention suddenly pinpoints to a shelf. "Are those...?"

I turn around, following his gaze. Two golden statuettes of a winged woman cradling an atom rest in proud display. "Yeah, those are my Emmys."

His grin overtakes his face. "You say that like those are bags of Doritos."

I hook an arm around his shoulder and lead him backwards towards my desk. "In your world, aren't Doritos equivalent to Emmys?"

"Quality, yes. But the former is a little harder to come by, Highland. I can't exactly go pick up an Emmy at the local Quickie-Mart."

My lips quirk. "Two is nothing. The producers who've been on *We Are Calloway* since the beginning have glass cases dedicated to their awards."

He shakes his head, confusion cresting his brown eyes. "Even one is a big deal, Jack." He says my name. Not a nickname, and it sobers the mood for a second. "Don't compare yourself to other people to minimize what that is." He points towards my shelf. "Give yourself more credit."

He's said that to me before. But *before* before. When we weren't dating or barely even a thing.

His words bring me back.

I think of the reception for the newest season of *We Are Calloway*. The one that recently aired and focused on the car crash, the aftermath within the families, and the trip to Greece.

The critical praise has been astronomical. Calling it, *"masterful art in documentary filmmaking"* and *"possibly the best season of the docuseries in its long, outstanding history"*—and the success is not all mine. It was the whole crew.

The best footage could turn into the worst show without the right vision, without the right team.

It wasn't just me.

But I know what Oscar is saying. It's still my triumph and feat.

He rests his ass against the edge of my desk, his hands low on my waist. Dragging down towards my back pockets.

I keep a hand on my head and take a shallow breath. Focusing on his gaze, I reply, "I know I've met a lot of success, especially by twenty-seven, but there's still more to do. More to achieve."

His brows furrow. "Won't there always be more? It sounds like you're setting yourself up to never enjoy what you have."

I drop my arm at my side. "Yeah, but I don't know how to rewire this"—I point to my temple—"to be satisfied with where I'm at and not seek more, the *it* project that quells all desires, the white whale." Quickly, I add, "And I'm not talking about *us.*" I laugh lightly. "You're actually the first person who makes me feel like... this is enough."

This is enough.

Those words quiet the air in a softness. A tranquility that draws something between him and me. His fingers brush gently against mine, and I lace our fingers in a feather-light hold.

"I didn't take you for a *Moby-Dick* reader," Oscar says softly.

"I took you for one," I say back. *He reads a lot of classic lit.* "You got the white whale reference then?"

"Yeah." He nods resolutely.

I let go of his hand to grip his shoulders. "You better watch your back, Os. One day you'll find a couple bags of Doritos on your shelf, and I'm going to make sure you don't touch them."

Oscar fights a smile. "You wouldn't."

"They're your Golden Doritos for being amazing." I cup the back of his head and kiss the corner of his mouth. "And hot." Our lips crush together.

He's grinning.

I'm smiling.

And after a deeper, rougher kiss, he tells me, "I get a thousand Golden Doritos for being hot, Highland." He grabs my ass.

My dick stirs. "A thousand then," I negotiate. "But you still can't eat them."

"Sounds like the opposite of an award," Oscar teases and unzips my jeans. Our ravenous kisses steal oxygen from my lungs. I slide a hand down his abs, lower, and grip hard to his bulge.

"*Fuck*," Oscar mumbles, breaking from my lips.

I harden at the sound, even more as he yanks my jeans to my muscular thighs and palms the outside of my boxer-briefs.

I swallow an aroused knot in my throat. My abs flex, head dizzying already.

Squeezing each other, we're moving in short, hungry strokes while our mouths fasten and explore. I don't feel like breathing tonight. Just give me Oscar.

I thrust my hips against him, creating more friction against his large hand. It feels so fucking good to be in his grip. Our breaths synchronize in heavy, panting waves, and we free ourselves from the last confines of fabric, tugging down our boxer-briefs.

Jesus, the feeling of his palm stroking my full length. I retreat in these pleasured feelings and pump him with my own firm force. "Highland." His voice is stern, along with his hands that push my shoulders down. Sexy. Sexy. Fuck, he's sexy.

I ease to my knees.

He's figured out that I love blowing him. I get amped whenever it leads here. For one, seeing and feeling him come turns me on. For another, I feel less selfish. I'm putting forth some effort to help him reach a peak.

Giving Oscar that eye-rolling, moan-inducing high is an achievement I want to unlock.

With my hand clutching his bare ass, he carefully guides himself between my lips. His movements are purposeful, forceful, like he's here to get off and nothing else and for some reason that blisters my senses. Lights me up.

I take him deeper than I did the first time I tried.

A noise rumbles through him.

I harden more.

Our eyes latch. His gaze melts in affection on me. Lips broken open with aching breath as I work him with my mouth.

"*God*," he moans, huskily. Deeply.

I pop him out of my mouth to breathe.

He laughs.

"Give me a sec." I inhale, exhale.

He caresses the side of my jaw. "Take your time. I'm not going anywhere."

I spread my knees more and grip him in a fist. Two more strokes, and he arches his hips, filling my mouth for me.

I flex my muscles as arousal slams against me with that one maneuver. He sees the contract of my abs, my biceps, my thighs.

His fingers suddenly tighten on the back of my head as he releases in a few shuddering jerks.

I swallow his load. *Holy shit.* He eases back.

I blow out a dizzying breath and rise to my feet.

"You've got something—" Oscar reaches out and wipes his thumb across my lip. Our gazes hold tighter. More heat boils between us. His hand drags down my abs and grips my length. I shut my eyes that almost roll.

Fuck, yeah. He's excellent at this.

Oscar starts stroking my erection. "Legitimately attracted to you." He eyes me in his hand. "You're really fucking hard, Long Beach."

I pant into a smile that falters in a staggered breath. I almost come— and then, my phone buzzes. *Fuck.*

It could be the other exec producers.

The verdict on my job.

"I have to take this." I lean closer to his muscular build, chest to chest, just to wrap my arms around his waist and grab the cell by the keyboard behind him. I'm taller than Oscar, so I can read the text from this position.

As I click into my phone, Oscar keeps moving his hand up and down my dick.

Pick-up shoots updated on the WAC schedule. Check your emails. — Ali

Shit.

"Everything alright?" Oscar asks. He pumps me in two long strokes, and I have to press my mouth to the top of his shoulder to stop a full-body shudder. My fingers slip off my phone and press into the table.

He stops suddenly.

"Keep going," I groan into his shoulder.

"But what was that?" He's already rubbing me again. "You look like Bambi died."

"Just work." I lay my palm flat on the table, eyes hooked to my phone that lights up with another unread message. "Work again." Not wanting the distraction, I flip my cell. I have such short windows of time with Oscar when he's off-duty, and I don't want texts or online hate to interrupt it.

His hand feels slicker, pre-cum increasing friction and my arousal. "Os." My voice catches, and I rock into him over and over until I'm almost at a release. He drops down and takes me into his mouth just as I reach my peak.

My breathing heavies for a long minute, and he climbs back to his feet. My head is spinning from the climax and incoming stresses. Two obliterating opposites.

He lifts up the elastic of his boxer-briefs and asks, "What were the texts?"

I pull up my pants, squeezing my cock back into my boxer briefs. "We're scheduling pick-ups which means we have to reshoot B-roll or make-up for bad footage."

I explain to him that if production fucks up, we can't ask Jane to go try on wedding dresses again. We just lose out on the moment.

We're not on a set. This is real life.

And I add, "More WAC filming means less Charlie filming, and at this point, even if I keep my job, I might not get the chance to *finish* the actual show. Or it'll end up being a rushed piece of trash." I circle around my desk, hunting for that old camcorder I left here last week.

"I've seen your work, Highland, it's not rushed. It's definitely not trash." Oscar zips up his pants. "You're putting too much pressure on this. Be like Elsa and just *let it go.*"

I catch the *Frozen* reference and laugh. "Well, Elsa makes that shit look easy." I search my desk drawers, and I wonder if he's worried I've put too many chips on Charlie. Bet too much on one losing number.

Oscar is gearing me up for the eventual fall. So I'll land softly.

But he hasn't realized that he's been a crash pad for me from the start. In a way, having him helps me take greater risks. Knowing that he'll be there at the end of it all. That's the best feeling.

"Thanks for coming tonight," I tell him. "When I texted, I didn't know if you'd be free. Is Charlie hanging back at his apartment?"

"No, he's at a club in the city."

Confused, I slowly stand up from a drawer. "So shouldn't you be with him?"

He shrugs. "I got a temp to cover for me." He says it like it's nothing, but if it's not a scheduled paid day off, Oscar doesn't go off-duty for just anything or anyone. "I figured my boyfriend, who doesn't text me while he's at a shoot, probably either wanted my dick or to talk. Either way, I'm here, bro."

My smile inches up. "Glad to know how I can't get your ass running to me." I dig in a filing cabinet. "After Jane's wedding, I'll be happy to never have to film another one for a good ten years. Maybe twelve."

Oscar bends down to grab his T-shirt off the floor. "What about your own? I assume marriage is probably in your ten-year portfolio plan. All lined up with the white picket fence. An apricot tree in the front yard."

I laugh. *Apricot tree.*

Found the camcorder.

I set the thing on the desk. "Maybe I should get you to redo my vision board, Os. It's definitely missing the apricot tree."

"You dodged that question fast, Highland."

He asked, *What about your own wedding?*

I tinker with the camcorder. "I guess I assumed I'd have a wedding. I thought whoever I was with would want one, and I'd do what I could to make them happy."

"Such a people-pleaser," Oscar teases, leaning slightly on the desk.

Closer now, my eyes trace the scar above his brow and the curls that touch his lashes. "I like pleasing people. You, mostly," I say into a smile.

He claps for me. "You've done well in that department."

I take a bow and smile brighter. "Really, if I could avoid having a wedding of my own, I would. I've attended so many at this point that it just feels...empty?" I search his eyes, realizing I want his answer to the same question. And I can't tell where he's leaning, so I just ask, "Have you dreamed about a wedding?"

Oscar slowly shakes his head. "Who's got the time?"

I laugh softly. "Don't I fucking know it." My brows rise. "Your parents wouldn't be upset?"

Oscar reattaches a radio on his waistband. "Maybe a little at first. But they have Quinn and Joana, and they know I'm busy as it is. They'd get it."

I can't be certain, but I think my parents would be the same way.

Oscar eyes the camcorder in my hands. "You fix that ancient piece of shit yet?"

"Almost." I slide in a new battery. "I had to buy a couple new—or I guess *old*—parts on eBay. Plus, this new battery." I click the power button and the side panel screen lights up with footage.

This...is not what I expected.

Kinney Hale sits anxiously on a four-poster ornately carved, black bed. Her dyed black hair is chopped with blunt bangs. She's twisting her hands together on bouncing knees.

"This is a security camcorder?" I have intense doubts about it now.

His heated stare punctures the screen. "Not a fucking chance."

"Okay," Kinney exhales. "This is video diary entry number...I can't even remember anymore. But something really intense happened to me in school, and I just need to get it off my chest—"

We shouldn't be listening to this.

I make a move to turn it off, but Oscar grabs my bicep, stopping me.

"—there's this boy in my grade, and he's a complete waste of space." She battles surging tears. "We have art together, and he followed me into the supply closet and told me *you can't know you're a lesbian, if you've never seen a dick.* So he pulled down his pants." She crosses her arms. "Yes, future self, I saw Tye Smith's penis, and I really, really hate that all I did was stand there. I should have throat-punched him! That's what Aunt Rose would've done." Her green eyes glass. "I just looked at him and said *still a lesbian.*" She pinches the bridge of her nose. "Then he told me *well, Kinney, you haven't touched it yet.* Then the bell rang, so he left. He left before I left! God, what's wrong with me? And like, I can't tell anyone because this is just so embarrassing." She grimaces and stands up quickly. "Uh, I can't." She strides to the camera and must shut it off because the footage goes dark.

I quickly hit the power button. "We shouldn't have seen that," I tell Oscar, my chest taut.

"You, keeper of all secrets, are worried about one more?" He's already pulling out his phone.

"It does get to me," I say. "Having other people's secrets isn't always easy."

He leans forward and puts a comforting hand on the back of my head. "You're not going to have to keep this one, Highland."

I have a secret I've been keeping from you. I should say it.

Right here.

Come on, dude.

I open my mouth. And I realize centering this situation on myself feels so wrong.

I bail on that idea and focus on the real issue.

Looking deeper in him, I ask, "What are you talking about?"

I can't imagine sharing what we learned here today with *anyone*. The diary was personal. Private. She didn't want anyone to see it, and I should have just shut it off from the jump.

"Kinney's *fourteen*," Oscar says. "That bastard should be expelled from her school, at the very least." He meets my shock. "I'm a bodyguard, Highland. Your job is to keep their secrets, but I have a duty to protect them. Right now, Tye Smith is a security threat. I'm calling her brother."

I know why he wouldn't reach out to her parents first. Maximoff is the safe place for the younger kids, so going to him first means Kinney won't feel betrayed by security.

33

Oscar Oliveira

I'M BRILLIANT, and so are my ideas. Historical evidence: I came up with the fake-dating strategy between Thatcher and Jane. Did not mean for them to hook up or get engaged. But a second reward just means I'm inadvertently even smarter than I realize.

So Maximoff didn't hesitate when I threw out another top-tier idea.

"Rainbow Brigade's first emergency meeting is coming to order," Kinney decrees, lighting a few candles on the table like this is a fucking séance.

Hey, we are unburying *feelings*.

All six of us are wedged in a corner booth in Superheroes & Scones, a comic-book coffee-shop hybrid in Philly. After-hours, the store is dead quiet. Most of the lights are turned off except for the one above the superhero-centric café area.

"First off," she says, "thank you all for coming on such short notice." She intakes a breath, and Maximoff extends an arm over his sister's bony shoulder.

It's been a long night.

Once I told Maximoff what happened, he approached Kinney, and she agreed to go to their parents together. The Hale family talked it out, and Kinney decided she didn't want to report the incident to Dalton Academy, even at the urging of her mom and dad.

In the end, they're agreeing to respect her wishes. They probably hope she'll change her mind, once she takes some time to think it over.

What was jarring was that Kinney kept this to herself. Didn't even tell the girl squad, her best friends. And Maximoff said that he wished she felt safe enough to open up to someone.

I had a light-bulb moment.

And here we are.

The first ever emergency Rainbow Brigade meeting.

Though we're not her own age or women, Kinney created the Rainbow Brigade to feel included among trusted family members and bodyguards who are LGBTQ. What better space for her to come to in a crisis than the one she built?

Great seating arrangement in the corner booth, as well. Kinney is in the middle with Tom and Maximoff on either side of her. Jack is close to me, my arm over his broad shoulders, and Farrow and I are sitting comfortably at either end.

Highland spreads his long legs more against mine, so he's not kicking the Hale prince across from us. *Love that for me too.*

"Secondly, I'd like to remind everyone that what you heard or saw on my camcorder stays *here*," Kinney says, pushing candles among the bottles of root beer. Those were provided by me and Jack after a gas station run. The pints of ice cream and spoons are Farrow and Maximoff's contribution.

Tom Cobalt just stole a Thor hammer off the merch wall.

We all promise Kinney to never tell a soul without her permission.

Tom raises a hand. "Question, Kinney-witchy-boo."

She glares at the nickname. "Ask." Her voice is deadpanned.

I swig the root beer like it's my popcorn.

Farrow is amused as fuck too. The famous ones bring endless entertainment, which always softens and lightens the raw, heavy parts.

Though, my boyfriend is a little more reserved than usual. I wonder if it's because of paparazzi tonight. When Jack and I exited his offices and walked to his car in a hurry, a cameraman shouted at him, *"Are you gay or bi, Jack?!"*

It's not the first time the media has pressured him to pick a label. They want some kind of confirmation that he's into me and it's not a publicity stunt. Like us kissing isn't fucking enough.

I hate that he's being pressured at all.

Tom edges forward in the booth. "When are we finding this Tye Smith guy?" he asks his question. "Because I propose we put bees in his locker. I know a dude—"

"No," Maximoff cuts in firmly.

Tom waves Thor's hammer like *what the hell*. "Then what's this meeting for if we're not going to plot revenge?"

"It's a safe place," Maximoff emphasizes the obvious. "For any of us to come and talk to each other."

We all have that already. Back when I was single, I've been to gay bars with Tom, Maximoff, and Farrow. And Tom will ask questions. He constantly goes to Maximoff for guidance. We're all willing to share in informal settings, but the formal one is needed too.

For Kinney and for moments where we're too busy to hit the bars or grab a coffee.

I loved the LGBTQ club I joined in college, and the famous ones don't trust easily. But they trust security. They trust production. They have us.

Maximoff continues, "And if you need advice or if something shitty happens and we feel like we can't go to our parents or our friends, we can come here."

"The Rainbow Brigade," Kinney says as she slides a button and pin to Jack. "Welcome to the club."

He picks up both, staring at the letters.

I squeeze him in a closer hug as his eyes redden with involuntary emotion. He seems surprised at his sudden surge of feelings.

I'd love to hear his thoughts, but he looks too choked to express them right now.

"Thanks…" Jack laughs into a brighter smile and lifts the button. "I'll wear this proudly, Kinney."

"Cool." She tries to act nonchalant. Girl is bad at acting because clearly this shit means something to her. And it means something to us, or else none of our asses would be here.

Farrow and Maximoff even left Ripley with his grandparents, all their attention focused on the Rainbow Brigade.

Tom twirls the plastic hammer. "Okay, but the bees—"

"No," Farrow and Maximoff say together.

"I'm in," I say, digging into a pint of Rocky Road.

Tom snaps his finger to me. "We've got one."

Maximoff blinks like his brain just malfunctioned. "I'm sorry, I just realized we have way too many Slytherins in this group."

"Eh, could use one less dork," Farrow says, smiling a smartass smile on his husband.

"Continuing on," Maximoff ignores him.

We all laugh.

"Our confessions," Kinney announces, and seriousness befalls on the booth. She smooths out lacy sleeves of her black dress. "We're all here to confess something that we've kept in."

That was my bright idea.

This can't work unless we're all willing to share here, or else Kinney will just feel like the Rainbow Brigade is for her and not *us*. So we're here knowing we're going to open up, and that's when Jack shifts against me. He sits up a little straighter. Runs a hand through his dark hair.

Should I be worried?

My eyes tighten on him with more concern.

"Do you want to start?" Maximoff asks his sister.

"No," she says flatly.

Tom lifts the hammer. "I'll go first."

Kinney looks relieved.

I pass my Rocky Road pint to Jack. He offers a half-hearted, *no thanks*, smile. Usually Highland will eat my snacks.

"So…" Tom scratches his head with the toy. "I still haven't found the *perfect* drummer to replace my old one. And the guy that got away is now playing for a mega-popular band that's blowing up—and that could've been me." He sighs out, and his eyes land on Maximoff. Tom looks like he's a second from exploding by whatever else he's holding in. "And I confess that I might've had a small, *tiny*...like so small you can't even really see it. Is it there? I don't think so. Yeah, that kind of crush on Farrow—*waaaay* before you two ever banged." His face turns into a wince. "Ahhhh, that didn't feel as good as I'd hoped."

Farrow is sucking in a breath that sounds like a cringe.

I'd be laughing my ass off if I wasn't worried about my boyfriend. Jack, though, looks more shocked at this revelation. I knew about Tom's crush.

Farrow knew.

And I'm pretty sure he already told his husband too.

"It's okay," Maximoff says, not caught off guard or jarred.

"Is it?" Tom has sunken forward, forehead on the table.

"Yeah, it was a long time ago."

Tom pops up, eyes on the ceiling. "My heart has definitively stopped beating."

"Man, lots of people had crushes on me." Farrow shrugs, and it's just so easy. I can't *not* take the swing. "I didn't," I say into a grin. "Not even for a half-a-second."

"That's because you have questionable taste, Oliveira." He holds out a hand to Jack. "Present company excluded."

"Appreciated," Jack says into a strong swig of root beer. Like he wishes that were actually liquid courage.

Tom starts to ease back. I wonder how long that has been weighing on him.

"Who's next?" Kinney asks.

Maximoff takes his turn. "I confess that in the twelfth grade, this guy on my swim team told me that being a slut must be hereditary, since I like to get it in the ass just like my mom. I guess he assumed I had already bottomed because I'm bi."

Wow, I'm shocked he shared that with anyone but Farrow.

Kinney looks overwhelmed. "You never told me that."

"Kin," he says. "You were eight."

"Oh. Right."

He nudges her shoulder. "I'm telling you now."

She nods a lot, thankful he opened up. My idea is working like a charm so far.

So I go ahead and speak. "I didn't have any LGBT friends in high school, so I looked up a lot online. My dad walked in on me searching the web for *How to Douche for Idiots*. Literally the title."

Farrow laughs, which lets the younger ones like Tom and Kinney feel free to laugh. I'm glad. It's a hilarious story as an adult, but damn was I mortified to hell as a teenager.

Jack smiles at me, but it fades too fast. And he rests a cement-block hand on my thigh. Trying to be cool, but I'm too perceptive to trick.

With the quick raise of two fingers, Farrow is next. "The idea of being a part of a clique is not my favorite thing. And being honest, this has always seemed like a clique." He tilts his head. "Technically, it still is. But I don't mind this little club. It's not half-bad."

I slow-clap. "That was weak sauce."

"Because you can't stomach hot sauce without shitting yourself."

I start to laugh, then mockingly cover Jack's ears. "Not in front of *meu raio de sol*."

Everyone laughs again, but Jack's fades into a sadder smile on me, like he's apologizing already.

What's wrong?

I drop my hands, about to excuse ourselves, but Kinney scoots forward.

Her turn. "Nothing I do to Tye Smith will help what I feel because all I wish is that I said or *did* something more in the moment."

"You think I always know what to say?" Maximoff tells his sister.

"You were in shock," Farrow chimes in.

Tom nods. "I've never seen a vagina in my life, and I still know I'm gay. What he did was wrong."

"Elephant in the room," I cut in, "he could be dropping his pants and pressuring other girls to touch his dick. What he did should meet some sort of school punishment, at the least."

She pokes a spoon in chocolate chip cookie dough. "I'm thinking about it." Her eyes flit to the last person who needs to share.

Everyone focuses on Jack.

He exhales a bigger breath, staring more at the Rainbow Brigade button. "I was scared to come here as part of the club. I thought I'd feel…" He shrugs. "Like a poser. You've all made sense of your sexuality so much sooner, and I feel like I lose some credibility by coming in late."

"You don't," Maximoff says strongly.

"Oscar kept telling me that too," Jack nods, his eyes on me with a loving, emotional look. And I remember the start of his journey, where he asked for my help. I didn't know if I'd be the right person for him, but I said I'd try.

I hold the back of his head, our foreheads pressed together in an intimate beat. My hand slides to his neck, and he says, "Kinney gave me the button, and I was surprised at how much I felt like I belonged." He inhales. "That's it."

Then why are you more tense now, Highland?

I hesitate to call him out in front of everyone. Luckily, I don't have to.

Jack turns more to me. "Can I have a minute alone with you?" To everyone, he says, "It's not about the Rainbow Brigade. I just need to talk with Oscar."

I nod. "Yeah, let's go."

Before I scoot, Farrow stands up on the other side. "You two stay."

Maximoff slips out next. "We're gonna watch a TV show upstairs in the loft before we leave."

The booth clears in under a minute. They leave the candles, the half-emptied root beers, and melting ice cream pints.

Rocky Road is sticky on my fingers. I try to wipe off my hands, but I'm really just eyeing Highland at this point. Confused as fuck, worried. Concerned. "What is it?" I ask.

He grimaces. "Don't hate me. Promise you won't hate me, dude."

Now I'm terrified. But my lovesick ass says, "I promise I won't hate you."

He runs his hands through his hair, keeps his palms on his head. "It's…"

"You're drawing this out and making this ten-times worse than it probably is." My heart is stuck in my throat like a boulder.

He cracks a pained smile. "I should've told you so much sooner. I had so many opportunities—and again, I missed them. Let them slip by, and now it feels like an actual conscious secret. *Fuck*, it is conscious."

Blood has drained from my face.

I think I'm near tears.

Motherfuck.

"What is it?" I ask again.

He cheated on me.

He doesn't actually love me.

He doesn't want to be with me long-term.

He's married to a woman.

He has a baby.

"I'm rich," he says.

It knocks me back for no other reason than it being *tame*. I just rode a fucking merry-go-round at a hundred miles per hour and jumped off. I'm gonna puke.

Legitimately.

"Oscar?"

"Oh my God, Highland." I lean forward again. "Don't ever do that to me again."

His lips falter. "You don't understand, Os."

I groan out the rest of my heightened pulse in the palms of my hand. Feeling better, I look over at my boyfriend. "I understand that you're rich."

"No, like *really* rich, Oscar."

I pause for a beat. "How rich are we talking about?"

"You know Charlie's apartment in the Saint-Germain-des-Prés neighborhood?" he breathes. "I could buy one of those."

Holy.

Shit.

Shock is a lump in my esophagus. I'd love to tell him that I don't care, but I really wish he felt like he could trust me with this sooner.

Jack rubs his jaw, set in a wince at my silence.

Little things are making more sense. Like why he got so upset when I paid for temp security to protect him when he has a lot of money.

I wipe up a melted puddle of Rocky Road. "So while you're taking all of my clothes, you could probably just buy the department store?" My eyes meet his. "That's what you're saying?"

He nods slowly. "It's inherited money. I have a trust fund. My parents are real estate developers."

"Millionaires?" I ask.

"Billionaires."

I choke on more surprise. Fucking shit. A billionaire. It doesn't change how I feel about him. It might change who's picking up the bar tab. Again, though, I can't believe it took him so long to tell me. Was he that nervous?

I ease into my feelings. "Did you ever tell the famous ones?" I ask first.

"Not until recently, I told Moffy, Jane, and Sulli," Jack admits. "I didn't feel like money is who I am, so there was no reason to talk about it. It's a trust fund. But my parents are proud of their successes. And I don't want to be ashamed of what they've given me. Plus, I eventually want you to see where I grew up, and my house in Long Beach is really nice."

"That has to be an understatement."

His smile flickers in and out. "I just want you to know everything about me. Sorry it took until now."

"Why is that?" I question. "Did you feel like I'd overreact?"

He pauses, gathering his thoughts. "I feel like...I missed the chance to come clean, and then after a while, it felt like something that could tear us apart."

I lean back and turn more to him, arm on the booth behind his shoulders. "I'm glad you told me now, but Highland, I'd much rather you trust me sooner than later. Don't be afraid to tell me anything. I want all your skeletons. Even the scrawny ones."

He lets out a soft laugh, then nods. "I'll save the scrawny skeletons for you, Os."

I grin. "Thank you. For the scrawny ones and for opening up now." I realize that Charlie's docuseries *Born into Fame* really is a passion project. There is no monetary reward for Jack. He doesn't even need his salary on *We Are Calloway*, which means that his career is so much more about the art.

Art is attached to the soul, and I don't want anything hurting him that deeply.

Jack grazes a hand along my neck, rising up my jaw. Our eyes dance over our features. We're about to go in for a kiss, and I swear to everything holy that cellphones are the toxin of my romantic existence.

His phone buzzes.

And his face falls. "It's the execs."

His job.

Where's Jack Highland going to land?

In my arms, probably.

34

Oscar Oliveira

THE SPORTS BAR IS PACKED tonight for a Phillies game, and Jack and I barely got a table, but it's squeezed right in the center of the room. Three TVs are in view, so I'm flying high tonight. I'm not even sweating pushing my way through the crowd as I return to our table with two mojitos.

"Bartender was not happy about making these." I slide my boyfriend his drink. "If it tastes like piss, tell me and I'll go have words." I sink down next to Jack and he wraps a casual arm over my shoulder.

He smells his drink and eyes me in a growing smile. "By all means, you can sip it first. You're older and hotter, so…" He pushes my glass closer to me. "Age and beauty first."

I crush some of the mint with my straw. "Flattery gets you everywhere." I grin just seeing his happiness. His honey-brown eyes smile a flirtatious, charismatic smile. We have reason to celebrate tonight.

Highland is still an exec producer. Production agreed that he's essential to the docuseries, and it'd be wrong to fire him over online hatred and trivial "integrity" issues. Who knows what really swayed them? Could've been the famous families vouching on Jack's behalf. Could've been Jack's own reasoning during the meeting.

In the end, he still has the career he spent so much time working towards. Clinking his glass in cheers, I take a sip from the drink. It's not too sour. "Not bad, actually. Some bartenders are way too pissy about making mojitos. You'd think I just ordered a fucking espresso martini."

Jack takes a giant swig from the drink.

I grin. "You looking to get wasted tonight, Long Beach?"

"Maybe." He smiles. "We're celebrating, right? For you and me. Your newest temp trainee finished her last course of training. She's fully-certified for temp bodyguard duty because of you." Training the temp is also why I have the night off, but I have to be back at work bright and early tomorrow. A few drinks won't hurt though.

"It's not a competition or anything, but pretty sure I've trained the most temps for Kitsuwon Securities. So we can definitely drink to that too. Emphasis on *too*." I hold up my glass. "We are both motherfucking badasses." The mojito goes down rough as I laugh at a thought. "Oh, fuck, you have to hear this. Back when Gabe completed the course, he asked me if there was a graduation walk."

Jack's face morphs into a pitying smile. "Ah, man. That's kind of sad. We could get him a cap and gown. Make it official."

"Only if you give the commencement speech, Highland." I pop a chip into my mouth, and he pulls the basket closer to his chest. I reach out for it. "Whoa! Uh-huh…these stay near me, meu raio de sol."

His eyes soften at the nickname, letting go of the chips too easily. "What does that mean exactly?"

I toss another chip in my mouth. "My sunshine."

He laughs into a brighter smile.

There it is. "Fits well."

He looks flattered for once, and then a homerun ignites the room and us in raucous screams.

We finish off our mojitos and get two more. Then three. And then a couple more. I can't remember being this happy. Or this drunk…in a long fucking time.

Jack's smile becomes more lopsided—and I don't know if that's because I'm wasted or he is—but he has an orange sucker in his mouth and keeps touching my face. "You've got something here," he tells me, his finger sliding down my lips.

"That's a mouth, Long Beach," I pretend to bite his finger. He pulls back and plants his hand on my crotch.

"This is a dick," he defines. "A hard dick."

I'm laughing so hard some blueberry mojito dribbles down my chin. I wipe it off with the back of my hand. "You're drunk." *We are fucking drunk.*

"Without a doubt." He shifts the sucker with his tongue. "At least we know that you're the less flirty drunk."

"Wait a minute." I lift my glass. "You think I'm less flirty? Are you sure you're not confusing flirty with sloppy?"

He smacks my chest, and his expression—kid you not—grows mockingly serious. "I'm not sloppy."

"Highland, your pants are wet. You spilled your second mojito on your crotch an hour ago."

He snorts like that's not true. Then he looks down at his pants, and stares at the wet spot for a long beat before looking at me. "Okay. Okay. I'm sloppy. But the better question is...why aren't you sloppier?"

"Because I'm *me*." I pop a blueberry in my mouth. "We can't all be this good at drinking."

Jack laughs and nods as he tries to put the straw into his mouth with a sucker still between his lips. So drunk. So cute.

The straw escapes him every time he tries. I can't stop laughing. "Here." I grab his glass, hold the straw steady for him, and he leans in to take a small slurp.

He swallows, pops the sucker out, and smacks his lips. "Nutty with a little aftertaste of citrus from the hills of Napa. Stellar. Five golden stars. A truly revolutionary taste." He grins. "And that would be my review for your cum."

Motherfuck. My smile hurts my face. "Get the fuck out of here." I point towards the door.

"Only if you come with me." He's tugging a fistful of my shirt, and I follow him out of the sports bar. We hook arms around each other, walking down the sidewalk and singing songs loud enough that people in their apartments yell at us to shut up.

We end up at a club where no one will scream at us, and we sing until our voices grow hoarse. We drink until we're holding each other up.

And still, I never want this night to end.

I WAKE TO A POUNDING IN MY HEAD THAT FEELS

like someone is auditioning to become Tom Cobalt's drummer in my brain. "Fuck," I groan groggily and rub the sleep from my eyes.

Where am I?

I blink awake. *Hell's Kitchen.* My studio apartment, I realize.

Jack sits on the edge of the pullout like he's been waiting for me to wake up. At the ready with a glass of water and a bottle of Advil. He gives me a tight smile that doesn't seem right. And then he passes me the water, but I'm not looking at the glass.

"*Highland.*" I stare at the shiny silver ring on his finger. That was definitely not there last night.

His eyes grow and he points upwards. *Shit.* My sister is here. Sleeping in the king-sized bed in the loft.

I scoot up the pullout, leather couch, avoiding looking at my own hand. No. No fucking way. I try to think back to last night, but it's all a messy blur after we reached the club. Quickly, I climb off the bed and grab his wrist, dragging him to the bathroom.

As soon as the door shuts, I take the plunge and look at my hand. Motherfucker! There's a ring on my finger.

A ring!

"Do you remember what happened?" I ask Jack, his dark hair is tousled from a hard, drunken sleep. My boyfriend leans a hip against the marble sink counter, arms threaded loosely over his chest.

"A little bit," he says, stiffly. "I was hoping we could talk it out and piece it together."

I place two hands on my head, chest rising and falling heavily. "Alright, so we were at the club."

"And then we left," Jack says.

"Okay…I vaguely remember stopping at a jewelry store?" I shake my head. "But that doesn't make sense because it was too late—everything would've been closed."

"No, that's right," Jack snaps his fingers. "You stopped at the store, and you called someone…"

I groan and sink onto the edge of the tub. "Had to have been Maggie. She's a friend from college. She works at Cobalt Diamonds."

Jack questions, "If you asked her to let you in after-hours, you think she'd open the store for you?"

I nod strongly. "She's done it before, mostly when I'm with Charlie." I swipe a hand through my bed-head hair. "But maybe this is a good thing? We just bought rings. We didn't actually get married."

Jack reaches into his back pocket. The same pants he was wearing last night. He passes me a crumpled piece of paper.

I'm staring at my motherfucking marriage license.

We both signed it.

"No one's talking about it on the internet," Jack tells me. "Which means we somehow did this without paparazzi or *people* noticing."

"Of course we fucking did." I fold the piece of paper. "I'm a strategic genius, Highland. I can get married without it being on the news the next day. Apparently, I'm so fucking good, I even hid it from myself." I start laughing, but it's a stressed, panicked sound.

Jack points to the paper in my hands. "The name of the officiant and the two witnesses are all fraternity brothers." He sucks in a breath. "So I'm just as much to blame. We must have run into them or something. I, honestly, don't remember."

I frown, the fuzzy parts starting to clear a little. "I think I do recall stumbling into some guy named Edgar. He wore an ugly plaid shirt that looked like vomit."

Jack laughs. "Yeah, he's a lawyer." He shakes his head. "The crazy thing, Oscar, is none of this would have happened if we both weren't so well-connected."

"Look at us," I say. "So popular we accidentally got hitched."

Silence finally seeps in, and it strains something between us.

He's my husband.

And I didn't even know his middle-effing name until seeing it on the marriage license. Until right now. "Your full name is Jack Arizona Highland?" I question. "*Arizona?*"

He makes a pained face. "I was conceived in Arizona, apparently."

I laugh, one that dies, but damn did I need that right now. The air sobers again. We stare at one another as the reality sinks and sinks.

Do I regret this? I'm a smart guy. Even drunk, I'm not going to do something I don't want. Deep down, I love Jack, and I can't imagine running to the courthouse to get it annulled. The thought causes my stomach to twist in tight, unthreadable knots.

But I also can't imagine this being okay for him. *Too soon* are words that ring in my head. Maybe he thinks I drunkenly married him for his money. *God, I hope not.*

I lick my dry lips, mouth parched. "We can get it annulled."

Jack doesn't blink as he asks, "Is that what you want?"

My phone rings. For a second, I worry I might've drunk dialed Farrow or Donnelly last night, but I see it's just Charlie.

I click into the call. "Hey."

"We're going to Vienna. I'm leaving in five." He hangs up.

And just like that, there's no time to discuss what to do. No time to even get an annulment if we wanted. We're headed to Austria.

35

Jack Highland

OSCAR AND I AGREE to pocket our rings and not speak about the marriage until we're alone again. A difficult task, seeing as how we spent ten hours on a private plane with Charlie.

I think *maybe* we'll get time to talk when we check into a two-bedroom suite in a five-star hotel. But we're there for less than two minutes, just enough time to drop our bags.

Charlie's true destination is a baroque palace, open to the public. Acres of gardens, an orangery, and fountains all landscape a historic, stunning structure.

"Johann Lukas von Hildebrandt was the architect," Charlie tells me as we stop in an area under a ceiling mural, chandeliers, and gold molding. Five windows have breathtaking views of the gardens. Charlie's eyes trace the painted ceiling. "It was commissioned as a summer home for Prince Eugene of Savoy." His voice carries a reverence whenever he talks about architecture or art.

Hands on my camera, I capture Charlie and the palace in an appealing frame. "What do you like about it?" I ask, eyeing him outside of the lens.

He smiles and says something in French. I glance over my shoulder, wishing Oscar were here to translate for me.

Currently, he's busy talking to the palace's security by the door. A few visitors strolling through have recognized Charlie, but after a quick autograph or photo, they've left him alone.

I'm about to ask Charlie another question when he lies down flat on the marble tile. Legs and arms spread out like he's creating a snow angel and stopped midway through. His eyes fasten on the mural like he's studying each brush stroke.

My curiosity piques, and I can only imagine others would feel the same seeing Charlie Cobalt now. He loves art. For someone so raw, this is one of the few *soft* things about him.

I zoom in.

And as noise pitches near the doors, I take a quick, concerned glimpse at Oscar.

Palace security is angrier. He waves an annoyed hand towards Charlie on the floor. Oscar nods over and over, and I start to distinguish their voices. But I don't know a single word of German besides *nein* which just means *no*.

Not helpful, dude.

One thing is clear: Oscar can speak fluent German.

Learned that new fact this morning when we checked into the hotel.

I should know all the languages my husband can speak *before* marrying him. That…did not happen. Structurally, this is off. We're at the end without finishing the middle. Learning new things about each other. Married. *My husband.*

Jesus fuck, I can't even process. The worst part is not being able to talk to Oscar about it. Having to spend the day pretending it never happened when we are very, *very* married.

The palace security guard leaves abruptly.

Oscar strides over with determined steps. He stops beside Charlie's black scuffed and worn down Bolvaint shoes, and Oscar lightly kicks the sole. "Get up, Charlie."

Charlie pats the ground. "Lie down, Oscar. Watch the clouds move."

Oscar's brows furrow and he squats down beside his client. I keep the camera rolling. "What'd you take?" he whispers.

"Just a couple booms."

"When?"

"Hotel."

"You have a bad trip, you tell me right away."

"Always."

Oscar stands up and meets my eyes.

"What are booms?" I whisper to him as we sidle to a middle window, leaving Charlie in the center of the room. On the floor.

"Mushrooms." Oscar's gaze intensely sweeps every entry into the marble-floored space. There are more doors and windows in this area than I think he'd probably prefer.

I'm not too surprised Charlie's high on mushrooms right now, considering he's experimented with hallucinogens before. He's not always quiet about that fact.

What draws my curiosity is Oscar's role in all of this. "Do you care that he does these kinds of drugs?"

Oscar's eyes fall to the camera in my hands. I'm ready for him to tell me he's not my subject, but then he says, "Not really." He crosses his arms over his chest. "I care more about *when* he does them. If I'm not around, he knows I'll be pissed."

He pauses for a second, considering something before he says, "The first time he took LSD, he tried to take off all his clothes and jump into a fountain." He snorts into a laugh at the memory. "He got a toe in the water before I intervened."

I smile. "Wish I was there."

"Me too. We could have laughed all night together." Oscar's lips slowly rise and his brown eyes flit to me. "I like having you here, Highland."

Softly, I brush my finger over an inside pocket of my blue bomber jacket, the one with patches sewn on the fabric. It should be here...

The ring...

Where's my ring?

Shit. *I don't feel anything.* Panic sets in and I stick my hand further inside the inner pocket.

Oscar frowns. "What's wrong?"

My shoulders sag in relief when I feel the cold metal. I take out the ring, not even thinking, just glad I didn't lose it. "I thought it fell out."

Oscar studies me for a long beat. "You would've been upset about that?"

I lay the ring flat in my palm, staring at the silver band—which I later realized is actually white gold. Oscar has the exact same band, three tiny diamonds set vertically in the center like an expensive notch.

Hazily, I remember Oscar at the jewelry store, saying drunkenly, "Three diamonds to express three classic words from a couple classic gentlemen…" He teed up with a long pause. "I. Love. You."

So I study the ring now. The tiny diamonds.

I. Love. You.

"Yeah, I would've been upset if I lost it." Glancing up at him, I meet his overwhelmed expression. My heart thumps louder in my chest. Warm breeze from the gardens blows through the opened window.

Right here, inside the most beautiful palace, next to the most beautiful man, I come to a clear understanding.

I have zero regrets.

No lie, I'm so close to combusting with these thoughts and feelings, and then a high-pitched squeal swerves our heads, our attention.

A girl recognizes Charlie.

Oscar taps into a vigilant state. He touches my shoulder in that *we'll talk in a second* way before he leaves my side. I watch him speak German again, and after a couple minutes, the girl nods, snaps a quick photo of Charlie—who's still just lying on the ground—and then she exits through another door.

Oscar returns to my side like he silently promised.

"You can speak fluent German," I say to him, brows raised. "Really well, I might add." I flash a smile. "It's impressive. So that's English, French, German, and Portuguese. Any other secrets up your sleeve?" I actually reach for his sleeve and pretend like I'm searching for something. It's just an excuse really to touch him.

Not that I need an excuse, I guess. He is my husband.

He's smiling, and he clasps my hand firmly. "Don't forget Spanish, Arizona."

Arizona. I shake my head with a wider smile. I confess, I never loved my middle name until this second. Hearing Oscar say it.

Like the entire state belongs to me.

I process, "So you're fluent in Spanish too."

"Yeah. Other languages, I can get by, like Italian, but I'm most fluent in those five. But Highland"—he sweeps me over for a long beat—"it's just as impressive that you can speak Tagalog. You and your brother grew up speaking it to each other?"

I nod and explain how our Lola doesn't know English, so we'd always speak in Tagalog around her, and Jesse and I just naturally started playfully speaking the language more to each other. Like it was a bond between us that transcended place and time. No matter if we were separated by miles or years.

When I finish, I ask, "When did you learn to speak French, German, and Spanish?"

"Spanish, I learned in high school. French, I learned when I was twenty-four and joined security. I started out on Ben Cobalt's detail, and all security guys on the Cobalts are recommended to know some French phrases. My try-hard ass decided I'd just learn it all."

I let out a laugh. "And you call me the overachiever?"

He grins. "That title still belongs to you, Long Beach. I wasn't overachieving. I just like doing my job well." His gaze refocuses on Charlie at those words, but he's still speaking to me. "German, I never planned to become fluent in. But when Charlie turned eighteen, he decided that he wanted to see every palace and museum in Austria." His lips lift. "Let's just say that year was a crash course in immersion."

Honestly, I'm realizing it feels better having this information. Like a checkmark in the *Oscar & Jack's Marriage: Not Too Soon* column. His eyes wash over me, breaking away from Charlie for a second.

I take the opportunity to hold up my camera. "Can you translate something?"

He nods, and I tap a few buttons to rewind an earlier clip.

Oscar leans into my shoulder. The weight of his body pressed up against me is this comforting relief that I can't quite fully explain.

On the footage, Charlie's gazing up at the ceiling, and my voice can be heard off-screen. "What do you like about it?" I ask him.

Charlie's response is in French, and my eyes are on Oscar. He slowly smiles.

"He said '*what's not to love?*' And that is a prime example of a non-answer from our man Charlie Keating Cobalt." His fondness of Charlie is clear. Maybe I'm a little bit clouded by the fact that Charlie did set me up with Oscar, but I've grown to feel the same.

Just as I think it, Charlie is up on his feet.

"And we're on the move," Oscar tells me, patting a hand to my chest. I train my camera back on Charlie. A part of me considers turning it off. *He's high.*

But the producer in me keeps rolling. He has final say in what makes air, anyway.

And instead of traipsing all over Vienna, Charlie wants to return to the hotel. When I hear those words, my smile explodes. Hotel equals privacy. Which means Oscar and I can *finally* talk about our marriage.

Passing swiftly through a ritzy lobby, vaulted ceilings and mammoth chandeliers overhead, we reach a gold-paneled elevator.

Should I be nervous or excited that *the talk* is almost about to happen? My body hums in this middle-ground stage of jitters.

Elevator doors glide closed, shutting us inside.

Not even ten-seconds in and Bad Timing spits in my face yet again. The entire elevator jerks to a shaky halt, and my excitement dies with the electrical groan.

I eye the floor-number, frozen on *5*.

"*No*," Charlie exclaims and reaches for the buttons, smacking a few. His yellow-green eyes are wide in panic, pupils dilated.

Oh no…

The horror of being trapped in an elevator never really registered with me. *Ride the swell.* But I forgot that Charlie wouldn't be as cool and collected.

"Calm down." Oscar pushes him back lightly and presses the red emergency button. A shrill alarm blares for a second before the sound cuts off.

Charlie steeples his fingers at his lips and stares haunted at the closed elevator door. I've never taken mushrooms before—but I can't imagine it helps the situation.

"We just have to wait," Oscar says. He looks to me. "You alright?"

Bummed that we can't talk, yeah. But on the positive side, I'm lucid and not going through a bad trip. Can't say the same for Charlie. My concern zeroes in on him. "Fine," I say to Oscar and then to Charlie, "Hey, maybe you should sit down."

He touches his throat, over and over. Rubbing his fingers over his Adam's apple. "Is it hot in here?" Charlie asks.

He's already shedding his shirt and his fingers fly to his pants.

"No, no, no." Oscar grabs his wrist. "You need to relax. *Charlie.*"

"I have a water bottle in here." I hurriedly unzip my backpack and rifle through camera equipment. *Found it.*

"Yeah, that's good." Oscar takes the PuraFons bottle from me. "Just sit down and have some water."

Charlie runs two hands through his hair, not reaching for the water. Panicked eyes return to his bodyguard. "You've got to get me out of here, Oscar."

"We're working on it," Oscar says.

Tears brim. "*Please.*" He chokes on a breath. "I can't be trapped here."

"It's just an elevator." Oscar stands in front of him and places a hand on his shoulder. "You're having a bad trip. It's amplifying your anxiety. Just take a deeper breath."

Charlie inhales deeply but never exhales. He holds in oxygen for an agonizing long minute.

"Breathe out, bro," Oscar says.

He gasps air. Silent tears slide down his cheek. His eyes flit from me to Oscar and back to me. "What does love feel like?"

My breath heavies, my eyes veering to Oscar. His gaze already glued to me.

Love?

All I know is my love for Oscar carries me like the water. A feeling of invincibility. The patience as the ocean laps underneath my body. The anticipation as the perfect wave rolls near. The cool excitement and power as I stand up. As I ride those impossible swells, and once I'm in the barrel, all the doubts and fears wash away. Leaving a bright burst of indescribable bliss.

That is his love to me.

But I struggle to articulate that to Charlie. "It's...hard to describe."

He swipes tear tracks off his cheeks. "I sometimes think that maybe it'll stop one day. This feeling inside me...frustration...all the fucking time." He blinks into more tears. "But it never really goes away, and... it has to be drowned out by something stronger. Either...pain or love."

I frown. "Is that why you let people hurt you?"

He blinks again, his tears welling and eyes growing bloodshot. "I need to talk to my dad." He rubs at his arms and shakes his limbs like he wants to crawl out of his skin. "Oscar—"

"I've got it." Oscar's dialing a number on his cell.

After filming Charlie for so long, I've realized he calls his dad any time he's feeling off. Like someone would call a therapist.

It's almost a daily phone call.

Oscar passes Charlie the phone. "Dad?" Charlie says, his voice controlled. "Can you just talk to me for a second?" He slides down the wall and tucks his head between his knees.

I touch my camera that's still around my neck. It's been rolling this whole time, and that fact knots my stomach.

"Hey." Oscar sidles next to me and his eyes skim my camera too.

After about a month of filming, I know this footage today is gold. It's a producer's dream to have their subject in such a vulnerable position. To confess something so personal. And yet, would Charlie have ever told me this without being under the influence? Without being trapped in an elevator?

I don't think so.

Ethically, morally, I feel stuck at a crossroads.

Before I make a decision, I have more questions, and they're not for Charlie. "Did you know?" I whisper to Oscar. "That that's the reason he lets people hurt him?"

Oscar nods. "If intelligence is a ladder," he tells me softly, "Charlie's trapped at the top. And it's a frustrating place to be."

A tortured genius. It feels like a hook for *Born into Fame*, and I hate it. I hate that I know it might sell. I hate even thinking about it here. I don't want to exploit Charlie. He's currently crying on the ground, high out of his mind, talking to his dad.

The elevator jerks.

Charlie's head pops out of his knees. "Oscar?"

"We're getting out of here," Oscar tells him.

36

Oscar Oliveira

"HE'S ASLEEP." I close our bedroom door in the suite. Charlie's safe and sound in his bed. His room is just across the living area. It's one of those times I'm glad we're staying in a ridiculously expensive hotel with giant multi-bedroom accommodations.

If he was staying in a normal hotel room, for my own conscience, I'd be standing outside his door in the hallway all night.

Luckily, I can relax here. Especially with Jack around.

My husband—if he even still wants to be that. He's got a hip against the window, drapes drawn back, like he's been watching the city streets, but right now, his eyes are on me.

I can't believe we haven't spoken about our marriage in over fifteen hours. It feels massively like my fault. If he drunkenly married any other guy, they'd have hashed it out immediately. Not put it on pause for a trip to fucking Austria.

I'm stiff against the door, air and silence separating us. Now that we're alone together it's almost like I can't find the words. I finish tying a rolled banana around my forehead and I say, "I wouldn't blame you, if you want to get an annulment, Highland."

His face cracks. "What?"

Pressure mounts on my chest. "I don't want you to feel pressured to stay in a marriage with me because of some drunken decision. So if you want to get an annulment, it won't change anything between us.

I promise you that. We'll just go back to how it was." I keep pushing the figurative window open for him in case he needs to escape this situation.

Jump back out.

Being with me isn't easy, and I don't want to trap him here after a drunken, stupid night. *I loved that stupid night.*

His expression is frozen in a perpetual wince. "I don't understand... do *you* want an annulment?"

No.

No hesitation. I want to stay married to Jack Highland, but I can't say those words. I run a hand through my thick curly hair. "Would it be alright if I didn't answer that?" I ask him. "Because if I say one way or the other, I'm going to feel like you're making a decision based on mine."

He looks me over. "But you have decided?"

I nod once.

He holds onto the window ledge. "You know that your non-answer is an answer, Os. You're a good guy, I know you'd be upfront and tell me that you want an annulment if that's where your head was at. So this is just to...what? Put the decision on my shoulders?"

"It is your decision, Highland."

He sucks in a tight breath. "This marriage is between *both* of us."

"And we couldn't even talk about it for over fifteen hours," I say into a bitter laugh. "Whose fault was that? *Mine.*" I point at my chest. "You really want to be married to someone who treats you like the *other* guy and not the main focus?" Tears threaten to rise. "I give so much of myself to my job, and unfortunately that job revolves around one person. Charlie. How could you want that?"

Realization washes over him. "Oscar, I've *never* felt like I'm in a competition with Charlie for your attention." He takes a step closer, but he stops. I take one and stop.

The strain in the room is like pushing two wrong ends of a magnet together. It hurts to move forward.

"I don't give you as much as I give him," I say, my insecurities bubbling to the surface.

Jack shakes his head. "That's not true." His confidence in that one statement sends a ripple through my body.

"Jack, you don't have to placate me—"

"I'm not feeding you a line, Oscar," he says, his voice choked. "I have all of you. Charlie gets Work Oscar. Bodyguard Oscar. Which is a very particularly endearing version of you, but it's not the complete package. You've given me *all* of you." He walks closer. "And yeah, it blows a little that we haven't had time to talk—I'm not going to sugarcoat that—but timing isn't our best friend. I'll get over it." He's inches away, but we don't reach out to touch.

"Maybe you shouldn't have to get over it," I tell him. "You could be married to someone else that'd give you more time."

"I don't want *time*," Jack breathes. "I want *you*. Your support. Emotional, mental, physical. I want it all."

Our fingers brush against one another, but we still don't crash together. Don't hold hands. Something feels unresolved between us. So I just ask, "But do you want to be married to me?"

Our eyes latch, and he winces again.

My heart crushes inside my chest. Smashed down to nothing. I can't breathe. I try to keep an impassive face. I told Jack that it wouldn't change things, if he wanted an annulment.

I'm trying to keep that promise.

"Oscar," Jack whispers. "I do want to be married to you, but..."

My chest rises and falls in his silence, and it takes all my energy not to run away from the pain compounding against me.

Jack's gaze washes over me. "I'm doing this wrong. I'm hurting you."

I don't deny that. "There's not really a right way to do it, Long Beach," I tell him. "Like I said, if you need the annulment, if this is *too soon*, I'm fine with that. I'll be okay."

"Will *we* be okay?" Jack wonders. He motions from his chest to mine.

My throat swells. "I think so."

His eyes redden, overwhelmed emotion passing between us. "I love you," he tells me. "I can actually see a future with you, Oscar. It's this crazy, high-adrenaline future where we're both running around the world together. I'm filming my docuseries, and you're protecting your client. And at the end of the day when we're both exhausted as fuck, we climb into bed together and hold each other and we don't even have to catch each other up on our day because we just know." He puts a hand to his chest. "*I* want that. So what I'm about to say has *nothing* to do with you or your job. Okay?"

Pain spindles between us because it feels like he's setting me up for the crash down. Not even a gentle let down. Like he's passing me a parachute before we both jump out of the plane.

"I need time to decide whether I want an annulment. Whether I feel like, for the both of us, it's the better option." He hugs his strong arms around his body, closing off.

Seeing him like that breaks my heart.

I finally reach for him, grabbing his wrist and separating his threaded arms. I pull him closer. Our knees knock, and my hand slides to his palm. His flies to my collarbones over my tattoos, planted in a way that feels like he's claiming me.

"I have to explain why," Jack breathes softly.

"Go ahead."

"We've been dating *one* month. Every article, every magazine, every voice on social media, they're all going to say our marriage is just more of a publicity stunt to combat the Oslie rumors." He grimaces. "I love you so fucking much, and having that type of negativity attached to a marriage feels *crushing*. You deserve confetti and congratulations and every *good* thing that comes with this type of announcement."

"You deserve that too, Highland."

He nods, but tears gather in his eyes. "Maybe if we wait to get married down the road. People won't be so critical. It's a possibility."

I know.

But I don't care about other people. I can be married now to him and face all those voices. Do I wish Jack is where I am? Sure, but we all have our own timelines, and I can't force his. Even if it hurts.

"The problem I'm having is that every time I consider getting the annulment, it makes me physically sick," Jack says into a deeper wince. "Which is why I probably need time to make the decision."

In his heart, I don't think Jack wants to end this marriage. I breathe easier knowing that, but it still doesn't change the fact that our rings are going to remain in our pockets for a good while. Maybe forever, depending on where his head lands.

"I'm good with that." Saying those words, I'm starting to feel it.

Because he needs time, and I need him to make this decision with a clear level-head. I want him to want this marriage completely and without reservations.

I add, "So we probably shouldn't tell anyone what happened."

"Would you be okay with that?" Jack asks. "Because I know you're close to Farrow and Donnelly—"

"They've kept so much shit from me, bro. Farrow dating Maximoff. Donnelly hooking up with Luna." I laugh softly. "It's *my* fucking turn." I lay a hand on top of his, the one that's planted on my collarbones.

A moment passes between us. Understanding. We're going to remain married, but for how long—who knows?

Jack edges closer, digging my back into the closed door. We grind in together like we're slowly mending something that fissured. His lips brush against my ear. "I'm sorry you have to wait for me." *To make a decision*, are the unsaid words.

"For you, I don't mind waiting," I whisper back. Our hands are roaming. Our bodies bucking into one another. Gripping his ass, I push him harder against me. His lips part against my neck.

"For anyone else," I tell him. "They can go fuck off."

I feel his lips rise into a smile, and he pulls back just enough to wedge his hand down between our bodies. He rubs my dick over the top of my pants. His eyes flit to mine, his smile turning into a full-on charming grin. "How do you feel about fucking a married man?"

"Depends," I say, kicking off from the door. I walk him back towards the gold four-poster bed with a cream comforter and fluffy décor pillows. His ass hits the mattress.

"On what?" His eyes fall to my lips.

"If that married man is married to me." I pick him up by the ass and he lets out a guttural aroused breath as I toss him further back on the mattress. I hop onto the bed and straddle him before he has time to move anywhere. His chest rises and falls, his hand on top of his head, winded, out of breath. All of the above.

He lies beneath me.

Gorgeous.

Tens across the board.

But we're playing with fire by talking about our marriage while we do this. Because it feels a little like twisting a rope around our hearts. Squeezing the organs until they rupture.

Still, I want to play this game because even if it's just tonight, I'd rather sink into the feeling of being married to Jack. Tomorrow, we could end it all, but at least we have this now.

Drinking him in, I only drag my eyes away to rip my shirt off over my head. He kicks off his pants. I help him with his shirt. We're hands and limbs and lips. Smoldering each other.

He breaks apart in a jagged breath. "*Os.*" His eyes veer towards our luggage by the door, and he puts a hand on my shoulder like he's about to push me off.

I put a hand to his shoulder. "You stay and keep looking beautiful. I've got it." Climbing off his athletic build, I strut buck-naked to my backpack. I grab the lube and condoms. When I return to the bed, Jack's already tugging himself.

I smile. "Hold up, Long Beach. Wait for me." I slide my hand under his, rub him a couple strokes, and kiss the hell out of his lips.

My cock aches, wanting inside him too badly to eke this out. I break apart and slide a condom on my hard shaft. When I glance back up, Jack's shivering.

"You cold?" I run a hand over his thigh.

He shakes his head. "No, I'm not cold."

My heart beats faster. "You nervous?"

"No." He blows out a breath. "This feels different than the other times. *Good* different. I'm just more…overwhelmed, I guess."

"I am, too."

His brows jump in surprise. "You are?"

I laugh. "Meu raio de sol, we're married. For tonight at least. I'm your husband."

That last statement charges a stronger voltage in the air. Arousal builds as our eyes search one another.

"And I'm your husband tonight," Jack says, amplifying the powerful current even more. He's still shivering, and I know how to heat him up.

Leaning down, I press my lips to his, guiding them open the same time as I open him below with my fingers. We fall into a rhythm as I lightly thrust against him. He deepens the kiss, and when he cuts away to let out a ragged, chopped breath, I have to pull my fingers out of him.

My erection throbs. I spread his legs open a little more and run a hand along his shaft. "You ready?"

"Please."

Fuck. I answer him by sinking inside him, slowly filling him. It feels too good for words, and my bliss is only heightened by the arousal in Jack's eyes. His hands fly to his head as I pump into him. Chests nearly flush, my lips press against the base of his jaw.

The bed rocks with my force, and my breath heavies and staggers as I push in and out, creating beautiful intoxicating friction. Jack's erection slides against my abs, and I reach down to give him a few pumps. Pre-cum coating my palm.

When I pull away, he has this tortured look in his eyes. He's about to reach down.

I slow my thrusts so that I can take his hand and put it back on his head. "Do me a favor, Long Beach," I say in heavy breath. "Keep your hands on your head."

A. It's fucking adorable.

B. I don't want him touching himself tonight.

He gives me a worried look. "Then I can't touch you, Os."

Ah, yes. This is his insecurity about being selfish. "You don't need to touch me," I tell him. "I'm inside you, Highland."

His face flames. "God." His muscles twitch. And he nods, a moan rough on its way out. "You feel good inside me."

I'm on a fucking ascent right now. Nerves pricking, blood cranked up. And I rock against him in two hard movements that cause his eyes to snap closed. "*Os.*"

"You alright?" I ease to a gentler rhythm.

His eyes open slowly, his hands fisting his hair. "Dude, please do that again."

I pump in two jackhammer movements that cause a deep, guttural groan from his chest. It blazes every nerve-ending in my body, and I press closer as I keep a steadier pace. Something that won't make him too sore tomorrow.

Thrusting my hips, flexing smoothly down and in.

My hand returns to his length. He shudders after two strokes, and I pull away again. The whimper on his lips sounds fragile. Our foreheads slide together. Breaths melding. "Os," he pleads.

"Not yet," I whisper.

My movements have slowed so much that I feel him trembling against me. Like he craves those two hard pumps either from my hand or my cock and I'm giving him neither.

But I want to eke out every last second of this.

If this is all we have.

Sweat coats our bodies, built between us like a blanket of heat. My hair sticks to my forehead, and Jack takes a hand off his head. Just to push my hair back for me. Tenderness wraps around us, and we're practically cradling each other as I rock in and out of him. His muscled chest glistens in sweat, and he leaves his palm on my head. Fingers threaded into my hair now. I'm thanking every star and moon and sun for sending him to me.

My body aches for a pleasured release, and when I up the pace, Jack's fingers coil in my hair. "*OsOsOs.*"

"*Fuck*," I moan and groan, grabbing onto the headboard as I push harder, wanting deeper.

He glances down at his erection like he wants that touch.

I press my lips to his forehead. "No hands, meu raio de sol."

Hand clutching the headboard, I thrust two more times with a firm, direct goal. I feel him shudder in a full-body release, and mine happens seconds later. The out-of-the-universe climax drains oxygen from my brain, and it takes a second to catch my bearings.

Slowly, I roll off him, and he immediately pulls me back into his arms. Hanging his bicep over my sweaty chest. We're curled up together. Limbs threaded. Neither of us bother getting underneath the covers. "Oscar," Jack breathes.

But that's all he says.

That's all he needs to say.

We just made love, and emotion still strings between us like a lit flame. His head buries against the crook of my neck. I am so in love with him.

And I'm so fucking scared of losing him.

37

Jack Highland

KEEPING OUR MARRIAGE quiet for over two weeks has been harder than I thought it'd be. Considering, I'm the one who wanted time to decide on an annulment, I shouldn't feel this need to *tell* people that Oscar Oliveira is my husband.

But there I was minding my own business at the WAC offices, eating a ham and cheese sandwich, casually scrolling through some entertainment sites, when I landed on an article about "the Pro" in Security Force Omega. Embedded in the story was a shirtless photo of Oscar. I recognized his yellow bathing suit trunks and the orange bandana. Sand beneath his feet. It was taken in California.

I scrolled to the comment section.

Oscar is HOTT.

Wow! He's got to be "the pro" in bed, right?

YUM. So when Oscar's done with Charlie and Jack? Can I get a bite of that?

And that last comment charged me up enough to almost type out the words: *You can't, I'm married to him.* Okay, I did type out the words, but I restrained myself from posting. Partly because it wouldn't change a thing.

I know that. Producer cred and all.

Still, I sit with these heavy feelings today. Jealousy mixed with indecision. And what am I jealous of? Some random person calling Oscar hot on the internet? Maybe I just want people to know that he's *really* mine forever. To finally believe me when they keep doubting the truth because of the Oslie rumors.

But I'm aware that yelling "Oscar Oliveira is my husband!" would be short-term bliss.

Some people will just take the marriage as a PR ploy. Warp it into something it's not. And that's why I ultimately need the time to think the annulment over. Maybe if we actually *wait* to get married down the road, people won't judge so harshly.

I hate that I'm factoring in other people in my future with Oscar. When really all I want is him, but it's been my life—my career—to understand outside perception. What it all means.

FYI: I looked up how long I have to decide before we can no longer get an annulment. Five years. So I have five whole years to live in this unbearable limbo.

Can't wait that long—that's all I know.

And at least I know something, right?

Finished with the WAC shoot today, I stuff my camera into its bag. Luna's wiping her swollen eyes with tissues I handed her. Sharpie drawings decorate a neon-green cast around her arm. The golf cart crash caused a bone fracture that's healing.

She's curled up on a beanbag in the loft of Superheroes & Scones. The store closed early so we could film here, and she's spent the last hour talking about all the headlines that surround her.

The ones that are obsessed with her nightly clubbing. How she's been "spotted" kissing different guys on the same night, sometimes at the same place.

I gently asked her if she wanted to discuss the other media headline. Tabloids hyper-focus on any of the famous ones' changes: tattoos, haircuts, weight-gains. And they've noticed that Luna has worn pants practically all summer long.

She didn't want to talk about it for the show, but she told me that Donnelly tattooed her leg, up to her hip, and she's afraid of her dad finding out.

I promised, like always, to keep the secret.

Hugging her another time, I tell Luna, "Remember, we don't have to air anything, if you don't want to." I'm referring to our talk about the nightclubs.

"When do I have to make a decision by?" She crumples the tissue.

"No deadline."

If she wants it in the show, it'll appear in the upcoming season. If she doesn't, I'll be the only person that ever sees this footage.

"Thanks, Jack." She tugs the string of her hoodie.

I stand and hook the strap of my bag over my shoulder. "Do you want me to call someone? Tom, Eliot, your older brother, maybe?"

She shakes her head. "I think I'm just gonna hang out alone for a little bit."

"Will I see you at the carnival later?"

H.M.C. Philanthropies is hosting a Carnival Fundraiser tonight, and I'm supposed to be filming Charlie there for *Born into Fame*. It already started about an hour ago, so Jesse's at the carnival in my place.

She nods. "I'm gonna stop by. I don't want to miss the Gravitron."

That eases me a bit. It'll be good for Luna to be around family.

"See you then." I take the spiral staircase to the bottom floor. Her bodyguard is the only person here. Quinn Oliveira sits in the red vinyl booth by a window, scrolling through his phone. He glances up when I'm about a foot away.

"She ready?"

I shake my head. "She wants to be alone." I readjust the bag as it slips off my shoulder. "How's the therapy going with Oscar?"

He makes a noise that sounds a lot like a sigh and a snort crossed together. "He didn't tell you?"

"He's told me some," I admit. "You guys don't talk during the sessions. Has that changed?"

Quinn messes with a saltshaker. "Why would it?"

I shrug with a warm smile. "Maybe the therapist broke through?"

Quinn narrows his eyes at me. "I know what you're doing, Jack. You can pretend to be nice and act like we're friends, but it's not working."

Alright then. "Quinn," I say. "I'm generally nice to everyone, and I know we're not friends. But if you don't want to talk, that's cool."

"I don't."

"Fine," I say into a tight nod. "I'll see you at the carnival."

38

Oscar Oliveira

THIS IS MY LEAST FAVORITE kind of carnival: ones that resemble state fairs with Ferris wheels, carousels, funhouses, and milk bottle games for entertainment.

Nothing really beats Carnaval in Brazil, a celebration that marks the beginning of Lent. The blocos alone are out of this world. Bouncing from one bloco to the next, each with different themes, music, and signature styles. Polka-dots, masks, ribbons. I've only been a couple times, but they're still some of my favorite memories. Doused in glitter, sometimes wearing costumes, drinking and dancing the night away. There's nothing like it.

Maybe one day I can take Jack.

That thought does a number on me. Because here I'm thinking about the future when we can barely scrape together what we are *now*.

A gust of funnel cake wafts in my direction. The heavenly, powder-sugary smell floods my senses. Changed my mind, I don't hate this kind of carnival because I do *love* their food. It's the eat-on-the-go goodness that my body craves.

But there's no time to eat.

Not when the fair grounds are jam-packed. Tickets sold out in less than an hour, and all the Hales, Meadows, and Cobalts are in attendance.

Comms chatter is soft in my ear, so I'm aware of everyone's location. How Maximoff and Farrow are on the Ferris wheel with their son, a bucket above Thatcher and Jane. Most of the Cobalts hang around the carnival game booths, and the Meadows family have been bopping around the higher adrenaline rides.

My main focus stays on the carousel.

For the past thirty minutes, my client has been lounging on one of the few double-bench chairs shaped like a boat. He's smoking a cigarette, reading a book, and ignoring the girls that try to converse with him from nearby carousel horses, bobbing up and down. I've lost count of the rotations the carousel has made, but no one tries to kick him off.

Normally, I'd be the one standing right next to Charlie. But these kinds of rides, even the slow-ass carousel make me want to puke. Instead, I've sent in Gabe to hug onto the pole next to Charlie's bench.

Evening approaches, but the sun hasn't set yet, making it easier to do my job.

Donnelly rounds the corner with a plate of funnel cake. My stomach lets out an audible groan. "Donnelly," I say. "Please say that's for me."

"Why else would I come over here?" He holds out the plate, and nods to Jesse. "Hey, little J."

Camera equipment weighs down Jack's little brother as he films a wide shot of Charlie on the carousel. Ten minutes ago, I took pity on the kid and grabbed one of the bags. It's heavy on my shoulder, but it won't break my back like Jesse.

"Where's Big J?" Donnelly asks me.

"*Jack*," I emphasize, "is heading over. He just got done shooting Luna." I rip off a chunk of the fried dough. "This smells fucking amazing, bro."

"The deal was dope, too. Some girl offered to give it to me. All I had to do was spit in her mouth."

Ugh. I drop the funnel cake piece back on the plate. "That's disgusting."

He picks my chunk and tosses the fried dough onto his tongue. "I didn't spit *in* the funnel cake, man." He licks powdered sugar off his thumb. "I spit in her mouth."

"Bro, I got that part. It's still gross. This wasn't yours."

"It is now," he says. "She only had like three bites before she gave it to me."

So gross. So fucking gross. I rub my hand down my pants, wishing I had some sanitizer right now. Love Donnelly, but I don't want to touch anything from someone who'd pay to spit in his mouth.

Jesse glances at us with a grimace. "Why did she want you to spit in her mouth?"

Donnelly shrugs. "I dunno. Said she thought the Ass-Kicker SFO bodyguard was hot. But pretty sure her friends dared her to do it." He smiles. "Jokes on them. I got this." He holds up the plate of funnel cake like it's made of gold.

Know the feeling.

Don't feel it now.

Donnelly's attention deviates to the carousel. "Are those dragons?"

"Yeah." Along with horses and boats, people can ride unicorns and dragons.

"Xander would've loved this." Donnelly glances around at the amassing people, the sun beginning to drop behind the rides and food stands. "Not these crowds though. Fuck me, there are a lot people here."

While Xander's at home, SFO put a temp on his detail, letting Donnelly join the carnival's security for the night.

Jesse nods to me. "I'm going to get a shot from the other side of the carousel."

He leaves, and Donnelly stares at the bag on my shoulder for a long beat.

"Bro, just spit it out."

"I was just thinking," Donnelly says, "that Kitsuwon's giant-sized manual clearly states not to carry production equipment for *We Are Calloway*. You a rulebreaker now or what?"

"Just a motherfucker in love."

"With Jesse?" Donnelly quips, whipping his head to where the little Highland just left. One thing people never get right when they first meet Donnelly: he's a smart motherfucker.

He plays dumb too well.

His smirk lands on me.

I let out a dry laugh. "That'd be funnier if you weren't eating someone's leftover funnel cake while you said it."

He sticks out his tongue, showing off chewed up funnel cake.

I grin. "You are seriously disgusting, bro."

He closes his mouth into a smile, and swallows down the rest of the food. Both of us suddenly grow quiet. An unspoken thing hanging.

Pinging and chiming sounds of carnival games and lively music from the nearby Tilt-A-Whirl fill the silence, but the strain isn't dissolved. We're dodging the unsaid topic. It sits between us like that funnel cake in his hands.

Crowds gather nearby around a ring toss stand. Tom and Eliot Cobalt bought giant bags of plastic rings and throw fistfuls at glass soda bottles.

When Donnelly focuses back on me, I just go ahead and ask, "How much money is Scottie taking from you?"

Donnelly chews slowly on the funnel cake. "He's not taking anything. I'm givin' it to him willingly."

So Scottie did want money. I'm at least right on that one.

"Semantics aside," I say. "Bro, how much?"

He shrugs.

"I'm not Redford," I remind him. "You didn't do me a solid. I didn't put you up at Yale. And if that doesn't convince you, I distinctly remember Redford calling you a viral mouth sore."

"Yeah, but he said it so fondly. What's not to love about being a viral mouth sore?" He laughs.

I smile. "Donnelly…"

"I give him my paycheck," he finally admits with an easy nonchalance. Like that was never a big deal at all. But the weight of the statement hits me hard. Crashes against my chest.

I almost rock back.

"Fuck."

"Nah, it's all good. I'm picking up some jobs on the side. Look." He fishes in his pocket and pulls out a hand-drawn business card. *Tattoos by Donnelly*. On the back is his phone number. "Been passing these out all night."

I wonder how many prank calls he'll get.

But I also know there will be lots of people who want a tattoo from *the Ass-Kicker SFO bodyguard*. Still makes me nauseous that he's essentially protecting Xander for free. Since he joined security, he's been doing tattoos on his own time because he loved it. Not because he needed the money.

"Boyfriend's here."

It takes me a minute to realize Donnelly is talking about *my* boyfriend. Or I guess my *husband*. But that could change, so Jack's like my short-term husband. Fuck, I hate even the sound of that.

Ugh. Need to come up with something better.

How about: Limited Edition Hottie Husband. Yeah, we're going with that one. I pass the business card back to Donnelly as Jack approaches.

Jack's eyes fall to the camera bag on my shoulders. "You shouldn't be carrying that. Where's Jesse?"

"It's not a problem, Highland." But I am passing him the bag anyway because the look in his eyes basically says *give it to me now*. "And he's around the other side of the carousel."

Comms light up in my ear. "Akara to Donnelly, head over to the ring toss. Eliot and Tom need extra security."

"Cobalts who slay together, stay together," Donnelly says as he leaves, throwing up a hand gesture that means *love you*.

Once out of earshot, I fill Jack in on what I learned about Donnelly.

"Shit," Jack breathes. "All of his money?"

"I'm more worried about what happens if Scottie starts asking for more." I swallow hard. It might happen, and Donnelly doesn't have more to give, but he's found creative ways to earn cash before. Some ways worse than others.

It's a mess. Especially because he won't ask for help. He'll reject it no matter how many times it's offered.

Darkness blankets over the carnival, colorful lights flashing brighter and the upbeat music growing louder. I quickly study Jack's face. He's quieter than normal, and I wonder if it has anything to do with his shoot with Luna. He usually gets like this after an emotional exchange—like he's working through his head what he heard.

He carries a lot of other people's secrets. I never pressure him for them, but there have been times he's volunteered some up *just* to me. Sometimes that makes him feel better. Other times, I think it's easier for him to keep them to himself, and seeing as how I've protected plenty of Charlie's secrets, I can understand and respect that.

"Your brother is doing a good job tonight, Highland. If you need a second before you start working—"

"Yeah," he says into a slow nod. "Yeah, I might need that."

I reach down and take his hand, squeezing tight. My attention trains back to Charlie, but my client is now on the move. I see him leave the carousel, and Gabe is about half a minute late on comms.

"Gabe to Oscar, Charlie's headed towards the teacups."

Fuck, another spin ride. I'd think Charlie was doing this on purpose, but 90% of the rides look like I'd hurl on them.

I click my mic. "Copy. I'm on my way." I step one foot in that direction, before I stop cold.

Quinn—my brother—he's charging towards me with long, determined strides. Luna is nowhere near him, and I think the worst. Something happened to her.

Jack squeezes my hand now.

"Quinn—" I start.

My brother must see the concern flash across my face. Quickly, he tells me, "Before you fucking blow your shit, Luna has a temp on her detail." He cringes in guilt when a young boy passes us, who heard him curse. His eyes fix back on me. "Akara's letting me take tonight off." He stuffs his hands in his pants pockets, thumbs out. "Can we talk?"

On instinct, my vigilant eyes dart to my client. Charlie's halfway to the teacups.

Quinn lets out a strained noise. "Fuck, bro. I'm asking for *ten minutes* of your time. Spare me that."

His words, his pained voice sends a shockwave of anguish through me. Quickly, I whisper in comms that I'm taking a break for the night. Prying the earpiece from my ear, I unclip my radio, hurriedly winding the cord around the device.

Quinn frowns. "What are you doing?"

"I'm going off-duty," I say. "If you want to talk, I don't want to put a time limit on it. You've got me for the night, Quinn." I don't know why he's chosen tonight, but I don't risk asking.

Jack shifts a camera to his left hand, then motions towards the teacups. "I'll let you guys catch up. I'm going to go film Char—"

"Wait," Quinn says swiftly. "Can you…I think…it'd just be best if you were around for this."

Same.

The likelihood of Quinn and I throwing fists at some part of this conversation is too high. We need a mediator, and I'm seconding the Jack Highland nomination.

Jack looks between us, sensing the tension. And he hikes the camera bag's strap higher up his shoulder. "Let's go somewhere quieter, then."

We end up on the plot of grass between a strongman game and the Gravitron, a domed ride where people line up and disappear inside. Our spot is out of the brighter lights, and for how busy the carnival fundraiser is tonight, this is as close to private as we'll find.

Quinn puts his hands on his head, elbows out like he just finished a 5K. His broken gaze drills into me. "I hate you, you know. Like I *really* hate you."

Those words slice me up worse than his fists ever have. I nod slowly. "Yeah, I've felt that," I tell him.

He grinds down on his teeth. His wavy hair blows in the wind. Jack unhooks his camera bag from his broad shoulder, dropping the thing to the grass. I meet understanding in his gaze, and he gives me a strong nod, shooting strength through my veins.

God, if I had to do this without him…I can't think it. Don't want to even imagine it. I realize it doesn't matter what he's here as—my boyfriend or some limited edition husband. It makes no difference. His support is still the same spellbinding force that carries me tonight.

I take a breath and turn to my brother.

Quinn drops his arms. "It used to be easier ignoring you and just letting the silence eat at us. But every time we're in therapy it's so fucking *unbearable*." He grinds down on his teeth. "Because I have to sit there knowing that you're the reason I still have a job. You did something good for me. You were willing to quit security for me." His eyes redden. "But I still can't stop hating you."

What did I do?

"Just tell me why you hate me so much. I want to know, Quinn." Desperation clings to my voice. "*Please.*"

Colorful lights dance across his cheek, across the scar beneath his eye. Someone in the distance cheers as they win the strongman game.

He waits for their celebration to end before speaking. "Telling you won't change a damn thing," he breathes. "Other than kill me and hurt you."

"This has already killed you, bro. It's already hurt me."

He chokes on a sob and presses a hand to his eyes.

I want to comfort him, but I'm afraid it'll just incite his anger. "Whatever it is," I end up saying, "you don't need to carry it on your own anymore. I'm here."

He lets out a staggered breath, nearing a panicked laugh. "You're here," he repeats and stares at the grass. "You know I used to idolize you. My big brother. Oscar Oliveira. The strongest, biggest badass I knew." His eyes meet mine, and he struggles with the next words. "I'd follow you around *everywhere*. You remember that? I'd tell you: "Quando eu crescer, quero ser como você." *When I grow up, I want to be like you.*

It hurts to breathe. "I remember." He was just a little kid. Five or six.

He twists the silver chain around his neck. Our mom gave him the necklace after his confirmation. A pendant of Saint Michael the Archangel is engraved in the middle. "What about when I was really little?" he asks me. "You remember how you'd bend down to my height and you'd put both hands on the top of my head, and you'd tell me: Eu sempre vou te proteger." *I'll always protect you.*

We're in an open field, but it feels like walls are closing in around me. I'm back in Vienna, trapped in an elevator. This time it's just me and my brother and the gnarled roots we've kept buried for years.

"I remember," I whisper.

His nose flares. "You'd say that over and over. Eu sempre vou te proteger. Eu sempre vou te proteger. Even when I was nine, and you left for Yale, I believed you." He ruptures into tears. "You kept telling it to me when you were hundreds of miles away, and I fucking believed you!"

I choke on my own breath. *What happened? What the fuck happened?!* I want to scream it. I want to protect him right now. I did something...I didn't do something. I'm so lost, but I feel his fucking pain, and I want it to end. "Quinn, I love you—you have to know that."

His hand goes to his heart, and he fists the fabric of his shirt like he's trying to stop the organ from beating. "Your love is weak, Oscar. It never protected me."

I blink back tears, a hand to my mouth. Jack edges close like he means to comfort me, but I just shake my head. No...no...my brother wants to hurt me. *Needs* to. I'm going to let him.

"You came home eventually," Quinn continues. "But it wasn't long before you joined security, and then you might as well have left all over again. *Eu sempre vou te proteger.* Fucking bullshit." He sucks in a harsh breath. "I was *fifteen*." He chokes. "Fifteen. You were twenty-fucking-five and you couldn't protect me!"

He just gave me an age...a timeline.

For the first moment in my life, I know when our relationship shattered. This news pulverizes me to the very core. "Fifteen?" I breathe, knowing this was *before*. Before he started training to box.

"High school was hard. Every day, I went there knowing I'd be shoved into a locker or railed on. Stupid shit that you'd think only happens in the movies," Quinn says, teeth clenching, "but I was the loser who landed into every fucking cliché."

"I don't understand. You were popular in high school," I say, desperate to make sense of this. "You were co-captain of the field hockey team." Though I know that sport got dropped as soon as he took up boxing.

"But you never saw the other co-captain slam me against the locker room walls. Never saw my teammates shove my face into the grass." He blinks. "You just assumed that I was popular because I played sports? My team *hated* me. They hated me for no fucking reason other than I cried when I got knocked down. Same reason dad spit-screamed into my face the first month of training." He shrugs but it's stiff like his whole body is made of iron. "And maybe I deserved it. I was just counting on my big brother to come save me or something." His eyes sink into mine. "But that never happened."

Eu sempre vou te proteger.

I will always protect you.

"If you would've called me—"

"You'd what? Drop everything to run home and help me? You never came home! These guys were fucking with me every goddamn day. Over and over. You couldn't stop what they already knew. I was weak. I had *no one*."

I'm hung up on the word *guys*. My stomach churns. "How many?" I ask.

He doesn't say anything.

"How many guys, Quinn?!" I scream, eyes burning.

His voice cracks into a cry. "I told you. The whole fucking team."

He didn't even have a chance. My brother...my baby brother was getting beat to shit, and I never knew. Never helped him. I was too busy protecting someone else. Someone who was paying for my protection, and I'd promised it to Quinn. Because he's my brother. He's my blood.

Dizziness sets in, and I squat down. Hands on my head.

Quinn takes a large breath, chest rising. "I don't need you anymore. I don't need anyone, bro. I got stronger than everyone in the family, so that I could finally protect myself." He jabs a finger at his chest.

I slowly rise. Colorful lights spinning around us are banging in my head. "Then why'd you quit boxing?" I always assumed he quit to follow me into security. But I know I'm wrong.

He wipes a hand across his jaw. "I couldn't stand it." He drops his hand, and he squeezes his fingers in a fist like he's trying to force something back. "Oscar, I don't just hate boxing. I fucking *loathe* it. People all around me *cheering* to hit him. Kill him. Harm another person. For what? Applause? A fucking trophy?"

The ring is violent. More than once have I been the recipient of those cries to murder. But we've grown up around the combat sport, it's just...normal to me.

Quinn grimaces into a shake of his head. "No. I'm not doing that."

"Then you could have gone to college," I tell him. "You could have made a different life for yourself."

"I want this!" Quinn points at the ground. "I want to defend people. Protect people. To be a force of *good*. You know why I go off comms like Farrow? Why I replicate his style of bodyguarding? Because he needs *no one*. Not any of the team. He can rely on himself, and that's all I've ever fucking wanted."

This need for self-reliance stems deep. All the way back to being bullied in high school. *Bullied.* Fuck, my baby brother was bullied. I want to cry or hug him. I fucking hate myself. Because never in a million years did I think Quinn—my brother who could knock me out—was once tormented every day by his peers. And he's right, if I'd been there for him, I would have put an end to every last fucker who laid a hand on him.

But I was barely around.

"Quinn—"

He cuts me off, "I realize now that I never would've been this good of a fighter, if you didn't fail at protecting me." Just like that, heat extinguishes from his gaze. "I guess I can thank you for that."

It's a final blow.

A knockout.

He is all that he is because of me. All that rage. All that pain.

"Quinn," I breathe. I have to try to mend this, and maybe I finally can now that I know what's broken. "I'm *so* fucking sorry. For the rest of my life, I'll always be sorry." I step closer. "I didn't protect you then, and I know it's too late now." We're near enough that I put a hand to the back of his head. He tries to shove me away, but it's not as hard or forceful as he's done before. I barely sway.

And I keep my hand rooted tight onto his head.

Tears stream down his cheeks.

"I love you," I tell him. "I should have never made you that promise, if I wasn't going to keep it." He claws at my shirt, and I can't tell if he's trying to push me away or hold on. "You don't have to stop hating me, but I'm not going anywhere."

He splinters into a sob and collapses in my arms. His forehead on my shoulder, he full-body heaves into tears. "I want to stop hating you," he mumbles into my shirt. "I just don't know how."

I keep my hand to the top of his head, trying to take his pain. "This is a start." *That's all that matters in the end.* A start. A beginning. We've been resting in purgatory for so long, unable to communicate with one another, that it felt like we'd never reach this point.

My own tears slide off my jaw, and I glance over his shoulder. I see Jack.

He wipes at his face, and he gives me a nod. *I love you,* he mouths. *I'm proud of you.*

That gets to me because I've questioned how I've handled my relationship with my brother for so many years. Jack has been a model big brother to Jesse. And having Jack's support and understanding through this is a beacon of light.

We both carry responsibility for being ten-years older than our brothers. He knows how my words back then, promising to protect Quinn, were like indelible ink in our bond.

I hug my brother tighter.

"Oscar!" Gabe's voice shocks both Quinn and me apart. The temp bodyguard runs towards us, and my brother and I quickly rub at our faces. I'm not ashamed for someone to see me cry, but this feels too personal to show.

Gabe skids to a halt beside me, out of breath with sweat running down his temple. "I've been looking for you everywhere." He huffs, hands to his knees. "I can't find Charlie."

Jack picks up his camera bag in a swift frenzy.

I try not to get worried. This has happened *plenty* of times before. But tonight feels different. Everything is different. I worry my brother will think this is a choice. Him or Charlie.

Quinn turns to me. "We can split up. It'll be faster." Our eyes lock, and I can't say forgiveness draws between us, but something closer to acceptance. We're both bodyguards. He's here to stay, and I'm finally at peace with that.

"That's a good idea," I tell him and start unwinding the wire off my radio. "You take the west side."

"Copy." He's about to jog off, but he stops for a second and turns to me. "Senti sua falta." *I've missed you.*

When he leaves, I expect to be left with relief. But I just feel guilty. Angry, even. Furious at myself. I should have pushed harder. I should have done more. I'm full of pent-up rage, and I know this isn't the right head space to do my job, but I still have a job to do.

39

Jack Highland

"WE'RE GOING TO FIND HIM," I assure Oscar with all my confidence. He hasn't said anything, but I know he's worried. His shoulders have curved forward, and his eyes carry a kind of scary, intense vigilance that I've only seen when crowds start amassing onto Charlie.

"I know we are," he says. "I'm just hoping he's in one piece."

We've split up from Gabe and Quinn, and Oscar has already radioed in to see if anyone has spotted his client. I text my brother and walk quickly. Are you around Charlie? I hit send.

My eyes are on my phone, so it jolts me when I collide with a hard body. I stumble back.

"Hey, watch it!" the man growls. He's waiting in line for cotton candy, an arm around his girlfriend.

Oscar stops two feet ahead and swerves around. "Watch yourself!"

"It's fine…" My voice trails off as my phone pings.

I left him a half hour ago at the teacups to grab B-roll. — Utoy

Fuck.

Oscar's not moving; he's throwing daggers with his eyes at the cotton candy guy. "He keeps on fucking smiling at us, bro. I'm about to lose it." His anger clearly stems from a deeper place. He just learned about Quinn's past and his role in it, and he's had exactly zero seconds to really sit with those feelings.

"Come on, Os." I pull him away from the cotton candy stand.

He misses sight of a teenager who rips the radio off his waistband with a laugh. The force yanks the earpiece from his ear and snaps the mic cord. Oscar curses, then casts out a hand to grab it back.

The teenager freaks. Drops the radio, and we both watch several feet stampede over the device, the crowd moving fast with shrieks as they spot the Calloway sisters together.

"*Fuck*," Oscar swears, picking up the battered radio.

That is very, very broken. He can't call security for back-up if we run into trouble. Truth is, he's often on his own around the world anyway.

Oscar tucks the pieces in his back pocket and looks off to where we were headed.

"Let's keep going, dude," I say. "Jesse hasn't seen him."

Oscar nods and follows my stride. Pace for pace. We stop behind every ride. Every booth. Every game. There's only one place we haven't looked.

Bumper cars.

Located in the far back of the carnival, all the lights are off. We pass an *out of order* sign set up a few yards from the tent. Looks like the sign has warded off people. Aluminum stairs lead up to the metal floor where brightly colored bumper cars sit motionless like a graveyard.

Stairs let out a squeak as Oscar and I jog up them, and it dawns on me how quieter it is over here. Metal poles jut from the backs of bumper cars to the ceiling of the tent. We weave between them like we're winding around an obstacle course.

When I pass a neon blue car, I hear heavy breaths and shuffled feet. And I see figures. Bodies. *Fuck, fuck.* We launch into a sprint.

Aimed for the back near pink and yellow bumper cars. Where Charlie is curled up on the floor. Three white guys in preppy shirts are kicking his ribs.

"GET OFF HIM!" Oscar yells. My legs pump beneath me.

Charlie holds his head, elbows curved in to protect his face.

Pulse speeding, I run faster, and we reach the guys. They turn on us, and Oscar blocks and dodges blows like a pro. Mostly all self-defense.

I just want to reach Charlie. One guy impedes my path, and his fist slams against my jaw before I even blink. Pain wells in my mouth. I spit out a wad of blood, splattering my shirt.

Jesus, *shit*. I drop my gear off me like it's not the most precious thing I have. I hear the *split* of my camera. Then a *crack*. But I can't tell if that comes from my equipment or Charlie's body as that same guy rotates and kicks him again.

"JACK!" Oscar shouts.

"I'm okay," I say in a shocked breath.

I've never been in a fistfight before. And I'm dating a boxer—no, I'm *married* to a boxer.

Come on.

I can't let this one guy beat up Charlie. Oscar is busy prying the weight of two stocky, preppy guys off him. Both try to physically drag him to the ground like sandbags.

And the third guy gears up to kick Charlie again.

"HEY!" I shove him hard, but he seizes my wrist. We wrestle standing up, pulse echoing in my ears, and his fist rams into my stomach in three successive waves.

Fuck.

I cough and cough. Keeled over, hands on my thighs.

"Jack, Jack, Jack," Oscar calls quickly, pained at my pain. Two guys still latch to his body—he's trying not to create a bloodbath and punch the guys to hell. He wrenches them off faster.

I battle for breath as the same guy turns on Charlie.

I go for him again.

To protect Charlie. No question. I'd do it for Jesse. I'd do it for Quinn.

"STOP!" I yell.

He whirls around and lunges at me. I push, he shoves, and he has better hold. He thrusts me forward with too much force. And my forehead collides with a metal pole.

Everything goes dark.

40

Oscar Oliveira

JACK COLLAPSES ON THE metal floor hard. Knocked out. KO'd. My heart bangs shrilly in my chest as I slam the bastard—the one who shoved Jack at a metal pole—right into a green bumper car. His two friends took off wheezing after I elbowed them in their windpipes.

He's the last threat.

Protocol: Restrain him. Zip tie him. Call authorities.

My husband lies unmoving feet away. My client hasn't stirred since the last kick to his ribs.

My fingers tighten around his preppy collar as he thrashes against my stronghold. Rage makes a home in my body, and I want to redo the past. Fix the mistakes I made with Quinn and beat the living shit out of this guy. But Jack's unconscious.

Jack's fucking *unconscious*.

That thought runs over and over, panicking me more.

Fuck, protocol.

I dig into his pockets, grab his wallet, and toss him to the ground like he weighs as much as a feather pillow. He's lighter than the other two. "Get the fuck out of here before I kill you," I growl.

He scrambles to his feet, stumbling as he sprints out of the tent. My chest rises and falls heavily as I reroute my attention. My eyes dart back and forth.

Jack.

Charlie.

I have to choose.

I'm sorry.

Every step I take is weighted with guilt and worry, until I'm on my knees beside Jack. His eyes are closed shut, and a bump already starts forming on his forehead. Blood stains his shirt, his lip busted open.

"Jack," I shake him a little. "Jack, come on."

He doesn't stir.

My throat swells. "Highland!" I yell, tears brimming. "Wake the fuck up!"

I should've protected him better.

I should've hit those guys harder to reach him faster.

"Oscar?" That groggy voice comes from the back of the tent. I glance over my shoulder, and see Charlie struggling to sit up.

"Charlie, stay there. Don't move. Are you alright?"

"Yeah…yeah. I think." He lets out a pained breath and favors an arm around his ribs. His eyes meet mine and then flit to Jack. He blinks back something. "Is he…?"

"He's fine."

He's fine. Fine. F.I.N.E. Spelling it in my head is not calming me down. I don't want to leave Jack at all, but he dropped his camera bag around here. He might have a water bottle stashed inside.

Just as I start climbing to my feet, his eyes begin to flutter.

I crouch back down. "Jack," I whisper, panicked desperation coating my voice. I kneel next to him, sliding a hand over his head.

He blinks awake slowly. "Os?" He tries to sit up, palm bracing his weight on the floor.

"Relax," I say. "You hit your head pretty bad there, Arizona. Do you know what day it is?"

"September 17th." He leans back against the bumper car, and his eyes sink into mine. Concern envelop them. "Your face."

I barely feel the pain in my cheekbone. One guy landed a single punch that my dad would have laughed at, but knuckles are knuckles and I'm sure there's a welt.

A fist connected with Jack's jaw too, but I'm more concerned about the blunt force against the pole.

Does he even remember we were in a fight? Maybe he's concussed. "Do you remember what happened?"

He gathers his bearings. "Yeah, of course, I just didn't see you get hit." He glances over at my client who's lifting up his button-down to inspect the deep bruises forming along his ribs. "Charlie, you okay?"

He nods once.

I reach for my radio to call the med team, then I remember it's mangled. *Good job, Oliveira.* Look what my anger got me.

Jack eases forward. "I'm alright." His lips, kid you not, curve into a smile. "Who would have thought my first fight would end with me knocked out by a pole?"

"Not me," I say honestly. "You vs. Pole. I'm putting all my money on you."

He smiles a little wider. "Here's the thing, Os, you'd put all your money on me no matter what." He stretches out his legs. "You're the president of my fan club."

"True," I say and eye that smile. "You sure you're feeling alright?"

He nods strongly. "Yeah." He rubs the back of his head.

I climb to my feet and hold out my palm. Helping Jack to a stance, I keep a hand on his shoulder, and I wait for a couple seconds. He's steady. Alert, even. But still, I ask, "Alright?"

"Yeah." His hand falls into mine and he squeezes before dropping it completely. His attention veers to his broken camera equipment on the ground, and my focus realigns to my client.

I squat next to Charlie. "Can you stand?"

"Maybe."

I help him up too, and as soon as his feet hit the floor, he careens into the nearest bumper car. *Fuck.* I support him around the waist before he falls.

I thought his ribs were the worst, but he might have actually fucked his leg again. "Hold on," he groans as he sits on the hood of a bumper car. "Let me take a breath." He winces as he inhales.

"What happened?" I ask the question I've been avoiding. I'm not sure I'm going to like the answer.

"They said they had weed." Charlie cringes. "They didn't. They robbed me." He nods a chin at a wallet on the ground. The wallet that I made that fucker give me before I let him go.

No. I bend down and pick it up. Immediately, I recognize the leather. Maybe I was too panicked before to comprehend the familiarity. But I flip it open and see Charlie's license. Fucking *shit,* I can't believe I made this mistake.

No ID of the threats.

They all escaped.

I'm going to get hell for this one. I pocket Charlie's wallet.

Jack scoops up his broken camera. "Charlie, why would you follow them without a bodyguard?"

"Yeah, Charlie, why would you do that?" I say mockingly, already knowing the answer.

He rolls his eyes. "I took the risk."

Because he doesn't give a shit if he gets hurt. Pain, right? It's greater than the frustration he feels on a daily basis. I don't know how to help him other than making sure he keeps talking to his dad.

All I can do is try to protect him, even if he doesn't want it.

I bend down to the graveyard of camera pieces, helping Jack pick up what's left. "Can it be fixed?" I ask him.

Charlie says, "I'll pay for it."

"It's not about the money," Jack sighs. "I lost whatever Jesse recorded earlier. But he still has a second cam on him right now, so whatever other footage he's grabbing at the carnival should still be usable."

Charlie pushes off the hood of the car and stumbles close before I can reach him. I see he's trying to help pick up a lens off the ground.

"I've got it," I tell him, but he's already on his knees, curling his fingers around the lens. He passes it to Jack.

"I'm sorry," Charlie breathes. It's one of the few times I've heard him verbalize an apology.

"Alright, you're concussed, Charlie," I say, flat-out. I help my client back to his feet and then wrap an arm underneath his, supporting his weight. "I'm getting you both to Farrow."

Jack zips up his camera bag, but I grab the strap before he can and hook it over my free shoulder. The three of us slowly walk down the aluminum stairs. Out of the bumper car tent.

Heading back to the main carnival, lights still glow and music thumps loudly.

Jack touches the bump on his head in a wince. "So this is what a fight feels like?" His glittering gaze slides to me. "Have to say, Oscar, I can't believe you used to do this for a living."

"Tell that to my baby sister who's still doing it for a living."

He lets out a soft sound with the shake of his head.

Gabe catches up to us, and I take his radio. *Sorry, Gabe.* Seniority and all. I fit in the earpiece and switch frequencies about the same time a familiar serious-ass voice sounds in my ear. "Thatcher to SFO, has anyone had eyes on Akara, Banks, or Sulli in the past twenty?"

What in the ever-loving hell?

My mind can't wrap around those three. For one, I thought Akara was in denial about his feelings for Sulli. So when she got her first boyfriend, I expected full-on Jealous Akara to gush his feelings once and for all. I grabbed my popcorn. Didn't happen.

Not even after Sulli broke up with her boyfriend.

What did happen? I overheard Banks say that Sulli is a "total stunner". Akara was there and just nodded. Couldn't tell if it was in agreement or if he short-circuited.

Putting that history aside, Sulli could be stuck challenging them to a basketball toss or squirt gun game right now. She's competitive, and Akara assigned Banks to her detail tonight too. Double-security. But Akara would respond on comms.

Unless another little bastard tried to rip his radio off him.

A chorus of *Negatives* and *No's* ring out in my ear. No one has seen them.

I manage to click my mic to get in a *no*. It takes one more minute before Donnelly says, "I saw them enter the funhouse a half hour ago."

Those three might be lost with no comms signal, but chances are someone from the med team will be over there in case something happened. And Charlie and Jack need a medical assessment.

At least now we have a destination, looking at the bright side.

WE REACH THE FUNHOUSE THE SAME TIME

Thatcher and Jane run up to the entrance where bulbs spell out *American Circus Funhouse*. They roll to a stop when they see Charlie in pain and welts on our faces.

"Merde," Jane curses in French. "What happened?" She changes course and reaches us with Thatcher jogging ahead. Her worry mounts as I unhook my arm from Charlie and ease her younger brother down to the grass.

"Life," Charlie says, eyes closed, pain cinching his face. "Stupid people, the aftereffects of my choices…walking backwards."

Stupid people, the aftereffects of my choices. Feeling that tonight like a motherfucker. I've made some mistakes that ended with me having a broken radio and caused Jack to head-butt a pole.

"Stay very still," Jane instructs, a hand on her brother's shoulder. If anyone asks, I'd say Jane Cobalt is a saint for her patience and kindness towards Charlie. She tries to take care of him, even when he actively pulls away from the family.

He's told me that he doesn't deserve his sister's love, but there are many times where he proves his own belief wrong. From joining the FanCon tour for her, to threatening her ex-friends-with-benefits so caustically that Nate never made a peep again.

And no one knows he did that but me.

I extend an arm around Jack as he sways slightly, too light-headed. My stomach clenches. "Take a seat, Highland."

Jack lowers to the grass and rests his forearms on his knees. Like he's taking a breather after high school PE.

He's okay, Oliveira.

But my eyes are on him like he's my job. I don't even care that he's my sole focus right now. Charlie has his family at this event.

Jack has me.

That's my husband.

He looks up at me with this weak smile that tries to strengthen. "You're staring at me like I'm your subject, Os."

"Who said you weren't?"

I watch a soft breath leave him and his smile grow. *Help him. Don't be distracted by his charm.* The thought kicks me into further action.

I adjust my earpiece and ask Thatcher, "Where's Redford?" And then I see a concierge doctor sprinting over to us, trauma bag thwacking his hip.

He's older. Ponytail at the base of his neck. That's Dr. Edward Keene, Farrow's father.

He squats down to Charlie and begins assessing. I'm not surprised he's on-call considering only the Keenes make-up the med team.

Thatcher answers me, "Farrow left the carnival early with Maximoff. Ripley didn't feel well. Teething issue." His gaze narrows onto the funhouse entrance.

I survey the onlookers, on alert.

Teens and adults loiter around the funhouse and take out their phones. Snapping photos. Filming. A good number of temps are thankfully keeping them at bay. Anyone who tries to approach is being told to stay back.

I'm about to ask Dr. Keene to check out Highland too, but Charlie is the one who says, "Can you look at Jack? He hit his head badly earlier."

"On what?" Dr. Keene immediately shifts to Jack.

"A metal bumper car pole," Jack answers. At least he remembers that. Puts me less on edge.

Dr. Keene shines a tiny light in Jack's eyes.

"What happened, really?" Jane asks Charlie again.

He stretches out his leg. "I was robbed."

"Robbed?" Shock widens her blue eyes. Thatcher has a comforting hand on her head, but his anger bears down on me.

Since Akara's not here, I knew I'd receive the wrath of the SFO lead.

He glares. "Where were you?"

"I had a temp on him because I went off-duty to talk to my brother, but Gabe lost sight of Charlie."

"Why didn't Gabe radio earlier that he was missing?"

I grimace, knowing what happened. "I told him that if I was ever in the vicinity, he didn't have to." I laugh but it's an odd sounding one, this night catching up to me. "You know what, I didn't realize that he thought being at the same carnival was considered *in* the vicinity. I should've been more specific."

My fucking bad.

"Where was *your* radio?"

I swallow an acidic taste. I've fumbled so royally hard tonight. "It's broken. I'm using Gabe's now."

Thatcher's shaking his head. His tightened eyes nail into the funhouse. I'd bet a hundred bucks he's worried about Akara and Banks.

I'm not used to being on the receiving end of disappointed, irate stares from Thatcher, and it lingers with me.

Even if Gabe is an idiot, it's my fault for not training him properly. But really, it's hard to put my brain in the brain of someone leagues below my intelligence. I obviously didn't factor in how he'd interpret some of my instructions.

"Both need to go to the hospital," Dr. Keene says. "Charlie for X-rays, and Jack for a CT scan." We start helping them up off the grass. I support Jack with an arm around the waist, and he hangs his bicep over my shoulder.

Thatcher keeps Charlie upright.

And then everyone's attention suddenly veers to a girl *sprinting* like her life depends on it…out of the funhouse.

"Sulli!" Jane screams and waves both her hands. Sulli redirects her target zone to our group, and as soon as she lands here, she grabs onto Jane's arm.

Where are her bodyguards?

I go still, on edge…should I be alarmed or do I need to go buy some kettle corn?

"Let's fucking get out of here. Right fucking now," Sulli says under her breath, her green eyes pinging to the camera phones. To the eager public eating this shit up. Can't fault them too hard.

I'm standing here thinking, *give me the tea. What's the drama?*

But also, *protect these ones.*

Thatcher and I motion for the temps to keep hold as the zealous audience tries to push closer.

"Why?" Jane's blue eyes grow wider. Their voices are hushed.

Sulli turns bright red. "I opened my big fucking mouth. That's why. I told Kits and Banks they're really fucking hot and they make me feel safe and comfortable, and that if I never have another boyfriend in my entire life, then it'd be cool to lose my virginity to one of them." She nods vigorously. "Yep, and I thought they'd take it like pals, you know like buddies. But they were fucking silent!" She waves a hand around. "So I ran, but then I ended up in the mirrors and I got lost and they were looking for me…and oh my fuck." Her gaze beelines to the funhouse exit where Akara and Banks are jogging out.

Oh yeah, this is a five-bucket kettle corn moment. I'd be grinning at the drama right now if people weren't hurt tonight.

"We're going," Jane tells her. "Right now. Let's go. Charlie?"

"I'll leave with Jack and Oscar. You go ahead."

"Are you positive?" she worries.

"Yes," Charlie says, standing on his own.

She hugs her brother. "We'll meet you at the hospital." She turns. "Thatcher?"

"Right in front of you, honey," Thatcher says, leading Jane and Sulli towards the parking lot.

I use comms and direct more temps onto them, and then Akara and Banks slow their jog as they reach us. My boss sees my client's injuries. "What happened?"

Comms chatter ignites. "Price to Akara, I've got word that Charlie's been robbed. Can you confirm?"

Akara glares, making me feel two-inches tall.

"He wasn't on my detail," Charlie defends me. "It was my fault. No one else's."

That's not how security works, but I appreciate Charlie trying to keep my ass off a hot seat.

I nod to Akara with confirmation. *Yes, my client was robbed.*

He clicks his mic and relays that back. SFO is never going to live this down.

Kitsuwon Securities 1 – Triple Shield 2.

The only reason we're really losing is because of me, and I feel like a bigger jackass. Bruising the reputation of SFO hurts all of our massive egos, but it'll hurt Akara the most. His name is on it. "Kitsuwon, I'm sorry," I tell him.

He shakes his head. "It's okay," he says, genuine. "It's been…a long night."

Now I *really* need the full story of what happened in that funhouse, but he's turning to Banks and they're already walking off together.

We start to head out too. But as we reach the Ferris wheel, Jesse approaches.

Pit stop #2.

"Where've you been?" Jack asks with the worry of a big brother.

"Where've *you* been?" Jesse motions to his brother's face, the welt, and me supporting him around the waist. "You look like you got in a fight, Kuya."

"It's a long story."

I upnod to Jesse. "Tell you at the hospital."

Jesse notices Charlie leaning awkwardly, and he instantly scoops an arm around my client. "You okay, dude?"

I manage to take Jesse's camera bag from him so he can brace Charlie. We continue our trek to the parking lot again.

"I'd be better if you overheard someone talking shit about Maximoff tonight," Charlie replies.

His wise-ass is coming out to play.

He's lucky Jane isn't here to snap at him.

"Uh...yeah, I have heard someone railing on him tonight." Jesse makes a confused face. "Why would you want to hear that? Did you guys get in a fight...I thought you two were cool now?"

Charlie suddenly looks too interested. His eyes laser-focus on Jesse. "What exactly have you heard?" Seriousness crosses my face, especially as he adds, "Have you caught any on film?"

Charlie.

Keating.

Motherfucking.

Cobalt.

Pieces of the overarching big-picture puzzle abruptly line up and connect too perfectly. My head spins. "Charlie..."

No one hears my whisper.

"Yeah, I shoot everything," Jesse says. "I can show you tonight's footage."

Jack exchanges a look with me.

This is it.

This is why Charlie wanted to do the docuseries. Besides set me up with Highland, *this* is the answer we've been waiting for all along.

"Is it an older man?" Charlie asks. "He'd only be at charity events like this one. And he'd have a proclivity for hating my cousin."

"Yeah," Jesse nods. "That sounds like him."

Ernest Mangold, the CEO of H.M.C. Philanthropies. Charlie wanted his head on a spike. That's my best theory, and I might've made dumb mistakes tonight—but I'm still an intelligent motherfucker.

41

Jack Highland

"*DID YOU HEAR THAT Maximoff left the carnival already? He didn't even take pictures with those boys at the Tunnel of Love ride...yeah...*"

Ernest Mangold.

I'm staring at him on my TV. I rolled it out of a closet and projected the camera footage from the carnival onto the big-screen. My brother, Oscar, Charlie, and I watch tensely in my apartment. We're all standing, even Charlie who leans on his crutches.

"*He was showing his son around the whole time. And he thinks he's good at charity work?*" His laughter is ugly.

My face is set in a perpetual cringe and confusion.

Whoever Ernest speaks to is standing out-of-frame. Carnival-goers pass in front of the camera. Obscuring Ernest and his friend. Sound quality is really poor but still audible.

"I didn't want to push any closer," Jesse defends the footage. "I have before, and he'll stop talking and make me shut off my camera."

I rest a hand on his head. "This is good, Jess. It's impressive you can hear anything at all with the music."

His lips begin to rise.

We look back at the TV.

No concussion, the hospital ruled—so I'm clear-headed as we watch Ernest loiter around the Tunnel of Love and run his mouth.

"…*he should've just left Ripley in the petting zoo. Yeah…yeah someone attach a sign to him that says 'pet me, I'm a meth-head baby'.*" He laughs again.

No one speaks.

Our silence deadens the room.

My muscles tense, sick to my stomach. I shake my head and meet Oscar's heated eyes. I tell him, "I've heard some weird, malicious things said 'in jest' behind their backs before, but nothing on that level, nothing from the inner-circle."

"It's disturbing," Oscar says, "and I'm sadly not disturbed by much anymore." We've seen it all.

The footage cuts to black a few seconds after that, and Oscar looks more concerned at me than anyone else.

I'm almost numb. Being hit with too many emotions at once. Fury at the douchebag CEO. Hurt for my friends, the famous families. Frustration at a project that I stuffed way too many hopes inside.

And more, so much more that I'm only starting to process.

We're standing entrenched in Charlie's main motive for the show. He was using the docuseries to capture evidence of Ernest's behavior. Charlie is outnumbered on the H.M.C. Philanthropies board, so this was the way he decided to unseat the CEO.

I wish his motive for the show were something else.

Something like he wanted to be the center of attention for once. A star among the gods. Egocentric. Anything that'd make *Born into Fame* feel long-term and not a blip that'll end once Charlie claims his prize.

Jesse looks between Oscar, Charlie, and me. He's tearing off a piece of funnel cake. My brother brought back tubs of carnival food while Charlie and I were at the hospital getting checked out, and he scored long-lasting points with Oscar when he tossed him a bag of kettle corn.

The scent of cotton candy and fried dough surrounds us as I power off the TV. "So you think he'll be fired for this?" Jesse asks.

"Unequivocally," Charlie says, eyes still on the black screen. I'm glad he'll be sacked. Maximoff never should've been kicked off to begin with, but I'm processing.

And processing.

"I have a question," I say what I always say, but this one contains so much more of my personal emotion. So much hurt. Yeah, I'm *fucking* hurt. I catch Charlie's yellow-green eyes. "Why didn't you just tell me?"

My dream is crumbling beneath me and everything is turning to dust.

Oscar has asked me before, *why this one?*

What's so special about this project? Why did I put my heart into it, knowing it was a risk? Like Charlie's answer for everything, mine wasn't that simple.

I put my heart in everything I do.

An opportunity to create my own show is one-in-a-million.

I love making art that speaks to the human condition.

To produce a documentary series about the most misunderstood Cobalt and make him understood…that feels more than rewarding.

Even thinking about how much I've invested emotionally into this project churns my stomach. Charlie's gaze washes over me. "Why didn't I tell you?" he repeats the question.

"Yeah," I say, hot anger fueling me for a second. "I understand you were upfront about the reason being a selfish one, and I appreciate that, but why not just tell me you needed footage of that asshole's behavior? We could have all made a plan together to take him down."

Oscar chimes in, "You know I would have helped you, bro."

Charlie blinks, his eyes on me. "I wasn't sure you'd do the show, if you knew I was using the footage to get a man fired. I couldn't take the risk."

My muscles stiffen. "Then why not just film Ernest yourself? Why go through this *whole* docuseries, Charlie?" I keep my voice steady, but I can even hear the thread of heat.

"I already told you why," Charlie's eyes soften, almost in hurt. "What benefit would me filming Ernest give Oscar? None."

Selfish and selfless. The room sobers for a second.

And I remember.

Working on the pilot to *Born into Fame* gave me the biggest opportunity of my life. I found love. Not just momentary love that passes like the seasons.

I found love that lasts even when the screen fades to black.

Charlie's docuseries put me on a collision course with Oscar Oliveira. It made me confront feelings and confusion about my sexuality that I let fester for too long.

Leaning more on his crutches, Charlie tells me, "And that's even if I could accomplish the task. Ernest is foul, but he's not a complete moron. He stifles his worst behavior whenever he sees me." He softens his gaze, and I know he's being sincere.

Charlie doesn't put on a facade for anyone.

"I still want to do the show, Jack," he expresses. "That hasn't changed."

I still want to do the show.

It should make me feel better, but all the walls are closing in on me. "The only reason you're agreeing to continue filming is *for me*. This no longer feels like a partnership, Charlie. It feels like I'm exploiting you."

"I'm letting you."

I run a hand through my hair. *That* definitely doesn't make me feel better. Charlie lets people beat the shit out of him. He'll surrender himself to pain because he doesn't care about his own life. I don't want to be the kind of producer that'd use that to my advantage. *I* care. Maybe I care enough *for* him.

Empathy. Don't lose it. Use it.

I don't want to lose it. I just don't.

Charlie must see me boarding up this project. Shipping it off to the land of unfinished and scrapped pilots. He quickly says, "Please don't make a decision now. At least think about it."

"I agree with Charlie," Oscar says. "Highland, it's been a long night. You literally hit your head and knocked yourself out. Just take a day. Maybe a couple more."

I hear his fear. For me. My dreams.

What does it all mean if it comes crashing down? I haven't pieced together that answer yet. All I know is that this might have been my one-and-only opportunity to have my own show. To have a subject as interesting and compelling as Charlie.

CHARLIE AGREES TO STAY IN MY APARTMENT
while I steal a moment with his bodyguard.

Side by side, our legs dangle off the metal grates of my building's fire escape outside my living room window. Oscar and I share a bag of kettle corn and watch Philadelphia below.

"I know," I start out, "you think you're not a good brother, Os." Our eyes lock for a strong beat. "But you were right to take care of yourself and go to Yale. You were right to figure out what you wanted and who you are, and Quinn is right to feel how he feels. And I hope now that he's opened up and you know he was bullied, therapy will be better for you both." I flash a warm smile. "I believe in the Oliveira brothers."

Oscar sniffs, then says, "Do me a favor, Highland." He grabs a water bottle. "Next time you give me a pep talk, warn me so I don't choke on popcorn."

We laugh.

He wipes his mouth with his bicep and nods. "I believe in the Oliveira brothers too."

I slide an arm around his waist. His ankle brushes mine as they hang in the nighttime air, and it's calming. Being with Oscar in a city. Even after a chaotic night—no, *especially* after a chaotic night.

"I asked Charlie if he'd even want me to air footage from Vienna," I admit to Oscar after I swallow a handful of sweet kettle corn.

"The footage from the elevator?" he asks.

"Yeah." I nod.

"Let me guess, he said, *yes, air it.*"

Oscar would guess right. I nod with a short breath. "Yeah. His exact words, *show it if you want. I don't care.*" I shake my head, conflicted. "I'm not sure he wants people to relate to him or even see him in a vulnerable state. He's not doing this for himself. He'd be doing it for me."

And again, it feels…wrong.

"You want him to say, *I need this*," Oscar realizes.

"Yeah." I look to him. "I love being a part of *We Are Calloway* because I'm able to help magnify peoples' truths that are usually drowned out with hate, but this pilot, this show, doesn't feel like it's purpose is for anything other than my ambition."

"Is that so bad?" Oscar wonders. "You don't have to give up on it."

I study the hard lines around his eyes. I slide him a warmer smile. "What are you, scared to see me fail?"

"Yeah, I am." His grin is a shadow that concern overtakes. "It feels like you're trapped in your own elevator tonight, and I don't know how to help you out of it."

Looking into him, Oscar looking into me—I feel like I'm paddling out and about to stand up on my board. Failure isn't as destructive as I thought it'd be. Because regardless of what happens, he's not going anywhere.

"I have you, don't I?" I breathe.

"That's not even a question, Long Beach."

So what's there to be afraid of?

His large hand encases my jaw, and I clasp the crook of his neck. Our lips skim, waiting out a longing kiss.

"Don't make a decision yet," Oscar whispers. "Sleep on it."

"As long as you're in my bed," I smile against his lips.

He grins back. "Oh, I'll be there. Don't you worry, meu raio de sol."

In this moment with Oscar, worry is so far away.

42

Oscar Oliveira

"YOU SURE YOU WANT to do that?" Charlie asks, watching me move the rook. Finger to his temple, he studies my play.

"Yeah, pretty certain I do."

Charlie paid for a public garden conservatory to close for a private event.

The event: Chess.

The players: Charlie Cobalt and Oscar Highland-Oliveira.

I'd like to say this is a special occasion, but really this happens at least once a month. The manager of the conservatory has even stopped asking when the other guests will show.

Red rose bushes surround us, and the chess set rests against a white iron table. It feels like we landed in the middle of Frances Hodgson Burnett's *The Secret Garden*.

It'd be a great location for Jack to film. And look at me, thinking about filming locations like I'm on production. How times have changed. How I've changed.

For the better. No doubt.

"Will you be at the ballet that's coming up?" Charlie asks as he moves his knight. He favors his left side slightly, three broken ribs from the fight at the carnival.

"For sure." I study the board. "Why wouldn't I be?"

"You said you're taking more time off."

My exact words were, *Charlie, you're going to have a temp on your detail more often.*

But he's not wrong.

I'm going to take more breaks. More time off. For myself, my husband, my brother and sister. I'm no longer going to grind so hard, and that decision comes on the wake of Charlie being beat up. I realize—timing, Oliveira. But I know now that there's no such thing as bad or good timing.

Just the time we're given.

You'd think Charlie would be upset by the news, but he's happy. He's wanted this for me ever since I lasted a year on his detail. Will I worry about him?

Every motherfucking day.

"I am going to take some time off, but maybe I won't tell you when," I say to my client. "Give you a little taste of how it feels. How about that?"

He's smiling, a heartfelt one. "Sounds the opposite of boring."

"Knew you'd think so." I shift a pawn. "And I'm still your 24/7 bodyguard, Charlie. That's not changing, okay?"

He frowns for a second. "Are you still my friend?"

We were never friends. Those words catch in my throat.

Charlie continues, "Jack still hasn't told me if he wants to continue *Born into Fame*. And I know he's upset about my reason. I just didn't know if that changed things between us?"

My mind skates through everything the two of us have been through. All the continents we've visited together. All the lunches, dinners, and plane rides we've shared. All the games of chess we've played and the languages we've conversed in. How much I care about him and his happiness.

How much he cares about mine.

We both wanted each other to fall in love, and he succeeded in helping me open a door that was right out of my reach.

It seems callous to continue denying the obvious.

"We'll always be friends," I tell him.

A smile reaches his eyes, and then he captures my pawn in a casual move. "I hope Jack will still do the show," he says. "I know how much it means to him, and that does mean something to me."

I sigh and shift my king. "Yeah, but I think it's bigger than what you or I want." I meet his yellow-green eyes. "If he ends up scraping it, he's not going to be around as much." It cuts me up to lose out on some moments, on traveling together, but I knew it might come to that if he's not filming Charlie anymore. "Especially since you're barely on *We Are Calloway*."

Charlie smiles. "Just ask me, Oscar."

"Ask you what?" I barely try to play coy.

We share a smile, knowing what's coming. "Alright, Charlie," I say into a bigger smile. "Would you consider being on *We Are Calloway* more?"

Charlie's grinning wider. "You hate having the cameras around. You're always complaining about them getting in your way."

"Still hate that," I laugh. "But I love him."

"Love," Charlie muses into a sad smile, almost longing. Wishing. I wish I could help open that door for him one day.

So he can reach the love of his life sooner rather than later.

He asks, "What's the difference between me being on *We Are Calloway* more and Jack just going ahead with the pilot? He's still filming me in both scenarios."

I asked the same question in my head. "That's why guys like you and me," I tell Charlie, "shouldn't be producers."

His lip curves. "Are you saying I lack a sense of morality?" *Yes.*

"I'm saying we both have our failings," I tell him. "Check."

This morning, he had a conversation with Maximoff about H.M.C. Philanthropies. With Ernest being officially gone from the company, the board instated Charlie as interim CEO. But Charlie has no desire to stay in that position.

I was there when he said to Maximoff, "It's yours, if you want it. If not, you can find someone else to fill the role. It's not something I want to do forever."

Maximoff nodded slowly. "I have to think about it."

"I knew you would," Charlie said into a laugh.

"Did you really do it for me?" Maximoff wondered.

Charlie paused for a moment. "Yes and no." He shrugged. "I hated Ernest, and I wanted him gone. But also...the company is yours. You should have never been fired in the first place, and it would have been a tragedy not to course correct."

Maximoff hugged him, and they kept hugging for a long beat. Farrow and I shared an eased look because our clients were at peace with each other. Can't beat love, in all forms, all kinds—and after a big dose of drama, all I want to do is surround myself in that feel-good, can't sleep, gotta keep my ass awake to sing the night away, kind of love.

In the garden, I watch Charlie study the chess board. It's those soft moments people don't see. The ones I cherish from Charlie. It's why I trust he'll find his way.

He defends his king with ease in two simple moves. His eyes return to me. "I'm fine with being on *We Are Calloway* more often. But the offer to film me traveling for a personal videography project still stands," Charlie tells me. "I know he probably won't take it because he wants a network deal. But it's on the table."

I don't ask whether it's something he really wants for himself or if he's just trying to help my work schedule overlap with Jack's.

It doesn't matter because I doubt Jack would agree to it.

"I'll let him know," I say. "There's one more thing. I have an idea, but I might need your help." There's something I need to do for Jack. Like all the other options, he might not take it. But I won't stop myself from at least trying to patch-up the holes in his boat of dreams and right it back to shore.

"I'm listening." Charlie moves his queen and it's staring down my king. "Checkmate," he says.

I'm not even that mad about it. Honestly, I love playing chess against Charlie.

He's the only person who's ever been able to beat me.

43

Jack Highland

"I BURNED IT."

Oscar blinks. "Come again?"

"I burned it, Os," I repeat in a whisper. "Like it's currently a pile of ash in a trashcan at my office." The curtains haven't been drawn for the ballet yet, but we're still sitting in Charlie's boxed seat. He pretends not to listen one row below us.

"All of it?" Oscar asks, studying my face.

All the days we spent together in Philly, New York, California, France, Greenland, Austria. It's charred to a crisp. That was the hardest part. Knowing that I was burning some of our memories.

But I couldn't store the footage if I'm not filming *Born into Fame* anymore. It's not safe to keep any video clips of Charlie when someone could get ahold of them. And that person might not have the same feelings or intentions as me.

"I didn't burn all of it," I whisper, being truthful. "I kept some of the footage where Charlie wasn't present." I smile at him.

He understands. "You kept the footage of us."

"Yeah."

Oscar grins, but his lips falter. "You're alright with ending this?"

I've learned a lot about Charlie and myself. I've met my limits on what I'm willing to do, and it's right here. I can't produce a show that's centered around someone who's self-destructive like him, who's too apathetic about his life being seen.

I'm ending the pilot. Ending the idea of creating my own show around him.

"It's not the one," I tell Oscar. "And it already gave me what I wanted. Just not what I expected."

He leans in and steals a kiss, one that melts us against each other, and we pull back as the curtains begin to rise. His hand stays in mine.

My chest rises, and I smile out at the performance of *Romeo & Juliet*. Barely watching, though. A strong sense of anticipation rolls through me. I can't stop visualizing how we ended up here.

How I fell in love with Oscar Highland-Oliveira.

Like someone hit *play* on the video of our lives. We're all over the fucking place. A big tortured slow-burn as I flirted my way into his heart and missed opportunity after opportunity to seize what I desired.

How we married in one drunken night.

How the annulment still lies on the metaphorical table between us.

In my head, it's already burned in the trash with Charlie's footage. There is no future where I'm not married to this man.

But I haven't articulated this to Oscar, and my pulse speeds even when he peeks over at me in the ballet. I use one of those times to whisper, "I figured it out."

His eyes rest on mine for longer.

"I'm pansexual," I breathe, knowing this has been what I've felt. I'm sexually, romantically attracted to people, regardless of sex and gender. I'm at peace with choosing the label as my own, and I know because I said it to myself in the mirror.

And fuck did I feel happy.

His mouth curves upward, pride in his eyes. "I really love you."

Emotion crashes into me. I didn't expect Oscar to say that. I wipe the corner of my eye. Smiling more.

He wipes it for me, then quietly he pops an orange tin on his lap. One that Audrey Cobalt gave him when we arrived at the theatre.

He tries to contain a laugh.

Do I use that as a reason to lean closer? *Of course I fucking do.* I lean into Oscar, my lips rising when I see the cookies inside the tin.

"How sweet of her," I smile brighter.

He contains another laugh. "She outdid herself this time."

I pick up a glazed sugar cookie. Orange icing is piped to resemble a glass of orange juice, and she scrawled the words, *Highveira*, in neat pink.

Our ship name.

We have fans outside the famous ones. Hate has died down as love for me and Oscar grows louder, and no one is happier than my parents, my brother. Mama even wears Highveira T-shirts to work. She's shown me proudly on FaceTime.

Oslie stans still exist, but there's a stronger fanbase around my relationship now. All because of one video.

Just one changed everything.

Paparazzi caught footage of Oscar spinning around my baseball cap and kissing me. We were grinning, and I might've slapped his ass. People decided that one was "authentic".

Fan sites popped up with headers and banners of orange juice. O & J—our initials.

"We have fans," I tell him into a bite of cookie.

While his eyes sweep the theatre, he whispers, "Just don't forget I'm still your number one fan, Highland."

"Don't forget I'm yours, Os."

His hand slips into mine, mine into his. Our grins bigger, and we try to focus on *Romeo & Juliet*. All the Hales, Meadows, and Cobalts are here today, some strewn in other boxes. Some seated in the orchestra section. Leo Valavanis is out sick, and Beckett is filling in as Romeo for maybe the only time all season.

My parents are also here.

And my brother. Along with Oscar's family. They're shadowed in the darkened theatre. All in their own boxes, watching the ballet. Waiting for the end.

Yet, it's not really the end for me.

The structure is all over the place, depending on the perspective. For some in the theatre, today is the rising action. For others, it's the fall.

Maybe for people like Charlie, it's eternally stuck at the beginning. And that's the frustration of it all.

Act 1, Scene 2, the Capulet family hosts a ball. The stage is full of ballerinas and—

Thump!

One goes down.

The audience lets out a collective gasp. Oscar is hawk-eyed more on Charlie, and I realize he's dropped the legs of his chair he'd been leaning back on. He's bowed forward.

The young ballerina quickly rises to her feet. We're close enough to see embarrassment shade her face. Hurrying, she continues the dance like nothing happened. She looks shorter than the girls next to her.

Charlie careens back to whisper to us, "Who is that?"

To free my hands, I bite onto the cookie I'm eating and flip through the program. Oscar is checking NDAs for her name on his cellphone. Since Beckett works here, the dancers have had background security checks.

Oscar finds her first. He leans forward and whispers, "Roxanne Ruiz. She's eighteen."

Charlie just turns forward, but I catch his smile.

Even with that *small* hiccup in Act 2, the ballet ends with a standing ovation, and pink flowers are tossed onto the stage for Beckett and the other dancers. I hear whistling from the audience, and I'm almost positive it's Jane Cobalt and Daisy Calloway.

The lobby.

We all wait for Beckett Cobalt in the lobby as the whole theatre begins to clear out. Security ushers some stragglers to the exit. They want to take more selfies with the Calloway sisters.

Oscar stays near Charlie, who loiters in the direct middle. On purpose. I asked him to.

I'm sweating bullets. And I unwrap a lime-flavored sucker and stick it in my mouth.

"Love that shirt," Oscar says, motioning to the white button-down I wear. *His* button-down. Everyone is in formal attire. "How many more are you going to steal from me, Long Beach?"

"Probably all of them," I smile widely, sucker up against my cheek. "You want it back?"

"I have a feeling that even if I say *yes*, I won't see it again."

"That's not true," I say with a bigger breath. I pull the sucker out of my mouth, and Oscar takes it. He slips the sucker between his lips.

I smile more. *That was hot.* Nerves start to subside.

"Why is that not true?"

"We're together, Oscar. You'll see your clothes again."

His grin softens to something more serious. Which is funny because he has a sucker in his mouth, and suckers aren't really an Oscar Oliveira thing.

I add, "They're just half-mine now."

Oscar laughs.

The lobby is really empty now. Just familiar faces, everyone chatting quietly. SFO laughs in the corner. Not needing to be as vigilant, no strangers in sight.

Popcorn machines rumble to a stop. Donnelly hops on the counter to start filling up a bag.

Jesse waves to me from one of the emerald couches. My mom already removes her tissues from her Louis Vuitton purse. The Oliveira family turns more to view us in the middle. Farrow, Maximoff, Ripley, and Jane and Thatcher have stopped talking, programs in their hands as they face us.

Even the Calloway sisters and their husbands watch.

Oscar's brows furrow. He notices.

He's too observant for this charade to last long.

And when his confused eyes land on me, I tell him, "Oscar."

"Jack?" The sucker is still in his mouth.

I smile like the next words exist deep inside me and have wanted to be set free for so, so long. "I was never rewriting my life when I met you. There was no rewrite, Oscar, because this is how it was always supposed to be written. I am supposed to be with you. You are supposed to be with me. Nothing else makes sense."

His eyes glass.

I continue on, "I love you. I love run-around-the-world Oscar. I love flirty Oscar, tactical bodyguard Oscar, snack monster Oscar"—everyone laughs, but I hold onto his laughter, his joyful tears that stream like mine—"my number one fan Oscar, sexy Oscar, intelligent as a motherfucker Oscar, a ride-or-die friend Oscar, a good brother Oscar, kiss me when the sun rises Oscar, my one and only Oscar…the love of my life Oscar."

He's nodding, overwhelmed, our cheeks wet with emotion.

"You're my everything Oscar."

He expels a, "Fuck, Highland." He takes out the sucker, about to bring me closer, but I drop to my knee. I hear sniffling from our family and friends.

"Oscar Felipe Highland-Oliveira. I love every part of who you are." I take his hand in mine and pull out a ring from my pocket. "Will you do me the honor of staying married to me?"

A collection of whispers sweeps the lobby, but I'm lost in Oscar's reaction. He falls to his knees, throws the sucker over his shoulder, and takes my face in his hands. "Yes," he says. "You're *my* everything Jack."

It balloons inside me. Like I'm floating in the air, sun shining down on us.

We kiss in a soulful force, cementing this marriage together.

Everyone claps around us, even if they're probably confused as hell. I didn't tell them we were already married, but I did invite them to the afternoon performance of *Romeo & Juliet* under the pretense of proposing.

Oscar pulls away and whispers to me, "Now I'm gonna need the details on how you made this happen."

I'm looking forward to the two-hour ride back to Philly where I can tell him all about it. It is hard to surprise the guy who's rarely surprised, but not impossible.

"I'm still holding your ring, Os." He's not letting me slip it on his finger.

"That one's yours."

"I didn't have yours to propose with…"

He's digging in his slack's pocket. He pulls out *his* ring, identical to mine. White gold. Three tiny diamonds.

I.

Love.

You.

My nose flares, more feelings balled up in me. "You've been carrying that around?"

"It hasn't left my side, Highland." He passes me his ring. I pass him mine.

Emotion tumbles between us. Knelt on the ground still, I slide his silver ring onto his finger. When he pushes the cold band along mine— it feels real finally.

Married.

Jack Arizona Highland-Oliveira.

It feels like this is the life I wrote myself. The one I wanted. The one I was too scared to chase, but thank everything in me that I did.

We kiss again, and as we climb to our feet together. Families swarm us. Congratulations sweep around us, along with the questions of *when, where, how?*

Oscar's parents speak in Portuguese, but with their smiles and uplifting tones, I'm pretty sure it's more of the same congratulatory sentiments.

I bring my Lola's hand to my forehead in respect and say, "Mano po, Lola." And then I wrap my arm around Jesse.

Farrow hugs Oscar and says with a grin, "You sneaky fucker. How the hell did you already marry him?" Donnelly shakes Oscar's shoulders, and the rest of SFO congregate around my husband. His brother and sister bound closer to him with their own grins and praises.

Maximoff, Jane, and Sulli come up and hug me. Smiling from ear-to-ear, and I receive top-marks from the Cobalts on my delivery and speech.

"Flawless," Audrey says.

I love, love, *love* people. I film them because I love them. We're all human.

Oscar raises a hand. "Alright, alright! We'll tell you all how Highland and I got hitched once we're back at the penthouse." He glances to Farrow. "You are throwing us a post-elopement engagement party, right?"

Farrow grins. "I'd ask you how you know but—"

"I'm always ten steps ahead," Oscar finishes. Everyone starts slowly making their way out of the building, gearing up for the penthouse.

I stop Jesse before he leaves. "Can we talk for a sec?"

"Yeah." Jesse can't hold shit in. He starts talking. "Can't believe you didn't tell Mama you got married. You're a bigger rebel than I thought, Kuya."

I laugh.

"They're not mad or anything," he continues. "I think this solidifies you as their *favorite* child because I'd never be able to pull this one off without landing major heat."

I elbow his side. "I'll use my power as favorite child for good."

"That's all I ask," Jesse smiles.

I hate that I took up his summer for not much of anything. He can't put *Born into Fame* on his resume since it doesn't exist. Jesse has told me ten times that he was just glad for the experience. The time spent with me.

But I want to give my brother a better opportunity.

"How busy do you think you'll be on the weekends, for the rest of your senior year?" I ask him.

Jesse shrugs, but a hopeful light reaches his eyes. "Not busy at all. Zero percent. *Unless*…something comes up?"

"Sulli wants to start free-soloing all her dad's old routes," I tell him.

Sulli announced this plan to her family yesterday at her dad's birthday party. The reaction was heavily mixed, not everyone in full support of her new goal. She's free-soloed before but conquering every mountain that Ryke Meadows has scaled (with no harness, no rope) is lofty and dangerous. It even freaks the fuck out of me.

I continue, "I'm going to need to film her for *We Are Calloway*, and I could use a PA that I trust a hundred-and-ten percent." Because filming her climbing is going to be a nail-biting, nerve-inducing ordeal.

"That's me right?" he asks, hopeful still.

I smile. "That's you, Utoy."

"*We Are Calloway*?" he asks in disbelief. "You're going to let me on a WAC production?"

"Only on the weekends," I say. "And Mama and I agreed that if it interferes with your school, it ends immediatl—"

He hugs me.

I wrap my arms around my little brother.

"Thank you," he mutters into my shirt.

We split apart. Everyone begins to go, and I end up in the passenger seat of the Black Widow. Oscar at the wheel.

Before we drive off, Oscar asks, "You were good with telling everyone we're married back there? No hesitations about what Oslie supporters might say about the marriage?"

"No hesitations." I smile. "All I want is to shout that you're my husband. Literally, I could fucking scream it out the window for two hours. Why hold anything in?"

We share a bigger smile.

"Yeah, I can definitely live with that answer." Oscar switches on the music. "Let's keep moving, Highland."

We drive and jam out to my favorite band. Singing smoothly at the top of our lungs, our hands clasped between our seats. He clutches the steering wheel with the other, and mine taps the car to the rhythm. Our gazes latch affectionately, powerfully in every other beat.

His love carries me through the barrel of every wave. I'm already up on the board.

I'm coasting on these feelings. Riding them to shore.

44

Oscar Oliveira

THE SUN SETS ON THE penthouse rooftop. Oranges bleed through the sky, and rays soak down on the most gorgeous guy.

That's right, my husband.

Our post-elopement engagement party is still in full swing, but we snuck away for a second to watch the sun drop behind the Philly skyline.

We're headed to the edge, but I seize his hand. Stopping him near the pool. A donut inflatable tube drifts over the blue water.

"I have to tell you something."

He frowns and spins more to me. Our buttons are popped on our shirts. Hot sauce stains his, thanks to my baby sis shaking a bottle too hard.

He couldn't be hotter. Or more confused.

"What's wrong?"

"Nothing." I laugh. "Nothing is wrong. This is legitimately the best day of my life." I know he can feel that because his smile is a thousand-watts of beauty. "But the something I want to tell you probably isn't on your radar, and I wanted to throw it out there."

"Okay," he nods to me. "Shoot your best shot, Oscar."

I grin at the words I've told him. "Charlie said that the personal videography project is still on the table. And before you say anything, I know why it wouldn't be appealing. You want to create a show, and it doesn't make sense to take on a personal project during off-seasons of *We Are Calloway*."

"Would I be traveling the world with you?" he asks with a growing smile.

It chokes me up. "Yeah, you would."

"Then okay. I'll take on some videography projects. It'll be fun."

"There's more."

He frowns, his lips falling. "What do you mean, *more*?"

"That wasn't my best shot, Long Beach. I'm shooting again." I hold his shoulders. "I want to be on camera."

"Os—"

"Let me pitch it to you," I say. "Our lives, our love. You're the creator of a documentary mini-series starring you and me, Oscar and Jack—the hottest bodyguard and flirtiest filmmaker. How we came to be suddenly famous."

His hand is on his head, shocked. "You'd want to be on camera? Why?"

There is only one phrase that makes sense.

Only one that comes to mind.

"Basta ikaw," I use his words now and translate, "as long as it's with you, because it's you."

He pulls me closer, our arms over each other's shoulders. "I'd have to pitch it to a network. We might have to film a pilot first…they might not want it."

"But you'd do it?"

"Yeah." His eyes glitter. "No question." He adds with that charming smile, "It was a perfect pitch, Oscar. I'd buy the show."

"Yeah, the network thought so too. We're straight to TV."

His breath catches, face drops. "What…? You pitched the show? How did you even get a meeting with the network?"

"Charlie. Benefits of being friends with an American god. He has more sway than a bodyguard."

Jack processes, his smile overwhelmed and rising and rising. "What are you going to say when I turn the camera on you now?"

"I'm your subject, Highland. And I can live the most *joyous* life knowing that."

We draw into a lively kiss. Hands on faces, chest pressed to chest. And the sun descends a little more. Glowing over our embrace, and we break to continue our trek across the rooftop.

As we move closer to the edge, Jack playfully hangs his arms over my shoulders from behind. I reach back and clasp his neck. We kiss again, and he smacks my ass before he comes next to me.

We're laughing. Smiling, and then we reach the brick side.

We look out at the sun again. At the Philly skyline. Our arms hooked around each other.

I've watched the sun set and rise in different cities, different countries, different continents with Jack. And each time, I feel like we've been chasing the day, catching up to the night. But right now, the world feels like ours. Like one enormous celebration of love.

Happiness. We hear the laughter of our families and friends, and our eyes return to each other. Rays brighten our joy as we lean in and kiss.

EPILOGUE

Jack Highland

OSCAR SHAKES OUT A BAG of Nagaraya original cracker nuts, his current favorite Filipino snack. Last week it was sour cream & onion Piattos, a lighter-style chip.

"You sure this won't mess with the sound quality?" he asks as he strides over, dipping beneath one of the softboxes that I set up in my living room. "Because I can ditch the snacks, if I need to."

I laugh. "You're serious?"

"I might complain about it, but I'll do it." His eyes sink into mine, and I'm lost in the deep browns for a solid moment. We're filming the first interview for *Suddenly Famous* today, our docuseries. Closed set. Only us. And I know this is a big deal. A first step to sharing our lives with the world. He gave me this.

The *one*.

I'm the creator of a show—a show about us, and my soul is already rooted in the film before the camera has rolled.

He shakes his bowl. "So verdict?"

"Keep your nuts."

He grins at the slight innuendo, and I dig a hand into the bowl. "This is about showing the real us. Plus, I have the best sound equipment that money can buy."

"Legitimately impressed that I married a billionaire." He touches his chest.

I slip him a smile.

"But you might want to spend some of that trust fund on a bigger apartment, Highland. You *still* don't fit in this one."

I laugh as I readjust one of the boom arms. "I'm surprised you never asked why I live in this apartment, since you know I have the trust fund."

He sinks down onto the couch, bowl on his lap. "I didn't need to ask. I figured out why."

My brows shoot up. "Really?"

"Really, Long Beach, you might surprise me a lot, but you are my husband. You're not that big of a secret anymore." His smooth confidence draws me in. Curly strands of hair touch his forehead, and he brushes them back. "You work so much. Most the time you're either at the WAC offices or on a shoot. In your head, there probably wasn't a big reason to upgrade from a shoebox when you're just here to shower and pass out."

My smile hurts my face. It's not just that Oscar knows me, but it's the certainty behind it. Like there's no doubt in his head that he could be wrong.

"But I have been thinking about upgrading the apartment." I slip behind one of the cameras and adjust the focus. I've got three different cameras positioned around the living room to give me varying shots.

His eyes widen. "Finally worried that the ceiling fan is going to knock you out? Because I've been eyeing that thing since the first time I stepped foot in here."

I let out a soft laugh, still standing and working on the boom. "No, I just figured we're married, dude."

Humor drains from his face replaced by that serious side that I've come to love. He sets aside the snack bowl and wraps an arm around the couch like his whole attention is mine.

"Explain, Long Beach."

"We're married." I open my hands.

"You said that already. I'm waiting for the description."

"Hold on," I say and purposefully glance down at the camera's screen to drag this out. He makes a noise while I take my sweet time focusing, adjusting, and making sure that his beautiful face is perfectly framed.

"Arizona, if you don't get your ass over here."

I break into a bigger grin. No lie, whenever he calls me Arizona, it feels like he's packaging the state and giving me a gift.

"I'm coming, just not too fast," I tell him. Feeling his grin behind me as I lock in the settings, click record, and sink down on the couch next to him.

Our knees knock together, turned into one another, and we both have an arm atop the couch.

"We're recording?" he asks.

"Yeah." I smile. "Something tells me we'll have the best blooper reel."

"Oh, by far." He chews on a cracker nut. "Best blooper reel, best show, best honeymoon." At our post-engagement-elopement party, we spun the globe in the penthouse's library and randomly landed on our honeymoon destination.

At first it was in the middle of the Pacific Ocean. We spun again and ended up on land. We came back from Auckland, New Zealand yesterday.

And I should've said that on camera. I should be *addressing* the camera. Looking straight ahead for the interview. But this is just as strange for me. To be on the other side of the lens.

I just start where we left off talking.

"Both of us have jobs that make us travel, which means we've never really talked about *moving in* together," I tell him the obvious. "Because what does that mean for guys like us? We're basically living together already, right? When we're in Philly, we sleep here. When we're in New York, we sleep at your studio. When we're in fuck-knows-where, we sleep there."

Oscar can't contain his smile.

He definitely knows where this is going.

I continue on, "So I figure, the only way for us to actually *feel* like we're living together as husbands would be to sell my apartment and get a place together in Philly. Even if we're never there, it's still ours." I search his eyes. "How does that sound?"

He nods. Love swells between us. "Sounds like our future. I'm there."

I'm grateful for the camera as it captures the light in Oscar's eyes in this second, this perfect frame of time.

ACKNOWLEDGEMENTS

First and foremost, we want to extend a special and deepest thanks to Lanie and Jenn. We'll always cherish the creation of this book because of both of you. You've been with us since the very beginning and rooted for us and given us and our books a sort of love that comes once in a lifetime. We wanted to write a Filipino-American family because we love you both, and we're so honored that we could bring Jack Highland to life with your invaluable input and help. You two have been our superheroes for years, and we'll always look back at *Charming Like Us* and remember the talks we had, the group chats, and learning more about two people we love most (that's you two!). Thank you for sharing your Filipino culture with us. Knowing pieces of you are in the Like Us saga is the greatest gift and treasure of all. It brings tears to our eyes. Thank you for absolutely everything throughout the years, and we hope we did you two proud.

Big thanks to those that helped us with bringing the Oliveira family to life. From our sensitivity reader to the translators, we're forever grateful for your input and expertise. And thank you to Andressa for answering our questions, for making beautiful art, and for being so sweet—we're so lucky you found our books!

Any mistakes and misrepresentations are our own.

Thanks to our mom for lending your editing powers and your constant support. Our books wouldn't be nearly as magical without you. We love you as each sun sets and rises!

Thanks to Marie for your continued help with the French translations. We're so happy to have you in our corner to make sure the Cobalt Empire continues to thrive. You are a goddess.

Thanks to Kimberly, our agent, for helping land this book in audio. We're so excited to hear Oscar and Jack in audio format.

Thank you to the bloggers and reviewers who continue to shout about this series at Book 7. We're forever honored that you've chosen to spend time spreading the word about the Like Us series. It's a dream having you all reach this point!

To the Fizzle Force, thank you for being a bright spot in our lives. Your love, memes, and edits are some of our favorite things and we're so grateful that you've found our books. Shout out to our admins, Jenn, Lanie and Shea for all your wonderful support and all you do to uplift us and these books. Thank you is never enough, but we shall always say a big overwhelming, thankyouthankyouthankyou.

To our patrons on Patreon, thank you for making our dreams come true by allowing us to write full-time, and for giving our dorky character-loving hearts a place to expand this world with bonus scenes. You've truly changed our lives, and we can't wait to add more and more content over there! Prepare yourselves!

And finally, thanks to you, the reader, for picking up *Charming Like Us*. This book is so special to us for a multitude of reasons, and we're so grateful that you took a chance on it and the Like Us series. We can't wait to bring you more epic romances in this world.

CPSIA information can be obtained
at www.ICGtesting.com
Printed in the USA
BVHW081207161221
624199BV00004B/92